HEAT
AND
LIGHT

ALSO BY JENNIFER HAIGH

Mrs. Kimble

Baker Towers

The Condition

Faith

News from Heaven

HEAT
AND
LIGHT

JENNIFER HAIGH

ecco

An Imprint of HarperCollins*Publishers*

HarperCollins books may be purchased for educational, business, or sales promotional use. For information please e-mail the Special Markets Department at SPsales@harpercollins.com.

FIRST EDITION

Designed by Suet Yee Chong
Illustrations by Jim Tierney

Library of Congress Cataloging-in-Publication Data has been applied for.

ISBN 978-0-06-176329-8

16 17 18 19 20 OV/RRD 10 9 8 7 6 5 4 3 2 1

For Rob Arnold

Our decision about energy will test the character of the
American people and the ability of the President and the
Congress to govern this Nation. This difficult effort will
be the moral equivalent of war.

—PRESIDENT JIMMY CARTER
   APRIL 18, 1977

Murmurs from the earth of this land, from the caves and craters,
from the bowl of darkness. Down watercourses of our
dragon childhood, where we ran barefoot.

—MURIEL RUKEYSER

HEAT
AND
LIGHT

By now these events are forgotten. No one is old enough to have witnessed them personally. According to Ada Thibodeaux, Saxon Manor's only centenarian, the story was repeated by candlelight in the fledgling mining camps, in the years before the county was electrified.

Ada heard the tale in childhood, from her own grandmother—like all the women of that clan, famously long-lived. This places her account nearly two centuries back, predating even the Baker brothers, who dug the first coal mine in the valley and named an entire town after themselves.

Ada's people came from two counties over, what had been Seneca land—given to Chief Cornplanter by the Commonwealth of Pennsylvania, for a few years anyway, until the state changed its mind and took it back. The white settlers were timbermen, French Canadians and Scots-Irish. They built churches and a sawmill. Up close, their post office and mercantile had a flimsy, provisional look, as though made of stage flats, easy to dismantle and reassemble elsewhere when the logging was done.

It was a small town, a nothing town, until the Colonel came.

He arrived on the back of the mail coach, which came twice a week from Pittsburgh—a tall stranger in city clothes, not young. He took a room above the mercantile and hired a wagon out to Pine Creek, to call on a farmer who lived there. Later he was seen poking around the creek bed on his knees—filling glass jars with water, according to the driver of the wagon, who became for a few days a kind of celebrity in this town where nothing happened and no one visited, a town in no way remarkable, except for its smell.

The odor seemed to emanate from Pine Creek—a smell of burning or, more precisely, of something long ago burnt.

More than most places, Pennsylvania is what lies beneath.

Rock oil was considered, then, a local nuisance, a malodorous black gunk that floated like a rumor down the creek, filthening whatever it touched: a farmer's overalls, a cow's hide, a child's shoes. Enterprising citizens tried to find some use for it. At the sawmill it served as a lubricant. The town doctor believed it had medicinal value. What it cured was not known.

On the banks of Pine Creek, Colonel Drake set up operations. A wooden tower was built. His hired man, known only as Uncle Billy, was spotted in the mercantile, buying tools and rope.

The tower resembled a hangman's gallows. A local wag called it Drake's Folly, and the name stuck. The Colonel's madness was a general topic, like the price of lumber or the weather—a point of universal agreement, until his well came in.

Overnight the little town changed unrecognizably. Strangers arrived in startling numbers, city men in a hurry. Wooden derricks sprang up like fast-growing trees. Finding rock oil became the local obsession. Professional smellers crawled along the ground, hoping for a whiff of it. Divining rods waggled portentously. Séances were held.

Along Oil Creek, as it was renamed, rowdy boomtowns burst to life. Fortunes were made and lost, made and lost, Fate's machine pumping like a bellows, an inhuman heart. Men arrived in wild hope and left angry or crazy. Before he shot the president, John Wilkes Booth came to Petrolia and drilled a duster. He wasn't the first.

The men came hungry and thirsty. Local merchants rushed in to meet their needs. Saloons were built, gambling parlors, a music hall. The Franklin Silver Cornet Band learned "The Petroleum Gallop" and "Coal Oil Tommy" and "Colonel Drake's Polka." Painted women appeared, bright and sudden as daffodils.

The towns were called Pithole, Petroleum Center, and Antwerp City—names the old-timers have forgotten and the young never learned, ghost towns that boomed once, when a well came in, then busted and stayed busted the rest of their days. Turkey City, Parker City, Rouseville, Oleantum. There may have been others.

Even Ada Thibodeaux can't remember their names.

THE POINT OF DYNAMISM

2010

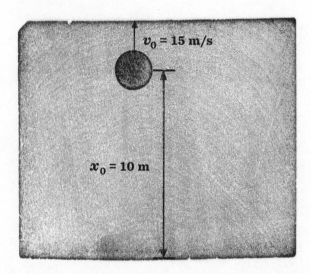

The first truck comes in springtime, a brand-new Dodge Ram with Texas plates. It trawls the township roads north of Bakerton, country lanes paved with red dog, piecrust roads that have never appeared on a map. The roads dip and weave for inscrutable reasons, disused mine trails, scarred and narrowed like the arteries of the very old. The driver, Bobby Frame, is as young as he looks, barely thirty, a big husky kid who might have played high school football. Up and down the Dutch Road, he is welcomed warmly—at the Fettersons', the Nortons', the Kiplers', Marlys Beale's.

Are you some kind of a salesman? he is asked at Friend-Lea Acres, the Mackey dairy farm.

No, ma'am. Just the opposite, Bobby says.

At Cob Krug's trailer, his first knock goes unanswered. When he knocks a second time, Cob rolls to the door in his wheelchair, brandishing a shotgun. Bobby never returns.

He bunks at the Days Inn on Colonel Drake Highway, room 211, the windows east-facing for an early start. Mornings he appears at the county courthouse as soon as it opens, clean-shaven, hair damp from his shower. He has a way with the clerk, a middle-aged lady who mothers and flatters him. Bobby hands her a printed list and waits for her to bring the books, the official record of who owns what.

His approach is always the same. *Beautiful property you've got here.* (This while removing his sunglasses, his eyes level blue and earnest in the morning glare.) Except for Cob Krug, folks listen as a matter of courtesy, after he shows his business card and explains why he came.

His explanation takes two minutes exactly. The shale lies a mile underground, has lain there since before there was a Pennsylvania, before a single human being walked the earth. Older than coal, older even than these mountains. It has an imperial name, the Marcellus. Deep in the bedrock of Saxon County, a sea of riches is waiting to be tapped.

Natural gas? The words repeated with some hesitation, the first lesson in a foreign language—vowels and consonants in odd permutations, awkward in the mouth. Those who know the local lore make immediate connections. There is a mountain spring, secret but famous, that bubbles for no reason. In the woods north of Deer Run, at a spot called the Huffs, heady vapors seep through the rocks. The Huffs are popular for underage drinking. Teenagers pretend to, or perhaps really do, get high on the fumes.

Buried treasure, says Bobby, feeling the poetry. The Marcellus Shale is Nature's safe-deposit box, its treasures locked away like insurance for the future. Now, at last, American ingenuity has found the key.

We drill a half mile down. Then we turn the bit sideways. We can drill for miles like that, right under your property. We're so far down you'll never know we're there.

You want to buy my land? the farmers ask, gobsmacked. As though Bobby has demanded a lung or a kidney, a piece of themselves God can't replace.

Not buy. Just lease it. You can keep on farming it like usual. You get a bonus up front, twenty-five

(later *one hundred*
five hundred

one thousand)

an acre. Once we start drilling, you get a percent.

Again and again, the same response: *What do I have to do?* Reminding him, always, that they are farmers—lives of servitude, unrelenting effort.

There's nothing to do, he says with a grandson's smile. *Sign the papers and wait for the check.*

RURAL PENNSYLVANIA DOESN'T FASCINATE THE WORLD, not generally. But cyclically, periodically, its innards are of interest. Bore it, strip it, set it on fire, a burnt offering to the collective need.

Bakerton understands this in its bones—a town named for a mining company, Baker Brothers, and not the other way around. Chester and Elias Baker threw the first shovel, bought up the farmland, and hired the men—Poles, Italians, Hungarians, Croats— who arrived in large numbers by wagon or train. The men slept in camps and, later, company houses. Their wives washed black coveralls and had babies, bought groceries with company scrip. The babies grew up, worked, married, were drafted. The lucky ones came back to mine coal. Union wages meant Fords and Chryslers, split-level houses. On Susquehanna Avenue, shops opened. The new public high school had an Olympic-size swimming pool.

When the mines failed, the reverse happened, like a film run backward. FOR SALE signs dotted the avenues. One by one the storefronts went dark. The miners, too, were extinguished, black lung or heart attacks or simple old age—never mind now, they are all equally dead. The children and grandchildren moved away, forgot everything. Only the widows remain. They will, if asked, point out the old mine roads, the clearings where tipples once stood: Baker One, Baker Four, Baker Seven, Baker Twelve.

This past holds no interest for Bobby Frame, though he owes his success to it—the distant memory of boom times, the ghost of prosperity that lingers in the town. Here, grand promises are met without skepticism. The landowners are churchgoers, people of faith. The agnostics—there are a few—need only look to history: Bakerton has been favored before, tapped by Industry's magic wand.

He lives a nomad's life, which is not for everyone. Four shale plays in six years: Barnett, Haynesville, Fayetteville, Marcellus. He is a star at the company, Dark Elephant Energy. Twice a year they fly him back to Houston and turn him loose at a training seminar. *This could be you someday,* the new recruits are told, and take notes.

If he's made sacrifices along the way—girlfriends who sent him packing, the college degree he didn't finish and now doesn't need. If he missed his high school reunion, family birthdays and holidays, weddings and funerals of people he loves. If regret can singe him without warning as he lies awake listening to motel noises, distant televisions, the ice machine down the hall. If all these things, so be it. In daylight the phantoms dissipate. He appears at the courthouse at eight-thirty promptly, his mind clear for the mission.

Beautiful property you've got here.

The new recruits take notes.

This Monday morning a trainee shadows him, Josh Wilkie from Boulder, Colorado. Bobby's had trainees before and appreciates the company. He's grown used to, but still dislikes, eating alone.

They meet in the Days Inn lobby and scan the breakfast buffet, which comes free with the room. Bobby selects a miniature box of cereal, a container of yogurt the size of a shot glass, four hard-boiled eggs, a paper bowl and plastic spoon.

"Once and done, that's the ideal. Two is okay, though. Two you can live with. Three visits, you're wasting your time. Still frozen inside." He tears open a Lender's bagel and lays it flat on the toaster. "Always. You have to put it through twice."

They watch the bagel's progress through the toaster, a horizontal grill that moves like a conveyor belt. A silvery scrape as it shoots out the bottom of the toaster. Hot in his hands as he returns it to the grill.

Late morning is best, Bobby explains, after the early chores. "Sometimes you get a wife, and you have to come back later to talk to the husband. That's not bad, to get the wife alone."

Josh Wilkie grins unwholesomely.

"Don't laugh. They're the decision makers, a lot of times. Get the wife on board, and you're home free." He thinks of Mrs. Mackey, the stubborn little woman who waved him off her porch as though swatting a fly. *Are you some kind of a salesman?*

"Get in, get out. It's that simple." It's the secret to his own success: on a good day he can get three leases signed before lunchtime. Five is his personal record. "Don't get hung up on the details. These people care about two things: what's in it for them, and how soon."

They set out for the courthouse, Josh riding shotgun, a curly-haired boy in need of a shave. He wears homemade bracelets on one wrist, woven from colored yarn. "Twenty-three," he says when Bobby asks. "I graduated last year." His degree is in horse crap, in Bobby's firm opinion. Also known as Recreation and Leisure Management.

"Resorts," Josh explains. "Health clubs, that kind of thing."

Horse crap.

"No kidding. How'd you settle on that?"

"I like to ski, you know? I'm great on skis. I've been skiing since I could walk." He is bright-eyed and pleased with himself, waiting to be praised

Bobby thinks, That is so impressive. Seriously, man: in the oil and gas business, skiing will be your secret weapon. It's almost an unfair advantage, when you think about it.

"No kidding," he says again.

The Saxon County courthouse sits at the center of town, three stories high and rambling, with tall columns in front. For a backwoods county it is an impressive structure—built a century ago, early in the coal boom. Today a third of it goes unused.

Bobby leads Josh Wilkie through the metal detector and up a creaking staircase—dark wood, the steps covered in linoleum streaked to look like marble. At the end of the corridor is the Registry of Deeds. The lights are on, the door propped open. The Seth Thomas clock above the counter reads 8:40. The clerk is not at her desk.

For a moment Bobby is confused. Then he sees the well-dressed man waiting on the bench. There is a sudden buzzing in his ears, like a distant alarm.

The sharp dresser gets to his feet. "Looks like I beat you to it."

Bobby feels a little queasy. He breaks out his salesman's smile. "Darling!" he says—breathlessly, like an ingénue in an old movie.

It's a bit of shtick that never gets old, at least for Bobby. This time it's for the benefit of Josh Wilkie, who stares at them, frowning.

"When did you roll into town?" says Bobby.

"Just last night. Rex Darling." He offers Josh Wilkie his hand.

The kid breaks into a goofy grin. "You guys know each other."

Bobby ignores him. He's had it with this kid, whom he blames for their disadvantage. They lost precious minutes at the Days Inn waiting for Josh's coffee: the urn ran empty, and the attendant took her time brewing a second pot. Having none himself, Bobby is severe about other people's vices—coffee, cigarettes, a drink to unwind. Needs that become the master of the man, dictating the architecture of his day.

He has never been on skis in his life.

Darling claps Bobby's shoulder. "I knew this joker in the Haynesville." *The Haynesville*, not *Louisiana*, the state of no interest beyond its shale play. Their two companies had done battle there, and a little horse-trading, swapping leases back and forth.

"Here you go." An unfamiliar clerk, a man, hands Darling a record book. Bobby glances sidelong at its spine.

"All right, then," says Darling. "You fellas have a good day."

He takes the book to a corner table and begins scribbling.

The clerk turns to Bobby, eyes him blankly like the stranger he is.

THEY ROLL ALONG NUMBER NINE ROAD, an old mining trail that intersects with the Dutch Road.

"How often do you shave?" Bobby asks.

Josh rubs at his chin. "Couple times a week."

"Not anymore. Now it's every day." There's more Bobby could say—*Grow up already. It's a sign of respect, numbnuts*—but he keeps quiet.

They turn onto the Dutch Road, past Jim Norton's pine forest. Carl Neugebauer's southern pasture sits at the top of the hill. Bobby signed both properties last week. "With Kipler to the east, that's six hundred acres, altogether," he tells Josh.

"Wow. Wow. That's amazing." The kid studies the topo map spread across his lap, and locates each property with his finger. "Kipler, Norton, and—Neugebauer. What's in between, though? It's a big one. Parcel one-twelve."

There is an awkward silence.

"That's Mackey. Dairy farmers. They need some time to think it over." Bobby keeps his eyes on the road. Both times Mrs. Mackey saw him coming and met him on the front porch. He hasn't, so far, made it into the house.

Quickly he changes the subject. Richard Devlin Jr. owns sixty acres. By all appearances, he's just sitting on it. Bobby drives slowly along the southern edge of the property. There is a newish suburban-type ranch house—prefab, from the looks of it—and behind it, a patch of neatly mown grass. Beyond lie acres of deciduous forest, a creek in need of dredging, a sloping pasture overrun with kudzu.

They pull into the gravel driveway. Up close the house looks naked, not a shrub or a tree around it, as though it dropped out of the sky. No porch, not even a sidewalk, just a single-story crackerbox wrapped in aluminum siding. Bobby knocks and waits. He hears voices inside, television noises. The door is opened by a young wife in a pink quilted bathrobe.

"Can I help you?" She looks younger than Bobby, older than Josh Wilkie but just barely—blond hair in a ponytail, glasses sliding down her nose.

"Mrs. Devlin?" Bobby introduces himself and Josh, whom he calls *my associate*. "I'm sorry to bother you so early."

In fact it's already ten in the morning, the sun blazing overhead. Mrs. Devlin doesn't keep farmers' hours. She squints in the bright light. "Oh, that's all right. Come on in."

The room is sparsely furnished in a way Bobby has seen before, the peculiar poverty of couples with young children. There is a couch, a giant television, and not much else. In one corner sits a plastic laundry basket filled with plastic toys. Mrs. Devlin leads them into the kitchen. Behind her back Josh gives Bobby a wink. It's easy to imagine slapping him, his stubbly face reddening. Bobby can hear it already, the seamy way Josh will tell the story—*Just out of the shower. She came to the door in her bathrobe*—and is irritated in advance.

The kitchen is sunny and airless, smelling of breakfast—toast crumbs on the counter, greasy dishes in the sink. At the table a girl child, three or four years old, eats saltines off a plastic plate.

"I stayed home from school," she announces.

Bobby sits beside her. Though it's already late August, the vinyl tablecloth is seasonal for Independence Day, with a stars-and-stripes motif.

"You look too little for school."

The child takes umbrage. "I'm in *kinnergarten*," she slurs, like a tiny, belligerent alcoholic.

"She's small for her age. Is it just me, or is it cold in here?" Mrs. Devlin hugs the bathrobe around her.

"It's pleasant," says Bobby, already sweating through his shirt.

Without asking, she pours them glasses of orange juice. "Rich worked a double. He should be back anytime now."

"Where does he work?" Bobby asks, drinking gratefully.

"Out the prison." Mrs. Devlin frowns, as though wondering for the first time what these strangers are doing in her house. "I thought you were friends of his." Her bathrobe is floor length, bulky as a down comforter. Beneath it, presumably, she has a body. Bobby thinks of women in Arab countries, draped head to toe in cloth.

"No, ma'am, though I look forward to meeting him. Your neighbor Carl Neugebauer thought Rich would be interested in doing some business." He launches into his pitch then, though it's a clear waste of effort. He'll have to rewind the whole thing when the husband gets home.

When he finishes, Mrs. Devlin looks flabbergasted. "On *our* land? Are you sure?"

Beneath the robe she could be anorexic or six months pregnant, a mermaid or a double amputee.

"Yes, ma'am. The geologists have already mapped the whole area. We'd have to do some additional testing, of course. Find the best spot to drill."

At last he hears an engine in the distance, a scattering of gravel. A moment later a screen door slams. Bobby gets to his feet just as Rich Devlin charges into the kitchen. He is Bobby's size, a big blond man in a green uniform. His eyes go from Bobby to Josh to his wife in her bathrobe. "Who the hell are you?"

"Beautiful property you've got here," Bobby says.

THAT EVENING, BACK AT THE DAYS INN, he takes papers from the safe: leases signed and unsigned, topo maps, internal memos, engineers' reports. He piles them methodically on the spare bed and settles in for the evening. The television plays constantly, its volume muted. Bobby senses rather than sees the images flickering across the screen. The shifting light is a live presence. It warms him like a blazing hearth.

Six years in motel rooms, you develop a system for living. He is a natural traveler, descended from pilgrims, his great-great-grandfather born on the trail from Nauvoo. Bobby needs nothing beyond what the Days Inn offers. He uses and appreciates each amenity: the magnifying mirror for shaving, the coffeemaker to heat water for his Cup O' Noodles, the plastic ice bucket to cool his Sprites, available at all hours from the machine down the hall. Years ago, in the Haynesville, he'd bunked at a Comfort Inn outside Baton Rouge, and learned the value of the in-room safe. That establishment was crawling with landmen—his rivals from Logistix, Diamond Energy, and Creek. He saw their faces each day at breakfast, and later at the county courthouse, a half-dozen opponents shadowing him. A recurrent nightmare plagued him: his door left open as the chambermaid vacuumed, his leases and maps in plain sight on the bed.

It is foolish to be surprised by Rex Darling's arrival in the Valley. His company, Energy Logistix, was Elephant's main competitor in the Fayetteville, and put up a good fight in the Barnett. For nearly a month Bobby has pressed his advantage in the Marcellus, signing more leases for less money than anyone in company history. Before another landman even set foot in Saxon County, the entire Dutch Road belonged to Bobby Frame.

And yet, this morning, Darling got the jump on him. Bobby thinks again of Josh Wilkie's coffee, the travel mug stinking up his truck. The odor disgusts him, an ancestral revulsion, the one speck of Mormon still left in him. The rest of his clan has shed it completely, by the looks of them—his sisters running wild, his father shrugging off the priesthood like an old sweater. Apostates, jack Mormons. It is hard to credit. Bobby's father had missed his whole childhood—busy, always, with some vague church business down at the stake.

From his briefcase he takes a signed contract. Rich Devlin had asked few questions. Left-handed, he signed carefully. He drew the letters deliberately, like a schoolboy who knows his penmanship is poor. He seemed surprised that his wife's signature was required, too.

Shelby Devlin, she'd written, in tiny round script.

Bobby glances at the TV screen. An actor playing a pathologist stands over a cadaver. He places an organ on a hanging scale, the kind used to weigh supermarket produce. Similar shows play at all hours, on multiple channels. Inexplicably, they are popular. People like to be grossed out.

He unfolds the topo map and spreads it across the bed, a hundred square miles of Saxon Valley. In the upper-left quadrant—Sector 1, where the Dutch Road curves westward—most properties are already shaded blue. He takes a blue highlighter and colors in the square marked DEVLIN. The property borders Neugebauer to the south. Both can be drilled from the same well pad, if the geology pans out.

Blue means a lease has been signed, the property not yet developed. Sector 1 shows, at the moment, two solid but separate blocks of blue: to the south, Fetterson, Norton, and Yahner; to the north, Devlin, Kipler, and Neugebauer. Around and between them are a few odd parcels, glaring white and irregularly shaped, like pieces of a puzzle. These are Bobby's failures, the defeats that haunt him—Mackey, Rouse, and Krug. Rouse and Krug he could have predicted: terse monosyllables, names for stubborn people. Bobby has noticed this time and again. The single syllables are unshakably convicted, a condition he knows intimately. His name, after all, is Frame.

He places Devlin's signed contract in the safe.

A horizontal well can stretch for two miles, beneath several properties. Drilling requires contiguous parcels, the signed consent of everyone involved. Arvis Kipler signed immediately; his three hundred acres are the linchpin. Farther to the south, Fetterson and Norton signed the very same morning, a sunny Monday. Feeling lucky, Bobby stopped next at Cob Krug's trailer.

He's been threatened before, but never by a man in a wheelchair.

The camera zooms in on the meat, a human heart with visible apertures. Bobby conjures up names from high school biology: auricle, ventricle, vena cava, aorta. Words he connects to the neat line drawings in his textbook, and not this revolting chunk of flesh.

The old cuss ran him off with a shotgun, twelve-gauge. The memory still stings him, the rudeness. Bobby was raised to value small kindnesses, the *please* and *thank you* and *have a nice day*.

And yet in the grand scheme Cob Krug does not matter. Like Rouse, the soybean farmer, Krug is an afterthought. Located at the far ends of the tract, neither property is a deal breaker. Mackey is the real problem. Mackey lies smack in the middle.

There's no way around it: he has to have Mackey.

The topo map is his daily accounting. Its companion, the stream map, depicts the kingdom to come. It shows the Dutch Road divided into parcels, a broken line connecting them. That broken line is code for pie in the sky, the company's wishful thinking, the elaborate fantasy of a team of engineers. The project—known internally as the Freeway—will connect Saxon County to the great neural network of interstate pipelines: the fabled Continental, the mighty Tennessee. These names are an incantation, their authority nearly biblical. Greater minds than Bobby's have planned the Freeway's spurs and junctions, its ultimate trajectory through the Lower 48. But only Bobby can make it happen. Thy Kingdom come.

The Mackey farm connects Kipler to Devlin/Neugebauer. Mackey makes all things possible.

Three visits, and you're wasting your time.

Occasionally—on restless nights, alone in his motel room—his yearnings overcome him. It is Bobby's version of drunkenness, or what he imagines drunkenness to be. He envisions a supertract,

Texas-size: Rouse, Kipler, Mackey, Devlin, Neugebauer, Krug, Fetterson, Norton, Yahner, Beale. The entire northern half of Carbon Township waiting to be drilled.

On the second floor of the Days Inn, Rex Darling sits in an identical room, studying his own map.

Let it begin.

The shareholders meet quietly on a sultry day in August, at a suburban Marriott ten miles from downtown Houston— a change instituted by Quentin Tanner, the new director of corporate communications. The former site, a huge Hyatt attached to the convention center, welcomed each group with much fanfare: announcements racing across a news ticker in the lobby, cheery greetings ("WELCOME BACK, DARK ELEPHANT SHAREHOLDERS!") on the outdoor marquee. The shareholders enjoyed the hoopla. They are a sociable group, disposed toward friendliness. As boys they joined fraternities and played on teams. They are businessmen in a sunny climate, where Business is revered alongside God and Country, the large, good things all sane people hold dear. They are proud of their association with Dark Elephant, unambivalent about its dealings. Quarterly profits are greeted with backslaps and broad Texas grins, a manly and uncomplicated delight.

Business in a sunny climate. It's an alien landscape to Tanner, a tenth-generation New Hampshire Yankee, congenitally taciturn, discreet on a cellular level; his native gifts honed by twelve years in Washington, chess with the masters: Big Tobacco, the NRA. Six months ago, a mendacious headhunter wooed him to Houston— charmless, treeless, a damp sinkhole with urban pretensions. A vast wasteland of concrete and melting blacktop, shimmering in the heat.

An hour before the meeting, the Alamo Ballroom quivers

with purposeful activity. Hotel employees wheel in urns of coffee, shrink-wrapped pastry trays the size of hula hoops. Tanner makes a minute adjustment to the podium. At the front table he lays out registration packets, neat rows of printed name tags, then stands off to the side with his arms crossed, watching the shareholders trickle in. He counts white men in three varieties, middle-aged, old, ancient. A few wear bolo ties without irony. He notes several pairs of cowboy boots, a smattering of western hats.

The name tags, it develops, are superfluous. At the buffet table men help themselves to coffee and pastry, hollering greetings like old friends. *Hey, buddy. How you been?* In Texas it is the standard form of address, equally appropriate to colleagues and rivals, superiors and underlings. Waiters are buddies, also mechanics, mailmen, bartenders, distant cousins. (*Amigo* may be substituted for janitors, or the young fella who mows your lawn.) In any social interaction, *buddy* strikes the right note—masculine, casual—and eliminates the need to remember anyone's name.

Tanner takes a seat at the registration table. The shareholders loom above him. Even correcting for hats and boots, they are a tall group. He is six one, a lanky man back east. In this room he is barely average. It's been studied, of course, this correlation between height and income. In Texas the effect, like all others, is exaggerated.

His cell phone buzzes in his pocket: his assistant, sounding panicked. "Quintin, I'm in the hotel, but I can't find the room to save my life. There are no signs anywhere."

"Excellent," Tanner says.

He directs her to a bank of elevators at the far end of the lobby. "We're on B Level, all the way down the hall. If you still can't find it, call me back."

He glances at the clock, does a quick head count, studies a registration packet: the day's agenda, second-quarter financials, a sheaf of photocopied magazine articles from *Forbes* and *Petroleum Week*. At his insistence, Polly included a dense, highly technical article by

Dr. Amy Rubin, published last fall in the academic journal *Structural Geology*.

I don't know, Quintin. Are they really going to read that?

I doubt they can *read it. Anyway, that's not the point.*

The point was to flatter Amy Rubin, who would be delivering the keynote.

Above Tanner's head, at a great height, the shareholders shake hands and slap shoulders. Natural selection? Bovine growth hormone?

Hey, buddy. How's bidness? In Texas it is a universal value, like rooting for the home team. Even janitors and landscapers are pro-Business.

Two years ago, the shareholders had never heard of Amy Rubin, a geology professor at a remote SUNY campus in upstate New York. Even now, few would recognize her name. And yet her *Structural Geology* article had set off a firestorm. With that one dry, impenetrable article, Amy Rubin had changed the fortunes of every man in the room.

At least, no Texan is *anti*-Business. It is as unthinkable as being anti-Jesus.

A moment later Polly charges in through a side door, carrying a cardboard banker's box. Tanner appreciates her from a distance, a big healthy girl of twenty-three who slightly resembles one of President Bush's twin daughters—charmingly awkward, today, in her pumps and grown-up suit. He's had countless assistants over the years, all brighter and more ambitious, but none as plucky and good-natured as Polly Granger. He hired her for her daughterly prettiness, wholesome and apple-cheeked; the toothy smile that appeared, for much of her adolescence, on the side of Fort Worth city buses, where her orthodontist father had purchased ad space. Tanner has observed her effect on the shareholders, the old goats flirting like rogue uncles, the sort of good-natured joshing that shreds his nerves. He suspects—hopes, really—that it hides some darker impulse, some geriatric carnal fascination he can't begin to grasp. To him Polly is sexless as a plush toy. She is simply too adorable to fuck.

She teeters toward him. "I swear I'm never going to find my way out of this place. I been carrying this thing for a half hour." She sets the box on the table and digs out the new issue of *Businessweek*. "It doesn't come out till Wednesday, but I got them to overnight us one. I made two hundred copies."

Tanner winces at the headline—THE NEW COWBOYS. Still, the cover photo is undeniably iconic: Kip "the Whip" Oliphant, Dark Elephant's flamboyant CEO, dressed head to toe in worn denim, astride a sand-colored horse. Tanner himself had arranged the shoot, dispatching a photo crew to Promised Land Ranch, the Whip's thousand-acre spread down south.

"I don't get it," says Polly. "Why are we hiding out in the basement?"

"It's a precaution. There are certain fringe elements. Polly, not everyone agrees with what this company does."

A blank stare greets him. Her degree, from Sam Houston State, is in communications. He sees no evidence that she's read a newspaper in the last six months, or ever in her life.

"Environmental groups, for example. There's been some controversy. The last thing we need is some kind of organized protest."

"Against a oil company," says Polly, getting her facts straight.

"It's been known to happen."

"In Texas," she says, making double sure.

Tanner feels suddenly ridiculous. "Well, perhaps not. But as a general principle: Why risk it? When we gain nothing at all by showing our hand. How's the article?" he demands, changing the subject. "Don't tell me you didn't read it."

"I looked at the pitchers. I'm no speed reader, Quintin. I had a half hour to burn off these copies and hustle over here."

Tanner flips to the article and reads.

The New Frontier

Ten years ago, natural gas deposits in shale rock were considered too costly to extract. Now, with the advent of **hydraulic fracturing** (graphic), a new generation of titans has opened a controversial frontier in energy exploration. Clifford "Kip" Oliphant, founder and CEO of Dark Elephant Energy, is leading the charge.

Polly reads over his shoulder, smelling of mint chewing gum and fruity shampoo. "*Clifford*? That's his name?"

"Dear God, woman. How long have you worked here?"

"I know, shame on me. But no one calls him that."

"Ah. I see." You sweet puppy, he thinks. You golden retriever of a girl. "But, Polly, I'm curious. What name did you imagine was written on his birth certificate? Kip? *Whip*?"

"I guess I never thought about it. They all have nicknames." She scans the rows of name tags. "Butch Rowe. Pooch McClure. Tuck Winans. Stop me when you hear a actual Christian name."

Tanner stares out over the hotel ballroom, two hundred alpha males juggling coffee cups and frosted pastry. The decibel level has risen. It's a bit like listening to the ocean, the rhythmic tumble of hearty greetings, the low roar of manly bluster and all-American good cheer.

A man who needs a nickname for a nickname. For occasions when *Kip* seems stuffy, unduly formal.

Hey, buddy, how's bidness?

It takes brass to wear a cowboy hat in the modern world. In Tanner's view, it is a confident look.

We are on the verge of a new inflection point.

Upstairs in the Lone Star Suite, the Whip is cracking, fortified by a successful morning: a swim in the hotel pool, twenty minutes of chi gung moves, his affirmations and breathing exercises, a pot of strong green tea. The shareholder buffet he avoids like kryptonite. His body is an advanced machine, precisely calibrated, accustomed to its rarefied fuel. The proof is in the mirror. His suntanned face looks thirty-five, not fifty. His body fat holds steady at 11 percent.

Now is the time to leverage our first-mover advantage, he tells the mirror. *To make strategic investments across the unconventional activity value chain.*

The Whip is a man of method. For the past twelve hours he's sequestered himself in this hotel room, preparing for battle. His wife has been instructed not to disturb him. "For any reason," he added for emphasis—yesterday afternoon as he headed for the door.

"For *any* reason?" Gretchen was at that moment watching a tennis match on television while striding furiously on her old Stair-Master. The machine was at high rev, whirring manically. She wore a strained, panicked look. "What if Allie is kidnapped? What if the house catches fire?"

The Whip said, "Call Pig."

His lawyer, Piggy Bunch, is on speed dial. In any variety of catastrophe, it's the only number he ever thinks to call.

He's explained it to her repeatedly, in simple terms. Life is a house with many rooms. He inhabits one room at a time; how can he do otherwise? And when he leaves a room, he turns off the light.

He is precise in his requirements, a quality that wears on her; though in public she attempts a positive spin: *Kip is very focused.* It is undeniably true, if reductive. Her husband's monomania is nearly mystical. He views the world as a static tableau with, at any given moment, a single moving part, an isolated point of dynamism. He trains his full attention on that point. With practice it is simple as a sing-along: follow the bouncing ball.

His garment bag contains a plain gray suit, impeccably tailored; new socks and underwear, still in the package; and two identical white shirts. He tries and rejects the first shirt. The sleeves feel, to him, a quarter inch too long.

There are no small decisions.

At that moment, the point of dynamism is located six floors below him, bouncing like a squash ball off the walls of the Alamo Ballroom, where two hundred wealthy men are stuffing themselves with peach Danish. The Whip's own remarkable life—his hundred intimate friends and thousand acquaintances; his one-of-a-kind house in the Houston suburbs, designed by the architect Milo Gabanis; the ranch in Hidalgo County, home to his four dogs and eleven of his best horses—does not, at this moment, exist. Even his wife and daughter have grown distant, receded like a distant shoreline. The successful life is a solo voyage, navigation a simple matter. He trains his telescope on the point of dynamism, glittering in the night sky.

The Next Big Play.

Houses in Umbria and Aspen; golf properties in Arizona and Scotland. The pro football team of which he owns a 20 percent share. A private hedge fund valued at eight hundred million; diverse business interests in and around Houston: the wine bar, the high-end steakhouse, the racetrack he financed and had a hand in designing, where one of his own horses, Count Your Blessings, won her first title.

The company name, Dark Elephant, is the Whip's own coinage—at once a play on his own name; a nod to the parent company, Darco Energy; and a clear signal of their politics. The track and restaurants, the hedge fund, are assets of Whipsmart Ventures, his own personal holding company. Eighteen employees—accountants, lawyers, assistants, and their assistants—manage his affairs.

How he got here is the opposite of a secret—a tale told so often, by so many, that it's no longer his story. Like a new religion, it belongs to the entire world. Twelve years ago, a Texarkana crackpot named Wade Dobie joined the Whip's engineering team, and sold him on horizontal drilling. Logistix had already done it, drilled sideways through bedrock, to squeeze the last drops out of some tired oil fields. The same technique could be applied to the gas patch.

Not even plumb sideways. A sixty-five-degree angle would do it, Wade Dobie claimed.

A cautious man would have dismissed the idea outright. But the Whip had, at the time, some land on his hands—a thousand leases along the Louisiana border, in a limestone formation called the Austin Chalk. He bet big when no one else would, on land no sane person would look twice at, on technology that never should have worked in the first place. It took some doing, a few disgruntled crews hired and fired, but the industry was in a slump and manpower was cheap and he always (always) had some land on his hands.

Dobie was wrong about the angle but right about everything else. The Chalk was a gold mine. While the rest of the industry was tanking, the Whip was standing in high cotton, Darco trading at eighty. (This in high summer, when every furnace in the Northern Hemisphere was gathering dust.) Deep into Louisiana, his landmen bought up leases. Contracts were signed, pads cleared, rigs sent. To fund the operation, he begged and borrowed. His stepfather complained about the massive debt, but without conviction. The Whip's strategy—borrow and buy, borrow and buy—had worked before, spectacularly. Dar had learned to stay out of the way.

Texas, Louisiana, Arkansas, Dakota. Wherever the Whip drilled, an entire industry followed: Logistix. Diamond Energy. Creek. He won by outrunning them.

Now is the time to leverage our first-mover advantage.

This morning he'll propose a major expansion, an aggressive strike into West Virginia and Pennsylvania, the mighty Marcellus. (Later, God and governor willing, New York will be ripe for the picking. But that's a conversation for another day.) For months his landmen have been signing leases. The Next Big Play.

We're on the verge of a new inflection point. Eyes closed, the Whip visualizes himself striding to the podium, the crowd applauding madly, rising to its feet. The front-and-center seats reserved, always, for his board of directors. Three are longtime cronies of his stepfather, family friends the Whip thinks of, collectively, as the Old Boys. The Old Boys vote as a block, their loyalty indisputable: if he wanted to send a drill rig to Mars, the Old Boys would be present at the launch. The rest of the board is a crapshoot. Pooch McClure can sometimes be bullied, Tuck Winans bribed into submission; but the others are beyond his reach. Floyd Whitty, the chair, has been a trial from day one—a hasty choice, brought on to fill an unexpected vacancy (the old chair's ill-timed mental breakdown, after an unusually brutal IRS audit). After a full year at his post, Floyd has yet to grasp the Whip's management style. Once in a while he'll listen to reason; but not always. With Floyd, you can never be sure.

Drilling a horizontal well in Pennsylvania costs three million dollars.

By his engineers' last count, six thousand wells are waiting to be drilled.

He runs a comb through his wet hair—a Whip trademark, shaggy blond and permanently windblown, as though he's just back from a regatta. In an industry run by crew cuts—bankers and ranchers, ex-military, Southern Baptists—it is an unorthodox look. But like every detail of his appearance, it is calculated for effect.

We are on the verge of a new inflection point.

He will speak directly to the point of dynamism—located front and center, in the vicinity of Floyd Whitty's groin.

In stocking feet, the Whip paces. He fires off a text message to Quentin Tanner, his new communications director: **locked and loaded!!!**

The same well could be drilled for two million in Texas, with its good weather and smiling regulators, its unorganized labor and friendly tax code.

As always, Tanner responds promptly. He is an odd duck, precise, conscientious. Even his texts sound formal: **Your adoring public awaits.** To the shareholders he is a cipher, soft-spoken and persnickety, a pasty beanpole in a dark suit. *That fruity fella,* the Old Boys call him.

The Whip protests—*nah, Quint's all right*—but in his heart he isn't sure. Tanner has never mentioned a girlfriend. Then again, he's never mentioned parents or siblings, friends or neighbors, a favorite sports team, a church, a dog. Such ordinary things; why make a secret of them? Why refuse to be a person like anyone else? This deliberate mysteriousness strikes the Whip as unnatural, though maybe it's normal in Connecticut or Massachusetts, where Tanner comes from. The small states with all the colleges. The land of Pilgrims and Division Three football, covered half the year in snow.

In his severe dark suits he seems to have stepped out of a painting, some long-dead Dutchman who's lost his hat.

At its next meeting, in three short weeks, the board will vote on the proposed expansion. Even with the Old Boys in his corner, and possibly Tuck Winans, the Whip takes nothing for granted. Floyd Whitty's support is key.

The point of dynamism coincides, always, with the Whip's own interests—a pattern observed over the years by certain of his wives and girlfriends, or by their therapists.

The Whip texts back: **time hack???** Tickled, still, by, this new way of communicating, learned from his preteen daughter. The immediacy of it delights him, a giddy throwback to the walkie-talkies of his youth.

Tanner's response comes instantly. **Showtime in ten.**

The Whip frowns. The word *showtime* troubles him. Maybe the

Old Boys are right; maybe Tanner is a gay. Though in Connecticut or Massachusetts, how could you tell?

He replies: **roger that—armed and ready!!!** His fondness for military lingo is another trademark. Though not himself a veteran, he considers it his birthright, his only inheritance from his actual father.

He has trouble discerning who is homosexual. Movie and TV actors all seem gay to him.

New socks and underwear are the cheapest kind of renewal. A fresh pair of socks puts a bounce in his step.

"I'LL HAND IT TO YOU, WHIP. That was some song and dance."

The hotel bar is quiet at this hour, the workday ended, the shareholders speeding off in all directions, toward home in its various incarnations: wives and children, mistresses, other bars. In short, an optimal moment to pour a drink down the throat of Floyd Whitty, a conversation long in coming. The Whip has done his homework. He knows what there is to know about Floyd's assets and liabilities, ex-wives and children, habits and allegiances; his tastes in liquor, women, and cigars.

Kip waits until the bartender brings their drinks. It's dunking day for Floyd, time to surrender to his personal Lord and Savior. Time for Floyd to come to Jesus.

"I need your support, buddy. Fish or cut bait."

Floyd gulps his bourbon and branch, half the glass in one go. "Weak," he says. "Listen, I know you got to spend money to make money. My question is the pace of it. Maybe stick our toe in before you dive us in headfirst."

Kip nods solemnly. "Floyd, I see your point." He excels at this part—the ego-soothing concessions, the pose of reasonableness. "But those leases are already bought and paid for. We got 'em cheap, but they weren't free. And we don't make a dime back till we start drilling."

"I know it." Floyd sighs audibly, the sad music of paternal disappointment, a sound that fills Kip with despair. "Though you might a thought of that before you went crazy signing them. If you don't mind my saying."

This gets Kip's back up. "Well, I guess I could have waited around for Logistix or Creek to get the same idea. Of course, then we say sayonara to twenty-five an acre." He drinks deeply. "Trust me on that one, Floyd. You weren't around for the Haynesville."

"I wadn't. But I heard." The Louisiana operation had devolved into a cattle auction, the project idling for years while the cagy Cajun landowners comparison shopped, everyone holding out for a better deal. "Still and all. Three million a well is some tab. Where's all that money going?"

Floyd sits back glowering as Kip explains the ways Pennsylvania isn't Texas. Well-boring is tricky in the freeze months. Winding mountain roads are lousy for truck traffic; God only knows how many will have to be widened or repaved. The one-horse towns are short on motel rooms and apartments. Thousands of roustabouts will need somewhere to sleep.

The old cheapskate nearly inhales his drink. "You mean to tell me we're paying for that, too?"

"Logistix did it up in Dakota. Prefab bunkhouses, two hundred beds apiece."

"You're kidding me. We're in the real estate bidness now?"

"There's an outfit in New Jersey that'll truck them in. A week to ship it, ten days to put it together. You got your bunkhouse inside a month. It's something to see." There is more, much more, he could say, having witnessed with his own eyes the raw miracle—the semis hauling huge sections of wall and roof, the twenty-man crew assembling the pieces right on site, basement, subfloor, plumbing, electrics, a geometry so intricate no human mind could have dreamed it. Watching, Kip felt his eyes fill. The spectacle moved him in ways he had no words for. He blessed the new century and its wonders,

understanding it to be a rare moment in history, like the building of
the Pyramids or the founding of Texas—an era of risk and prospect,
an age when men are gods.

Floyd's eyes narrow. "And all this is included in the price tag?
That three million a well."

"The worker housing is extra. But think what we saved—"

"On those leases. I heard you the first ten times." Floyd rises.
"All right, then. You made your case, Whip. Let me study on it."

He drains his glass and puts on his hat.

With Floyd gone, gravity shifts abruptly. Kip becomes aware,
again, of his surroundings, the point of dynamism darting around
the room like a june bug. When did Amy Rubin come into the
bar? Possibly she's been there all along, reading *Time* magazine at
a corner table, a highball glass at her elbow, an immense leather
pocketbook on the chair opposite, like a stand-in dinner date. She
is small and dark-haired, with the round, delicate features of a silent
film actress, an archaic sort of prettiness to which women no longer aspire: porcelain skin, a rosebud mouth. Kip watches her turn a
page and hold it at arm's length, and feels a hot pang of recognition.
Despite his wife's nagging, he is offended at the very idea of reading
glasses. To wear them even at home seems a capitulation. He studies restaurant menus ahead of time, on the Internet, to avoid public
embarrassment. He wonders, now, if anyone is fooled.

Kip ambles toward her table. He's worked with geologists for
half his life—rumpled, whiskery men, palpably uncomfortable in
polite society, like farm animals brought indoors. The female version, by all rights, should be ugly as homemade sin. But Amy Rubin
is attractive, for her age anyway. He's never dated or married a
woman old enough to need reading glasses.

"Everything all right here? You look like you seen a ghost."

She sets down *Time* and stares as though she can't quite place
him. Come off it, lady, he thinks. This is my company. You're here
on my dime.

He extends his hand. "Kip Oliphant. Happy to meet you, Miss Rubin. Is it Miss?"

"Doctor. Or Amy is fine."

Old maid, he guesses, and not happy about it. "Amy, I want to thank you for coming all the way down here. You were a big help to us."

In truth, the keynote had gone on longer than necessary. With the lights dimmed for her PowerPoint presentation, more than one shareholder had seized the opportunity for a nap. It had taken all Kip's self-control to avoid hollering: *Wake up, boys! She's coming to the good part.* And sure enough, in the end, the number roused them. It would have roused a corpse. The number was so staggeringly large that the room gasped audibly. Rubin had upped her estimate. The Marcellus Shale held more gas than anyone had imagined: by her calculations, a mind-blowing *fifty trillion cubic feet.*

Now she glares at Kip like he called her a sonofabitch. "I'm a scientist. I'm always happy to talk about my research."

"Let me buy you a drink. It's the least I can do." He grins. "In a year or two, you'll a bought me another ranch."

She flinches as though he slapped her.

"Thanks, but I can't." She stands, stuffing *Time* into her giant pocketbook. "I have a plane to catch."

WELCOME TO NOWHERE

SPRING 2012

1.

The town is named for its coal mines. The prison guard is named for his father. Both feel the weight of their naming, the ancestral burden: congenital defects, secondhand hopes. Condemned, like all namesakes, to carry another's history, the bloopers and missteps, the lost promise. The concessions of age, its bitter surrenders; the rare and fleeting moments of grace.

At Deer Run Correctional Institute, on a Friday morning in May, Richard Devlin Jr. walks the length of F Block, making his rounds.

"A man needs privacy," Hops says from behind the sheet. "I've explained this before."

The sheet—bleach-smelling, washed thin—is stretched across the front-facing bars of his cell. It's a stunt he's pulled before, though never on Devlin's watch.

Devlin waits, his arms crossed. From somewhere behind him, an odd noise—a metallic chinking, like the tap of an ice pick—echoes through the corridor.

"I'm talking about a human right. A basic need like food and shelter. I'm getting aggravated."

The prison is named for the road it sits on—years ago, a winding country lane scattered with red dog, bordered by forest and traveled mainly in buck season. Smoothly paved now, and widened, a four-lane highway the COs call Roadkill Run.

Devlin says, "I don't make the rules."

Hops steps closer to the sheet and speaks in a low voice. "Tell me one thing. You got a door on the bedroom at home? The baffroom?"

"This isn't about me." Devlin, too, lowers his voice. There is a certain intimacy to speaking through the sheet. They are emboldened by its presence, like a Hasidic couple making love.

What the hell is that noise?

"You got a wife, boss? You let her see you on the crapper?"

Devlin is practiced at deflecting such questions. In his ten years at Deer Run, he has never spoken of Shelby or the kids, never once. "Sorry, Hops. Didn't know you had a wife in here."

From the next cell comes a stifled laugh. "Give it up, man," someone calls.

"All right, fine. You win, boss." Hops pulls down the sheet with a flourish. He is older than Devlin, by decades possibly. Or possibly not: his brown skin is unwrinkled, his braids more black than gray. His cheekbones are dotted with freckles that looked painted on, round as pencil erasers and nearly as large.

The chinking gets louder, as though somewhere on the cell block, a secret operation—salt mining, the carving of festive ice sculptures—is taking place.

"Thanks, Hops. I appreciate it." It's a lesson Devlin learned long ago: the inmates respond to simple courtesy, like anyone else. And yet few of the COs bother with *please* and *thank you*. The reality, which he'd been slow to understand, is that not everyone wants peace. Some guys—most, maybe—are in it for the fight.

Ignoring his sciatica—also inherited, another gift from his father—he continues on his rounds. At the end of the row he finds the source of the noise: Charles Polley, known as Cholley, clipping his toenails. Offill, his cell mate, picks idly at a guitar.

"Devlin? I thought Schrey was on today." Offill eyes with displeasure the flying shards of toenail.

"Tonight. I'll tell him you missed him."

Phil Schrey is a recent hire. Like most new COs he came in with a swagger, a pose the men saw through instantly. Naturally they pushed back, which only made him swing harder. It's a common mistake, but the smart rookie figures it out eventually. Schrey is not smart.

Cholley moves on to his left foot, a calculated hit on the big toe. A sliver of nail shoots across the room.

Offill brushes it away. "Fuck, man. How many toes you got?"

Devlin continues on his rounds. In the next cell Weems lies on his bunk reading a dog-eared paperback. Weems is always reading. In the afternoons he works in the prison library, and comes back with an armload of books.

What are you reading? Devlin would ask anyone else; but Weems doesn't welcome conversation. He is a local kid, possibly the quietest inmate Devlin has ever encountered. It's hard to imagine him doing any of what's in his jacket, all meth-related. More and more, Deer Run seems overrun with meth heads, skinny, wasted men with stubbed teeth like jack-o'-lanterns. Weems looks better than most of them; he looks perfectly normal. A guy you wouldn't look at twice if he passed you on the street.

F Block is black, white, Hispanic. Except for Weems, they are city hoodlums from Pittsburgh and Philadelphia; men who'd never heard of Saxon County until the Department of Corrections sent them here. Deer Run is medium security, a designation that means nothing. Violent offenders, dope fiends, gangbangers, smash-and-grabbers: virtually anyone can land here, for virtually any reason. For no reason at all, if a judge decrees it so.

Next door Wanda sits barefoot on her bunk, rubbing lotion into her bare feet. She wears the same prison blues as everyone else, with a few modifications: shirttails knotted above her navel, waistband rolled down to her hips. Her eyes are circled with black liner, her lips painted frosty pink.

"Hi, sweetheart," she calls. It's impossible to sneak up on her; she is gifted with superhuman hearing and eyesight.

"You heard me coming."

"Honey, I hear them all coming." Her other superpower is the ability to make anything sound sexual. The COs find this disconcerting. Her simple presence provokes them, her languorous movements, her odd falsetto voice. Despite the bright makeup, the eyebrows plucked thin and arched into half circles, it is altogether too easy to see how she looked as a man: the clefted chin, the heavy jaw. Some—Schrey, for example—persist in calling her Juan. *Still got his prick, don't he?* It's a question Devlin can't answer, and wouldn't; something he'd rather not think about.

They chat for a few minutes, the Pirates losing to Cleveland, the summery weather. It's a basic lesson of the job, how anything can become normal. Compared with some of them, Wanda is a pleasure—no beefs, no attitude.

"You hear about that boy in the balloon? Out west somewhere. They had the radio on in the kitchen." Wanda works the early shift, prepping for breakfast. Devlin can see, across her forehead, the faint red line left by her hairnet.

"He went to some air show with his parents and stowed away on a hot air balloon. He out there floating all by hisself."

"Still?" says Devlin.

"What kind of mother, is my question."

"You can't watch them every minute."

"True that." The arched eyebrows give her a startled look, as though she's seen everything and decided, in the interest of efficiency, to remain surprised.

By the standards of the world she is not an attractive woman. Not a woman at all, in point of fact; and yet Devlin looks forward to seeing her each morning, a realization that unsettled him at first. Her bright face is a relief from the drab functionality of the prison, its unrelenting maleness. Though not technically a woman, she is womanlike; and he would rather look at women than men.

She rubs the lotion into her hands, her elbows. "The dishwasher is broken. We was scrubbing pots for a solid hour. You think I'm kidding." She shows him her fingernails, the red polish chipped in places.

It's unclear who smuggles in her makeup. Every few months, her sister comes from Philadelphia for a visit. Strictly speaking, the cosmetics are contraband, though Devlin is willing to look the other way. For another CO, it might be reason enough to toss her cell. Wanda is a kind of inkblot test for the COs. The decent ones treat her kindly. For the shitbirds—Schrey, Ianello, Poblocki on a bad day—she is an easy target.

Late in the day, from a certain angle, her face looks shadowed, mustache and sideburns coming in.

"Okay, Wanda. I need to shove off. Don't forget, there's a fire drill later."

"Wait, wait." She approaches the bars. "Boss, I need to ax you a question."

"Hit me."

"It's a delicate matter. Come here, I won't bite." She smiles, showing her gold tooth. "Unless you like that sort of thing."

Devlin approaches the bars.

"Officer Devlin, you have always treated me with respect. I appreciate that. These other ones, don't get me started." Wanda lowers her voice. "I am in a situation. Somebody stole my pills."

He catches a whiff of her vanilla-scented lotion, the same kind his wife uses. "You're not on the med list."

"You know what I mean."

Unhappily, he does. It's common knowledge that Mulraney supplies Wanda with birth control pills, to meet the mysterious hormonal needs of a man who wants to be a woman. What Wanda gives him in return is conjectured, but not known.

"It's the middle of my cycle. I can't be skipping pills. There are consequences." Intelligence in her eyes, a basic awareness: Wanda, a man in lipstick and false eyelashes, is saner than most.

Devlin speaks in a low voice. "How long have they been missing?" The question itself shows poor judgment. By acknowledging that the pills exist, he has already compromised himself.

"Since yesterday. Somebody came in here while I was at work." At this distance, despite the makeup, she looks neither masculine nor feminine. Viewed up close, Devlin thinks, everyone is just a person.

"And you're sure they're gone? You couldn't have misplaced them somewhere?"

Wanda looks meaningfully around the cell, ten feet square. There is a chair, a desk, a toilet, a bed.

Devlin says, "I'll see what I can do."

THE REST OF HIS TOUR IS UNEVENTFUL—no missing, no hang-ups. He has encountered both before and certainly will again, a thought he beats back each morning as he crosses the sally port into the low-slung bunker—overheated, fluorescent lit, a building that smells of its floors.

The men speak their own language, which only sounds like English. *Inmate* is what a CO calls you. *Prisoner* is what you call yourself. *Convict* is a term of respect, reserved for old-timers. A convict doesn't lie or game or cop or snitch. A convict settles beefs honorably, and holds his mud.

He has seen their papers, all of them. Cholley held up a department store on Christmas Eve. Offill has been down four separate times, for every offense imaginable—most recently, shooting a man in a meth beef. The last judge, smarter than most, gave him twenty years.

A *ding* is a head case, an inmate who acts crazy. They're all crazy, but most can dial it down when they need to. Not so the dings.

Hops was nabbed in Montgomery County for armed robbery, a Wawa convenience store. When a beat cop spotted him Hops gave chase, and took a bullet in the hip—causing, forever after, the trademark hitch in his step.

A ding's outburst can land him in the Ding Wing.

Wanda was pulled over on the Pennsylvania Turnpike in a tricked-out Pontiac Sunbird, registered in the name Andre Tibbs. "My boyfriend," she told the arresting officer—who, after she failed the Breathalyzer, had probable cause to pop the trunk.

Andre Tibbs was a big man. The medical examiner testified that he'd been bludgeoned in his sleep—250 pounds of deadweight, by the time Wanda crammed him into the trunk.

I am in a situation. Four hundred angry men locked up in cages, exactly one pair of breasts in sight. Yes, Wanda: you are in a situation.

Long ago the job seemed exciting, part of the larger something. If you'd watched enough television; if you came of age in a basement rec room, sprawled on shag carpet, gorging on cop shows and private detectives—Kojak and Columbo, Rockford and McMillan, gruff, charming men known by their last names. If you'd absorbed, along the way, the underlying lesson: that crime is the essential human experience, the most compelling and significant. That fighting crime is how heroes are made.

This is how a person becomes a prison guard.

At 7:50 the loudspeaker crackles: ten-minute movement. The dings shuffle downstairs to the med line.

The real mystery is where Mulraney gets the pills to begin with. Steals them from his wife, the COs joke, and maybe it's true. Steph Mulraney is pregnant for the fifth time. Sooner or later, the punch line goes, she'll figure out why.

After the movement, Devlin runs showers. A temporary procedure, supposedly, put in place after a series of incidents. Mainly it's been a success, though the COs still grouse about it. (*What next, we hold their dicks when they piss?*) The complaints are inevitable, wholly predictable—at Deer Run, any new policy is guaranteed to provoke a shitstorm. This is true no matter how effortless the change, how obviously necessary, how small.

Today half his inmates are on the shower list. At each cell he radios the control room; Gary Rizzo buzzes open the door; and Devlin walks the guy to the shower. Rinse, repeat, rinse, repeat. You imagine growing up to be Rockford or Columbo, and end up walking guys to the john.

The dings wait in line for their ding biscuits.

Wanda is booking whammers. Devlin is sure of it, though he's never witnessed one in progress.

You COs are off the hook, Hops said to him once. *What kind of fool come to the joint on purpose?*

Unless he sees one in progress, no action is required.

He understands, too late, that guarding prisoners isn't crime-fighting. It's crime-cleanup. The COs are janitors of the system, curators of its waste.

It isn't a forever thing. That's what you tell yourself. Like Wanda, he has served ten years.

He has never witnessed one in progress, which is all that matters. It is the CO's first lesson, the difference between what you know is happening and what you actually see. At least once each shift, Devlin puts somebody on notice: *Don't make me see it.* The inmates understand it is a matter of respect.

They are the smartest people he's ever met, and the dumbest. With one or two exceptions they are rash, impulsive, prone to flashes of anger and acts of monumental stupidity: the fistfight, the verbal threat, the ding fit. Yet they are inventive in ways regular citizens would never imagine, a creeping intelligence that can still dazzle him, a twisted kind of genius. Until Mulraney shut him down, Cholley ran a clandestine snack bar out of his cell, specializing in what he called a *chi chi:* nacho chips from the vending machine, crushed and mixed with water. The whole mess cooked right in the bag, on a steaming radiator—a salty orange-colored pancake with the distinctive Doritos flavor, *a zesty blend of spices and cheese.* Out in the world, he'd be a celebrity chef with his own TV show.

They work in the kitchen or laundry, lift weights, watch television. They go to AA meetings and earn GEDs. Do people on the outside do any more with their freedom? No; they do less. Devlin is thinking of Booby Marstellar and Nick Blick, the great friends of his childhood: one on permanent disability for phantom back pain, the other forty years old and living with his parents, still playing guitar in a band. Devlin's own brother spent years shooting heroin in the slums of Baltimore, the exact number of years unknown by anyone. All three, in Devlin's opinion, would be better off in jail.

Ten years ago he was in a similar situation, an unincarcerated prisoner—driving, at minimum wage, a truck for Miners Medical, delivering oxygen tanks to old geezers slowly suffocating from black lung. The days punctuated by a sound he couldn't forget, the old miners' wheezing and gasping. Like the doomed drip of a leaky faucet, it was a persistent reminder of his own life passing. His youth draining away a drop at a time, a deliberate, inexorable waste.

When the prison opened, half of Bakerton had answered the ad in the paper, five hundred applicants for the sixty full-time slots. A CO made union scale, the best-paying job for miles. Of the sixty men hired, fifty-six were veterans: men already inured to long hours, arbitrary rules and regulations, the palpable, ever-present threat. Not the smartest guys, maybe, but did it matter? Nobody was solving equations at Deer Run.

At 3:55 Schrey comes to relieve him. He is a beefy guy with a shaved head and a reddish goatee that resembles, from a distance, a scabbed-over brush burn, as though he's fallen on his face.

"All quiet, dude?" Schrey's fondness for the word is, like the goatee, a strike against him.

"Yep. Nothing to worry about." Devlin doesn't mention Hops's sheet trick or Wanda's pills. Why would he?

Don't make me see any (drugging, fistfights, contraband lipstick). Any (dick-sucking, stabbings, cooking of snack foods). Do what you have to do, assholes. Just don't make me see it.

It isn't a forever thing. You have an exit strategy, a plan for the future. This is what you tell yourself.

Devlin's solution didn't fall from the sky, not exactly. It will, very soon, rise up from the ground.

THAT NIGHT, LIKE MOST NIGHTS, he helps his dad, tending bar at the Commercial Hotel. Friday night, the start of the holiday weekend: every stool taken, men standing three-deep around the bar. Rich keeps his back to the drillers but can't help hearing them, the drawling blowhards shouting over the music. This particular crew, he's seen before—one greasy ponytail, one fat Mexican, a sawed-off muscleman and a pockmarked skinhead, his neck and arms covered with tattoos.

The ponytail is red-faced, half in the bag. "So we're laying there without a stitch on—"

"Do I want to hear this?" the Mexican says.

The ponytail raises a finger, professorial: "—without a stitch on, and she says, 'You can't stay. I got a dog.'"

"Besides you," says the muscleman.

"Besides me," the ponytail says.

A year ago they'd have attracted attention, their accents and soaring bar tabs, their brand-new pickup trucks racing around at all hours, more DUIs than the town cop could process. Recently the state police have stepped in, setting up a sobriety checkpoint on Colonel Drake Highway, a road busy with tank trucks.

The ponytail says, "I got a big dog and he don't like men."

Rich reaches under the counter and turns up the music, Gregg Allman singing: *Now she's with one of my good-time buddies. They're drinkin' in some cross-town bar.*

His dad comes out of the stockroom with an unfamiliar bottle. "Pour those guys a couple shots, will you?"

Rich studies the label. "Since when do you stock *cognac*?"

In the kitchen a telephone rings.

"I'll stock antifreeze if someone will drink it." Dick limps off to the kitchen favoring his left leg, the bum knee a souvenir of his years underground. He's been on his feet since 10:00 A.M. In the past year the lunch crowd has doubled, engineers and company men with expense accounts.

"A big motherfucker. A Doberman," the ponytail says.

A screaming wind of guitar, the song building to a climax: *Sometimes I feel like I've been tied to the whipping post.* Teenage Gregg groaning like a fifty-year-old bluesman, drunk and heartsick, beat down by life. A kid himself when he discovered the song, Rich hadn't fully appreciated the vocals. The other Allman, Duane, had been his hero, his and Booby's and Nick's, the three friends holed up with their guitars in the Marstellars' garage. They called their band Sportster, after Duane Allman's motorcycle: three guitars, no bass, no drums. They all wanted to be Duane.

"Now, normally that'd be a good sign." The ponytail shouts over the music. "It means she's conversant with male behavior."

"It means she'll pick up big piles of shit," the muscleman says.

Three Duanes: that's what they should have called themselves. They practiced for a year or two, though only Nick had shown actual talent. For all the good it had done him, or ever would.

Sometimes I feel like I've been tied to the whipping post.

Rich pulls an Iron City and sends it down the bar to his neighbor Peachy Rouse—hunched and bleary, spitting tobacco into a styrofoam coffee cup. "Hey, Peach. How you been?"

"Not so hot, Richard. We had some excitement out to my place." Peachy spits again, a quiet, practiced hocking. "Some kid broke into the barn and stole my fertilizer. Some goddamn drug addict."

"Jesus," Rich says.

"I don't care about the anhydrous. That costs me a buck a gallon. But now I got a busted valve and a couple sliced hoses. I have to replace the whole goddamn tank."

Rich nods silently—glad, for a moment, that his grandfather

isn't here to witness such a thing, Pap who lived on his farm for fifty years without a lock on the front door. "Did they get the guy?"

"Not this time." Peachy lowers his voice. "There was another one back in April. Tapped my wagon tank. I don't advertise it, because it was my own goddamn fault. I never should've left it out overnight."

Dick returns from the kitchen with a tray of Buffalo wings. "That was Shelby on the phone. I said you'd call her back."

"Jesus, now what?" Rich had left his cell phone in the truck, hoping for a few hours' peace. "I told her not to call here."

"Why don't you shove off early? Gia's around here somewhere. She can help me close."

Gia is always around somewhere, a world-class waitress when she remembers to show up for work. Like other local girls popular with the drill crews, she seems to live her whole life in or near a bar.

"It's her night off," says Rich.

"She won't mind." Dick makes a quick pass down the bar, collecting the fives and singles and stuffing them into Rich's shirt pocket. "You earned it, buddy. Now get out of here before I change my mind."

Rich grabs his keys and slips out the back door. All along Baker Street, every parking space is taken, pickup trucks with out-of-state plates and the occasional bumper sticker: DON'T MESS WITH TEXAS. DERRICKHANDS KNOW HOW TO TREAT A HOLE. A half dozen have crowded into the small lot behind the Commercial, despite the sign Rich hung there: EMPLOYEE PARKING ONLY. (*What employees?* Dick protested. *Half the time it's just my car out there. Richard, don't be a prick.*)

Rich heads for his truck, parked at the far end of the lot. Directly opposite, ten feet away, sits a red Mazda—locked in a stare-down, grille-to-grille, with Rich's truck. Even with its windows closed, he can hear its radio blasting hip-hop. The tattooed skinhead sprawls behind the wheel, leaning back against the headrest—eyes closed, sleeping off his drink.

Rich gets into his truck and flicks on the lights. A second later, a head pops up from beneath the Mazda's dashboard. Gia Bernardi squints into the headlights, her hair in disarray, her blouse undone.

Rich squeals out of the parking lot into the street.

He takes the long way home, avoiding the drunks on Drake Highway. The extra driving doesn't bother him—it's a relief, actually, after sixteen hours on his feet. Forty-two, he thinks. This is what forty-two feels like. If he's this beat at forty-two, how must his father feel? Dick at the stage in life where, if he were a car, you'd junk him before the transmission went.

In five minutes the lights of the town are no longer visible. Rich drives and thinks of Gia Bernardi, servicing strange men in the parking lot of the Commercial. His dad's favorite waitress, beloved like a daughter. If Dick ever found out, it would break his heart.

Forty-two feels like the midpoint of something. His dad will be seventy-six next month. Duane Allman was dead at twenty-four, his Sportster creamed by a flatbed truck.

Number Twelve Road is high and winding, unlit, the rusted tipple looming in the distance like a dinosaur's skeleton, all that remains of the old Baker Twelve. Beyond it lies a valley of dense forest still known as Swedetown, though the mining camp is long gone and no Swede has lived there in a hundred years. The valley belongs, now, to the Prines and Thibodeaux, clans connected by marriage but eternally feuding, each sequestered in its own ramshackle compound of junk cars and sagging sheds and stationary trailer homes, the whole mess wrapped in razor wire and guarded by rottweilers, as though anybody is fighting to get in. The families are known in town, easily recognized: the long Thibodeaux face replicated through the generations with uncanny accuracy; the pale and white-blond Prines. For a few years, in elementary school, Rich knew kids from both tribes, a marauding band of cousins who roamed whooping and barefoot through the forest until they grew into their parents, impulsive, semiliterate, precociously sexual, and heavily armed.

He takes the curves quickly. In his peripheral vision, a burst of light: the Prines or Thibodeaux are setting off fireworks. The forest is loud with canine excitement.

Another burst of light.

Finally the road curves eastward, through cleared farmland. He's maybe fifty yards past Peachy Rouse's when he sees a county sheriff's car parked at the side of the road, a uniformed deputy at the wheel. In the passenger seat is Chief Carnicella, the town cop, miles outside his jurisdiction. Remembering the stolen fertilizer, Rich gives him a wave.

He pulls into his driveway, gravel crunching, bouncing over potholes he's been meaning to fill. A light is on in the kitchen. Inside he finds Shelby at the kitchen table, staring at her laptop. She wears ancient gray sweatpants and an old flannel shirt.

"Olivia was sick after supper," she tells him. "She threw up twice. I'm so tired I don't know what to do."

He leans in for a kiss and gets her forehead. "Again?"

"She has a nervous stomach."

"What does she have to be nervous about?" He opens the fridge, locates and unwraps a leftover chicken leg.

"Let me get you a plate."

"Nah, that's okay." He eats standing over the sink.

"The bank called. I took a message. It's here somewhere." Shelby riffles through the clutter on the table—junk mail, clipped coupons—and hands him a yellow Post-it note.

Rich takes it without looking and tucks it into his pocket.

"You're exhausted," says Shelby. "You can't keep doing this."

"Dad needs the help." His father is healthy, mainly, though he spends more and more time running to doctors—the knee, a lingering cold, recurring appointments for what his doctor calls *blood work* (what exactly they're hoping to find in Dick's blood, Rich isn't sure). The Commercial is too much for a man his age, and yet he'll never let go of it. Dick Devlin is that rare thing in Bakerton, a success story: a respected businessman, president of the Borough Council. His old union buddies scrape by on Black Lung and hold court in the Legion, drinking to kill the day.

"He needs to hire someone," says Shelby.

"He shouldn't have to. It's a family business. Darren could do it."

This is not a new conversation. Unlike his sisters, who disappeared long ago into marriages and children, Rich's kid brother—eternally single, earning chicken feed as a drug counselor in Baltimore—has nothing better to do. He'd make more money and live cheaper and better, helping Dick run the bar. It's the least he can do, in Rich's view, Darren who caused their parents more grief than the other three kids combined.

"He'd never move back here," says Shelby.

"Why the hell not?"

"No bones in the disposal, sweetie. Remember last time."

He throws the drumstick in the trash.

"You're home early," says Shelby. "That's good, anyway."

He takes the last beer from the fridge. "Yeah, well. Gia's helping Dad close. Supposedly. It's her night off." Just saying her name has an immediate effect on him. He can nearly feel the weight of her head in his lap, though he's never, in actual fact, experienced such a thing, a warm mouth in a parked car. Shelby isn't adventurous that way, or any other way he can think of.

"So why is she hanging around there?" Shelby turns her attention back to the screen. "She told me she quit drinking."

"I didn't actually see her drinking. None of my business what she puts in her mouth."

Shelby looks puzzled.

"She was talking to those drillers. Just, you know, being social."

His wife frowns, as though it's an alien concept. As though they hadn't—before they were married, a lifetime ago—closed a few bars together: Rich and Shelby, Gia and whatever dirtbag she happened to be dating at the time. Back when Shelby and Gia were too young to order their own drinks, Rich—fresh out of the navy, newly divorced—had paid for them both, liking how it looked. They had seemed, at first, like two versions of the same thing, one brunette, the other blond. At a certain point he had to choose between them. Shelby had seemed the safer choice, a quiet, pretty girl who could be trusted.

"I worry about her," says Shelby. "She's going to end up like my mother." Shelby's mother works, for the moment, as a paid companion to a mean paraplegic. She lives in the man's house, feeds and dresses and takes him to the toilet, tasks complicated by the fact that both are blind drunk most of the day.

Rich stands behind Shelby's chair, rubs deeply at her shoulders. She gives a little sigh of pleasure.

"Oh, that feels good. I'm taking Olivia off dairy products. I think she's allergic, like me. It says right here—"

"Do we have to talk about this now?"

She turns to face him, frowning unattractively. When they first met, her heart-shaped face had a solemn quality, sweetly symmetrical, the delicate profile of a cameo brooch. Over the years she's acquired a collection of grimaces, lopsided frowns, and puckers. The expressions are unsightly but eloquent, a timid girl's silent language. His wife's dominant emotions—irritation, resignation, an outsize disappointment—are written clearly on her face.

"Oh, excuse me. Your daughter has been miserable all night. I thought you might be interested. And you know I don't feel well."

He takes a deep breath. "Shelby, there's nothing wrong with her. She's been drinking milk her whole life. All kids do."

"But it says here—"

Rich throws up his hands. "You know what? I give up. You're turning her into an invalid. She's *seven years old.*"

He takes his beer out the back door and stands a long moment on the deck, staring up at the sky. *You know I don't feel well.* He knows, he knows: the migraines and allergies, the menstrual cramps. For five days each month Shelby lives on the couch, clutching Olivia in her arms like a doll. *My little girl is sensitive,* he's heard Shelby tell her mother. *If I'm sick, she feels what I feel.*

The night is silent, the moon glowing almost imperceptibly through the fog. Gingerly he stretches his lower back. He can still smell prison on himself. Usually a shower gets rid of it, but not always. The smell is trapped in his nasal passages. After ten years the place has seeped into him, his skin and hair, his blood and bone.

He breathes deeply. He built the deck himself last summer, a sturdy platform of engineered wood—the flimsy house's one attractive feature, better than it deserves. Looking out over his grandfather's land, sixty acres of fields and rolling pasture, he feels instantly cleaner. The best hours of his boyhood were spent here, fishing the creek, riding the back of Pap's snowmobile. When Pap died and the farm was divided among the four grandchildren, only Rich loved the place enough to keep it. He imagined living in the old farmhouse with his new wife and future children—four or even five, though Shelby would take some convincing. As a family they'd get the business up and running—dairy cows, like Pap had raised.

You have an exit strategy, a plan for the future. This is what you tell yourself.

He borrowed enough to buy out his sisters, who'd moved away and had families to raise and needed the money more than the land. His brother, too, was eager to sell. The smartest Devlin by far, Darren had landed a scholarship to Johns Hopkins, half tuition, though he wasn't smart enough to figure out how to pay the other half.

Buy him out, for heaven's sake! Rich's mother urged. Darren, the baby, had always been her favorite. *He needs the money for school.*

He needs the money for something. Rich didn't actually know—he only suspected—that Darren had expensive habits. (How quickly and dangerously he could burn through sixty thousand dollars. The high times so much money could buy.) But in the end Rich gave in; Darren got his money and flunked out of Hopkins and didn't call home for two years. By then their mother was dead, and it was Dick who paid for Darren's rehab—not once but twice—at the clinic where Darren still works.

It would have been better for everyone—for Darren especially—if he'd simply *given* Rich the land.

An exit strategy, a plan for the future. Not now, but soon.

He is patient by nature, which is both a strength and a weakness. As a boy he studied the Sears catalog in the weeks before Christmas, making extensive lists of the toys he coveted: the Evel Knievel action figure with its collection of motorcycles, precise replicas of the bikes Evel rode in real life. Now, in the same spirit, he trawls online message boards. All his research points to the Honiger 4000, a state-of-the-art milking system—to his adult self, the equivalent of Evel Knievel's chopper. Lesser systems would kill you with repair costs and lost milking days, but the Honiger is a miracle of Swiss engineering, reliable as the sun. A brand-new system, installed, runs a hundred thousand; but with a little research, used components can be had. At this very moment, a dairy farmer in Somerset County is about to retire. He's looking to sell his Honiger, only eight years old. Rich can swing a wrench as well as the next guy, and his dad knows a plumber who'll work for cheap. Not including animals, he could be up and running for fifty grand. For a guy at his pay grade, it's still a lot of cake; but all that can change in an instant. Can and will, once his wells go in.

Two summers ago, he'd driven home from work on a Monday morning, dead tired after an all-night lockdown, to find a strange pickup parked in his driveway. His first thought would later shame him: his wife, alone all night, had been entertaining a visitor, another man in his bed. Flooded with adrenaline, he circled the truck. The out-of-state plate seemed, at the time, exotic. He'd known Texans in the navy. Never once had he encountered one in Bakerton.

He rushed into the house and found Shelby in her bathrobe, drinking orange juice with two strange men. She didn't look guilty or even nervous; she seemed excited, as though she'd been given a surprise gift. The guy put Rich at ease right away—the folksy drawl, maybe, or the way he was dressed: khaki pants, a denim shirt rolled to the elbows. He looked like a guy who worked with his hands.

He signed the contract immediately, stunned at his good fortune. Suddenly all things seemed possible. He called Saxon Savings and refinanced his mortgage. The reward was immediate, a year and a half of lower payments. By the time the balloon payments kicked in, his wells would be producing, and he'd have cash to spare.

He hadn't counted on the waiting. In that time he'd learned a few things. The gas company's offer, which had seemed simple and generous, was neither. He'd been a fool to fall for their opening gambit—twenty-five bucks an acre, plus 12.5 percent of the profits, the minimum allowed by law. *You played me,* he imagined telling Bobby Frame, the slick salesman who'd taken advantage of his ignorance. But Bobby Frame was long gone.

Then, four months ago, Rich's balloon payments kicked in, and his monthly tab nearly doubled. With no other options, he borrowed ten grand from his dad—who, after years of paying suppliers with his own Black Lung checks, finally had a little cash to spare.

I'm good for it, Rich promised. *I signed a gas lease.* It was all he could think to say. He was nearly mute with shame.

Now he takes the Post-it note from his pocket. *Beth at Saxon Savings. Call her back ASAP.* His current payment is three weeks late. His dad's check will take two more days to clear.

Tonight he will dream of digging.

As a boy he'd been haunted by the story of the Number Twelve collapse, eight miners crushed after a freak methane explosion. For an entire summer, in dreams, Richie Devlin led the search team digging through the rubble, uncovering bodies piece by piece—a severed foot, a terrible grasping hand. Now, once again, he dreams of digging. His dream self digs a hole and fills it with cash, bundles of fifties and hundreds going right into the ground.

The kitchen door opens behind him. Shelby stands in the doorway in the quilted bathrobe he hates. "I'm exhausted. I'm going to bed."

Surprise, surprise.

"I'm taking Braden with me on Sunday," he tells her. "Dad wants to go fishing."

She looks pained. "What about church?"

After ten years of marriage, there are no new conversations. Rich could have had this one with himself.

"It's just one Sunday. Anyways, I already told Brady he could come."

She hugs the robe around her. "Great. Thanks for that. He's already decided that church is for girls."

"I wonder where he got that idea."

Her face twists into a look he's seen before, one that particularly dismays him: left eye squeezed shut, mouth tucked to the left, as though she's suffered a debilitating stroke.

"Sorry. It just seems weird to me. A lady preacher. I didn't grow up that way."

Shelby says, "Nobody did."

"Look, Dad wants to go fishing with his grandson. What was I supposed to say? He's not getting any younger." Rich stares up at the sky. It occurs to him that Shelby, raised without one, doesn't understand the point of a father. "Who knows how many fishing trips he's got left?"

This ends the discussion, as he knew it would. The door clicks shut behind her.

Shelby brushes Olivia's hair, counting the strokes. The house is quiet around them, no cartoons playing, no video games or Braden noises. Her son is the sort of boy who produces a near-constant stream of sound, like the world's most irritating radio station: machine-gun blasts, guttural and plosive; ringing cartoon farts; monkey shrieks. She thinks of a hip-hop group, popular when she was a teenager, whose front man was called the Human Beat Box. Using nothing but his mouth, the Box produced pulsing bass lines and rhythmic drumming. The Box, if he'd been more ambitious, could have put entire orchestras out of work. Now, raising a son, Shelby understands that the Human Beat Box was nothing special. He simply did what boys do.

Eighteen, nineteen, twenty. A mother is judged by her child's appearance. This is a known fact.

Usually Olivia complains about the brushing. Today she barely notices, absorbed in recounting a dream that becomes, in the telling, no longer a dream but a thing that actually happened. Its convoluted plot involves witches, several girls from her first-grade class, the neighbor's dog, and its new puppies. At the center of the story is Olivia herself, transformed for dream purposes into Ariel, the Little Mermaid.

"And then the witch—" says Olivia.

"And then the black puppy—"

"And then I—"

Her small clear voice vibrates with certainty. It's horrible and somehow marvelous, the conviction with which a seven-year-old can lie. Does Olivia even know she's lying? Shelby thinks she does. She remembers the feeling from her own childhood, the exhilaration of fibbing outrageously and getting away with it. *No kidding,* her mother would say, and that would be the end of it. Roxanne put no particular stock in truthfulness.

"Twenty-nine," says Shelby. "Thirty." Walking into church with her two well-groomed children is the high point of her week. The rest of the week is notably lacking in high points. Years ago, when she worked at Saxon Manor, there was the elaborate daily ritual of choosing her outfit, heating the curling iron, applying makeup. Her day at Saxon Manor went downhill from there.

Thirty-one, thirty-two. A fact known by people everywhere, with the exception of her own mother. Shelby and her sister had run wild in the neighborhood, feral girls, unbrushed and unbraided. Once, a neighbor lady came out of her house with a damp washrag to wipe Shelby's dirty face.

"Forty-nine, fifty!" she says aloud, ending with a flourish. A hundred strokes was expected, a hundred was the standard. But on Olivia's baby hair, fine as cobwebs, a hundred strokes would seem like a punishment. Fifty is more than enough.

She parts Olivia's hair and begins braiding.

"Not too tight," Olivia says.

In a small wavering voice she sings a wisp of a song she learned in Sunday school: *Who built the park? Noah! Noah!* She has a habit of mishearing song lyrics, which worried Shelby at first. But Dr. Stusick has tested her hearing and swears that Olivia's ears are fine.

"Something smells," Olivia says.

Shelby sniffs. "Daddy left the coffeemaker plugged in." Most Sundays, Rich is gone before sunrise. In early winter he goes hunting, doe, buck, rabbit. Later, it's the snowmobile. The rest of the year he drives north to Yellow Creek, to catch-and-release whatever is in season: rainbows in springtime, walleyes in summer, steelies in fall.

Her supervisor at Saxon Manor, a man named Larry Stransky, had complimented her appearance. A small thing, but it had brightened her day.

Olivia is getting squirrelly, squirming in her chair. "Why does Braden get to go fishing?"

"You can go next time, when you're feeling better. Today we have church."

Church is for girls. Rich, predictably, had found Braden's comment amusing. The memory washes over Shelby like nausea.

"Ow."

"Sorry, baby."

"Your hands are shaking."

Shelby rubs them together, as if to warm them. The tremor comes and goes without warning. No one but Olivia has ever noticed. She is a sensitive child, uncannily attuned to her mother's symptoms—a quality notably lacking in her father and brother and even their family doctor. Olivia, one day, will make a wonderful doctor. Of this her mother is sure.

After her marriage, Larry Stransky took a disliking to her.

Shelby ties off the braids with blue ribbons. "All done. Now can you stay put for two minutes while Mommy gets dressed? And no more juice, sweetie. We don't want you spilling on yourself."

He got that idea from you, she could have said, but didn't. *If you ever came with us, even on Christmas. Ever, even once.*

In the kitchen she shuts off the coffeemaker. The coffee is thick as motor oil, but she pours a cup anyway. At least it will keep her awake in church. Like the burnt coffee, her exhaustion is Rich's fault. She lay awake for hours until he came to bed. She couldn't relax with him prowling around the house.

She couldn't fall asleep because she worried that he would wake her.

Except for the odd wedding or funeral, he never sets foot in a church of any kind. The world, Shelby knows, is filled with such people, for whom a personal relationship with Jesus Christ is inadequate enticement. Rich would rather sit around waiting for a fish he isn't even going to eat.

When he came to bed she held very still, breathing slow and regular. Any deviation in her breathing would be noticed. But he had left her alone.

It wasn't always like this. In the beginning she felt lit up by the knowledge that he wanted her, shocked to life by the force of his want. But there was a difference between wanting and expecting. When he climbs on top of her she feels the terrible weight of obligation. Letting him touch her solves nothing. Letting him touch her is throwing dimes and nickels at a debt so large it can never be repaid.

Now and then he invites her to stop by the bar while he is working, as though bartending were a movie or a sports match, some kind of performance she might want to watch.

For a couple their age, three times a week is a normal amount of lovemaking. She read this in a magazine.

With Larry Stransky she did nothing. He did it all himself. Long ago, before her marriage, her only action was to meet him in his car at the dinner break. *Let me look at you,* he said while he finished himself off. Ten minutes later she was back in the building.

He did it all himself.

THEY GET INTO THE VAN, Olivia in the backseat. On the front seat is an arrangement of yellow carnations, an all-purpose flower.

Living Waters is in the center of town, in an old storefront. *That's not a church,* Rich likes to say, and it's true that the building looks deserted, its plate glass windows covered in butcher paper. The sign out front was dismantled long ago, but the ghost of the words is still visible, the old-fashioned cursive: *Friedman's Furniture.*

Heads turn as they enter the church. In her white dress Olivia is an angel, which is all that matters. Shelby had no time to fix her own hair or put in contact lenses, but she is just the mother. No one is looking at her.

A mother is judged by her child's appearance. This is an established fact.

The church is as full as it ever gets, though Pastor Jess, eternally hopeful, sets out a dozen extra chairs. Shelby leaves her jacket and purse on her usual chair in the front row. She likes a clear view of the pastor—beautifully dressed, always, in an elegant pants suit. That surprised her at first, Shelby who'd always worn dresses to church. Now she sees the wisdom of it. A pastor shouldn't have to worry about a run in her stockings, or her slip showing. She should move in her clothing as easily as men do, freeing her mind for higher things.

She leads Olivia downstairs for the Children's Service, songs, and a Bible reading and a discussion of the day's lesson. Later they'd have milk and cookies while the adults enjoyed their coffee upstairs. A half-dozen little ones are already there, sitting cross-legged on colorful squares of carpet. The walls are decorated with their drawings, recognizable as Bible scenes because all the men have beards.

Upstairs she takes her seat and gratefully closes her eyes. For years her own prayer had been an afterthought; she spent the hour dispensing toys and whispered scoldings, sitting between Braden and Olivia to keep them from acting up. Now, each Sunday, she feels her soul opening—moved in new ways, touched in places she has never been touched. It's a thing no male minister would ever think of, that a person might actually pay attention to the service if her children were safely occupied elsewhere. If she were, for one blessed hour a week, left in peace.

Even Pastor Wes—rest his soul—had never thought of such a thing.

When Braden was born with the hole in his heart, it was Pastor

Wes who sat at the hospital with Shelby. Who, during the surgery, held her hand in the waiting room, their heads bowed in prayer. It was the most significant event of her adult life, and yet no one remembered it. Not Rich, who pretended it had never happened; and certainly not Braden, transformed overnight from a sickly baby to a hyperactive toddler, full of mischief. Only Pastor Wes had been a true witness to her suffering, the waiting and wondering, the episodes of panic and dread. Certain that her baby was dying, she never guessed (nobody did) that in a few years Pastor Wes would be dead himself, of some young man's cancer no one knew he had.

The only true witness to her suffering. And Pastor Wes is gone, gone.

The opening hymn is an old one Shelby remembers. It isn't one she particularly cares for, and yet she finds herself moved by the words as she sings them.

> Even though it be a cross that raiseth me,
> still all my song shall be
> nearer, my God, to Thee

When Pastor Jess rises to give the lesson, Shelby leans forward in her seat. The pastor speaks to the congregation one person at a time, her eyes moving from face to face as though she notices everything about you: whether you're peaceful or troubled; if you got a good night's sleep or sat up half the night with a sick child; if your husband made love to you or fell asleep on the couch. Whichever happens to be true, she looks at you with compassion and deep understanding, as though your worst transgressions are already forgiven; as though grace is something you actually deserve.

The service ended, she helps Lois Fetterson at the refreshments table. The social runs from ten to eleven—for Shelby, an anxious hour. She helps herself to coffee but skips the doughnuts. Chewing in public unnerves her.

"Doesn't Olivia look sweet?" Lois says with her mouth full. "Where's your boy this morning?"

"Rich took him fishing." Shelby's tone discourages further questions. Lois Fetterson is a notorious gossip. Shelby's life is in no way gossip-worthy, and yet she feels a strong urge to conceal facts from Lois, for the simple pleasure of denying her.

"Wally saw Rich last night at the Commercial. He's a good son, helping Dick like that."

Shelby ignores the comment. It's just like Lois to remind her that her husband is a bartender. Never mind the fact, well known in town, that Wally Fetterson spends every evening in one beer garden or another. Rich, at least, was helping his father. Lois's husband has no excuse.

This Sunday, as on all others, a small crowd surrounds Pastor Jess. Shelby approaches, carrying the yellow carnations. "For Pastor Wes. I thought we could go together."

Pastor Jess looks confused. "Oh, the *cemetery*," she says at last. "For Memorial Day."

Shelby stands there awkwardly, holding the flower arrangement, which she left in the minivan during the service. It looks a little wilted from the heat.

"That's kind of you, Shelby, but I can't leave just yet. You go on without me. I hate to keep you waiting."

Shelby says, "I don't mind."

TO EXPLAIN PASTOR WES you have to start at the beginning. In the beginning Shelby's mother worked at the Moose. In Bakerton a moose is not an animal but a tavern, smoke-filled, where men shoot pool or play cards in the back room or stare at the television above the bar.

For most of Shelby's childhood they lived in the upstairs apartment, Roxanne's answer to babysitting: Shelby and Crystal could, in theory, come find her in case of emergency. Of course, they never did. Because what, for Roxanne, would constitute an emergency? About nightmares and scraped knees, she was unfailingly casual. In case of fire or a masked intruder, Shelby would have called the police.

Roxanne was not a motherly name. Even as a child Shelby knew this, in the same way she knew that bartending was not a normal job for a woman.

The hidden life of the bar, its daily rhythms. In the morning trucks idled out front, painted with familiar logos: Pabst Blue Ribbon, Iron City, Stroh's. With the front door propped open, the Moose exhaled its sour beer breath, sharpened by the pine-scented cleaner Roxanne used to mop the floor.

In the afternoon the jukebox played sad men, George Jones and Merle Haggard clearly audible in the upstairs apartment, the slow thump of the bass like a heartbeat in the floor. The bar's TV tuned, always, to some sports match. In a faraway stadium a crowd cheered. An announcer explained the action in a scolding tone, insisting that you care.

When dark fell the music changed, guitars screeching and wailing. Between songs Shelby heard snatches of conversation, pool balls colliding with a dry crack. A comforting noise as she lay waiting for sleep next to her sister, on the foldout couch in the living room.

Their mother came home long after midnight, tiptoeing around furniture. She was so quiet that Shelby might have stayed asleep, if not for the smell—cigarette smoke, the deep fryer—Roxanne wore like perfume. It was a more concentrated version of the odor already lingering in the apartment, a smell that rose up through the floorboards.

The smell clung to Shelby and her sister, their hair and clothes. She learned this one day while riding the school bus next to Patti Wojick who, to Shelby's horror, leaned over to sniff her and said, "You smell like French fries."

Now Rich comes home smelling the exactsame way.

Shelby understands that he isn't really a bartender, that he is only helping his father. Still, she doesn't particularly want to watch.

They were clever girls, resourceful, independent. On summer afternoons they haunted the town swimming pool. Later—sunburned, chlorine-smelling—they roamed the neighborhoods and made fast friendships. The new friends had curfews and allowances, grassy yards, bicycles. They had kind mothers who sometimes cooked extra, delicious casseroles and meat loaves served at a table, on matching plates.

Sturdy girls, practical, resilient. Uncomplaining, because complaining got them nowhere. Roxanne was immovable, a slab of granite. Small sicknesses did not impress her. To colds and bellyaches her response was predictable: *go to school, you'll feel better.* The girls went to school with mumps, with strep throat, with pinkeye. Shelby infected her entire second-grade class with chicken pox.

And so it's hard to say when Crystal's illness actually started. She was a docile child, sweet tempered; a fair-haired girl whose sunburns turned to rashes, whose fingertips went blue in the cold. When, at eleven or twelve, she became suddenly and permanently tired, achy, and listless, she went to school but did not feel better. Shelby was awakened in the night by Crystal's fevers, the heat rising off her in waves.

After Crystal died, it was Shelby who studied the class pictures, taken each year by a visiting photographer in the first week of school. In her fifth-grade picture Crystal looked healthy and suntanned. A year later the red stain was visible across her cheeks. The butterfly rash was the signature symptom of lupus. A responsible mother would have noticed. But by the time Roxanne took her to a doctor, Crystal's feet were swollen, her kidneys failing. Overnight, everything changed. Three times a week, Buzz Wenturine drove Crystal to the county hospital twenty miles away, which had a dialysis machine.

Buzz Wenturine was Roxanne's boyfriend, a big bald-headed

man with a handlebar mustache. Like most men, he had been a
miner. More recently he drove a yellow bus, which Shelby and Crystal had ridden to middle school. Back then Roxanne had a different
boyfriend, and so the girls paid little attention to the nameless bus
driver, a gruff man who never changed his clothes.

When Roxanne brought him home, three or four years later, he
was wearing the exactsame green plaid shirt.

Buzz Wenturine's car smelled of aftershave and breath mints.
For the first week Roxanne rode along beside him. Then the treatments were rescheduled for late afternoon, after school let out, so
that Shelby could go in her place. Buzz drove in silence, hunched
over the wheel in his camouflage jacket, listening to a ball game on
the radio. The sisters sat together in the backseat, speaking in whispers, pretending he wasn't there.

The treatment room was blocked off with a plastic curtain.
Shelby sat in the armchair beside Crystal's bed. A treatment took
four hours. While her sister slept, Shelby watched the tiny television bolted to the ceiling, *The Young and the Restless* and *As the World
Turns*.

At the hospital Crystal was showered with kindness. The
Ladies Auxiliary offered home-baked cookies. Candy stripers dispensed small gifts—lip balm and chocolate bars, a pocket-size book
of crosswords—from a wheeled cart.

Every Friday after her treatment, while Crystal saw the doctor, Shelby did homework in a waiting room down the hall. The
waiting room was often crowded. She saw children and even adults
crying, as though something tragic had occurred. Over time she
recognized certain faces. A particular small, slight man was often
present, dressed in a cardigan sweater. He sat with his head bowed
and spoke in a soft voice. Weeks passed before Shelby understood
that he was praying. She had never witnessed such a thing.

He didn't care if you were a man, woman, or child. He bowed
his head and took your hand.

One Friday he spoke to her. "What are you writing?"

The waiting room was crowded and he had sat beside her, their shoulders nearly touching. He was pale and handsome, his eyelashes long as a girl's.

"A report. For Pennsylvania History." Unused to such questions, she wondered how much of an answer was required. "It's about Colonel Drake. You know, the oil rush."

He leaned close to her and read from the notebook on her lap: "*When the world's first oil well was drilled in right here in western Pennsylvania, Colonel Edwin Drake was given all the credit.* That's very good," he said, smiling. "How is your sister feeling?"

Shyness overcame her. "How did you know she was my sister?"

"You look just alike."

This pleased her unreasonably. Shelby was not unpretty, but Crystal was a beauty. Everyone said so, and Shelby accepted it as fact.

"Dialysis is grueling. She's lucky to have you with her." His voice was gentle and melodic, a step away from singing.

"She has lupus."

"It's a terrible illness."

They sat for a long moment, staring at the television, tuned to a local channel that aired announcements. SAXON COUNTY FAIR TRACTOR PULL CONTEST. FIREMEN'S FESTIVAL BATTLE OF THE BARREL.

"I'd be happy to pray with you," said the Reverend Wesley Peacock.

He said, "It must be very difficult for you."

He had no idea. The cookies and crosswords, the cooing volunteers who smoothed Crystal's hair and called her *sweetie*. Shelby was a starving child forced to watch another's gluttony.

As she'd seen him do with everybody, he bowed his head and took her hand.

Her mother slept late on Sunday mornings, and so it was easy enough to sneak out of the apartment wearing the one nice dress she hadn't outgrown. Fourteen and still growing, a late bloomer; Roxanne could barely keep her in blue jeans. Shelby's old clothes were handed down to Crystal, who would never wear them. Who would spend her remaining days in shortie pajamas, under an afghan on the couch.

That first Sunday, Shelby chose an unobtrusive spot in a middle row. The church was full of families, parents and children praying together. They seemed unsure what to make of her, a young girl sitting alone.

From the pulpit Pastor Wes spoke to her directly. "I'd like to welcome all those new to our congregation. We're very glad you're here."

After the service, in the vestibule, he had a smile and a word for everyone. Shelby studied them from a distance, Pastor Wes and the woman at his side. His sister, Shelby thought at first. She had the same shiny dark hair, the gentle brown eyes.

Pastor Wes seemed delighted to see her. "Jess, this is Shelby, the girl I told you about. My wife, Jessie."

He was a grown man, a pastor with his own church. Of course he was old enough to have a wife.

"We have a little social after the service," he told Shelby. "You can meet some of the other young folks."

"I need to get home," she stammered. "To my sister." It wasn't true, not remotely: Crystal would spend the day sleeping and watching television, whether Shelby was there or not. But Pastor Wes gave her a look of such melting kindness that she was glad she'd said it.

"Crystal is on dialysis," he told his wife. "Shelby is by her side the whole time. You've never seen a more devoted sister."

At home Shelby changed out of her church clothes. Her mother, still asleep, hadn't even noticed she was gone. Deceiving her was so effortless that Shelby could have done it forever, if not for the day at Rite Aid.

Because only an adult could refill Crystal's prescriptions, Shelby and Roxanne went to Rite Aid together. As she always did—in stores, the bank, the post office—Shelby pointed out the NO SMOK-ING sign.

As she always did, Roxanne lit a Virginia Slim.

A moment later Shelby saw him. They passed side by side through the automatic doors, Shelby and her mother through the IN door, Pastor Wes through the OUT. Spotting Shelby, he grinned and waved.

"Who's that?" Roxanne said.

They dawdled a moment on the threshold, their weight on the rubber mat holding the door wide open. Finally they went into the store and, awkwardly, turned around and came back outside.

Pastor Wes was waiting for them on the sidewalk, a crisp shirt and tie under his cardigan sweater. "Shelby, is this your mother?"

"Who wants to know?" said Roxanne—in cutoff shorts, braless, a cigarette dangling from her mouth.

Shelby offered a clumsy introduction. Roxanne took a final drag of her cigarette and ground it beneath her heel.

"I don't like him," she told Shelby later as they waited at the pharmacy counter. "He looks like a preacher."

"He *is* a preacher."

"He's a grown man. What does he want with you?"

"He's teaching me scripture."

Roxanne seemed disappointed by this explanation. Shelby wished, too late, that she'd invented a better story.

"He helps me with my homework. My Colonel Drake report. Anyway, he has a wife."

"They all have wives."

After that there was no need for sneaking, though Roxanne occasionally teased her: *Are you going to see your boyfriend?* Though some months later, when he offered his church for Crystal's funeral, Roxanne changed her tune and pronounced him *harmless*—as though it were a personal failing, an irreparable character flaw.

Was a man supposed to be harmful? Except for silent Buzz

Wenturine, Shelby didn't know any men. She'd lived her whole life in a two-room apartment where you could shower with the door open, it didn't matter, because they were all girls.

Even Roxanne had to admit that the service was beautiful. Pastor Wes's eulogy was full of personal anecdotes, as though he'd known Crystal all her life. In fact they had never met. He simply remembered what Shelby had told him.

Buzz Wenturine sometimes left bruises on her mother.

Pastor Wes remembered everything Shelby told him, and had never left a bruise on anyone. She knew this beyond all doubt.

Of course he'd never met Crystal. Shelby's sister was desperately shy, timid around strangers. The treatments left her too weak for visitors. These excuses and others, Pastor Wes accepted without question, and remained Shelby's alone.

Yellow carnations, an all-purpose flower. She lays the flowers on his grave.

2.

There are no accidents. Everything happens for a reason. Rich's wife is constantly spouting such truisms. *Horseshit,* he tells her, though he wishes he were wrong. And maybe he is: because one afternoon, as he's coming out of the stockroom at the Commercial, he spots Bobby Frame sitting alone in a corner booth, tapping out a text message on his cell phone.

"Hey," Rich calls.

Frame looks up, startled. The detritus of his lunch sits before him, saltine wrappers, a crumpled paper napkin, a half-eaten pickle.

"You don't remember me, do you? Rich Devlin. You were at my house. I signed a gas lease."

"Sure I remember," he says smoothly. "Nice to see you."

Rich ignores the pleasantry. "I'd understand if you don't, because that was a while back. A year ago in August. Coming up on two."

"That sounds about right." Frame smiles warmly, but his eyes look panicked, as though he's been accosted by a crazy person. As, in a way, he has.

"I'm surprised to see you here," says Rich. "I figured you were long gone by now."

"I was. I came back to testify in a court case. Never mind that. That's not important," Frame adds hastily. He eyes the pickle with regret, then opens his wallet and leaves a bill on the table. "Take care, Mr. Devlin. Give my best to your wife."

"Whoa, wait a minute." Rich nearly puts his hands on the guy—not to hurt him, just to keep him from running away. He's having a hard time expressing himself. "About my lease. What exactly is the holdup? My neighbor Wally Fetterson got drilled a year ago."

"Have a seat, Mr. Devlin. This is going to take a minute." Frame reaches over to the next table for an unused napkin. "You have, what, sixty acres? If I remember correctly."

He takes a pen from his breast pocket and sketches a quick map.

"So this is you." He draws a square, marks it with the letter *D*. "And this, to the south, is your neighbor Mr. Neugebauer. Mr. Kipler is a ways over to the west. All three of you have signed leases, which is great news. What we'd like to do—what we need to do—is drill all of you from the same well pad."

"Okay," Rich says.

"But here's our problem." Frame draws another square and shades it with cross-hatching. "This here is Friend-Lea Acres. Owned by your neighbors, the Mackeys. Their farm sets right smack in the middle of where we'd need to put that pad. And the Mackeys refuse to sign."

It is the great, deflating lesson of Rich's adulthood: nothing, but nothing, is simple. "I don't get it. Can't you just put the pad on my land?"

"Mr. Devlin, I'd love to. Nothing would make me happier. But for just sixty acres it isn't cost effective. Now Mr. Kipler, over here"—he draws a long rectangle—"has four hundred acres. If we absolutely had to, we might could bring in a rig just for him. But the smaller properties—yours and Mr. Neugebauer's—we'd need to bundle them somehow." He draws another square at the edge of the napkin. "This here is your neighbor, Mr. Krug. Now if we could get him on board—Devlin, Neugebauer, and Krug—that's a decent parcel. That might be worth our while."

Rich is suddenly tired. It figures perfectly—it's just his luck—that the deal hinges on Cob Krug, a known crackpot, an angry crank who scares small children, a notorious hermit and hoarder. A man of complicated opinions, paranoid theories that require much explaining on *Open Mike,* the local radio station's call-in show. Cob is the sort of eccentric who gets stranger with age, and he's been old as long as Rich can remember.

Cob Krug, of all people, holds the keys to his future.

"Let me guess. Cob wouldn't sign."

"Said no and meant it. Damn near blew my head off. I don't think there's any changing his mind."

"Which leaves Mackey." Mack and Rena—the lesbian dairy farmers who run Friend-Lea Acres—are locally famous, though nobody in town actually knows them. In the way of rural neighbors, Rich sees them only at a distance, barreling down Number Nine Road in their battered pickup truck. He knows nothing about them beyond the local gossip.

"Bingo. And they're—well, I only met the one. She's a pretty stubborn lady. Believe me, I've tried." Bobby gets to his feet. "You're not the only one, if that's any consolation. Your neighbors are all in the same boat."

"So there's nothing I can do?" The injustice stuns him: his entire future—his kids' future—wiped out by a neighbor's whim.

Bobby Frame eyes him with pity. "Look, I get it. If I was in your shoes, I'd be aggravated, too." He claps Rich's shoulder. "You want my advice? Go have a talk with the Mackeys. I did my best, but I'm just some guy from Texas. It will mean more coming from you."

MACK IS DREDGING THE CREEK, up to her ankles in cold water, when the truck turns down the lane. It's an old Chevy with round headlights and a wide smiling grille, like the face of a friendly dog. At the wheel is her neighbor Carl Neugebauer. Beside him is a younger man she doesn't, at first, recognize: Hank Becker's grandson, her neighbor to the south.

The three sit on the porch drinking cold beer from the can. Mack is barefoot, her boots on the brick stoop drying in the sun. She is happy about the beer, the company, the simple animal pleasure of dry feet. The afternoon is hot and still.

Carl Neugebauer has aged, his wrinkly throat like something hanging off a turkey. He is closer to eighty than seventy. Mack hasn't seen him in a couple years. Except for rare trips to town—Amway, barbershop, hardware store—she is a homebody, though she's always glad to bump into a neighbor she's known since childhood, the vanishing cohort of old-timers who knew her pop. She has always preferred the company of men.

Carl takes a can of snuff from his pocket and offers her a pinch. "How you been, Susan? I never see you around town."

It's a name no one calls her, a name she's always hated. But Carl was a friend of Pop's. He can call her whatever he wants.

Hank's grandson is named Devlin. Mack has seen it on his mailbox.

"Busy," she says. "The vet was here all morning. Second time this week."

It's as much small talk as either can muster. The pleasantries out of the way, Carl wastes no time. "I guess you've made up your mind about this drilling business."

"Pretty much." Mack takes the spit can from under her chair and places it on the table, equidistant from them both. Devlin, she notices, does not chew.

Carl nods gravely. "I wonder what your pop would say. He was no kind of businessman, but he never would've left that kind of money setting on the table."

Mack flinches, insulted on Pop's behalf. And yet she knows it's true: he left Friend-Lea Acres in a precarious financial position. If he'd lived five more years, he'd have run the farm into the ground.

"They'll pay you fifteen percent over the life of the well," says

Carl. "More, if you play your cards right. I guess Wally Fetterson has made a million already. A million dollars without lifting a finger."

To Mack the sum is unimaginable. You couldn't argue with that kind of money—though Rena, if she were here, would try.

"We're not asking anyone to agree with us," she says. "We never have."

"I guess that's true," Carl says.

Better that Rena isn't here. Even if she could hold her tongue (unlikely), her simple presence would make Mack uncomfortable. To sit side by side on their porch swing, in the presence of neighbors, would be revealing too much of themselves.

"Seems like you're the one trying to talk *us* into something." Mack reaches for the spit can. "We want the same thing everybody else wants. To run our farm in peace."

Carl seems to consider this.

"You girls run a clean operation. I respect that. And if you want to pass up an opportunity, well, I guess that's your business. But once you start taking money out of my pocket, I got to say something." He spits deliberately. "Your land sets right in the middle of where they need to run them wells. I'm getting wells, Richard here is getting wells. Hell, even Jim Norton is getting wells, with the little spread he has. But until you sign that paper, none of us are going to see a dime."

Mack glances skyward. The sun is sinking, the unmistakable slanted sunlight of late afternoon. Rena will be home any minute, in her Monday mood. On Monday evenings anything is possible, Rena weepy or angry or brooding after her visit to the prison, the agonizing hour she spends with her son.

Mack puts on her boots, warm inside, and gets to her feet. "Well, I should get back to it. Thanks for stopping by."

She walks the men to their truck. Devlin, who hasn't spoken a single word, shakes her hand.

"Will you at least think about it?" says Carl.

"Sure," says Mack. "Sure I will."

The old truck bounces down the lane, raising dust.

IN THE WEEK BEFORE THE INCIDENT, there were warnings. Nothing so dramatic as a flaming shitbag left on their doorstep, but clear signs that something was amiss. Rena explains this to the town cop, Chief Carnicella. They are sitting in the police station, a square wood-paneled room in the basement of Saxon Savings and Loan, just large enough for a desk and two chairs.

"Signs." The chief doodles on a yellow legal pad. His stubby fingers grip the pen like a hammer or screwdriver. He hasn't, so far, written anything down. "What kind of signs?"

They are dressed illustratively, like life-size dolls. Their clothing explains who they are and what they do. His navy blue pants and uniform shirt, which gapes between the buttons. Her baggy smock and faded scrub pants, freshly laundered, a blank canvas for whatever the ER has in store for her—blood, urine, vomit, tears.

Chief Carnicella listens, frowning. His hair, what's left of it, is darker than it should be, longish and wispy, combed over his bald spot and pasted into place. In high school he was a star wrestler, the sort of boy who seemed older than everybody else—like many of the young Italians, the victim of a spectacular early puberty. In the team's yearbook photo he is the only freshman with chest hair. By graduation he had a receding hairline and a five o'clock shadow, like somebody's dad.

Behind Rena the door clicks open. The borough secretary sticks in her head. "I'm going to lunch, Chief. You need anything?"

Chief. All of Bakerton calls him this, without irony. In fact he is the entire police department, its only employee. No one but Rena seems to find this comical.

"Nah, I'm good. Sorry," the chief tells Rena. "Continue."

The first sign came last Monday, the neighbors' visit. "They were nice about it," says Rena, "but they weren't happy. 'Until you sign that paper, none of us are going to see a dime.' Those were his exact words."

The chief frowns. "That's a true fact?"

Rena nods.

"It don't seem right."

"That's not the point." She sees, already, that the conversation is going nowhere, which is not surprising. Filing a police report was Mack's idea, Mack who believes in law and order. Rena, personally, has no faith in cops.

The second incident came last Tuesday. Late for her shift at the hospital, she'd backed halfway down the lane before she realized her front tires were slashed.

Finally the chief writes something. "What was the total damage to the vehicle? I'm going to say two hundred a tire."

"Sure. Whatever," Rena says.

The third incident was the fire on their doorstep. Mack had stamped it out, cursing, realizing too late what was inside the flaming bag. It might have come from a neighbor's cow, or even one of their own. A stranger might have stepped through their fence and filled a sack with it. There are a half-dozen dairy farms in this part of Saxon County. Cow dung is in plentiful supply.

"It's harassment," says Rena.

The chief looks unimpressed. "You're saying there's a connection. A common perpetrator."

"Well, no. It could be different people. But they're all sending the same message."

"Which is?"

"I explained this already. They want us to sign a gas lease." She has a sudden, powerful urge to muss his lacquered hair. "I mean, what else could it be?"

"From a law enforcement perspective, my professional opinion is you've got some bored juveniles making mischief." He pauses significantly. "How's your boy?"

"He's fine."

"They treating him good up there?"

"He's fine."

There is a silence. Finally the chief gets to his feet.

"Sorry, Rena. I wish I could help you. I can file a report on the vehicle. But from where I sit, this looks like a couple unrelated acts of vandalism. Nothing much I can do about that."

SO, FINE. YOU TOOK POSITIONS that were unpopular. Not a new situation, Mack and Rena reminded each other.

As if they could forget.

They live on the farm as though it were an island. Periodically one of them—Rena, usually—rows to shore for supplies. On the farm it's Mack who is truly indispensable. Rena's most valuable contribution happens elsewhere. It's Rena who brings home the steady paycheck, who has, once again, a full-time job at Miners' Hospital. Which demands that, five days a week, she row to shore.

Five days is a recent development. Until last summer she worked part-time. They got by on her smaller salary, just barely. Then, in October, their fuel costs doubled.

"*Doubled?* How is that possible?" Despite years of habituation, Mack is always surprised by bad news. Rena is never surprised. It's Rena who grapples with each month's bleak mathematics, confronting in the end an untenable equation: the volatile dairy market on one side, the hundred small and large expenses, constantly fluctuating, on the other.

"We can't go on like this," she said and said and said, until finally Mack heard her. "I need to go full-time. I don't mind." It was partly true. Rena minded the hospital, she minded it terribly; but full-time would be no worse than part-time had been. Now she's a floater, working whichever department is shorthanded: Surgical, Medical,

Emergency. Second shift—three to eleven—leaves her mornings free to help Mack with the milking. By the time she leaves for the hospital, the daily chores are done.

YESTERDAY, HER DAY OFF, Rena spent in Pittsburgh. Her first stop was Verdant. She met with Natalie Lavender in the office above the restaurant—an airy, sun-filled room with blond wood floors, its perimeter ringed with green plants. Glorious smells wafted up through the floorboards: bacon, sautéed onions. A cool breeze floated through the open windows, the hum of urban traffic.

"I'm sorry, Rena. It's nothing personal. Friend-Lea makes a marvelous product."

Natalie resembled an aging movie actress: tall, slender, her hair a silver blond not found in nature. Rena studied her face in duplicate. There was the real Natalie at her immaculate desk, cool and composed in a pale linen dress; and hanging on the wall behind her, a recent cover of *Three Rivers* magazine, Natalie in her white chef's jacket beneath a bold headline: *FARM TO TABLE STAR CHEF BRINGS LOCAVORE EATING TO THE BURGH.*

"Was it something we did?" As always in Natalie's presence, she felt disheveled, a dowdy farm wife in worn sandals and a cotton skirt she'd made herself, badly, the flowered pattern mismatched at the seams.

"Our customers read the newspaper. They know what's going on in your part of the world." *Your pat of the wuld.* Natalie was from Australia or New Zealand; Rena could never remember which.

"I don't understand." Up at dawn to help with the milking; then numbed by hours of highway driving, rattled by the search for a parking space, queasy from the strong coffee served by Natalie's assistant. Rena was not at her best.

"Verdant is completely transparent about its sourcing." Natalie handed over a sheet of paper. "This is tonight's menu."

Rena read aloud. *"Angus filet with local microgreens, 30. Diamond*

Farms grass-fed beef, Lorain County, OH. That's a lot of information."

"Our customers want to know exactly what they're eating, and where it comes from."

Rena scanned the page. An item on the dessert menu caught her eye. "*Profiteroles with Seasonal Berries, 10. Potter County strawberries, Hillsdale Farm, Eastfield, PA. Saxon County Cream, Friend-Lea Dairy, Bakerton, PA.* What are profit rolls?"

"Cream puffs," Natalie said.

"Who could eat ten of them?"

"No, that's the price. Ten dollars."

"For cream puffs."

"It's an ambitious price point for Pittsburgh, but our customers are willing to pay it." Apologetic smile. "That's part of the issue, really. If you've spent a couple hundred dollars on dinner, you feel entitled to ask the farmer a few questions. Such as, where does your water come from?"

Rena's face went hot—a regular occurrence in recent months, and stress only made it worse. "We have a well."

"Which is fed by the water table. Which lies beneath your farm and all the surrounding properties." Natalie paused significantly. "How many of your neighbors have signed gas leases?"

"A few."

"Yes. And can you guarantee that none of those chemicals are leaching into the water your animals are drinking?"

"Okay, but what can we do? Should we have the water tested?"

"I would, if I were you. But regardless." Natalie turned her lovely hands palm up. "That doesn't solve *my* problem. When customers see Saxon County on the menu, they think gas drilling. Not all of them, certainly. But the ones who do are quite vocal about it. And I'm not sure they're wrong."

"Our land is clean." The flush spread across Rena's chest, her throat. "We've had gas guys knocking at our door for two years now. I can't tell you how many. I don't even let them in the house."

"But your neighbors do."

There was no arguing that point.

"I'm sorry, Rena. Friend-Lea milk is the best I've found anywhere. I'll have a hard time replacing it." Natalie offered her hand. "Good luck to you."

Rena left the restaurant through the back door, feeling or imagining the pitying looks of the kitchen staff. She drove around the block to a convenience store parking lot, then dialed Mack's cell phone. The phone lived in a basket on the kitchen table, a catchall for Mack's personal clutter: snuff tins, sweaty bandannas, the odd can of Bag Balm. Rena imagined it ringing in the empty house.

"Verdant dumped us," she told the voice mail. "I'll explain later. It's kind of complicated."

What was the point of having a mobile phone, if you never took it with you?

Somewhere behind her, a car alarm shrieked.

The shift to organic had been Rena's idea entirely. While Mack's father was alive, such a thing would have been impossible: Pete had fixed ideas in all matters, and Mack, who idolized him, had inherited his blind spots. Until his death, and for a long time after, she viewed any sort of change as a betrayal of his memory. *You want to do what?*

Organic, Rena said, feeling audacious. She was not, herself, a true farmer. A coal miner's daughter, she'd spent her childhood in a back yard the size of a sandbox, behind a company house on Polish Hill. Her young self had envisioned a different future entirely—a city life, like people on television.

Like everything else, that changed when she fell in love with Mack.

As couples did, they split the daily chores according to their aptitudes and interests. Mack's distaste for business matters— indifference verging on hostility—meant that it was Rena who read *Farm News* and *Dairy Week* and *Graze;* who put in for federal

MILC payments; who manned the ledger, money in, money out. In this particular argument, it gave her a clear advantage. While Mack squirmed like a restless schoolboy, Rena made the case for organic, with hard numbers: the higher base price for fluid milk, the lower input costs of rotational grazing, the savings in freight and vet bills.

She wasn't wrong. For nine years her plan had worked. More than worked, according to Mack: it had made farming fun again. Their decisions were no longer made by feed and fertilizer salesmen. To Pete's herd of grade Holsteins, Mack added Jerseys and Jersey crosses. To boost their forages, they rented extra acreage from Peachy Rouse. Within three years, Friend-Lea Acres was certified organic. Their milk check nearly doubled. There was no going back, or so it had seemed.

Rena drove, brooding. Verdant had been a reach for them. They'd landed the account completely by accident, had never heard of the restaurant until Natalie Lavender came to *them*. She'd been buying Friend-Lea milk from a neighborhood health food store, the Village Greengrocer, and was tired of paying the retail markup. She was interested, too, in other products: whipping cream, sour cream. When she called the farm—they still had no separate phone number for the business—Mack was skeptical; but Rena saw a rare opportunity. If Natalie Lavender—author of a popular cookbook, a frequent guest on TV cooking shows—chose Friend-Lea milk and cream, other restaurants would follow. Besides, Rena told Mack, they were already delivering to Pittsburgh. An extra stop at Verdant wouldn't cost them anything.

And just as she predicted, more accounts followed: a gourmet deli, a pastry shop; a new French restaurant, wildly popular, its every table booked until Christmas. Fifty gallons a week, a hundred. How long before those customers were scared away, too?

As many things did, the thought made Rena perspire. She fiddled with the truck's air conditioner, which needed a freon recharge.

The fan blew a feeble stream of tepid air. In the restaurant business, reputation was everything. Did their other customers know that Friend-Lea Acres was surrounded by gas wells? What exactly were people saying?

Ronny Zimmerman would know.

His store, the Village Greengrocer, had been their first Pittsburgh account. Back then Rena had delivered his milk herself, packed into Igloo coolers at the back of her station wagon. Of all her customers, he was the only one she'd call a friend.

She parked in the tiny lot behind the store and went in through the back door. Inside, a lone customer browsed the shelves of supplements and homeopathics, teas, dried herbs, and weird-smelling soaps. A small refrigerated case was stocked with Friend-Lea milk and yogurt. Despite its name, the store sold no other actual food.

She found Ronny at the cash register, hunched over a newspaper, in an old concert T-shirt and his trademark rainbow suspenders—dressed exactly as he had in 1978, possibly in the same actual clothes. Like its owner, the store was resistant to change. The Nag Champa incense he burned to hide his pot smoking; the walls plastered with homemade flyers advertising guitar lessons, vegan potluck suppers, midwives to deliver your baby at home. Faded Tibetan prayer flags gave the place a defeated air, like a used car lot gone out of business.

Ronny looked up from his paper. "Rena! What brings you to my humble emporium?"

"I had a meeting in town. I need to talk to you."

"You look like you could use some enlightening refreshment." He reached under the counter for his rolling papers. At that moment, the door opened. "Hey, man!" he called over her shoulder. "Rena, have you met my buddy Lorne?"

She turned.

The man was her own age, lean and wiry, handsome in a long-haired way. He carried a stack of green paper. Later she would try to reconstruct the moment, her first sight of him—the alert dark eyes, the loose grace of his walk. At the time she noticed none of this; she was simply irritated at the intrusion. Ronny's hippie friends could rant for hours about local politics, the evils of artificial sweeteners, the nutritional bankruptcy of school lunches, diatribes that bled one into another as the joint was passed.

"Lorne Trexler," he said, offering his hand.

"Rena's my farmer friend. The Friend-Lea Dairy lady. Let me see that." Ronny plucked a sheet of green paper from Lorne's stack. "Hey, not bad! 'GET THE FRACK OUT OF PENNSYLVANIA.' I came up with that myself. Clever, right?"

"You're a genius, Ronny." Trexler handed Rena a flyer. "Sorry to interrupt. But as a landowner, you might be interested."

Tell the governor we've had enough! she read. *Get Big Gas out of* **OUR BACK YARD!**

"There's a protest in Harrisburg next month," said Trexler. "If there's enough interest we're going to hire a bus. Are you in?"

"No. Maybe. I don't know much about it." She blotted her forehead with one of Mack's bandannas, stashed in her purse for this purpose.

"You're in luck, Rena. Lorne is an expert. Maybe the greatest living authority on hydro-fracking, water contamination, the whole clusterfuck."

"That's an exaggeration." Trexler smiled disarmingly. "I'm just a geologist. And, I guess, a community organizer, though that's a recent development. Where's your farm?"

"Saxon County."

He regarded her with new interest. "Lots of drilling up there, and it's only going to get worse. Half the county is under lease."

"No shit? You never told me that." Ronny eyed her suspiciously, mistrust written on his face, creeping doubts about the purity of Friend-Lea milk. Another account they were destined to lose.

"Well, it's not *that* bad. But I think some people have signed leases." Rena thought of the neighbors who'd come calling, Mack's newfound ambivalence: *It's good money, Rena. We could use it.* "Not everyone, though. Not us."

"If the community is divided, it's the perfect time to organize."

"I'm not very political," said Rena.

"Nobody is, until it's too late." Trexler seemed to be studying her, which was disconcerting. She couldn't remember the last time a man had looked at her.

"This is where to find me, if you change your mind." He handed her a business card from his pocket: LORNE TREXLER, CHAIR, DEPARTMENT OF GEOLOGY, STIRLING COLLEGE. Rena had never met a professor before. Her nursing instructors at the community college—all local, all female—somehow didn't count.

Ronny pinned the flyer to the bulletin board. "Tell her, Lorne. There's people out west who can light their tap water on fire."

"That's impossible," said Rena.

"Oh, yeah? Stay tuned." Lorne Trexler had a particular way of smiling. His smile took three full seconds to develop. Later Rena would time it, the slow smile she'd always associate with him.

"Remember Love Canal? In a couple years that's going to look like a neighborhood nuisance. They're fracking in twenty states. This is ecological disaster on a grand scale."

"Love what?"

Ronny gaped. "Love Canal? Toxic waste? Dioxins? *Not In My Back Yard?*"

A lick of sweat trailed down Rena's back. "I must've missed that."

"Forgive her, Lorne." Ronny's hands were busy under the counter rolling a surreptitious joint. "Here's the *Reader's Digest* version: they drained the canal and turned it into a dump. Twenty thousand tons of chemical waste buried there, and what did they do? They built a school on it."

"How do you do that without looking?" Rena said.

"The trees died. The grass died. Black sludge in people's basements. Was that you?"

They all stared at Rena's abdomen. Again her stomach made a creaking noise, like a barn door swinging open. Ronny lit the joint.

"I should get some lunch," she said, edging toward the door. Mack, who disapproved of pot smoking, might smell it on her clothes.

"Cancer," said Ronny. "Epilepsy. Asthma. Birth defects."

"Hold on. That was toxic waste. You're saying fracking causes the same problems?"

Ronny inhaled deeply. "I'm saying it's *possible*. I'm saying, who the fuck knows? I'm saying we should probably find out before we turn the whole state into a gas patch."

"I'm going now. Nice to meet you." She waved away the joint Ronny offered. "If I smoke any of that, I'll never find my way home."

On the outskirts of Oakland she made one more stop: Whole Harvest, the giant natural foods store Ronny viewed, with typical grandiosity, as a competitor. She made two tours of the parking lot before finding a space. At that hour—at every hour—the store was crowded with shoppers: women in suits, in workout tights, in Birkenstocks; a large number of forty-year-old mothers carrying babies in slings. Rena wandered the aisles, studying the inventory. The variety was stunning. A fair number of items (bonito flakes?) she couldn't begin to identify. Her usual store was the Bakerton Food Giant, notable for limp produce and a large selection of prepared Jell-O salads, its deli counter run by friendly women sturdy as loggers, cheerily hefting giant blocks of lunch meat. Rena's own mother had been one of them—twenty years in a smock and hairnet, slicing ring bologna and Dutch loaf.

(What was Dutch loaf, exactly? Rena was tempted to ask the dreadlocked boy who ran the deli counter at Whole Harvest, who almost certainly would not know.)

At the refrigerator case she mulled the offerings. Organic milk at several price points, from four to five dollars a half gallon. Yet even at those prices, people were buying. She watched a pregnant woman load up on organic yogurt. A scrawny man in running shorts chose a half gallon of skim. Neither looked, to Rena, especially wealthy (as though she'd know what wealth looked like). And yet they were paying extra for organic, fully double the price of conventional milk in a grocery store. In Bakerton such a thing was unimaginable: Friend-Lea had priced itself out of the local market. Virtually all their milk was trucked to Pittsburgh, Altoona, State College. Bakerton shoppers might conceivably choose organic milk, but not at twice the price.

She watched two girls, college age, approach the dairy case hand in hand. They were similarly dressed in boots and pegged jeans, their stringy hair cut into bangs. Lesbians holding hands in public— another thing you didn't see in Bakerton, as foreign as bonito flakes.

She bought a sandwich and ate it at one of the tables at the front of the store, studying the other customers: a black man with extravagant braids; a Chinese mother with small twin daughters; two Muslim women in head scarves talking on cell phones. All would seem exotic in Bakerton, where everyone looked more or less the same.

The lesbians at the dairy case were neither feminine nor masculine. They were just girls. Rena wondered how Mack would see them, Mack who'd never, herself, been a girl.

She drove home feeling vaguely depressed. Unlike Mack, who despised cities, she enjoyed her trips to Pittsburgh. And yet they left her in a somber mood. In cities there were too many options on display, reminders of the many lives you'd never get to live.

Years in, years out, a crash and slow backslide like waves breaking.

Fifty-four was older than she'd ever imagined being, decades lost in a fog of child rearing and farm chores, Rena and Mack like close-planted trees, their roots so braided together that there could be no untangling them. How and why they'd come together, that long-ago moment of choosing each other, now seemed both distant and unlikely, like a remembered dream. Each had brought to the relationship an incorrigible problem child: Mack's farm. Rena's son. They coupled swiftly and unconditionally, in the fevered certainty of youth. Not understanding then, or for a long time afterward, that no merger was absolute, that the totality of their union was an illusion.

That Friend-Lea Acres would never be Rena's farm.

That Calvin would never be Mack's son.

When she arrived home, Mack—wild-eyed, red-faced—met her at the door with a shotgun.

"For God's sake!" Rena cried. "What's the matter with you?"

Mack put down the gun. "Sorry, baby. I thought they came back."

"*What?* Who?"

And Mack showed her what was left of the shitsack, the reeking mess at their back door.

FROM THE POLICE STATION Rena goes straight to the hospital. The Emergency Room is quiet, the waiting room empty except for a mother and child. A pregnant nurse named Steph Mulraney is doing intakes. She hands Rena a clipboard.

"Urgent stomachache. Emergency queasiness." Steph is reliably grumpy about this kind of thing, Bakerton's poor and uninsured treating the ER as their own personal family doctor. It's true, of course: they see a dozen colds and earaches for every heart attack.

Rena glances at the paperwork. The stomachache, unusually, has Blue Cross. Her father works for the Department of Corrections, which means a top-drawer policy paid for by the state. Rena notes this with interest. Then she notices the child's name.

"Olivia Devlin. This is my neighbors' kid."

"Yep. She's a regular customer." Steph sits back in her chair, hands folded across her belly, a woman so often pregnant that it seems her natural state. "The mother is kind of a nutcase. We call her Chicken Little. You know: the sky is falling."

In the waiting room Rena calls Olivia's name. "I live up the road from you," she tells Mrs. Devlin, who looks not the slightest bit familiar. Who looks, in fact, too young to be anyone's mother, though in Bakerton this is not unusual. Her clothing—a skirt and high heels, careful makeup—makes her seem even younger, like a child playing dress-up. Olivia is a pretty little girl, a corn silk blonde. Her pale skin seems nearly transparent. A blue vein is visible at her temple.

Rena leads them to an exam room. "How are you feeling, honey?"

"She vomited twice this morning," Mrs. Devlin says.

Rena takes the child's vitals. Height, four feet one-half inch. Weight, forty-nine pounds. "Small for age seven."

"She's in the thirty-third percentile. I was the same way. I guess she takes after me." Mrs. Devlin rattles off Olivia's symptoms: daily stomachaches, frequent nausea. "I know for a fact she has food allergies. Dairy products, peppers, tomatoes, and wheat, for sure. And maybe eggs and corn. She needs a complete GI workup."

"Wow," says Rena. "Are you a nurse?"

"Oh, no." Mrs. Devlin flushes dramatically but seems pleased by the question. "I used to work at Saxon Manor, in Medical Records. Now I'm just a mom."

"All right, Mom. The doctor will be right with you." Rena gets to her feet. "Dr. Stusick is out this week. Dr. Finney is on tonight."

"I know. I called ahead." Mrs. Devlin hands over a folded sheet of paper, a fact sheet printed from a website. "I did some research. This is exactly what she needs."

"Reglan? Yikes, that's a pretty heavy-duty drug for a seven-year-old." Rena ticks off the commonest side effects—diarrhea, constipation, drowsiness. "It's basically a last resort."

"That's what Dr. Stusick said." Mrs. Devlin smooths Olivia's hair. "But I've already changed her diet. I don't know what else to try."

"Let's see what Dr. Finney has to say." Rena hands back the paper. "Has he seen Olivia before?"

"No, but I remember him from Saxon Manor." Mrs. Devlin leans forward confidentially. "I always thought I'd go back to school and get my RN. Then I had kids and, you know."

"I know," Rena says.

Back at the desk, Steph is eating a candy bar. "How'd it go with Chicken Little?"

Rena hesitates. Years ago, when Calvin was small, she herself had been a Chicken Little—like any nursing student with a young child, alert to ominous symptoms, hideously aware of all that could go wrong. Steph, pregnant with her fifth, is by necessity a different kind of mother. If she ran to the doctor every time one had a stomachache, she would do nothing else.

"She's a little—intense. But Olivia is tiny, malnourished probably. Which makes sense, if she can't keep her food down. Honestly, I'd be worried, too."

Rena settles in at the desk. Like many afternoons, the ER is quiet, and she finds herself wishing for patients—nothing too serious or scary; a sprain or splinter, a broken bone maybe. Her shift stretches endlessly before her. Back at the farm, a hundred chores need her attention. It's worse than ridiculous—it's a kind of torture—to sit here for hours with nothing to do.

Steph hands her an admission sheet. "Was this your patient? Monday afternoon."

Rena hands it back. "Not mine. I was out getting tires." She'd used up a precious sick day sitting in a tire shop in Altoona. "I had to get all new ones."

"They couldn't patch them?"

"I didn't want to risk it. That's all I need, to get a flat on the way to Pittsburgh."

"I can't believe you drive there. That traffic scares the crap out of me."

Mack says the same thing, Rena could have answered but didn't. It's the way normal people make conversation, something she isn't able to do.

Hours pass. Steph takes her dinner break. Mrs. Devlin and Olivia leave with a prescription for Reglan. Rena sees a roofer who fell from a ladder and dislocated his shoulder; a case of weeping eczema; a four-year-old boy with multiple bee stings, wailing like an air raid siren. Around nine o'clock the change will happen: people becoming their nighttime selves, the colds and stomachaches giving way to different kinds of impairments. The car crashes and bar fights; the wives with fresh bruises and questionable stories. Nearly everyone will seem drunk and disoriented. The change is most apparent on weekends, though lately Thursday is not so different from Friday. More and more, people treat it the same way, as though having worked four days entitles them to celebrate. Thursday is now the start of the weekend, with all the deliberate foolishness that entails.

She watches the clock. Steph returns from the cafeteria with a chocolate cupcake on a plate. "For later," she says.

Rena gathers up her purse and sweater. The cafeteria is notoriously freezing, the one part of the hospital where the air-conditioning works too well.

"I'd skip the lasagna if I were you," says Steph. "I'm already regretting it."

At that moment two men burst through the automatic doors. Rena smells them before she sees them—a chemical smell, intensely sweet and not entirely unpleasant. The odor puts her in mind of the old Cambria Confection plant, defunct now, whose specialty, a marshmallow candy bar rolled in peanuts, had been a favorite of her son's. Years ago, she drove past the factory every evening on her way to the community college. Even with the windows closed, the marshmallow smell had seeped into her car.

The men approach the desk. "My buddy needs a doctor," says the older one, a short muscle-bound guy with a barrel chest.

The younger one—chubby, dark-skinned—looks soaking wet. Steph sets down her cupcake. "Go. I'll take this."

Later, Rena will replay the moment a hundred times, thinking *It should have been me.* But it was Steph who took the patient to an exam room, stripped off his sodden clothes, and stuffed them into plastic bags.

At the time Rena knows none of this. But when she returns from the cafeteria twenty minutes later, Steph's chair is empty. The chocolate cupcake sits untouched on the desk.

3.

The camp sulks at the edge of town, plainly visible from the highway, a cluster of squat barracks fenced off with chain-link. The grounds are paved with macadam. Armed security guards man the gate. Inside the fence are two large dormitories; a third building holds a Laundromat, cafeteria, and gym. The compound resembles, from a distance, a maximum-security community college—an enlightened institution for lepers or convicted killers, men guilty of, or infected with, something lethally bad.

Denny Tilsit is the camp manager, a job he'd wish on no one, though he's done it twice before, in Wyoming and Dakota. *Welcome to nowhere,* he tells the new arrivals, and rattles off the rules. No drugs or drinking, no firearms, no females on the premises. They think he's kidding about that last one, until they get a look around and understand the rule is unnecessary. No female would be caught dead here.

Each dormitory sleeps two hundred. A bedroom is the size of a gas-station restroom, with a cable TV bolted to the ceiling, a narrow bed, and a desk. Each pair of rooms is joined by a shared bathroom—an arrangement known elsewhere as a *jack and jill,* though in the all-male camp it's more like a *jack and jack,* a joke Denny has stopped making. Here you don't even joke about guys jacking each other. The men are sensitive about that kind of thing.

A dormitory packed with two hundred men, you'd expect it to smell bad. It does, but not the way you'd think. The corridors reek of pesticide and newness, the manufactured smell of trash bags, cheap lawn furniture, Tupperware, balloons. If anyone asked, Denny would explain that the walls are made of plastic, a special polymer that resists mold and warping. The pesticide odor is self-explanatory. But nobody asks.

A name, DAYBREAK, is emblazoned across the towels and sheets, the comforter and pillowcase. Have no doubt who owns that bath mat. Never forget where and whose you are.

Day or night, the corridors are quiet. Always someone is sleeping. The men keep exotic hours. Shifts start at noon, at midnight, at 4:00 P.M., at dawn. The cafeteria, which never closes, serves bacon and eggs at all hours. It's always breakfast time for someone.

Daybreak LLC is a subsidiary of Darco Energy. The company logo, a stylized sunrise, appears on napkins and dinner plates.

In the hallway outside the cafeteria are four public computers, for the middle-aged and elderly. All the young guys bring their own. The shared computers are used for video chats with wives and children; for checking weather and sports scores; for compulsive bouts of online poker. For porn, though, you'd have to finish yourself off in private. They're not ideal for porn.

The cafeteria smells of chicken nuggets, twenty-four/seven. Other foods are served, hamburgers and pizza, but the nugget smell dominates. Exhaust fans blow it into the blacktop courtyard; intake fans suck it into the bedrooms. The fans run constantly, a loud rush of air like the camp's own weather, its sirocco and mistral. The wind carries the camp's chronic halitosis: plastic and pesticides, chicken nuggets and cigarettes.

A girl in California cavorts before a webcam, at least she says it's California. It could be Saskatoon or Gary, Indiana, any place with tanning beds.

No jills in the camp, no jills whatsoever. A secretary helps Denny in the front office, a local woman named Brenda Hoff. She is fifty and squat as a dishwasher; her eyes bulge froggily. Brenda Hoff is not sexy, has never heard of sexy. Still the men find excuses to stop by the office, an anthropology lesson, as though Brenda Hoff is, quite literally, the last woman on earth.

It could be Riga or Bangkok or Mexico City. Any place with board-certified plastic surgeons, or their unlicensed equivalent.

The game room has a pool table, couches, and another TV, in case you get tired of watching your own. Men sit talking and smoking. The new arrivals watch baseball; the veterans have given up on baseball. They are men who'd rather be sleeping, insomniacs winding down from their shifts.

The middle-aged and elderly finish themselves off in private.

The Laundromat smells of chicken nuggets and detergent, the twenty-pound boxes of soap powder the camp provides.

IN TOWN THERE ARE WHISPERS, unholy rumors. The security guards speak with southern accents. The supply vans have out-of-state plates.

The camp is full of illegal Mexicans, army deserters, Afghan terrorists from Gitmo. Armed marshals escort the prisoners to work. The chain-link fence hums with high-voltage current. The security guards have orders to shoot on sight.

The camp is a hotbed of drugs and prostitution. Local girls are scouted for this purpose, recruited and hired by Brenda Hoff. Girls arrive by the half dozen, at all hours, crowded into a Mercedes: a six-pack of prostitutes, provocatively dressed.

The men are white separatists, mercenaries, paramilitary. The camp is protected by its own militia, the fence built to keep the world out. The men's needs are serviced by licensed contractors. Supply vans come and go. The camp's trash is carted away to a secret incinerator. Even its shit is proprietary: the toilets drain into a private septic system somewhere on the grounds.

The prostitutes are kept in a bunker beneath the building. This explains why they are never seen.

IT IS BACKBREAKING WORK, punishing to the body. There are no soft jobs on a drill rig. A mud motor weighs six hundred pounds. The hoisting system uses steel rope. The men yank and drag and push and pull. Twelve hours a day they hump and heave. Some work injured, numbed by painkillers. After twelve hours they'd rather sleep than drink or eat or talk to their families. With a few youthful exceptions, they would rather sleep than fuck.

They are well paid, naturally. A high school dropout can earn six figures if he is strong and willing. If nothing goes very wrong.

Now sleeping is the Bravo crew—the first tour, or most of it: Mickey Phipps the tool pusher, Vince Legrand the derrick man, the roughnecks Brando and Jorge. Their rig manager, who makes more money, has decamped to the Days Inn. For months Herc was a vibrant complainer—the thin towels and acrid coffee, the nugget smell. The public service announcements on every flat surface, framed posters of drill rigs, the company slogan: S.A.F.E. (STAY ACCIDENT FREE EVERYDAY) DRILLING.

It's not even English, he'd grumble. *What kind of pidgin language is that?*

No one else comments on the posters. They grouse about the food, their knees and backs. Except for Mickey Phipps, who is Christian, they complain about the dearth of women—even Brando, who is known to have solved that problem. For him, for all of them, horniness is a conversation starter, a neutral topic like baseball. They spend half their time working, half exactly: seven days a week, twelve-hour shifts. When the shift ends, second tour comes to relieve them. The drilling literally never stops.

Who has time for baseball, with its long season? For the spectator, it is a demanding sport.

They work two weeks straight, then pack their bags. The camp is for on-duty workers only. Other men need those beds. The company runs a free shuttle to the Pittsburgh airport, where Mickey Phipps catches a flight to Houston. The others keep the local bartenders busy, and find somewhere to sleep off their liquor—in a woman's bed if they're lucky, on Herc's floor at the Days Inn if they're not.

Brando is always lucky.

Back at the camp, Denny Tilsit guards the schedule. It's his own private nightmare, summarized on a detailed spreadsheet: room numbers, arrivals and departures, cleaning crews in and out. When the men return, others will have slept in their beds, watched their televisions, shaved at their sinks. To Herc, the rig manager, it's another argument in favor of the Days Inn.

What does he care? says Jorge. *They clean the room so good I can't tell the difference.*

It's four-thirty in the morning, and the men assemble sack lunches in the pantry behind the kitchen. The camp provides bread and cold cuts for this purpose, industrial-size jars of mustard and mayonnaise.

Seriously, man. They change the sheets and shit. What does he care?

Jorge is twenty-four and caffeinated, unbothered by waking in the dark. The others are silent and irritable. Brando lights a cigarette. Vince Legrand swallows Motrin for his back.

Mickey Phipps, who is Christian, does not comment. The truth, he knows, is harder and simpler: Herc doesn't want to leave Pennsylvania every two weeks, doesn't want to fly back to his wife in Texas. He's happy right where he is, or not happy. Anyway, he doesn't want to go home.

THE MORNING IS DIM AND MOONLESS. First tour starts at five. A convoy of pickup trucks rolls down Number Nine Road, past a few scattered houses, still dark at this hour. Up and down the Dutch Road, dogs begin to bark.

The drill site, Fetterson 2H, glows in the distance, lit up like a stadium at night. Herc's company truck is already there, parked behind the operator's trailer; a magnetic sign—STREAM SOLUTIONS—stuck to the driver-side door. He sits on the hood drinking coffee from a Days Inn cup. Jorge and Legrand park on either side.

In the trailer they gear up—safety goggles, hard hats—and climb the hundredsome-odd stairs. The rig floor is a platform suspended in midair, at the height of a three-story building. As he does each morning, Jorge reads aloud: DANGER HIGH VOLTAGE. WARNING HIGH NOISE LEVEL HEARING PROTECTION REQUIRED.

The signs are Herc's pet peeve, one his crew has picked up on. There are signs on the railings and catwalk and V-door, signs in the trailers, the doghouse, the john.

NOTICE AUTHORIZED PERSONNEL ONLY

AVISO SOLAMENTA PERSONAL AUTORIZADO

It's a petty complaint; Herc knows this. He understands that his irritation is out of all proportion, and yet he can't help himself. The signs offend him personally: the bright colors, the capital letters. The repetition in English and Spanish, as in the educational television his kids watched when they were small.

By six the sun is up, the air warming. The Bravo crew is tripping pipe. According to procedure it takes five men to change a drill bit, five men to pull the drill string from the hole. The actual truth is somewhat different. Three joints of drilling pipe weigh more than a pickup truck, and yet the floor hands, Brando and Jorge, do all the lifting. This is true of racking pipe, true of most things. A drill rig is a hierarchy like the rest of the world.

The trip goes smoothly, it would seem to the only observers, the darting barn swallows, the numberless gnats rising in clouds. Seen from above, the men are larger than birds and bugs, but only a bit larger. A drill rig isn't scaled for humans. Like a sailor on an aircraft carrier, a roughneck crossing the catwalk looks aphid-size.

Legrand leans out from the monkey board and throws a line around the pipe.

The roughnecks are both strong: Brando tall and wiry, Jorge low and heavy. It takes all their combined force to swing the kelly over the rat hole and unhook the swivel bale from the hook. They attach the elevator to the pipe and step back, panting, like boxers at the bell.

While they catch their breath, Mickey steps into the booth and grabs the joystick. The hoisting system kicks in, raising the pipe from the hole. One, two, three joints clear the opening. Then another scramble as Brando and Jorge set the slips. With tongs and a spinning wrench, they break off three joints' worth. A hundred feet above their heads, Legrand fits the top end into the fingerboard. A satisfying clank as they drop the pipe in the mast.

The trip completed, Herc calls a coffee break. The men are feeling conversational. Like women in a beauty parlor they stand around yakking. Brando ignores their chitchat, tedious shit about Mickey's kids, a caper involving Legrand and a waitress in the next town over. There's always a waitress in the next town over. Figments, possibly, of Legrand's drunken imagination, this army of waitresses no one has ever seen.

There are ten times more signs than there used to be, though only Herc has been around long enough to note the difference. This rig, brand-new, is particularly rich in reading material. New OSHA regulations? A punishing lawsuit, more costly than previous lawsuits?

WARNING NO ENTRY WITHOUT SUPERVISOR

DANGER PINCH POINT

Herc has yet to see a sign that tells the simple truth: of all the calamities that can happen on a drill rig, falling is the likeliest. The easiest way to kill yourself is simply missing a step. He has seen up close what a three-story fall can do to a body. He'd do anything to wipe that picture from his mind.

DANGER

AVISO

PELIGRO

It's a truth most people never have to learn, that the human body is simply a bag of blood.

THEY END THE DAY at the loud end of the bar, with mugs of Iron City. After ten months in Pennsylvania they've developed a taste for it. Herc, who spent the afternoon at the Emergency Room with Jorge, orders a shot to catch up.

The Commercial is packed for a Thursday, every seat taken. Men stand three-deep around the bar waiting for drinks. Brando glares at the bartender, who pretends not to see him. "What, U.S. currency's no good here?"

The guy pulls one Iron City, then another. He slides them down the bar to where the locals sit, two greasers in ball caps staring at the TV screen.

"Who is this shithead?" says Brando, loud enough for the bartender to hear.

"Oh, he's all right," says Herc, though there's no mistaking the attitude. "He don't know us, is all." The owner, a surly old cuss, is no friendlier—never a smile or a *Hey, how you doin?*—but at least he's quick with a drink.

"He's the old coot's son," says Legrand, who could use a shower himself. Even in the dim light his ponytail looks lank and greasy, his face flushed with booze and a week's sunburn. "I think he's some kind of a cop."

Herc studies the bartender, taller and younger than he is, but probably not as strong. He's done this since childhood, the runt's habit of sizing up his tormentors, though these days Herc is all lats and deltoids and nobody has given him trouble in years.

"He's a guard at the prison," says Jorge, who looks pretty good, all things considered, for a hazmat casualty about to star in his own OSHA report. "I seen him in his uniform."

At that moment a cell phone rings in Brando's pocket. Barks, actually, deep and resonant like a German shepherd.

"What the hell is that?" Legrand says.

"That's nobody." Brando turns off the phone, which has been barking since lunchtime. It emits strange noises all day long, beeps and peals and snatches of music. Once it even farted, the thunderous ripping fart of a dyspeptic old man. "Hey, officer. Another shot over here."

"To *Law and Order*," says Herc, raising his shot glass—a dig at Mickey Phipps who, being Christian, spends every night alone in his room staring at the TV. It's the first time in months they've gotten him out for a drink. "You must a seen every episode by now."

"I guess I have," Mickey says, grinning. He is the steadiest of the crew, easy and good-natured. The rest have done their share of acting out, Brando and Legrand especially: bar fights, drunken capers, women. After ten years working rigs, Herc has seen it all before. Send a man a thousand miles from home; work him like a mule for two weeks straight; then let him loose with money in his pocket. Only a saint like Mickey Phipps will avoid making a fool of himself. This time tomorrow he'll be on a plane back to Houston, drinking ginger ale and reading from his pocket Bible, a man who wants nothing more from life than to spend every spare minute with his wife and kids.

Mickey pretend-sips his beer, still full after half an hour. "How 'bout you? Any plans for the weekend?"

Only Mickey would ask such a question and expect an answer.

"Oh, I don't know. Might could drive up to Canoe Creek."

"You get a fishing license?"

"Not yet."

Legrand howls. "Who you kidding? You'll be propping up the bar at the Days Inn like usual, and I'll be setting there with you." He raises his glass to Herc. "Fishing, my ass."

Herc knocks back his shot, knowing he'll regret it in the morning. Drinking with Legrand has already subtracted years from his life. Vince has this effect on all who know him, the several ex-wives, the identical twin brother dead already, in some hideous freak accident involving liquor and heavy equipment and God knows what all. Probably it can be expressed mathematically, what his friendship does to your life expectancy. Insurance companies have formulas for it.

A girl makes her way through the crowd. *Eye-talian Gia*, the roughnecks call her. Usually she is behind the bar, a stunning dark-eyed girl with long curly hair.

Brando spots her first. "Jesus fucking Christ."

Mickey flinches visibly. Herc, sitting between them, wants to slug them both: the holy roller with his ladylike sensibilities, the arrogant punk running at the mouth.

Brando runs a hand over his stubbly hair. A year out, he still keeps it army-short. "It's supposed to be her night off. I can't get away from that bitch. What does she want from me?"

"Your daddy ought to have explained that to you," Legrand says.

"Hey, boys. Where have you been?" Gia asks Brando. "I just called you. I've been texting you all day."

She's a little skinny for Herc's taste—he likes voluptuous women—but still, a beautiful girl.

"I forgot my phone," Brando says.

Gia frowns. "You never go anywhere without that thing."

"The battery's dead." He lies effortlessly, without blinking or fumbling, as though he doesn't care whether anyone believes him or not. Herc watches his performance with a kind of awe. He hired the kid against his better judgment—even in a job interview, Brando was all tattoos and attitude. But he served a tour each in Iraq and Afghanistan, which ought to count for something. This was Herc's thinking at the time.

"I need to talk to you," says Gia. "Can we go outside?"

"Now?"

"It's important."

Brando chugs the rest of his beer, half a glass in a few gulps. He drops a crumpled five on the bar. "Be right back."

"I doubt it," says Jorge, watching them go.

"Can't say I feel too bad for him." Legrand drains his glass. "I'd say that's a good problem to have."

AT MIDNIGHT JORGE AND LEGRAND ORDER ANOTHER ROUND. Herc excuses himself to take a leak.

"Amateur," says Legrand, who is famous for never urinating—a skill so valuable, in a derrickman, that they ought to screen for it in the job interview, right along with the drug test. By this measure Legrand is a consummate professional. Never once has Herc shut down the whole show so Vince could descend the hundred-foot mast to piss.

"Time to get your pisser checked," says Legrand. "Get you some Stream Solutions."

"Don't give me that," says Herc. "I know you keep an empty Coke bottle up there."

"You have insulted my honor," Legrand says.

From the men's room Herc heads out the back door, to the rear parking lot. In his truck he dials his home number. Colleen answers on the first ring. Sitting, probably, in her usual spot on the sectional, nursing a wine cooler and watching a movie on the Lifetime network, another sensitive melodrama about noble women and the men who abuse them. *The wife-beater channel,* she calls it. She seems to have a limitless appetite for such stories. He's stopped wondering why.

"Honey, it's me."

Dead silence.

"I wanted to say hi to the boys."

"It's eleven o'clock."

Shit. Even with the time difference, his kids have been in bed for hours. And yet the delay was necessary. He's a better liar with a few drinks in him.

"I guess this means you're not coming." Colleen sounds fed up, weary. "When were you going to tell me?"

They've had the same conversation, with minor variations, since last summer, through the fall and endless winter. In those months Herc has seen his family exactly three times. Colleen reminds him, often, that this isn't what he promised. Mickey Phipps spends two weeks per month in Texas. Herc, if he wanted to, could do the same.

If.

"I'm telling you now. I got to work next week."

"No kidding. How'd that happen, Marshall?" As pissed as he knew she'd be. She must be, to use his full name.

Herc pauses for a breath, remembering Brando—deadpan, perfectly relaxed—at the bar. "We're stretched pretty thin here. Nothing I can do about it. My guys aren't too happy, I can tell you that."

"Oh, *really?* Because I ran into Didi Phipps at the store. She says Mickey's coming home."

Shit, shit, shit.

"Mickey's not working," he says, backpedaling. "I got another tool pusher up here can do it. It's the rig manager that's out. I got no one else to run that crew."

"What's wrong with him?"

Herc's mind races. Food poisoning? Threw his back out?

"I don't know," he says irritably. "What do I care what's wrong with him? The point is, I got to work. That's going to be forty-two days without a break. Shit fire, Colleen. You think I'm happy about it?"

His irritation seems to convince her. He's been short with her lately; she has come to expect it. Again he thinks of Brando: when all else fails, be a prick.

He's known Colleen exactly two-thirds of his life, since they were both fifteen. She knows him better than anybody ever has or will, and there is comfort in that. There is also boredom, resentment, disappointment, and shame. After so many years, she knows what he is and isn't; the limits of his abilities, his character, and even his love.

"Aw, baby, I'm sorry," she says softly. "I just miss you is all."

Herc closes his eyes. "I miss you, too."

"What do you boys do for fun up there?"

"*Law and Order* is on the TV."

Colleen laughs low in her throat. "It's always on. You need to get out of that room. Maybe one of the guys will go drink a beer with you."

"That's an idea. Tomorrow night, maybe."

"All right, then. I'm running out of steam here. I been up since six." She makes a kiss noise into the phone. "Call me tomorrow, okay?"

"Will do," Herc says.

HE'S WORKED IN PENNSYLVANIA TEN MONTHS: long enough to have a small affection for the place, not long enough for it to take the slightest notice of him. The town was welcoming at first, his Texas plates an easy conversation-starter: *It's a work truck. We're up here drilling.* As the leaves fell, the local mood shifted with the weather, turning cold and sharp. People groused about the detours and roadwork, the truck traffic. The same thing had happened in Shreveport, but in Louisiana he didn't feel like a foreigner. Not since the air force, his year on Okinawa, has he felt so far from home.

And yet home is its own kind of heartache. After two weeks on the rig he forgets how to talk to people, his wife especially. When Colleen meets him at the airport, she seems exhausted, worn down by the kids and, it seems to Herc, a long list of grievances: everything he missed in the last two weeks, every essential chore he failed to do. Only his boys seem excited to see him. The boys are the good part—their natural and generous enthusiasm, their authentic, uncomplicated joy.

He waited longer and longer to buy his ticket, until the inevitable happened: at Thanksgiving, at the last minute, every flight was booked. He took his licks from Colleen, then booked a room at the Days Inn and spent the holiday getting hammered with Vince Legrand, whose latest wife had kicked him out for good. Herc spent his hangover sleeping and watching television, savoring the indifference of his motel room, its clean anonymous quiet. This was a new version of himself, or maybe an old one he'd forgotten. As a boy he'd been happiest on horseback, far away from everyone.

His two weeks of freedom stretched before him, eventless days. He rose early no matter his condition, spent two hours in what the Days Inn called the *fitness suite,* a windowless basement room with a battered treadmill and weight bench. He'd lifted weights since high school, the short man's salvation. (He's five six on tiptoe.) This one discipline made him feel better about everything, as though it canceled out whatever nonsense he'd been up to the night before. In the afternoons he took long drives, or wandered the aisles of Walmart. It was in no way a pleasant place to spend time; it was simply unpleasant in a familiar way. In recent years he'd loitered at Walmarts in Shreveport, in Fayetteville, in Casper, Wyoming. Each offered the same merchandise, the same signage, the same sort of friendly old person greeting folks at the door. The clientele, too, was the same: lone women, elderly couples, young mothers with children strapped into shopping carts, clamoring for candy or toys. The sort of regular life a person stops seeing, doing the work he does. Watching them, Herc was acutely aware of his own perversity, spying on regular families in Walmart when his own regular family was waiting for him in Houston.

The sameness of days. The monotony was curiously restorative.

He couldn't say why, but two weeks alone was exactly what he'd needed. For the first time in years he recalled his scripture: *On the seventh day, he rested.* As a boy he'd decided this was pure human invention, that God, being God, wouldn't need to take a break. The Sabbath was a fabrication by the man wielding the pen, the unnamed Israelite who dreamed up the creation story. Tuckered out by long weeks of fishing the Galilee or growing wheat in the desert, he embroidered this elaborate fantasy, this mother of all excuses, just to get a day off work.

You had to hand it to him.

At Full Gospel Sunday school such insights were unwelcome. By age twelve Herc had the God beat out of him; his father, the preacher, had done the beating himself. Hanging from a hook in the pastor's basement workshop was a wooden paddle he called the Grace Stick, a two-foot length of polished oak he'd carved with those words. And yet grace was God's gift, something you were supposed to want.

Herc could not imagine hitting his own children for any reason. It seemed the opposite of grace.

He might never have stepped inside a church again, if not for Mickey Phipps. Seven weeks ago, the Pittsburgh airport closed for a late-season snowstorm, Mickey had slept on Herc's floor at the Days Inn. When Sunday morning came, he asked the desk clerk about a church. *Not Catholic, not Lutheran. Just plain Christian,* said Mickey. *That's all I am.* Overcome by the black despair of a crippling hangover, Herc agreed to tag along.

They wondered, at first, if they'd botched the directions. Two Hundred Susquehanna Avenue was an empty storefront. Then Mickey spotted a handbill on the plate glass door, printed on somebody's home computer:

Living Waters, a Bible Fellowship.
The Rev. Jess Peacock, Pastor

Inside, a small crowd of locals waited on folding chairs. The plywood altar was draped with a white cloth. No organ, no choir: music was supplied by a boom box set on the floor. The whole business had an improvised feel, a child's playacting. Herc thought of himself at five or six, playing preacher in the barn loft. He'd saved several playmates from eternal damnation, baptizing them solemnly in the creek behind the barn.

When a pretty dark-haired lady rose to the pulpit, it took him a minute to understand what he was seeing. The Reverend Jess Peacock was a woman.

She was dressed in a gray pants suit, the sort of outfit Hillary Clinton had worn in her presidential campaign. His wife, who hated Hillary Clinton, had called the pants suits hideous, but Herc secretly liked them. His upbringing, probably: he liked to see women modestly dressed. Colleen still wore the short skirts she'd favored in high school. Somewhere along the way, she'd gotten the idea he liked them. Maybe he'd complimented her once, to make her happy; maybe he'd even meant it at the time.

Marriage in middle age: living in a house made of shit you've said over the years.

The actual content of the service, the prayers and Bible readings, are vague in his memory. He remembers only the pastor herself, taller than Colleen, and shapely—Snow White from the Disney cartoon, the live-action version.

"You must listen for God's promises and stand on them." She spelled out the word, her voice vibrating with sincerity: "S-T-A-N-D. And by *stand* I mean something very specific. I mean Speak Them All Night and Day."

Against his will Herc thought, *Stay Accident Free Everyday Drilling.*

When the pastor stood for the final hymn, he was struck again by her height. In truth she was not unusually tall, but he'd always gone for petite women. He wouldn't look twice at a lanky super-model, no matter how stunning. What would be the point?

When the music stopped she gave a hopeful smile. "Please join us for coffee and fellowship after the service."

Well, all right, Herc thought. He could've used a little fellowship, no question; but Mickey Phipps was already heading for the door. Herc followed hesitantly, avoiding the pastor's eyes. He felt like a heel for skipping out. It seemed callous to disappoint her, a sweet serious child playing preacher, by refusing to play along.

They drove back to the Days Inn, Mickey at the wheel. "Nothing wrong with her preaching. It just don't seem right to me." He smiled tightly. They had worked together ten months, through exhaustion, horizontal snowstorms, a broken mud motor, a bad case of bronchitis that nearly killed them both. This was the first time Herc had seen him angry.

"Reverend Jess Peacock," said Mickey. "It sure sounds like a man. Kind of makes you wonder."

"Wonder what?"

"She could have picked it on purpose." Again the tight smile. He was really, really mad.

"Maybe," Herc said. "Or, you know, maybe it's just her name."

STAY ACCIDENT FREE EVERYDAY DRILLING.

Herc has no talent for paperwork. It is, without a doubt, his least favorite part of the job. When he can put it off no longer, he brews a pot of coffee and holes up in the office trailer, studying OSHA reports. His own safety record is respectable, if you don't go too far back.

The distracted employee is an accident waiting to happen. The waitress in the next town over, who just might be pregnant. (She says.) The wife who will not, will not stop calling. The hangover to end all hangovers: the pulsating headache, the lurching stomach, the runs.

He studies OSHA reports while talking to Colleen, who is watching television. It's hard not to conclude that they both have better things to do. His cell phone is hot in his hands, as though warmed by her anger. It bothers her that he never sends greeting cards.

```
Report ID: 0419921
Injury While Sandblasting Derrick

Employee #1 was sandblasting the derrick. A
sudden movement of his supply hose caused him to
lose balance. As he steadied himself, the nozzle
caught in the gauntlet of his glove and his left
forearm was injected with sand and air.
```

Nature: Puncture

Degree: Hospitalized injury

Keywords: sandblasting, glove, hose, arm, derrick

Colleen herself sends cards for every occasion—birthdays, holidays, marriage, sickness, and death. She has an uncanny knack—she prides herself on this—for picking the perfect card.

On her birthday, which was today, he sent flowers, a gift certificate good at all Chili's locations, and a pair of earrings he chose from a catalog, with help from Eye-talian Gia. He felt he'd done pretty well until he described the gifts to Mickey Phipps, who is Christian. *Well, it's the thought that counts*, Mickey said.

```
Report ID: 0422920
Employee Struck and Killed by Unsecured
Counterbalance


Report ID: 0499337
Employee Caught Between Kelly and Mast
```

He paid extra to have the earrings gift wrapped. He shouldn't have bothered. It doesn't count, according to Colleen, unless he wrapped the box himself.

He is fourteen hundred miles away, on a drill rig.

The cell phone is probably giving him brain cancer.

"Sorry, baby," he says, because it's just fucking easier. "I should have sent a card."

In Houston, a satisfied silence. They have their best conversations after Herc admits to being a shitheel.

"So we'll see you next weekend?"

He remembers, then: next Sunday is Father's Day, a holiday he hates. He's given up trying to explain why. The whole notion depresses him, his children's pure love manipulated by advertising, the boys guilted into spending their tiny allowances to prove their affection for him. Only Mother's Day is more vile, thanks mainly to its higher price tag, the cynical machinations of jewelers and florists.

"Sure," he says, cornered. "See you then."

THERE'S SOME KIND OF HULLABALOO AT WALMART. A half-dozen shoppers cluster in the front lobby, near the gumball machines. They seem to be watching something. Herc cranes his neck to see a uniformed cop talking to a scrawny bottle-blonde, not young, in cutoff shorts and a tube top. A wreck of a woman, but if you squint just the right way, it's possible to see a trace of lost sexiness, a ghostly remnant of the bombshell she must have been before hard living took her looks.

The cop places a hand at her back. "All right, Roxanne. Follow me, please."

"Get your hands off me."

The crowd parts to let them pass. Herc watches them head toward the office at the front of the store. "What happened?" he asks no one in particular.

Heads turn in his direction, but no one answers. It's as though he's speaking a foreign language. Red-faced, he heads into the store.

"Welcome to Walmart," says the greeter, an old coot he's seen here before.

Normally Herc is stumped for an answer. This time he asks, "What was all that fuss about?"

The coot shrugs. "Shoplifters, prolly. We get them once in a while."

"That's too bad," Herc says.

Inside, he wanders the aisles. He had a vague idea of checking out the fishing gear but can't seem to find it. He is loitering in Home & Garden when he spots the lady preacher pushing a cart into the grocery section. She wears a different pants suit, cream colored. He follows a few paces behind.

She heads straight for the bakery and picks out two big tubs of cookies. Herc watches from a discreet distance.

Abruptly she turns. "Are you following me?"

"No, ma'am," he stammers—noticing, too late, his reflection in the round fisheye mirror above the bakery counter.

She smiles disarmingly, like a teacher who means to scold you and then changes her mind. "I recognize you. You've been to my Sunday service."

A moment of hot confusion: she had noticed him. "I enjoyed your preaching very much."

"Herc," she repeats when he introduces himself. "How do you spell that?"

He spells it. "It's a nickname. From Hercules. It's asinine. My real name is Marshall."

"Marshall." She seems to be studying him. "You're not from around here. You work for one of the gas companies?"

"Stream Solutions. That's Dark Elephant," he adds, like an idiot. "Which is Darco."

"You work for all of them?"

"You could say that."

And somehow it feels perfectly natural to follow her to the express checkout lane, to pay for his five-pound drum of FierceCut protein powder.

"You're a long way from home," she says. "That must be difficult."

"I'm used to it. I was in Arkansas last summer. Loosiana before that."

Such ordinary answers, and yet they seem to fascinate her. Every question leads to two more. They linger on the sidewalk in front of the store, her shopping cart between them.

"Marshall, I'd love to talk some more, but I'm on my way to Bible study. That's what the cookies are for. Would you like to join us?"

"I can't tonight. I have plans." It is an actual lie: he has nothing, nothing at all, to do. But he's out of practice conversing with a woman, and tense from the effort. If he says anything more he is sure to spoil it. Better to quit before he makes a fool of himself.

She eyes the plastic jar under his arm. "What do you do with that stuff, anyway?"

"Mix it with water. It's not bad." He grins. "Yes, it is. It's revolting. I can't lie to a woman of God."

She laughs then, an exhilarating sound. A thing he had forgotten, the simple joy of making a woman laugh.

Her next words stun him completely.

"Are you free for dinner on Friday? I'm guessing it's been a while since you had a home-cooked meal." She reaches into her pocketbook and hands him a business card. "That's my home address. Come at seven."

He takes the card.

"MOM, WHAT ARE YOU DOING HERE?"

Roxanne's daughter looks surprised to see her. No: surprised is an understatement. Shelby seems near death from the shock of it. Her eyes are ready to pop out of her head.

"I was in the neighborhood," Roxanne lies. There is no neighborhood. Shelby and Rich live out in the sticks, miles from anything. "I figured I could see my grandbabies."

"Braden is at practice. And Olivia is taking a nap."

"At her age?" It's better not to specify a number. Olivia is six years old, or possibly eight or ten.

"She isn't feeling well."

"Aren't you going to invite me in?"

"I'm kind of in the middle of supper." Shelby's hair is pulled back in a ponytail, so tight her forehead looks stretched. Typically, she wears no makeup. Her face looks scrubbed, serious, and very young.

"At three in the afternoon?" says Roxanne.

"I make it ahead of time. I have Bible study later."

Roxanne says, "I can help."

Shelby frowns grotesquely.

"Shelby Elizabeth, if you don't stop it, your face is going to get stuck that way." It is only a slight exaggeration. Not even thirty, and already she's got some wacky expression lines, on exactly half her face.

Shelby steps aside to let her in. It isn't much of a welcome, but you've got to be somewhere. Roxanne needs to collect herself before going back to Peanut's. Walmart rattled her, the public embarrassment, though in the end the cop had let her go. She drove away shaky with relief. Another court date is the last thing she needs.

"How's Peanut?" Shelby asks.

"He's all right." It isn't exactly true. Peanut isn't exactly all right. For reasons unknown, his disability check is two days late. This happened once before, last winter. Roxanne wishes the federal government would get its act together.

Living with Peanut is not all that different from being married, as far as she can recall, though her experience with that institution is distant and brief. When she cashes Peanut's check she keeps half for herself. She earns her share doing what needs to be done: laundry, emptying ashtrays, heating Hot Pockets in the microwave. Mornings she drives his van around town, doing errands. *Basic necessities,* he said when she was first hired. *Groceries, Rite Aid, that kind of thing.* That was—two years ago? Three? In that time her job description has narrowed. The definition of *basic necessities* has narrowed.

What she does now, mainly, is buy meth.

Peanut has never been married—to Roxanne's knowledge, never even had a girlfriend. Until age fifty he lived with his mother. When his mother died, Peanut got MS. *He's got to be queer,* says Roxanne's sister, but really, what does it matter? It's hard (also unpleasant) to imagine Peanut having sex with anyone. Hard to imagine him doing anything but watching TV, smoking cigarettes, and getting high.

"What's all that business out on the Dutch Road?" Roxanne asks. "There are trucks everywhere."

"They're drilling for gas."

What a fucking mess, Roxanne thinks but doesn't say. Shelby is always scolding her about her language, even when there are no kids in the room.

Shelby studies her. "What happened to your tooth?"

"I left it in an apple."

"Did you go to the dentist?"

Shelby is always bugging her about this kind of thing: flu shots, cholesterol. Last year, for Christmas, she gave Roxanne a set of nicotine patches. All Shelby's gifts were like that. They all told you what was wrong with you.

Roxanne sits at the kitchen table and watches Shelby open a can of mushroom soup, store brand. She has a cute little figure, not that you'd know it from the way she dresses. Her baggy sweatshirt hangs nearly to her knees. "Where's your handsome husband?"

"He's helping Dick at the Commercial. He'll be back in a couple hours."

Altogether, it is disappointing news. Rich, if he were here, would at least offer her a beer.

Squinting, Shelby reads from the can: *"Half teaspoon onion powder."* Is it strange that she reminds Roxanne of her own mother? Louise the knitter, the churchgoer, the clipper of coupons. Near-sighted from thirty years in the dress factory, she had the exactsame squint.

Roxanne excuses herself to the bathroom. Idly she opens the medicine chest. Her son-in-law—did she imagine this?—has back trouble. With luck he'll have Vicodin or at least a Percocet.

Shelby's medicine chest is like an entire aisle at Rite Aid. There is a selection of salves and ointments, a vast wardrobe of Band-Aids in different sizes. There are Tums, throat lozenges, and chewable vitamins; bottles of Robitussin, children's Tylenol, Pepto-Bismol, and syrup of ipecac. In other words, there is nothing of interest. Once again Roxanne thinks of her mother, with her joyless old-fashioned remedies: milk of magnesia, Mercurochrome, castor oil, Doan's Pills.

She closes the medicine chest.

Because there's no reason not to, she wanders into Shelby's bedroom. The bed is neatly made with a quilted coverlet. Atop the bureau are framed photos of the children and one of Shelby's wedding. Nineteen years old, and happy. She was a beautiful bride.

Roxanne stands very still, listening. From the kitchen she hears the sound of frying, like rain on a tin roof. Because there's no reason not to, she opens the top bureau drawer.

Her daughter's underwear depresses her—the plain white briefs, the ugly bras with thick elastic straps, more bra than Shelby actually needs. (She has never been voluptuous.) Roxanne riffles through the drawer thinking, What a waste.

Roxanne herself keeps an envelope of cash in her underwear drawer, an old bartender habit. For most of her life she has lived on tips.

A waste of a cute figure, a good-looking husband. She'd like to grab Shelby by the shoulders and shake her. To make her understand how quickly these things will disappear, Roxanne who is no longer young.

She feels around, but there is no envelope. She is closing the drawer of sad underwear when the bedroom door creaks open.

"Mommy?" The tiny voice, the small blond-haired girl in a flowered nightgown: for a second, really just a second, it is her Crystal, in the yellow nightie she was wearing when she died.

Roxanne nearly weeps.

"No, baby," she says, recovering herself. "It's just your granny Rox."

"What are you doing?"

"Just putting away some laundry, to help your mommy. Go back to bed now."

"Okay."

Olivia closes the door behind her. Only then does Roxanne notice Shelby's pocketbook hanging from the knob.

4.

The forest is a century old, mixed hardwoods, trunks thick as rain barrels—the childhood gymnasium of four generations, prime real estate for tree houses and tire swings. The forest ringing with war whoops, high-pitched laughter, *Ollie Ollie Oxen Free*. There have been epic games of Red Rover, Red Rover; hide-and-seek invitationals that lasted for hours. There have been acts of boyish heroism, stealth attacks on tree forts, death-defying climbs. It is a province of children, a place adults do not venture—the coffee-drinkers and newspaper-readers, the taxpayers and insurance-buyers, the wearers of lipstick and ties. A kingdom governed by ancient laws, passed down through the ages, Dibs and Three Strikes and Tag, You're It.

From the surrounding neighborhoods—at suppertime, at dusk—come the distant calls of parents. Among the kids there is an unspoken protocol: the first two calls are to be ignored.

Endless summer days.

The forest is cut with a Chisholm 600, the industry standard. From a distance it resembles a giant's power sander. It severs each trunk at ground level, with a blade the size of a merry-go-round.

Above the blade, mechanized claws grab the cut timber. They toss it aside like Mothra having a tantrum, the temperamental star of a Japanese horror film.

The earthmovers come next, to dig the containment pond—a

half acre wide and nine feet deep, larger than the town swimming pool. Finally they carve out a clearing the size of a shopping mall. The bare space waits patiently, like a throne for a visiting dignitary. This is where the drill rig will sit.

The drill pad is leveled and laid with gravel. Then the well is dug.

A well starts with a cellar, a hole six feet deep. From the cellar a deeper hole is dug. If witnessed more than one hundred times, this operation may seem natural, commonplace. If witnessed fewer than one hundred times, it will look and sound obscene. The low whine of the augur, its throaty mechanical pleasure. The giant grooved phallus boring ninety feet into the earth.

Into the hole goes a length of conductor pipe.

Two more holes are drilled, staging areas. The rathole holds the kelly. The mousehole holds, on standby, the next section of drilling pipe.

A pit is dug to hold the cuttings. A cutting is an earth turd, a chunk of dirt that goes flying. A cutting is whatever spews from the hole once the drilling has begun.

The mud pit is half the size of a football field—Olympic-size, if there were an Olympic event that involved mud.

CO DEVLIN IS FINISHING HIS ROUNDS when Gary Rizzo buzzes him on the radio. "Sorry, man. She says it's an emergency."

In the front office he picks up the phone.

"Where have you been?" Shelby wails. "I kept trying your cell phone."

"It's in my glove box. Where it always is. For Christ's sake, what's the matter? Are the kids okay?"

"They're fine." She inhales sharply, a moist snotty sound. "The trucks are here. It's—oh God, I can't describe it. The noise is unbelievable. They're cutting down all the trees."

His heart soars.

For weeks he's carried a scrap of paper in his wallet, inscribed with his own jagged handwriting: *Honiger 8 yrs old 40K.* Beneath the words, the phone number of the dairy farmer in Somerset County, a number he now knows by heart.

Devlin's exit strategy, his plan for the future. If the Honiger is still available. If he's not too late.

HOW IT ALL CAME TO BE is a question worth asking. One rainy morning just before dawn, Rena Koval heard sirens. She rushed out of the milk parlor just in time to see an ambulance race down Number Nine Road. It turned the corner onto the Dutch Road, in the direction of Cob Krug's trailer.

She found Mack in the barn running the footbath. A few of the girls have chronic heel wart. "Something's happening over at Cob's," said Rena. "Nothing good."

He'd been dead just a few hours. That his body was found so quickly—that it was found at all—is a story already famous, destined for years of repetition around the bar at the Commercial Hotel. The discovery is credited to Cob's dogs, a couple of mangy German shepherds. Later versions of the story will have them running to a neighbor's house, barking urgently like Lassie on television, but this is apocryphal. In fact they were simply seen running loose through Jim Norton's woods. Jim's wife knew—everyone did—that Cob loved those dogs like children. Sensing trouble, she called 911.

Cob's death—a heart attack, though it might have been anything—surprised no one. The surprise was the sudden reappearance of his wife, whom he'd driven off thirty years before. They had married young and briefly, so long ago that the town had forgotten her name. And yet there it was, on the deed to Cob's trailer and his forty acres: **Lynette Jean Krug.** They had never gotten around to divorcing. At his funeral she rode in Rocco Bernardi's hearse. At the graveside, Dick Devlin handed her a folded flag.

The funeral was surprisingly well attended. Men in suits offered the widow their condolences. Several asked to meet with her privately, but Bobby Frame—that morning at the Days Inn, where Lynette was also staying—had beat them to it.

THE LADY PREACHER LIVES in an ordinary rancher, a split-level or split-entry—Herc can never remember the difference, if there is one—wrapped in aluminum siding, its living room perched atop a double garage. He notes the immaculate yard, the novelty mailbox shaped like an old-timey barn and marked with her name, PEA-COCK, as though a miniature species of that bird might live inside.

His new sports coat is tight in the shoulders. He rings the door-bell and waits, holding a yellow box. A plane buzzes overhead. In his guilty imagination it flies south and west, with one empty window seat, the nonrefundable ticket to Houston he paid for but did not use.

He studies the box in his hand. *It's no surprise that our Whitman's Sampler® is America's favorite box of chocolates. A special treat for any occasion!* He was raised never to arrive empty-handed, and yet you couldn't exactly bring a bottle of wine to a preacher. Flowers, too, seemed risky, all that business about what the different colors were supposed to mean. The color, in Herc's view, is beside the point: unless she's in a hospital or a cemetery, bringing a woman flowers of any color means you're hoping for something. At least it used to, back when he was single and had some insight into such matters. After fourteen years of marriage his instincts have withered from disuse. For instance: the lady preacher offered to cook him dinner. In his single days, that meant only one thing.

Movement in the house, a curtain shimmering. The door opens. The pastor is flushed, a little breathless—barefoot, in blue jeans and a tank top. It's the way his wife dresses while cleaning the house.

"Welcome! Oh, lovely," she says, taking the box from his hand.

"I overdressed," he says, feeling like a jackass.

"Not at all. You look great. Please come in."

He follows her up a short staircase, struck by the weird intimacy of the situation. (Her shoes lined up along the steps—worn flip-flops, a pair of sneakers with balled-up sweat socks tucked inside.) Also unsettling: she is taller than he remembered. They stand eye to eye, though she is barefoot and he wears cowboy boots.

"This is a beautiful house," he says, though *beautiful* isn't the right word. Comfortable, maybe. The living room is lined with book-cases. Photographs and framed diplomas—Hambley Bible College, Calvary Theological Seminary—decorate the walls. All the knick-knacks and personal memorabilia make him slightly claustropho-bic, though probably his perspective is skewed. He works outdoors, sleeps on motel sheets, eats in restaurants. He can't remember the last time he set foot in an actual person's house.

"I'll give you the tour after dinner. There's a whole finished basement. I do pastoral counseling down there."

"That must be—interesting." Once, years ago, Colleen had dragged him to a marriage counselor. He'd sat mostly silent, answer-ing in monosyllables. They never went back.

"Sometimes." She gathers up books, papers, a pair of eyeglasses left on the couch. "I was just working on my Father's Day sermon. I don't suppose you have any thoughts on the subject?"

"I doubt your congregation would appreciate my thoughts on the subject." He speaks without thinking, his last conversation with Colleen still rattling around in his brain.

I don't care if you hate Father's Day. The boys don't care either. They care that you're not here.

The pastor smiles broadly. "I know, right? I'm not a parent, of course, but I've always thought it was a bogus holiday. I hope you like fish. I made salmon."

"Yes, ma'am. I like everything." He is conscious of her bare shoulders, an errant bra strap. He didn't expect to see quite so much of her. Flummoxed, he turns to the bookshelves. *The Historical Jesus. Scripture in the Modern World.* "You sure have a lot of books."

"My personal stash is in the guest room. Those are mostly text-books. You'd find the same ones in any pastor's house."

"I'll have to fight you on that one. My daddy was a pastor. Except for the Bible, I don't think we had a single book in the house."

This seems to delight her. "You're a preacher's kid? I should have guessed."

"Why's that?" His shirt collar is very tight, strangling him. He feels the flush spreading across his cheeks.

"You're very—polite."

"I was raised to respect the cloth. Daddy was the Pastor. That's what my mother called him. *The Pastor is very disappointed in you, Marshall. You'll have to talk to the Pastor about that.* So, you know, I'm not even sure what I'm supposed to call you."

"How about 'Jess'?"

"Well, now. I'm not sure that's proper." He leans in to study a framed photograph: a much younger Jess, arm in arm with a pale dark-haired boy. They wear identical gray sweatshirts, lettered in navy blue: HAMBLEY. "Your brother?"

"My husband."

His face must have betrayed something, some shame or horror or mortal regret, because she adds quickly: "I'm a widow. That was taken when we were in college. He died seven years ago."

An awkward silence.

"I'm sorry," Herc says. "I don't know why I thought he was your brother."

"A lot of people did. I guess we did, you know, look alike. Wes and Jess."

He studies the photo. In fact the resemblance is a little creepy: the same goofy smile, the same warm brown eyes. They look too young to be college students. In the matching sweatshirts they might have been fraternal twins, raised by a doting mother who insisted on dressing them alike.

"Thyroid cancer," she says.

"Beg pardon?"

"People want to know, but they never ask. Wes had thyroid cancer. He was—we both were—thirty-four."

"Good Lord. That's too young to be a widow."

"It was. You know, I used to avoid that word. Now—" She shrugs. "It's just what I am."

The table is already set, salad and potatoes and, to his relief, a sweating bottle of wine. She opens it effortlessly, spinning the corkscrew with practiced ease.

"I've been hoping for months that some of you guys would wander into my church. You and your friend were the first takers. He never came back, though."

"He was a little—surprised. You know, a lady preacher."

"A lot of people are. Have a seat." She reappears with a platter of salmon. "Me included. I sort of backed into it, if you want to know the truth. I was perfectly happy being a pastor's wife, until Wes got sick." She fills their wineglasses. "He wouldn't give up his church, so I did what I could to help him. By the end I was writing his sermons. After he died, I went back to school. I needed something. It seemed like the natural thing to do."

Herc drinks deeply, relaxing a little. "And then you started the church?"

"Not right away, no. Nobody was going to hire a female minister, so I started a Bible study group out there in the living room. In the beginning it was all women. Eventually a few husbands got dragged along." It was one of the husbands, she explains, who convinced her to rent the old Friedman's Furniture and, recently, to buy an actual church. In Bakerton such buildings were cheap and plentiful, the local Catholic diocese having closed a half-dozen small parishes. Living Waters had bought the old St. Casmir's at auction for almost nothing, a bargain despite its settling foundation, its leaking roof.

"Right now we're raising money for the renovation. Car washes and bake sales." She grins. "You're a preacher's kid. You know all about this stuff."

"Yes indeed," says Herc, recalling years of Youth Group fundraisers: magazines and cookware, raffle tickets and hook-a-rug kits, chocolate bars, scented candles, Christmas decorations, and blocks of cheese. "There's more I'm forgetting, but those were the major ones. It's a miracle I didn't end up a salesman."

She loads his plate with salmon and potatoes. "Have you always been a—what is it called?"

"Rig manager. I guess I worked up to it. I've been roughnecking since I was a kid." Twenty-three when he first started, younger than Brando or Jorge. It makes him tired, and somehow sad, to think how long ago that was.

"You must like it, then."

"It's all right. But, you know, there's more to life." He nearly tells her how, a few years back, his brother Dinky proposed going into business together, hiring themselves out as fishing guides on the Brazos. The startup costs would be minimal: some gear, a few repairs on Dinky's boat. Herc was already making good money at Stream Solutions, but the constant travel wore on him: his boys growing up without him, his whole life racing by like so much scenery, the blurry view from a high-speed train. He'd been all set to raid his 401K when Colleen put her foot down. *Dink can catch a fish, but that doesn't mean he can run a business. You Bonner boys! Neither one of you has any sense.* In the end Dinky did it without him, and proved Colleen right, losing all the money he'd borrowed and more besides. Yet Herc can't shake the feeling that things might have turned out differently; that if his wife believed in him even a little, he might be capable of more than running a drill crew. As a young man he'd been full of ideas. He hasn't thought of himself that way in years.

He raises the glass to his lips and finds it empty. "Tell me about the new church," he says, hoping she didn't notice.

Jess refills his glass. "We're almost ready to move in. The roof is the final thing. I can't wait to get out of that storefront."

"Well, that was a surprise, too."

She covers her eyes with her hand. "It's hideous, I know. That carpet."

"I didn't notice the carpet."

"You're lying. It's disgusting. I'm amazed anyone comes back."

"I came back."

She treats him to a full, dazzling smile. "Yes, you did. But not for a couple weeks."

"I had to work."

"On Sunday morning?"

"First tour starts at five."

"What's a tower?"

"A shift. Sorry. A rig has its own lingo. It's like being in the military. You forget how to talk to regular people."

She chews thoughtfully. "You've been in Bakerton what, a year now?"

"Ten months."

"Ten months. And how many actual conversations have you had with people from town?"

"One. You, in Walmart. I guess tonight makes two."

"My point exactly. If you're going to be here, you might as well be part of the community."

"I'd say that's a minority opinion. Most folks want us to get lost." Herc helps himself to more fish. "The ones who've got leases are in a hurry to get their money. But once we tear up their property, they want us to get lost, too."

She drinks meditatively. "It's complicated, Marshall. Change is hard, especially if you didn't choose it. Most people here didn't. And the town has definitely changed."

Herc recalls Bakerton as he first saw it, the empty storefronts.

What is it that people miss, exactly? In another ten years it would have become a ghost town.

"A few people are making a lot of money," she says. "Good for them, but everyone else is affected, too. The noise, the road construction. The other day I could swear I felt an earthquake."

"People always think that. That's just seismic testing. It's nothing to worry about."

She looks unconvinced.

"And what about the water supply? I've read about this. There are people out west who can set their tap water on fire."

"The water will be fine. Trust me. That's a load of—propaganda." Herc stops himself, just barely, from saying *horseshit*. "Environmental nut jobs trying to scare you. Greenpeace or whoever."

There's more he wants to say. *I care about these things, too. Nobody wants to dirty up the water.* Hard experience has taught him to keep his mouth shut. Environmentalists aren't reasonable people. To Herc they are fussy housekeepers like his mother-in-law, who lives in a retirement community so tidy it's intolerable to visit: dustcovers on the sofa, lamp shades wrapped in plastic.

There is a silence.

"You don't believe me," he says.

"It doesn't matter what I think. I don't have enough land for anyone to drill here. But if I did? No way would I sign a lease."

"I'm not going to try to change your mind. But really, it's not that bad." He drains his glass. "Okay, it's bad, but only for a little while. A few months total."

"From your perspective, I guess that's true. But the town is being changed *permanently*. To be honest, it's bringing out the worst in some people." She refills their glasses. "Bakerton was decimated when the mines closed. Some of those guys still aren't working. Imagine you've been unemployed for months or years, and you see a bunch of workers brought in from Texas or wherever."

"I never thought of that." Herc thinks of the rude chambermaid at the Days Inn, the surly locals at the Commercial, the bartender's attitude. "No offense, but it isn't the friendliest town."

"Is that so surprising? People feel they've been passed over. You're taking their jobs. And if you happen to be black or Hispanic, it can get ugly. I've heard comments I wouldn't repeat, from people who should know better: *I'm not racist, but . . .*" She drinks. "There was a case a few years ago, maybe fifty miles from here. Four high school football players beat a Mexican man to death. Apparently they got angry when he spoke Spanish to them. The jury acquitted them. They said it was a street fight that got out of hand."

Herc thinks of the pregnant nurse at the Emergency Room, who eyed Jorge up and down and asked if he was a U.S. citizen. What if he hadn't been? Would she have sent him away?

"The irony is, Bakerton used to be an immigrant town. Polish, Italian, Hungarian. Those people didn't speak English either. Now it's their kids and grandkids who are getting all worked up about immigration." Jess shifts in her chair. "I don't mean to tar everyone with the same brush. Most people here are lovely. But the ones who aren't tend to be the loudest."

"Like everywhere," Herc says.

"Then there are the logistical problems. We have a tiny little hospital, a volunteer fire department. Did you know there's only one policeman for all of Bakerton? Nobody even locks their doors here. We've had zero crime, until now."

"Are you sure about that? I bunk over at the Days Inn. I can't tell you how many times somebody's broke into a welding truck in the parking lot. Welding leads are made of copper," he explains. "Drug addicts steal them and sell them for scrap."

"Drug addicts? In *Bakerton*?" She looks flabbergasted and something else—injured, disappointed, or maybe he's reading too much into it. He recalls the Sunday he and Mickey walked out of her church, skipping the social. Once again, he feels like a heel.

"It's a nice town," he says quickly. "I like it. But every place has its problems. The fish is delicious." In fact it is a little dry; he took seconds just to please her.

He eyes the wine bottle, nearly empty now.

"That's a relief. I was shooting for edible. I'm a little rusty in the kitchen. You get lazy living alone. When Wes was sick it didn't seem important. Most of the time he had no appetite."

"My granddad had stomach cancer," says Herc. "He always said the treatment was worse than the disease."

"Yes, that. But not just that." She is quiet long enough to make him nervous. "Cancer changed him. It changes everybody, I guess, but Wes went a little crazy. He was desperate to know why it happened. I mean, it's a reasonable question. He was so very young."

Her hand lies palm up on the table. Only now does Herc notice that she still wears a ring. He thinks of his own wedding band, lost years ago on a rig in Arkansas and never replaced.

"I feel a little strange telling you this. Like I'm breaking a confidence. Which, after all this time, is ridiculous."

How had he failed to notice? Seven years widowed, and still a ring.

"It's none of my business," he says quickly. "We don't have to talk about it."

"No, I want to. It's healthy, right?" She lifts her glass and finds it empty. "I'm drinking too much."

"Or not enough." He pours the last splash of wine into her glass. "To Wes."

Her eyes are suddenly moist. "Oh, you're lovely. Yes. To Wes."

They clink glasses.

"So, okay. He had certain theories." She drinks deeply. "Remember Three Mile Island?"

"The nucular plant?"

"Yes. He grew up—we both did—right near there. I mean, *right near*. You could see the plant from their back yard."

"Good Lord."

"The Peacocks lived next door to us. My mom was pregnant, so we had to evacuate; but Wes's parents stayed. I guess they thought it would be all right. At least, his dad did. Who knows what his mother thought. It was that kind of marriage."

Herc thinks of his own mother, who was given a weekly allowance like one of the children, the five- and ten-dollar bills kept in an old tin atop the refrigerator—SAYRE'S BOILED PEANUTS—along with a pocket notepad. Cleaning house after her death, he'd flipped through the pages, years of small household expenses faithfully recorded—*Milk man 3 dollars*—in his mother's careful hand.

"Anyway, when he got sick, it took him five seconds to decide that was the reason."

Herc frowns.

"The radiation," she says.

"Oh. Sure. Well, was it?"

She shrugs elaborately. "His doctor said no, it couldn't have been. But Wes was convinced. He read everything he could get his hands on. By the end he had file cabinets full of papers. Medical studies and so on. But nobody believed him."

"Did you?"

A long pause.

"I believe he believed it." She stands to clear the table, stacking their empty plates. "Yikes, I'm a little tipsy."

Herc rises to help. Later he will try to reconstruct exactly how it happened. He must have taken the platter from her hands before he took her in his arms.

NORMAL
ACCIDENTS
1979

I t is a work of genius, alive as a human body, the dream of a
scientist with the intellect of God. But the scientist himself did
not design it. The engineers who designed it have never run it.
The operators can't, themselves, maintain it. The maintenance crew
has no idea what they're maintaining. They perform procedures outlined in the Handbook, written by someone. They follow the schedule and complete the checklist and hang the yellow tag.

The miracle sits on an island at a bend in the river, three miles
downstream from the town. A generation ago, vacation cabins were
built here. Farmers grew corn and tomatoes and sent the harvest
to the capital by barge. Unit One came online five years ago, a
good time for a miracle: cars idling for hours at the Pennzoil, the
president kicked out of the White House, Patty Hearst pointing a
machine gun in her Communist beret.

Today Unit One is down for refueling. Unit Two has been
online just three months. For five weeks it has run at full capacity,
powering schools and hospitals, factories and airports, the utility
recouping its investment. Unit Two cost seven hundred million dollars. Miracles are not free.

The plant has uncountable moving parts, God's wristwatch:
acres of tanks and engines and pumps and chambers, variously
heating and cooling, humming and spinning, each calibrated for
its single mission, the unique and infinitesimally precise action, the
step-turn-dip in the dance. Miles of piping, a small city of valves

opening and closing. A thousand moving parts for each symbol in the equation, a declarative sentence in a wordless language no one actually understands.

In the containment building stands the Babcock & Wilcox reactor, forty feet high and fifteen across, a massive cylinder of reinforced steel. The reactor is the Ark of the Covenant, a receptacle of high purpose. Inside is the uranium core. The core contains fuel rods, a hundred tons' worth: thirty-six thousand tubes coated with zircon cladding, each packed with radioactive pellets. The core generates a lunatic heat; water runs constantly through it. The water turns to steam and is piped to a generator, which powers a turbine.

Which runs to a generator, which feeds a transformer, which connects to the grid.

The grid powers televisions in three states. Eight-track tape players and Weedwackers. The Wear-Ever Popcorn Pumper. The Atari 5600 game console.

The plant is self-regulating, entirely self-sufficient. The lobster shift runs eleven to seven. Two night operators man the controls. The control room is large as an auditorium, bright as an operating theater. The panels add extra illumination: red lights, blue lights, white, green, gold. The panels cover three walls, floor to ceiling. Altogether there are nine hundred square feet of buttons and switches and dials and gauges, tracking each shiver in the system. All in service of the equation, the wordless sentence, the numeric koan in the secret language of God.

Of the six thousand indicators in the control panel, seven hundred fifty are alarms.

An hour before dawn, the two night operators drink coffee and talk about the movie. One has seen it, one has not.

"Pure horseshit," says the first man. "Looks real, though. The instrumentation and all." The movie, about a disaster at a nuclear plant, opened twelve days ago. He saw it with his wife, who clutched his arm in rapt and fluttering fascination: *Is it really like that?* Showing, for the first time in years, an interest in his work, in him period, the familiar husband transformed into something larger than he'd been that morning, the chronic snorer in a stained undershirt, the bathroom slob.

Yeah, pretty much. He felt a rush of manful pride, as though he'd taken her for a spin in a sports car.

"I wonder where they filmed it," says the second man. "What kind of a plant would let them do that?"

The alarm lights run across the top of the back panel, seven hundred fifty glass windows, each three by five inches. When a window illuminates, a message is displayed: PRESSURIZER LO. REACTOR COOLANT PUMP VIBRATION HI. The panes are lettered in block capitals, like Valentine candy hearts.

If an alarm trips, the light flashes off and on until the problem is acknowledged. Then it glows steadily until the issue is resolved.

The plant is self-regulating, entirely self-sufficient. Its marvelous autonomy is the central tenet of the Handbook. The maintenance crew knows otherwise, the sixteen men in constant motion. That Wednesday morning, in the turbine room, a tech services a feedwater polisher. The feedwater system cools the reactor. It also owns his soul. To the feedwater system he is a whore on retainer. He services each tank and pump without favoritism, diligent, quietly hostile, a slave to the collective need.

The turbine room is dark and noisy, ribbed with piping. His client at the moment is Polisher 4 (also known as a demineralizer, also known as an ion-exchange tank; this fucker has aliases like a master criminal, wanted in all fifty states). There are eight such polishers, each filled with resin beads to scrub the feedwater. The beads are changed every twenty-eight days exactly, as outlined in the Handbook.

The Handbook weighs nine and a half pounds.

The equation is vision and hallucination, dreamed by wizards who can't change a tire. He'd pay good money to watch them unclog a feedwater polisher, a hulking piece of junk that clots regularly, in menstrual fashion; the fucking thing worth more than his car, probably, and yet.

Changing the beads is an arduous process. At one time or another, each of the polishers has clogged. The tech flushes them with water and compressed air, as directed by the Handbook. This works only sometimes. At 4:00 A.M. the shift foreman comes downstairs to help. He clambers up on a pipe and peers through a sight glass.

He's getting too old for this.

For a brief second the pipe quivers beneath him. He recoils instinctively, and just in time. The pipe lurches free of its mounting. The noise is deafening, like a massive engine backfiring. Water races through the compressed air line in machine-gun bursts.

The feedwater valves are controlled pneumatically. A second later, every valve in the system slams shut.

Upstairs, the control room quakes like a plane caught in turbulence. The two night operators are shaken from their chairs. It is thirty-seven seconds past 4:00 A.M. A siren wails like a cat set on fire. All across the back panel the white lights are flashing.

The night operators are startled, but not worried. There are systems in place for just such eventualities. For all eventualities. In every situation imaginable, the plant itself knows what to do.

There are a thousand parts for each symbol in the equation, a declarative sentence in a wordless language no one need understand.

In a matter of seconds, the plant itself takes action. First the turbine shuts down. The bypass valves open, dumping steam into the condenser, circumventing the turbine. This series of events is described in the Handbook, an article of faith.

Then—for inscrutable reasons—the reactor itself shuts down.

The operators stare in disbelief.

All around them the panels are flashing like fireworks: red lights, blue lights, white, green, and gold. In training drills, systems fail one at a time; there's never a question where to focus. But now the turbine has tripped. The reactor has tripped. The feedwater system has shut down completely. Temperature and pressure are rising. The operators are surrounded by flashing lights, above and below and behind them.

The shift supervisor makes an announcement over the P.A., as directed by the Handbook. *Unit Two, turbine trip, reactor trip.* Years ago, in the navy, he ran a submarine reactor. He repeats it twice for good measure, his voice strong and confident, militarily gruff.

One after another, safety systems activate. Relief valve. Makeup pumps. Injection pumps. These devices act automatically, at the precise right moment. The Handbook decrees it so.

FIFTEEN THOUSAND PEOPLE LIVE within a mile of the plant. They have seen the miracle only from a distance—the four cement cooling towers, massive and bell shaped, exhaling steam.

To the fifteen thousand the thing has not yet happened. Showers are taken, breakfasts eaten. (The Remington electric shaver. The Amana Touch Radarange.)

A feed salesman is driving to work, the plant visible in his rearview. He notes absently that no steam rises from the towers. Then he blows his nose and takes a Dristan. His son brought home a cold—from where, the salesman can't imagine. The kid is homeschooled, shy of the neighborhood children. Left to his own devices, he would never leave the house.

This morning is no different. The boy Wesley Peacock plays a board game in his pajamas, cross-legged on the living room floor. The game involves building a complicated mousetrap, a Rube Goldberg–like creation. There are twenty-three plastic parts in red, blue, green, and gold. He rolls the die and lands on a white space, then adds the plastic crank to the trap.

The box says *TWO TO FOUR PLAYERS*, but the clever only child learns to ignore such instructions. Wesley takes a turn for the blue mouse, a turn for the green one. He is used to playing against himself.

It's fun to build this comical wonder, but woe to the mouse who gets caught under! FOR AGES 8 to 14, says the box.

IN THE CONTROL ROOM several things are happening, all impossible.

The emergency pumps have started, yet the temperature keeps rising.

The temperature is rising, yet a white light flashes: PRESSUR-IZER LO.

The pressure is dropping, yet a white light flashes: PRESSUR-IZER WATER LEVEL HI.

According to the Handbook, these things cannot happen. Either the instruments are lying, or the Handbook is full of shit.

In the pump house building, a tech stares at a drain in the floor. A second later he hears a smack of footsteps, the radiation chemistry tech running down the hall. *"Get the hell out! Get your stuff and get out!"*

Still the water keeps coming, welling up through the drain in the floor.

In the control room men crowd in shoulder to shoulder, after-shave and coffee breath and sharp apocrine sweat, one another's personal smells. What is remembered. The base workings of the limbic brain, the black box recorder always running, taste touch smell hearing, the substance of felt life. Years from now, when the day's events have been deconstructed and debated and reduced to a caption, this data will be missing from the record, the human texture the photographs will not convey.

Across the panel, lights of all colors are flashing. Ominous realities are becoming clear. Steam has overflowed the quench tank. The containment building is flooded with reactor water. In the dome of the building, radiation levels are skyrocketing. Radioactive water seeps into the pump house building, rising up through the drains in the floor.

From the shift supervisor's office, phone calls are made per the Handbook. First things first: the American Nuclear Insurers Company. Next the state police, the county Civil Defense, the Pennsylvania Bureau of Radiological Health.

The final call is to the Nuclear Regulatory Commission, its regional office in the Philadelphia suburbs. The line rings and rings. At last the supervisor leaves a message on an answering machine. No one is there to pick up the phone.

THE FEED SALESMAN'S WIFE IS QUEASY, a fact she will remember later. She has never had a temperamental stomach, a temperamental anything. She is the firstborn daughter of a large family, raised on farm chores.

She dries the fry pan and eats a cracker for her stomach. Wesley is in the living room and blessedly quiet, playing a game in front of the TV. Her husband disapproves of television and occasionally scolds her—*Bernadette, you know my feelings on this.* But to Bernadette the TV is a help and a comfort, a fact that shames her. Her own parents are Mennonite and have never owned a set. Her mother raised eight children without *Sesame Street* or *Mister Rogers' Neighborhood,* without babysitters or disposable diapers. At one point or another Bernadette has used all these things, has used every crutch in existence, to raise her one well-behaved boy.

Mister Rogers is a pastor, which makes a difference. She is grateful to have another adult in the house. Mister Rogers makes himself available for a half hour each morning, to occupy the boy while Bernadette takes a shower or mixes bread dough or mops the kitchen floor, tasks her mother had managed without any help at all, because her mother didn't have a Wesley. The boy is constantly underfoot, hungry for company, amusement, comfort. Bernadette understands that she has raised a clingy child. She has no one to blame but herself.

Some mornings—she has never told Gene this—she allows Wesley an extra program before she begins his lessons, *Card Sharks* or *The $20,000 Pyramid*. The games are loud and crass but better than the morning soap operas, full of steamy kissing and bosomy women and dialogue that makes her blush.

Wesley comes into the kitchen, his brow puckered. "They took off my program."

She follows him into the living room. A man in a suit speaks directly to the camera. "It's just the news, sweetie. Let's change the channel."

"It's on every channel," says the boy Wesley Peacock.

A state of emergency has been declared on Three Mile Island. There was a small release of radiation to the environment. All safety equipment functioned properly.

Bernadette's stomach does a little leap. She sits on the couch to watch.

ELEVEN MILES AWAY, in the state capital, six men stand before a pale blue curtain. At the podium is the lieutenant governor, handsome as a movie actor, the youngest in the history of the Commonwealth. He reads from a prepared statement. "The incident occurred due to a malfunction in the turbine system. There was a small release of radiation to the environment. All safety equipment functioned properly."

There is a chorus of voices, a show of hands. The reporters are like eager schoolchildren. He calls on a pretty young woman at the back of the room.

"What is a small release?"

The lieutenant governor finds this question unsettling. His mustache and modish haircut were a hit with young voters. He's been in office two and a half months. "We have no way of telling exactly how much radiation was released."

"Then how do you know it's small?"

The state Department of Environmental Protection has supplied a nuclear engineer to answer such questions, a baby-faced man in a mustard-colored turtleneck. He wears notable sideburns, a hangdog look. "The utility sent investigators across the river, since the wind was blowing that way, to take a reading. They detected a small amount of radioactive iodine on the ground."

He pronounces the word *iodin*.

"Can you spell that?" a reporter calls.

"Io-DYNE!" a voice booms from the front row. It's the irritable voice of a man used to shouting; his wife is hard of hearing. "He means io-DYNE."

The engineer continues. "They have been continually monitoring in both locations and they have determined that the levels are less than one millirem per hour."

There is a general commotion. "One *what* per hour?"

The engineer is asked to spell it. The irritable man repeats after him: *m–i–l–l–i–r–e–m.*

"Per what?" the irritable man barks.

"Per hour."

"Per hour," the irritable man repeats. "Well, what does that mean?"

The engineer gives the definition of *millirem*.

A bearded reporter interrupts him. "The statement says there was a malfunction in the turbine system. What kind of a malfunction?"

"The plant was operating at a hundred percent power, and some fault in the—the nonsafety system, the turbine plant, caused the valves going to the turbine to shut." The engineer is aware of his voice trembling. An hour ago he was riding in a National Guard

helicopter, a mile downwind of the plant. "This is a normal, antici-
pated transient."

The irritable man spells the word *transient*.

A female reporter gets to her feet, the feisty one who scared off
the lieutenant governor. "Well, how did the company discover the
problem? Is there some kind of a system that alerts them?"

The engineer struggles visibly with this question. He thinks of
the six thousand indicator lights in the control room, the seven hundred fifty alarms. He is ready to laugh or weep.

"They could tell from their instrumentation." The absurdity of
his own words nearly undoes him. He tries again. "Well, the plant
is designed to withstand this particular transient."

At the back of the room—he is sure of it—reporters are beginning to laugh.

Male reporter: "It sounds like you rely heavily on the instruments and reports from the utility company. Is there any reason why
we should doubt the credibility of that?"

The engineer admits that no one has verified the company's data.

"So you're just taking what they tell you?" says the feisty woman.

"Yes."

In the front row the irritable man lights a pipe. He sucks vigorously to get the thing going, three hearty puffs of smoke.

The room gets louder and louder. A few reporters still shout out
questions but most have lost interest in the engineer, now speaking
through a cloud of smoke. He explains again what the turbine does,
what the relief valves do, but no one is listening. He wishes someone
would knock him unconscious.

Finally a reporter asks a question he can answer.

"No, I haven't seen the movie," he says.

ALL DAY LONG, civil defense trucks roll through the neighborhoods.
The trucks are impressive, military-issue. They seem built for some
strategic purpose, attack or rescue, the distribution of vital supplies

or arms. Today they simply make announcements: *A state of emergency has been declared on Three Mile Island. Please stay indoors with your windows closed.*

To the boy Wesley Peacock, it seems an arbitrary request. "Why can't we open the windows?"

"Air pollution," his mother calls back. She is sitting at the kitchen table with their neighbor Audrey Hershberger. In the living room Wesley plays Mousetrap with Audrey's daughter. Wesley is the green mouse. Jessie is the red.

"Hydrogen is flammable," says Audrey. "If the bubble keeps growing there could be an explosion."

Bernadette cuts two more slices of cinnamon cake. They've each eaten a slice already, talking about the bubble. It's been a struggle to keep Wesley away from the television. She was relieved when Audrey and Jessie showed up at the door.

"We saw the movie," says Audrey. "Bern, aren't you curious?"

"A little," she admits. "But Gene would never. He says everybody should simmer down."

Audrey takes the smaller piece of cake. "Like I need this. Ned says I'm big as a bus. Oh, so guess who else is expecting? Bonnie Hoover."

Bernadette thinks, Again?

"Pregnant," she says softly. "Are you sure?" Honestly, how is it possible? Bernadette is grateful as a beggar for her one child. Bonnie Hoover is her own age, and already on number four.

"Keeping the windows closed," says Audrey. "What good is that going to do?"

Ralph and Bonnie Hoover must be at it all the time.

In the living room Wesley rolls the die. He and Jessie are in the thick of the game, the trap built halfway. He snaps the plastic gutter into place.

"It's not pollution," says Jessie. "It's radiation. They told us in school."

She is a quiet pretty girl, dark-haired. She and Wesley are sum-
mertime friends. From Memorial Day to Labor Day they are insep-
arable. Then, each September, Jessie disappears into school and
dance lessons, weekend sleepovers with girls Wesley doesn't want to
know. Girls in groups make him nervous. He is happiest—in fact,
completely happy—with Jessie alone.

In the kitchen the mothers finish their coffee. "Are the windows
made of lead?" says Audrey. "Because lead is the only thing that
stops radiation. We need to get home and finish packing. Ned wants
to hit the road at four."

When the guests have gone, Wesley sits at the kitchen table
with his phonics workbook. Bernadette takes pork chops from the
freezer. A crazy person pounds at the front door.

Bernadette rises to answer it. Her neighbor Digger Farrell
stands on the porch, wild-eyed and red-faced. She can smell the
liquor on his breath.

"What are you doing here?" Digger shouts. "I thought for sure
Gene would of got you out."

"Oh, no. We're fine right here."

"What do you mean? Didn't you hear? Preschool children."

Bernadette flushes. Wesley is small for his age, but not that
small. "Oh, no. Wesley is school age."

"Then how come he don't go to school?" To her relief Digger
doesn't wait for an answer. "We're loading up the truck right now.
There's room for you both. We're heading down to Kentucky to
Marla's parents'."

Bernadette lowers her voice and hopes Digger will do the same.
"Digger, that's kind of you. We're going to stay put for now. We can
go later, if we need to."

Digger looks dumbstruck. "What if you can't get on the highway? If they put up barriers on the entrance ramps? I got guns and
a chain saw. I can get through if I have to. But what are you going
to do?"

"That's kind of you, but we're going to sit tight for now," she says, almost whispering. "I appreciate the concern."

Firmly she closes the door.

THE A&P IS EERILY DESERTED. Bernadette pushes her cart up and down the aisles. It's like shopping in wartime, the shelves empty of bread, sugar, candles, canned peas and corn. The Maxwell House coffee is gone, so she settles for a can of Folgers. She looks for items that don't require cooking or refrigeration, as instructed by the radio, and leaves with a strange assortment: beef jerky, a box of doughnuts, jarred sauerkraut and beets.

Gene says Folgers tastes burnt.

That night the family eats dinner in silence, knives and forks loud on the plate. "Don't you think they would tell us?" says Gene.

"They *are* telling us. It's all over the radio."

"They're saying preschool children. He's not preschool. Pre-school and pregnant women."

Bernadette punished—again—for failing to be pregnant.

"Well, does that make sense to you? How is it bad for them and not for us?"

Wesley ignores his pork chop but eats his green beans as a concession. Without enthusiasm he asks to be excused. He is expected to play outdoors after dinner. He takes his jacket from its peg near the door with an air of weary resignation, like a miner heading underground.

"Not tonight, sweetie," says his mother. "Go in your room and play your game."

Last year on his birthday, his mother let him watch a movie on television, *The Boy in the Plastic Bubble*. The boy, played by John Travolta, had no immune system. He couldn't live in a world full of germs, so he stayed in a plastic oxygen tent inside his bedroom. To Wesley it is the greatest life imaginable.

He rolls the die for green and assembles the staircase.

The bubble had a TV and stereo, like the boy's own groovy apartment. Inside it he wore funny hats and raised hamsters and even danced (disco moves John Travolta later made famous in *Saturday Night Fever*, a film Wesley wasn't allowed to see).

You know, the Bubble Boy told his doctor, *I'm not so unhappy in here as all of you think.*

To Wesley it was a thrilling notion. The words rang in his ears like a manifesto, a singing affirmation that he was not wrong.

The blue mouse lands on the space marked GO TO CHEESE—a wasted opportunity for the green mouse, since the trap is only half-built. He rolls the die for green and attaches the shoe to the lamp-post. Then he rolls the die for blue. Radiation is worse if the wind blows it at you, according to Jessie's teacher. Those people, the down-winders, will die in a matter of weeks. Everybody else will get cancer, which takes a while.

He wonders why anyone wants to go to school.

IN TOWN THE REPORTERS KEEP COMING. Teams arrive from France, England, Japan, West Germany. It's a kind of disaster Olympics. They set up camp in roadside motels.

Protestors arrive by the busload. It's a Thursday morning, a workday; yet hundreds of long-haired people have nothing better to do. "It goes to show you," the feed salesman tells his customers. "Idleness is the devil's workshop." On the sidewalk in front of the dime store, braless college girls offer him bumper stickers. A man in braids hands out pamphlets from his truck. NO NUKES NEVER AGAIN. The salesman understands that the world has gone mental, his wife included. Bernadette is a high-strung woman, prone to upsets. He is grateful to be at work.

The salesman himself is a model of industry. He gets an early start and skips his lunch break, eats a sandwich listening to the radio in his car. After the radioactive iodine was detected in Goldsboro, the county agricultural extension issued a directive. The AM stations repeat it on the half hour: *all livestock should be on stored feed until further notice.*

He sells more feed in a day than he has in six months.

How to play and build the
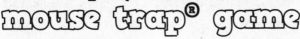

Player turns crank Ⓐ which rotates gears Ⓑ causing lever Ⓒ to move and push stop sign against shoe Ⓓ. Shoe tips bucket holding metal ball Ⓔ. Ball rolls down rickety stairs Ⓕ and into rain pipe Ⓖ which leads it to hit helping hand rod Ⓗ. This causes bowling ball Ⓘ to fall from top of helping hand rod through thing-a-ma-jig Ⓙ and bathtub Ⓚ to land on diving board Ⓛ. Weight of bowling ball catapults diver Ⓜ through the air and right into washtub Ⓝ causing cage Ⓞ to fall from top of post Ⓟ and trap unsuspecting mouse.

FRIDAY THE SUN RISES as though nothing unusual has happened. The stock price of Columbia Pictures rises 8 percent. Every few hours someone holds a press conference.

The uranium core was never uncovered. Dauphin County will not be evacuated.

Children are to stay indoors.

The core was uncovered for several minutes. For several hours. For an undetermined period. People of all ages should stay indoors until midnight. A quarter of the fuel rods have melted, but this is no cause for alarm.

Radiation has been confined to the reactor building. To Unit

Two only. Radiation has been confined to the island. Forty thousand gallons of radioactive water have been released to the river, but this poses no danger to public health.

A small pocket of hydrogen has been detected in the reactor, a harmless bubble. Evacuation is unnecessary at this time.

Sixty percent of the fuel rods are damaged. Schools are closed until further notice. Pregnant women and preschool children should leave the area. Please note that this is not an evacuation. There is no Chinese syndrome.

The hydrogen bubble appears to be growing.

Residents are asked to remain calm.

n the Dairy Queen two radios are playing. The one out front is for the customers, a hushed male voice Mack recognizes: *A warm wind's blowing, the stars are out, and I'd really love to see you tonight.* Standing at the counter, it's just possible to hear the second radio, or maybe it's a television, playing in the kitchen. A newscaster is speaking, a grave male voice: *Federal regulators descended on Harrisburg today to assess the ongoing situation at Three Mile Island.*

"You're back," says the girl behind the counter. She wears a red uniform and visor and a plastic name tag: HOW MAY I HELP YOU? RENA. "My first customer of the day."

"I get hungry early. I can't help it." Flushing, stammering, Mack orders the same lunch as last time: two double burgers with bacon, large fries, vanilla milk shake. Rena writes the order on a pad. Her penmanship is neat, her hand small as a child's.

The Pennsylvania Emergency Management Agency has reported a new, uncontrolled release of radiation.

Rena stands very still, listening.

"You're not worried about that, are you?" says Mack.

"There's a bubble." Rena tears the sheet off her order pad and clips it to a metal carousel on the counter behind her. "We're downwinders. Well, maybe. It depends on which way the wind blows. It was on the news."

The radio voice returns. *In a press conference today, the governor urged residents to stay calm.*

Rena snorts. "Wow, that's so helpful. Thank God for the governor. How else would we know what to do in a nuclear meltdown? To stay calm." Rena punches numbers into the cash register. "Calm, my ass."

Her ass is curved and impossibly compact, like two halves of a cantaloupe. It makes Mack wonder about the rest of her, knees shoulders thighs breasts, the matched parts small and rounded and perfectly formed.

Mack hands her four dollars. "I remember you from high school. I was two years behind you. You had a boyfriend, Ted or Fred or something."

Rena hands back two dimes and says, "Freddy Weems."

"My hair was longer then. I played basketball," Mack adds stupidly, as though the two facts are related. "It's okay if you don't remember. You don't look too busy. Come sit with me while I eat."

"We're not supposed to do that." Rena glances over her shoulder. "Maybe for a minute, though."

They choose one of the two booths. The indoor seating is a recent addition. The Dairy Queen started out as a summer joint, a roadside custard stand with a patio and a few picnic tables out front. Mack unwraps the cheeseburgers and set the fries in the middle of the table. "Have some."

"I'd be big as a house if I ate like that."

"I burn it off," says Mack, who is big but not as big as a house and, anyway, has never wanted to be small. "I've been up working since five o'clock. Have some."

"Five in the *morning*? Geez Louise. Where do you work?"

"My dad's farm. For now," Mack adds hastily. "I'm home from college. It's spring break."

Rena shakes out a dollop of ketchup. "College. Do you like it?"

A silence in which Mack considers what to say about college. The truth seems too complicated: that college crushes and then remakes you. That it's where your life actually begins.

Rena doesn't wait for an answer. "I almost went. I saved money and everything. But it's hard with a kid."

"You have a kid?"

Rena shakes out a dollop of ketchup. Already she's made serious inroads into the pile of fries. "He's four now. I don't regret it, but you can't do everything."

A sudden draft as a customer comes in the front door—Rocco Bernardi, the town undertaker. The DQ is a half mile from the cemetery. A few times a week Rocco comes in for lunch.

"I should go. I have a customer."

"All right." Mack slides the paper boat across the table. "That one's yours."

"I can't eat your last one."

"Bet you can."

Rena pops the French fry into her mouth.

MACK TAKES THE LONG WAY OUT OF TOWN, Susquehanna Avenue to Drake Highway to the Dutch Road, the curving cow path that leads to the farm. The lane is sloppy, slick with spring mud. She stops to check the mailbox, which is empty. Eight months ago, she got a letter from Liz Harvey, a woman with pretty handwriting. When Mack realized who the sender was, she tore up the letter and threw it in the trash. Later she regretted this. Now she checks the mailbox every day, but a second letter has never come.

When Mack knew her, her mother was called Betty. Mack never heard the name of the man she ran off with. He drove a lemon-yellow Chevy stately as an ocean liner, full bodied and extravagantly finned. Mack remembers watching it from the porch swing. Given the chronology of events, she must have been five years old.

When she and her mother got into the car, the man looked displeased. *What did you bring her for?* He wore a stiff new shirt fresh out of the package, his hair backcombed with some fragrant pomade. He looked like a cowboy who'd cleaned up for church.

What else was I going to do with her?

They drove with the windows down, the high winding road that led to Garman Lake, where Mack was told to get out and play. The adults sat in the car watching her like a drive-in movie. When she got back in the car her mother had been crying.

By the end of summer—it might have been a week later, or a month—her mother was gone.

Mack closes the empty mailbox and continues up the lane. Pop is coming out of the barn, favoring his left leg, his step heavy and lurching—a tall man still, despite his stoop.

"Susan!" he shouts. "I been looking for you."

No one else calls her this.

Mack rolls down the window. "Sorry, Pop. I stopped to get some lunch."

"My work light crapped out. I can't get up there to change it." It pains him to say it, pains his daughter to hear it. Her entire happy childhood was built on the myth of his omnipotence.

She follows him into the barn, where a ladder is waiting. Beneath the dark work lamp, a small motor lies in pieces. She shimmies up the ladder and replaces the bulb.

Her childhood was happy. Pete didn't know how to raise a girl, never having been one or understood or liked them much, so he raised her as a boy. He wanted a son, and Susan, by glad coincidence, wanted to be one.

When she comes down he's already bent over the engine. He's still good with his hands. He doesn't thank her and she doesn't expect him to. It was only a lightbulb.

"See you later, Pop."

He grunts in assent, glad to be about his business. Life is filled, increasingly, with these piss-ant frustrations. He's always been a capable man, impatient with those less shiningly competent, a category that once included everyone he knew. But age has diminished him, sixty years of farmwork, arthritis in his knees, hips, and back.

That the great Pete Mackey can no longer change a lightbulb is a truth too awful to mention. A hired hand—a younger, stronger man to witness his failures—is a humiliation he will not tolerate. Only his daughter can help him in a way that doesn't shame him. She divines his wishes without being asked.

He offers her a pinch of snuff.

Susan needs no instructions, accepts no payment, expects no gratitude. She allows him the illusion that he did it all himself.

THE FARM CALLS HER, the farm needs her. Pop is glad to have her back. This should have settled the matter, and it does, mainly. Only rarely does Mack remember college, a period in her life that now seems imaginary, like something she once dreamed.

She left Penn State a year ago. What she told the Dairy Queen girl was slightly true, that one part of it: her departure coincided with spring break. The timing shocked her coach, her teammates. Track and field was a spring sport, their season just about to begin.

The women's team had been, for fifty years, a quiet intramural program, noticed by no one. Then came Title Nine, a flood of federal dollars, and suddenly they were a varsity sport. Coaches brought over from the men's side were asked to do the impossible. Female bodies weren't designed for throwing the javelin, a point the coaches agreed on. Female bodies were designed for a purpose they did not mention, though it was always on their minds.

Mack was Coach's personal discovery. He'd spotted her in the gym one morning, a rising freshman in the summer basketball camp. The sport, she told him, didn't interest her. Football would have been her pick. In junior high she'd been an unstoppable running back, the first and last girl in Bakerton history to play on the boys' team. At nineteen she was still fast, despite her size. In stocking feet she was Coach's height. Her morning weight was two hundred pounds. Had she been a boy, someone would have seen that she was a born thrower: the titanic thighs and shoulders, the instinctual rhythm and grace. Coach let her try all the throws, but her destiny was obvious the instant she held the shot.

Of course she'd watched Bruce Jenner win the decathlon. Everybody had. Now the unthinkable had become thinkable and so Mack thought it: *That could be me.*

Track and field lived together, ate together, trained together. On weekends they drank together. It was alcohol that caused the disaster, unleashing a series of events.

There was a problem about a girl.

A day later Mack was on a bus back to Bakerton. Now she hasn't picked up the shot in more than a year, though she throws it nearly every night, in dreams.

A YEAR PASSES QUICKLY ON A FARM. From dawn till supper, Mack's days are packed with chores. Winter was hard on the fences. All day Saturday, Pop unrolls lengths of chicken wire. Thinking of the Dairy Queen girl, Mack hammers in the posts as lunchtime comes and goes.

The DQ is closed on Sundays.

On Monday she is waiting in the parking lot at 10:50. She's been hungry all morning, woke up hungry, as though she hasn't eaten in days.

At eleven the neon sign illuminates: OPEN. Mack gets out of her truck. Inside, the place is empty except for a small blond-haired boy. He sits in one of the booths, hunched over a picture book.

"Hiya," Mack says.

The boy doesn't answer, which is fine. Mack treats children like live grenades. When she was fifteen and sensitive, a distant cousin had visited the farm at Christmas, bringing her small daughter. The child studied Mack openly, glaring as if displeased. *Are you a boy or a girl?*

Mack is recalling this when Rena comes out of the kitchen. "You're still here. I figured you'd be back at college by now."

Mack gropes for words. She considers and rejects *What happened to your eye?* Because, really, only one thing could have happened to Rena's eye.

"Are you all right?" she says instead.

Rena's hand goes to her eye and then away, as though she's been instructed not to touch it. "It's nothing."

The bruise is clearly visible through her makeup—new, but not brand-new. It's had some time to blossom, a day anyway, to reach its full purple.

"Is that your boy?" Mack says.

"I had to bring him with me. I'm not supposed to. He usually goes to his gram's. But under the circumstances."

"Your mom?"

"His other gram. Freddy's mom. So, you know, awkward." Again her hand goes to her eye. Finally she takes the order pad from her pocket. "Two bacon doubles, large fry, large shake?"

"Yeah." Mack looks at the wall clock—11:02—and reads the signs: **A DILLY OF A BAR!** *HOT AND JUICY BRAZIER.* She studies the tile floor, the soft-serve machine behind the counter, the three sizes of paper cups stacked in towers, small medium large. Having run out of things to look at, she allows herself another glance at Rena's eye.

"Have a seat," says Rena. "I'll bring it out to you."

Because she is supposed to, Mack sits at the table across from the boy, now writing in his book with a green pencil. "What's your name?" she says.

The boy doesn't answer. He puts down the green pencil and picks up a blue one. Mack wonders if he's hard of hearing.

Rena comes to the table with a paper sack, Mack's lunch wrapped and ready. She sits gingerly, making Mack wonder what was done to the rest of her body. The black eye is the only damage you can see.

"Calvin," Rena says to the boy. "You shouldn't write in your book."

The boy shrugs. Except for his hair, which is wispy and blond, he is the image of his mother: the pointed chin, the Cupid's-bow mouth.

Mack feels compelled to say something. "What are you reading?"

Rena leans over the boy's shoulder, pointing to words on the page. In a clear childish voice Calvin reads: *"This is the dog who scared the cat who chased the rat who ate the malt who lived in the house that Jack built."*

"You should eat," says Rena. "It isn't good cold."

Mack unwraps her hamburgers, the boy's eyes following her. "Can he have some French fries?"

Calvin looks up at Rena.

"Go wash your hands," she says, and slides over so the boy can wriggle out of the booth. "He's shy with strangers."

"Who did this to you?"

Rena ignores the question. "Calvin was in bed when it happened. But nobody could have slept through that." She takes the blue pencil and draws in the boy's book, a detailed butterfly. "Here's what's crazy: he's pretending like he doesn't notice. He wakes up and his mom has a black eye and he doesn't even ask."

"Did you call the cops?"

"They don't do anything."

Don't, not *didn't*. As though this were a regular occurrence, the sort of thing that happened from time to time.

They watch the boy come out of the restroom.

"I quit school," Mack says suddenly. "A year ago. I live here now."

"I thought you were on spring break."

"I was. A year ago."

"You're kind of a strange person," says Rena.

"You have no idea," Mack says.

They're all assholes. It's the first learning of the weekend.

"You're here today because your life doesn't work. You're an asshole because you pretend that it does." The maestro paces the makeshift stage, silent in his shoes. A young woman hovers at the edge of the stage, waiting to refill his water glass. In each corner of the room stands a burly security guard.

The hotel ballroom is windowless, aggressively air-conditioned. It might be a hundred degrees outside, or ten below; it might be noon or midnight or anytime in between. In fact it is a Saturday afternoon in early spring, San Francisco Bay lost in fog. In the fourth row a surfer kid squirms in his clothes, Dacron dress slacks that make his legs itch.

"Your life doesn't work and YOU. ARE. RESPONSIBLE." The maestro is lean and preternaturally handsome—a genuine celebrity, a regular on the talk show circuit, a man thanked at awards shows. "In this training you will get that you didn't just happen to be lying there on the tracks when the train came. You are the asshole who put yourself there."

The assholes fidget in their straight-backed chairs—utilitarian, stackable—and await further insights.

They have paid their three hundred dollars, and made certain agreements. There will be no tape recording or note taking during the training, no eating or drinking or trips to the bathroom.

The agreements are famous. Like the profanity, the dressing-down, they are part of the mythology: the pronouncements delivered with unassailable authority, a stranger's wholesale dismissal of all they are and all they do.

"Most people go through their whole lives standing on the freeway, waving the traffic in the opposite direction to the way it's going." His tone is thoughtful, conversational—as though his words have been chosen for these particular assholes, and them alone. "Well, I got news for you. Traffic is going where it's going. It doesn't give a shit how you feel about it, and neither does life."

A man in the front row raises his hand. He wears horn-rimmed glasses like Henry Kissinger. His name tag reads HAROLD. "I'm a physician," he begins. "And while I certainly *appreciate* this notion of personal responsibility—"

"Harold APPRECIATES it." The maestro's voice is plump with sarcasm. "Also, Harold wants all of you to know that he went to medical school, he makes more money than you do, and his opinion matters more than any other opinion in this room. All right, Harold. We get it. You may continue."

Harold blinks furiously behind his glasses. "Can I ask my question?"

"Please."

Harold clears his throat. "Considering what's happening in the world right now, how does any of this apply? Personal responsibility, fine, but what about those people in Pennsylvania? If they die of radiation poisoning, how are they responsible?"

The maestro frowns as though he doesn't understand the question.

"There's a bubble," Harold says.

The maestro dismisses this with a wave of his hand. "Don't talk to me about bubbles. Those assholes in Pennsylvania—"

The room inhales sharply. The shock is actually audible.

"Wait," says Harold. "They're assholes, too?"

The maestro smiles enigmatically.

"Am I getting this right?" Harold looks dumbstruck. "Those downwinders who could die an agonizing death if the core melts, they're responsible for what happens to them?"

"If that's what you get."

The surfer kid is dazzled. He is nineteen and prone to misplaced compassion. In ways he's just beginning to understand, this has made him a victim and a fool. Recent events have confirmed his congenital gullibility, his vulnerability to manipulation. *If you believe that, you've got a hole in your screen door.* It's what his mother is always telling him, never mind that she's usually the one doing the manipulating. It's the fundamental flaw in his character, serious, possibly fatal. Beggars on the street smell him coming, the stink of patsyhood rising off him, one part credulity and one part embarrassment: a rich boy ashamed of his private-school softness, his stepfather's munificence.

In the front row a fat man raises his hand. "I'll be honest, I'm not thrilled about paying three hundred bucks to be called an asshole."

The maestro sips his water. "Fabulous," he says, an all-purpose response. If you call him a sonofabitch, he will answer in one of four ways. *I get it. I hear you. Thank you. Fabulous.*

"Also: why do you get to drink water?"

"I get to drink water because I didn't make an agreement not to." He pronounces it *wooder,* still a Philly street kid despite the hundred-dollar haircut.

DO YOU HAVE A PERSISTENT, NAGGING PROBLEM? Do you have too many to count? Choose one, then. Bodily sensations are good. Migraines, insomnia, back pain. You fear airplanes or public speaking. Your wife's genitals turn your stomach. Leaving your house gives you panic attacks.

Choose one, asshole. Your pack-a-day habit, your shoplifting.

Your nail biting or freebasing cocaine. Pick a symptom or a troubling emotion. A destructive behavior you can't seem to stop.

Choose one, and call it your item. Sharing is encouraged. Join
the other assholes taking turns at the mike. Paolo's item is betrayal.
(His wife gave him herpes.) Julie fears abandonment. (She fakes
orgasms.) Assholes, remember your agreements: each revelation is
to be acknowledged with applause.

The assholes can't stop sharing. For hours on end they take turns
at the mike. Time stands still in the hotel ballroom. Civilizations
rise and fall. Lifetimes pass.

Gilbert steals his mother's painkillers. Jerry dreams, vividly, of
fucking his sister-in-law. Kay's husband likes wearing her clothes.

It is, altogether, a fail-safe antidote to excessive compassion.
Spend sixty hours in this room, and you will hate every one of these
people. The surfer kid, who has never so much as made a fist in
anger, is ready to beat them all senseless.

The maestro quizzes each asshole with rabbinic patience. Can
you locate the sensation in your body? What is its shape and color,
its provenance? The mother who locked you in a closet; the horny
babysitter. Childhood is a minefield, clearly. No one comes out
intact.

The surfer kid studies him, mesmerized. Abruptly he gets to
his feet. A volunteer rushes in with a mike. "My item is anger," he
begins, surprising himself. He is known for his sunny disposition,
his unwavering benevolence.

The maestro interrupts him. "Where's your name tag?"

Almost imperceptibly, the security guards advance.

"I didn't get a nayame tag," says the kid, hearing his own Texas
twang.

The maestro flashes his famous smile. "He didn't get a name tag."

Another volunteer—a blond girl, stunningly beautiful—rushes
in with a Sharpie marker. "What's your name?" she whispers, her
breath tickling his ear.

"Kip," he whispers back.

She writes it in block capitals, large enough to be seen from the stage, and presses the name tag to his chest. Undoubtedly she feels his heart pounding through his shirt.

"Yeah, so—" Kip hesitates. More than anything in life he wants to sit back down, but the blond girl is watching. He feels the ghost of her hand in the vicinity of his heart.

"Last year I got into West Point. I'd be there right now, except that my girlfriend got pregnant. I offered to marry her. For the baby, you know. It seemed like the right thing to do." His face feels very hot. He is ready to puke or pass out or both.

"So I refused the appointment. I stayed in Houston and went to work for my stepdad, which I swore I would never." He feels suddenly bone-tired, weak with hunger, exhausted by the effort of explaining himself. "Never mind that part. That part's a whole nother story. Point is, last fall I find out she's seeing this other guy. The baby isn't even mine."

The maestro stares at him blankly. "So why are you angry?"

"What do you mean, why am I angry? She lied to me. She ruined my life."

"*Ohhh.* I get it." The maestro's voice drops to a stage whisper. "That is a colossal load of crap."

Kip's ears ring loudly, as though a deafening wave is breaking over his head.

"If your life is ruined, you ruined it. You're a failure, and you're pissed at the girl because she stole your excuse." His stare is perforating. For a moment, Kip is the only asshole in the room.

"She wrecked your chance to be a hero. Out of the goodness of your heart you *offered* to marry her. What, she's supposed to be grateful? Of course she's fucking some other guy. Good for her." He waves a hand, the girl's deception and treason summarily dismissed.

Kip sinks back into his chair.

"Stand up. I'm not done with you. How long did you want to go to West Point?"

Kip stands. "All my life." His eyes are burning, the greatest shame imaginable. He'd sooner wet himself than cry in public.

"Bullshit. If you wanted to go, you'd have gone."

Kip's stomach lurches. His one visit to the Academy sparked recurrent nightmares, a truth he's confided to no one. The dismal corridors, the grim plebes in their gray uniforms, the stern interviewer so like his father. The gruff, belligerent firsties, dead-eyed boys who used to be human. *Huah.* In a single year, they promised, Kip would be similarly transformed.

The packed ballroom awaits his next words. The microphone quivers in his shaking hand.

"I been hearing about that place my whole life," he tells 250 total strangers. "My dad went. It was the best thing that ever happened to him." His dad the Colonel calls twice a year, Christmas and Kip's birthday, though he usually gets the date wrong: a month early, two days late. Last Christmas their conversation lasted nine minutes, eight of which involved West Point. This Christmas the Colonel didn't call.

"Fuck him," says the maestro. "Why should you go to West Point, just because he did?"

Kip's heart swells with unfamiliar emotion. There is nothing else to call it—he realizes this later—but love.

Werner Erhard has already changed his life.

EIGHT MONTHS LATER, in Houston, the traffic backs up for miles. Late for a meeting, Kip Oliphant leans on his horn.

He can see his destination, a mirrored office tower that nearly blinds him with reflected sunlight: the world headquarters of Darco Energy, his stepfather's company. He can see it; he just can't get there. Fumes rise from the pavement, a dizzying wave of exhaust. Last summer in San Francisco, with gas lines stretching around the block, drivers cut their engines to conserve fuel. Here, Cadillacs and pickup trucks idle in every lane, huffing hotly, a string of red brake lights as far as he can see.

Finally he pulls into a parking lot and sets out walking, attracting curious glances: a clean-cut young man in a cream-colored Stetson, suit jacket over one arm, his city look. In deference to local custom, he has cut off his ponytail. Still his hair is inches longer than other men's, covering his collar and bleached nearly white at the ends—the last traces of his old life as a stoned surfer bum, the endless months of indolence.

The morning is bright, warm for November. He lopes along at a comfortable pace, easily passing the cars stuck in gridlocked traffic. On Jefferson Street he sees the cause of the commotion, a crowd assembled on the cement plaza outside Dresser Tower. "What's going on?" he asks a man coming out of a doughnut shop.

"That's the Iranian consulate," the man answers, still chewing his doughnut. "They been out there all week."

Kip thinks: The what? He wonders briefly what it says about him, and about Houston, that he lived here twenty years not knowing the city possessed such a thing.

The cars crawl along Jefferson Street.

Outside a gas station he spots a phone booth. He digs a dime from his pocket and calls the office. His stepfather, Darby Butters, is not available; predictably, his direct line is busy. For six solid months he's been on the phone. Boom times in Houston, a year of record profits; and the debacle in Iran will only drive prices higher. President Carter's embargo is good news for Darco. Iranian imports have been stopped cold.

"Tell him I'm hung up in traffic," Kip tells Dar's secretary. "Some kind of a protest, I guess."

He hangs up and continues down Jefferson Street toward the plaza. The demonstrators are mostly young, mostly male. A few carry makeshift signs. AMERICAN CARS RUN BETTER ON AMERICAN OIL.

LET'S PLAY COWBOYS AND IRANIANS! The image rendered in broad cartoon strokes, a swarthy man in a head scarf, garroted and hanging from a tree.

Suddenly the crowd bursts into applause. Passing motorists honk their horns.

"What happened?" Kip asks no one in particular. Two old men in ten-gallon hats, brothers possibly, stand watching, thumbs hooked identically through their belt loops. There are several women in white uniforms, nurses on their lunch break. St. Joseph Hospital is just a few blocks away.

Kip makes his way through the crowd. He sees, finally, the cause of the commotion: a red, white, and green flag burning hot, as though it's been doused with lighter fluid.

Behind him a boy and girl hoot and holler. They are dressed alike, in blue jeans and western shirts, and old enough that they ought to be in school. Each holds one end of a sign, high over their heads. Puzzlingly, it shows a head shot of John Wayne, blown up bigger than life size.

"Is that the Duke?" Kip asks.

The kids look at him like he's bonkers. "Yessir," the boy says.

All around him signs are brandished like weapons.

DEPORT TRAITORS NOW

GO TO HELL AND TAKE YOUR OIL

KEEP THE SHAH AND SEND THEM CARTER

At the head of the crowd the nurses begin singing. It's a feeble effort at first, high pitched and warbling. The old men doff their ten-gallon hats and join in for the chorus, in deep, rumbling baritones: *America, America, God shed his grace on thee.*

"You never seen anything like it," Kip tells Dar later. They are sitting in the engineers' room, a cramped closet thirty-six floors above the sidewalks of downtown, its walls plastered with topo maps slightly faded by the sun. Dar spends most of his time here, preferring it to his own office, a gleaming corner suite with impressive views on both sides. The clutter comforts him, the piles of paper, the engineers' half-empty coffee cups. It calls to mind the rented space above a warehouse where a much younger Darby Butters hung out his shingle. The new company was his entirely, and in the local fashion he named it after himself.

"I don't care if they *are* Ayrabs. I don't believe in burning anybody's flag." Dar drums his fat fingers on the desk, a sign he's getting antsy. He is a squat homely man with the jowly underbite of an English bulldog, bald as a snow globe, and rich enough that it doesn't matter, which entirely explains his marriage to Kip's mother.

Darco was as good a name as any. The alternative, Buttco, was not a viable option.

"A course they did spit in our eye," says Dar, "and Carter let them."

Kip is barely listening. He scans the engineers' shelves for an atlas. The point of dynamism is eight time zones away, in a country he really should locate on a map. In the streets of Houston the horns are still honking.

"Then again," Dar adds, stating the obvious. "It's good for bidness."

The press attaché wears a striped dress shirt, a rim of undershirt visible beneath it. Imagine him dressing for work four days ago, fortified by coffee, slipping the shirt off its hanger, and running through his to-do list, the memos and meetings and phone calls, the ordinary day.

Now he is brought out before the cameras, still wearing the shirt. Two of his captors—scruffy young men, students presumably—hold his elbows. Inside the American embassy his colleagues are still alive. Blindfolded, he feels the crowd gathering, its anger swelling like a weather system, raining insults in Farsi and English.

On Taleghani Street, business is booming. Vendors hawk caps and sweatshirts, bottled water and boiled sugar beets. From a wheeled cart, a boy and his father sell videotapes of Sunday's invasion, the mob of students scaling the embassy wall.

In the States it is still yesterday. The press attaché is watched from sectional sofas, from BarcaLoungers, the living rooms of deep America: shag carpet and track lighting, hi-fis, tropical fish in tanks. In Manhattan and the outer boroughs, his name is repeated wonderingly. *Barry Rosen.* The name says grandson and nephew, lavished with tutors and orthodontia and lovingly bar mitzvahed, a family's hope. There is concern for his parents, the poor Rosens no longer kvelling. *(My son the diplomat. In the State Department, can you imagine?)* It makes you stop and think. It makes you grateful for your own underachieving offspring, the assistant managers. The lazy boy and timid girl rapidly aging, still working retail. You think of the poor Rosens, and give thanks.

An outrageous act, a shocking violation. The press attaché does not speak. He is displayed like a well-behaved child, the mannerly boy he once was. Barry Rosen is seen and not heard, escorted off, stage left.

AN OUTRAGEOUS ACT, but not without precedent. Nine months ago—Valentine's Day, at the very same embassy—a secretary filled a glass dish with candy hearts. An hour later the embassy was attacked, the ambassador held hostage.

BE MINE. SWEET ON YOU.

Panic at the State Department, a flurry of briefings. At the Pentagon men conferred behind closed doors. By evening, to everyone's surprise, the ambassador was released. Washington slept deeply, rose early, and made prudent adjustments: the ambassador recalled to Washington, the embassy staff in Teheran cut to a skeleton crew of sixty. The front windows of the building were replaced with bulletproof glass.

Nine months later, the bulletproof glass is useless. An angry crowd engulfs the embassy. A girl cuts the chains at the gate on Taleghani Street, with metal cutters stashed beneath her chador.

Like a parade of worker ants, students pour over the wall.

Night after night America watches from its couches. All three networks run the same footage, the Imam's face reproduced on fifty-foot banners, his beard and turban, his fierce black brow. Immense crowds cheer him: Super Bowl–size, ominously foreign. Bearded men, women swathed in fabric. Some carry homemade placards, in that diabolical curling cursive no one can read.

The U.N. Security Council calls a closed session.

In Teheran the Imam makes an announcement: the hostages' fate will be decided by the Iranian Parliament.

The Iranian Parliament is not yet elected.

In Oregon and California and Michigan and Ohio, Muslim students hold protests. *SEND HIM BACK! THE SHAH MUST STAND TRIAL.* In Minnesota they are hit with snowballs. In Massachusetts they are pelted with rocks. A Cleveland sportscaster sets fire, on camera, to a red-white-and-green flag. The station gets six hundred calls from viewers. Only one is a complaint.

In New York a champion boxer holds a press conference. A famous Muslim, he offers himself in exchange for the hostages.

All three networks cover the press conference. A boy in Pennsylvania is barely listening. He rolls the die and moves the mouse around the board.

NOT IN
MY BACK YARD
JULY 2012

5.

There's a new hire at Wellways. Darren Devlin knows this by the smell of his shit. In the staff restroom, on three consecutive mornings, three similar-smelling bowel movements have occurred. This is no trick of bad sushi or Mexican food, no stomach virus. There can be no doubt: a new shitter has joined the team.

It is an addict's superpower, this awareness of shit, not extrasensory perception but its opposite, deeply sensory, an animal intuition. An aptitude modern plumbing has rendered obsolete; a vestigial sixth sense humans have, for the most part, evolved beyond. The opiate addict being a special category of human.

For many years, in the depths of Darren's own addiction, shitting was a memory so faint, so distant, it might have come from a past life. He'd gone months or possibly years without ever sitting on a toilet—a claim few in the developed world could make, opiate addicts excepted. His morning Group has proven, definitively, that it is impossible to die of constipation. If it were possible, Darren and most of his clients would already be dead.

In detox, of course, the reverse happened: a tsunami of diarrhea, two or five or ten years' worth of impacted fecal matter released with unspeakable urgency, a notable (but by no means the only) bodily humiliation of heroin withdrawal. Kicking for the last time, Darren had been astonished by its volume. Where did it come from? For years he had scarcely eaten. His daily rations—sugary,

insubstantial—came from convenience stores: Popsicles and lemon-
ade, candy bars and shrink-wrapped Rice Krispies Treats.

Not long ago, he came across the intake papers from his first stay
at Wellways. Height, five feet eleven inches. Weight, 130 pounds.

His morning Group is generous with such stories—its bodily
debacles, its sicknesses. Only the newcomers are reticent, not yet
understanding that public debasement is the coin of the realm.

He is on his way to morning Group when Patricia, the director, stops him in the hallway. "I've been looking all over for you."
Her hand lingers on his shoulder. She is a sturdy little woman,
fifty-something, with forearms like an army mess sergeant. Like all
women who flirt with him, she is old enough to be his mother. "We
have a problem. It's about your vacation."

"I haven't taken any vacation."

"That's the problem. Are you aware that in four years you have
taken not one single vacation day?"

"I wasn't," he says. "Aware."

"At the moment, we owe you eight weeks of paid vacation.
Reliance is requiring that you take it before your anniversary date.
Which is August twentieth."

Requiring?

"What happens if I don't take it?"

"Mandatory furlough."

"Wait, *what?*" The word conjures up images of wartime: soldiers
in gray homespun, riding home to sweethearts a week before Get-
tysburg. A tender interlude, then death by bayonet.

"Sweetie, it's simple. You need to take eight weeks' paid vacation. Or, if you prefer, eight weeks' unpaid. That part is up to you."

"That makes no sense."

"Correct." Patricia gives her happy zombie look—glassy eyes,
a terrifying frozen smile. Last winter Wellways was acquired by
Reliance Healthcare, an immense multinational that runs clinics
and small hospitals in twenty states and the District of Columbia.

Since then new policies have been implemented, outlined in Patricia's weekly memos, which go straight into Darren's recycling bin. When forced to speak of the new initiatives, Patricia refrains from comment. Her exasperation is conveyed by the happy zombie look.

"You can take your eight weeks all at once, or in increments. Your paycheck will be direct-deposited every other Friday on the usual schedule. Unless you opt for the furlough. In which case nothing will be deposited." Again the zombie smile.

He stares at her dumbfounded. "What you're saying is I can't come to work."

"That's what I'm saying."

"But who will take my groups? The new guy?"

"How did you know there was a new guy?"

He does not answer this question.

"Have fun, Darren. Get some sun or something." A playful punch on his shoulder. "Live a little, why don't you?"

He smiles weakly, though his shoulder is smarting. For a small woman Patricia packs a wallop.

"I'M DARREN, THE HEAD COUNSELOR ON THIS UNIT. And I'm an addict."

Twenty men answer in unison, like gravelly voiced first-graders: "Hi, Darren." The youngest, a skateboard kid from Catonsville, is fifteen. The oldest, a Catholic priest hooked on Vicodin, is seventy-four.

He begins by welcoming two new clients. Tony is a wizened grandfather, Latino or Italian. Alvin resembles a retired NBA player, a large, sad-eyed black man with a shiny bald head. Unusually, both are alcoholics. Intake rarely sends him the drinkers. Mainly he gets what the medical director deems the hard cases—which, in Baltimore, means opiates. Of the counselors, only Darren is a graduate of the program, which is believed to give him cred with the clients.

That he graduated twice is never mentioned.

He invites the new guys to tell their stories. Alvin requires some prodding. Tony, a more typical alcoholic, poses the opposite problem; there is simply no shutting him up. Given the choice, Darren would take a junkie any day, though he knows better than to express a preference. At Wellways it is a point of doctrine, incontrovertible: addicts are more alike than different. The same modalities (individual cognitive/behavioral counseling, Twelve Step group work, medical intervention where appropriate) are effective for all.

Like everything else in rehab, the stories are interminable. The men can barely stay awake. The skateboard kid looks catatonic. The priest's lips move silently.

Interminable.

When you quit drugs, you learn how long a day is. For years Darren had lived outside time, his days crowded with purposeful activity: scrounging for money, copping, shooting. Slipping, when all was finished, into that blessed state where time had no meaning at all. By comparison, sober days were cavernous. Six years later, they still are.

He filled them, at first, with meetings, two and sometimes three a day, anything to avoid his empty apartment, linked forever in his mind to the old life's squalid pleasures. The apartment in Charles Village, a few blocks from the Hopkins campus, where his seduction had occurred and occurred and occurred, the whole demented carnival of craving and rapture and despair.

What did people do all day, if they didn't do drugs?

Sobriety was effortless—meaningless, too—if you'd never been high.

Early in his recovery, he'd found projects. It was as though he'd awakened from a long nap, blinking and disoriented, and found himself in a dilapidated shack: the windows broken, the roof leaking, the walls crumbling. It was figuratively true, if not literally (though his housekeeping had, in fact, deteriorated). His disease had left his life in ruins, the adult life that had started without him noticing.

Unmedicated, he faced the smoldering wreckage of his academic career, his credit rating, his health. The people he'd avoided, lied to, stolen from, betrayed. The roommate he'd bailed on, a girl who loved him. His academic adviser. His lab partner. His dad.

He hadn't been sober since the ninth grade, an age at which sobriety wasn't a choice but, like virginity, a state you were cursed with. Darren at fourteen: a skinny dork hooked on chess and crosswords and, incongruously, the music of Public Enemy. In his lily-white hometown, rap music was automatically suspect, embraced only by a few shameless posers. Darren listened covertly, under headphones, and felt defibrillated. The driving beats, the fierce lyrics, were the testosterone shot his young self badly needed. He felt, fleetingly but powerfully, like a man.

Half of sobriety was wishing you'd never started: if you'd never taken that first drink, first bump, you could have stayed clean forever with no sweat at all. Instead, it became your life's work. Six years in, Darren is gravely aware of what recovery has cost him: his own time and other people's money, the nearly superhuman effort. The crushing, virtually incalculable cost of getting well.

He could have cured cancer by now, if he'd never gotten high.

Newly sober, he embarked on a massive salvage operation. A new apartment, night classes at the community college (a humbling experience, when you'd blown a golden ticket at Johns Hopkins). He worked a lunch counter at the Baltimore Convention Center, as many shifts as they'd give him, selling overpriced sandwiches to salesmen from Cleveland or Wichita. He gave up red meat, he gave up all meat. Paid his old parking tickets, opened a bank account, saw a dentist. Swallowed vitamins and joined a gym. On Sundays he called his father, who'd subsidized his treatment. Who'd believed despite overwhelming evidence that Darren would someday get clean.

Tony is winding up for his grand finale. "Eighty-three years old. She's in a walker, okay? She call that county van for the disabled, they come and get her. That's how bad she want to leave me."

Eight weeks of paid vacation. Eight weeks is fifty-six days.

The other half of sobriety was wishing you'd never stopped. The job at Wellways meets Darren's one overarching need: it expands to fill the space available. He can spend the day at the clinic and then, if he is bored or lonely, drop in at night or on weekends. He's been called—by coworkers, by Patricia herself—a workaholic, an idea he finds ludicrous. They're addictions counselors: Can't they see his behavior for what it is? The addict replacing one substance with another, desperate to fill the day.

He gave up meat because what was meat to him?

Of course he's never taken a vacation. Why would he? Why would anyone, with no heroin to shoot?

"Sixty years of marriage," says Tony. "I guess she finally had enough."

How else could a person fill fifty-six empty days? Six years since his last fix, Darren can imagine no other way.

HE LEAVES BALTIMORE on Friday afternoon, joining the slow parade of refugees fleeing the city for the summer weekend, Route 70 backed up all the way to Fredneck. Beside him, on the passenger seat, are his laptop, duffel bag, and *The Big Book of Alcoholics Anonymous*, its plain black cover faded and worn. At the Pennsylvania border he peels off the highway. The day is clear and bright, the view transporting. A rainy spring had worked its magic, turning the valley lush and green. *I'm overdue for a visit*, he'd told his father, a laughable understatement. He hasn't set foot in Bakerton in years.

And yet the route is deeply familiar, the tollbooths and truck stops, potholes in all the old places. The sameness of everything allows him to pretend, briefly, that no time has passed. That it's still thirteen years ago, his first-ever trip to Hopkins: sprawled in the backseat of his parents' Crown Vic, his few possessions (the chess set, the Public Enemy CDs) piled in milk crates beside him, his water pipe and rolling papers hidden in a duffel bag. Eighteen years old and thoroughly stoned, the only way he could imagine spending three hours in the car with his parents.

Now he'd give a year of his life—more—to be back in that car.

His mother still living, his own addiction still in front of him. Time, still, to circumvent it. To take another road.

The rest stops and Cracker Barrels, the bright signage advertising gasoline and fast food, outlet shopping, Amish quilts. The sameness isn't merely unsettling. In some way that makes no sense, it offends him personally. He feels affronted by the world's denial, its stubborn refusal to acknowledge all that has been broken, snuffed out, wasted, lost. And so, when he spots two unfamiliar billboards at the crest of a hill, on either side of Drake Highway, he feels compelled to stop and examine them, concrete evidence—at last—that time has passed.

He puts on his hazards and gets out of the car. The billboards are identically sized. One shows a pastoral scene, a grassy meadow. Emblazoned across it is a boldfaced slogan: CLEAN ENERGY FOR AMERICA'S FUTURE. At the center of the meadow stands an unobtrusive metal canister, man-size, painted dark green.

Across the road, the other billboard shows a swarthy man's face the size of a trampoline. He looks down on motorists with an expression of infinite sadness, as though they have disappointed him profoundly. A FRACKING NIGHTMARE? CALL PAUL ZACHARIAS, ATTORNEY-AT-LAW.

He gets back into his car.

Fracking. The word sounds subliminally obscene, a genteel euphemism for *fucking.* Darren remembers, vaguely, a Public Radio segment he once heard on the way to work. Fracking contaminated the water supply, or caused earthquakes or possibly cancer. Did it also kill wildlife? Dick Cheney, somehow, was to blame.

How distant the world has grown, its problems secondary,

always, to his own dysfunction. His entire attention absorbed, forever, by the not-using of drugs.

His old fuel stop is a Sheetz convenience store on the outskirts of Bakerton, the cheapest gas for miles. His tiny tank can be filled for pocket change. The parking lot is crowded, cars and pickups and, off to the side, two huge trucks idling at the diesel pump. Darren pulls up to the pump and goes inside to pay, nearly knocking over a display of bottle openers stamped with the Pittsburgh Steelers logo. Scotch-taped to the cash register is a hand-lettered sign: SUDAFED LIMIT 2 PER CUSTOMER NO EXCEPTIONS.

Behind the counter, in red Sheetz smocks, stand a man and a woman he vaguely recognizes—MARTY and ALYSSA, according to their name tags. Either or both might have been his classmates, though to Darren they look middle-aged. Like everybody in town, they're probably younger than they look.

Alyssa stares out the window. "What kind of a car is that?"

"A smart car."

Marty guffaws. "Where's the rest of it?"

"It's good on gas."

"Christ, I hope so."

Darren hands over his cash. "I've never seen this place so busy."

"It's always like this."

Darren looks over his shoulder at a long line of men in work boots, waiting to be fed.

He takes the slow route through town, past the dress factory, closed now, and the old train depot, unused in fifty years. Above it the famous sign is still standing, the familiar words now barely legible: BAKERTON COAL LIGHTS THE WORLD. He performs this ritual each time he returns, counting the newly empty storefronts like a doctor making rounds, measuring the health of the town or more properly, the rate of its decline. Arriving, always, at the same conclusion: Bakerton is a terminal patient, barely hanging on.

Crossing town ought to take five minutes—six at the outside, if all four traffic lights happen to be red. But today, inexplicably, traffic has stopped. A Ford pickup idles in front of him, an even larger truck ahead. Craning his neck, Darren sees the reason for the slowdown: an orange DETOUR sign at the intersection, Baker Street blocked off with sawhorses.

A *detour* in Bakerton?

Darren turns down a side street and cuts south, in the direction of his dad's house, thinking how a detour presumes two things: traffic and its need to get somewhere in particular. Neither condition, in Bakerton, generally applies.

His parents' house is a tidy split-level, yellow brick. Darren idles a moment in the driveway. The house looks strange to him. A moment later he understands the reason. All the flowers are gone.

His mother had been crazy for flowers. Hanging baskets of petunias and impatiens, cement urns filled with geraniums and marigolds, beds of tulips and daffodils she planted each fall, never doubting that spring would come. His dad isn't the type to fuss over flowers. He keeps the lawn close-cropped. The porch's only decoration is an American flag.

Darren idles a moment in the driveway. The house's windows are dark, Dick's car gone. Darren, who has no house key, backs out of the driveway and heads back toward town.

Years ago, when his mother was living, they changed the locks on him, a security measure that was necessary at the time.

In town he parks in front of the Commercial and cuts the engine. It's still early, the blinding late afternoon of high summer. With any luck the place will be empty. He'll borrow Dick's house key and be out of there in five minutes.

The bar is cool and dim inside. It smells of beer and floor polish and brass cleaner, a smell of Darren's late childhood. He was thirteen when his dad and uncle bought the place, flush with Uncle Pat's settlement money. A beefy man stands behind the bar, alternately eating French fries and drying beer steins with a dirty towel.

"Is my dad around? I'm Darren."

The bartender eyes him blankly.

"Devlin," he adds. "The other son."

"Oh. Sure." The guy eats a French fry and wipes his hands on his pants. "Dick's at the funeral home. He should be back any minute, if you want to wait."

Darren remembers, then: the AmVets. Anytime a veteran dies, a couple of the old guys are dispatched to the wake. Flags are involved. What exactly is done with them, Darren is unsure.

He sits at the end of the bar, opposite a giant TV screen.

"I didn't know there was another son. Sorry, buddy." The bartender pours an Iron City and sets it at Darren's elbow. "On the house."

I'm not a beer drinker, he could have said, if he wanted to make things even more awkward. "Thanks," he says instead.

A commercial flashes across the television: an animatronic lizard standing on its hind legs, speaking in an Australian accent. *Are you paying too much for car insurance?* Darren, who cares nothing about lizards or Australians or insurance, stares entranced. There is no looking away from it. The average American watches an ungodly amount of television, four or six hours a day, a habit Darren understands completely. If he owned a set he'd spend his entire life in this hypnotized state, gaping dumbly at commercials.

The lizard drives away on a tiny motorcycle.

A German sedan races along a mountain road, whipping around corners. *The Mercedes E Class,* a man intones with the gravity of a priest.

A heartsick man speaks directly to the camera. *For forty years, I've stood up for the little guy.* His heavy-lidded eyes are eerily familiar. An unusual name, vaguely biblical, flashes across the screen: **Paul Zacharias, Attorney-at-Law**.

"Who is that guy?" Darren asks the bartender. "I've seen him somewhere."

"You and everybody. Those ads have been running day and night."

If you and your family are caught in a fracking nightmare, you have valuable legal rights.

The bartender snorts. "You sign a lease, you take your chances, is my feeling. If I had some land, I'd do it in a minute. Where the hell is Gia?" he shouts into the kitchen.

"Gia Bernardi?" A name Darren hasn't said in many years. "She works here?"

"Supposedly. Who do you like?" the bartender asks, nodding toward the screen.

It takes Darren a moment to understand the question. One team wears red hats, the other blue. The things people fill their lives with. A lifetime ago, in college, he read novels in French. *Ça meuble la vie.* He can't recall authors or titles, characters or situations; he can scarcely form a sentence in that language, but all these years later the phrase is still lodged in his memory. *Meubler,* to furnish. To fill up a life the way a sofa fills up a room.

"I always go with the underdog," Darren says.

"Ignore him, Budd. He has no clue what he's talking about." Gia Bernardi charges in through the back door at high speed, generating a perfumed breeze. Short denim skirt, the sleek suntanned legs of a high school cheerleader. She is more beautiful than he remembered. The picture he still carries in his head is eighteen-year-old Gia: the face rounder, eyes rimmed with black liner, a hairdo wider than her shoulders. Grown-up Gia is lean and sinewy. She looks freshly scrubbed and glowing, her hair in a ponytail as though she's just come from the gym.

"Whoa, Gia." He gets to his feet. "You look great."

They embrace briefly, her skin outdoor-warm. She smells like Gia, cigarettes and coconut suntan lotion. Her head fits neatly—he forgot this—in the crook of his shoulder.

From somewhere near his sternum comes a bright electronic melody with a catchy backbeat. "What the hell is that?"

"My ringtone." She takes a cell phone from her purse, glances at it briefly, and stashes it beneath the bar. "I can't believe it's you! Where the fuck is your hair?"

Darren passes a hand over his head. His hairline had begun receding in college. Some years later, during his first stay at Wellways, he noticed a yarmulke-size bald spot on top. Possibly it had been there for some time. During his second stay at Wellways, he gave up and shaved his head.

"I must have left it somewhere."

"I like it this way," Gia says.

She busies herself behind the bar. Ignoring the beer at his elbow, Darren inquires politely about people he barely remembers, Gia's many brothers, her ancient father. "Hold that thought," she says periodically, rushing off to serve a customer. He doesn't mind the interruptions. The spectacle pleases him: Gia racing up and down the bar, pulling beers, flirting with patrons, pocketing tips. If he had a video camera he'd have recorded it. That would be a reason to buy a television: Gia Bernardi on a continuous loop, Gia's bare suntanned legs in the short denim skirt.

Ignoring the beer is not difficult. He never was a beer drinker. Never a drinker, period.

A beaming woman in a negligee lies on what looks like a hospital bed. *My sleep number is fourteen,* she says ecstatically.

Beneath the bar Gia's cell phone rings.

Four hours a day. Darren is a single guy with no hobbies or pets, no girlfriend, not even a lawn to mow. And yet even his empty life holds no space for such a time-consuming habit. Television watching is like the earring he wore in high school: once you gave it up, the hole simply closed.

"Whew, I'm beat." Gia takes Darren's cigarettes from his chest pocket and tucks one behind her ear, a gesture he remembers with a pang. It would be a lie to say he's thought about her in the last six years. Even sober—especially sober—he is a master at not thinking about the past.

"I'm tired just watching you. Business is good, I guess." Darren eyes the portrait above the bar, his father and uncle arm in arm, Pat's eyes sunken and unnaturally bright, the terrible avidity of end-stage sickness. His settlement check arrived in April. Mesothelioma would kill him the day before Christmas. That summer the brothers made an offer on the old Commercial Hotel, fulfilling a lifelong dream.

"The last six months have been crazy. Gas guys, mostly."

Darren glances around the room. None of the faces looks familiar. "In Bakerton? They're, what do you call it, fracking? *Here?*"

She stares at him as though he's been living on some distant planet. As, of course, he has. "Seriously? Jesus, Devlin. Ask your brother about it. He signed a lease."

"*Rich* did?"

"He didn't tell you?"

"Er, no." The brothers had spoken a few Christmases ago. Born ten years apart, with two sisters in between, they had never been close. "He's going to let them drill on the *farm?*"

"Sure. Why not?"

No short answer to that question, and Gia doesn't have time for the long one—not that he'd be able to articulate it. (Cancer? Earthquakes? Dick Cheney?) At the far end of the bar a man holds up his empty glass. Darren reaches for his wallet.

"You're not *leaving!*" Gia screeches.

He is aware of grinning like an idiot. "Nah. Just showing my appreciation for the excellent service." He places a five on the counter, remembering that he can actually afford to get drunk in Bakerton. It's a dangerous thought.

"Your sister was up for a visit, a couple weeks ago," says Gia. "With the baby. I saw her at Walmart. I guess she told you."

Weirdly, she had not.

"She said you have a girlfriend."

"I don't." Darren feels his face heat. He'd talked too much about the receptionist at work, making it sound like more than it was—part of his ongoing campaign to reassure Kate that he managed some semblance of a normal life. "There was this woman, but it was nothing. I'm surprised she mentioned it."

"I asked her."

Clocks reverse direction. The earth pauses in its orbit, momentarily confused. It hovers there for weeks or months while Darren formulates a response.

Why, Gia? Why do you want to know?

But before he can speak the words, her attention shifts palpably. Like a sunbather under a passing cloud, he feels a sudden chill. Darren looks over his shoulder. In the doorway a guy is scoping out the room. Buzz cut, long ugly face, two thick gold chains around his neck. It's an exotic look for Bakerton, though he'd fit right in at Wellways—a garden-variety Baltimore street hood, lurking in the lobby waiting for his juice.

The guy lopes toward them, taking the empty stool next to Darren's. "Hey, girl," he says to Gia. "What up?"

"Brando, this is Darren. My old friend from high school."

"Hey." Brando wears shorts and a frayed black T-shirt with the sleeves cut off. He's lean and sinewy—the way Darren might look with a little muscle. It's hard not to notice this, impossible really, since most of his visible skin is covered with tattoos: a motorcycle, a sunburst, a detailed scorpion.

Gia sets, at Brando's elbow, a shot of whiskey he didn't order. Clearly she knows what he likes. She races down the bar to serve a customer at the far end. Darren and Brando sit in silence.

"Nice ink," Darren says finally, a line he's used with sullen clients. People loved to talk about their tattoos.

Brando grunts but doesn't speak, so Darren tries again: "You get them around here?"

"Nah, all over. Texas mostly."

"How many do you have?"

"Eleven, if you count this one. It's pretty fucking small." Brando extends a hairy foot, bare except for a flip-flop. On the instep is a replica of a military dog tag, actual size. "I got it before I redeployed. My serial number is on there, in case I lose it."

"The dog tag?"

"The foot." Brando knocks back his shot and calls to Gia. "I got your jumper cables out in the car."

Jumper cables? Darren is immediately wary. It's a line he never thought of, himself. *I've got to hit the head. Smoke a cigarette. Make a phone call.* All the ways you excused yourself to go get high.

"I have a smoke break coming." Gia looks around the room for Budd, who sits watching the ball game in a corner. She signals him as though hailing a cab, something she has almost certainly never done.

"Deployed," says Darren. "You were in Afghanistan?"

"Iraq before that." He pronounces it *Eye-rack*.

Darren thinks, Never mind that. Tell me about Afghanistan.

"Be right back," Gia tells Darren, briefly touching his hand.

Brando follows her out the door. Darren watches mutely, his hand burning where she touched it.

The room has gotten louder. Every stool is occupied, the overflow crowd spilling into the dining room. From their place above the gantry, his dad and Uncle Pat beam down at the scene.

Since childhood, apparently, they'd dreamed of owning a bar.

Pat worked for twenty years on an assembly line in Cleveland, making insulated windows. In the basement of the factory, another line churned out fireproof doors. His case was complicated by the fact that only the doors had contained asbestos. In the end the company settled—for Pat, just in time.

The beer sits at Darren's elbow, sweating slightly, doing what beers do. He stares idly at the TV screen. A dark-eyed woman, vaguely ethnic, smiles encouragingly at the camera. *Are you a home-school family? Get your kids hooked on phonics!*

Even after they changed the locks, his mother had tried to help him, behind Dick's back when necessary. Every few months she sent care packages of clothes and food, until Darren moved without telling her.

For most Americans—he knows this—Afghanistan represents something other than an abundant supply of cheap heroin.

A moment later Gia returns. "Hey, sorry about that. His battery died the other night. I told him to keep them for a day or two, just in case." She lowers her voice. "What kind of shit-for-brains drives around without jumper cables?"

"I don't have jumper cables."

"Exactly my point."

Darren eyes her suspiciously. She is an accomplished liar, historically; but this story has the ring of truth. He remembers a time, years ago, when she changed a tire for him, teasing him all the while: *Devlin, you are such a girl.*

She had never been his girlfriend. In high school they hadn't spoken; he was simply aware of her, as boys were. They met properly a week after graduation, while working for KeystoneCorps—a state-funded program that provided summer jobs for underemployed youth, which in Bakerton was pretty much everyone. The assignments were predictable, transparently sexist: the boys worked on road crews, the girls as cleaners or kitchen slaves. The few college-bound males were placed with the girls. Darren and Gia were both sent to Saxon Manor, the county nursing home, a grim holding pen for the indigent old.

They worked in the laundry, a stifling basement room loud with dryers. At orientation they learned to operate the huge machines. They learned which solutions removed blood or feces or Jell-O—the residents ate vast quantities of Jell-O—from soiled sheets. At each set of instructions, Gia's shoulders shook violently. In Darren's fractured state—he'd smoked a joint on the way to work—her laughter was contagious. By the end of the morning his side ached.

In the way of small towns, he knew of her family. For three generations, Bakerton's dead Catholics had been embalmed at Bernardi's. Gia drove to work each morning in her father's cast-off hearse. In the rear parking lot at Saxon Manor, Darren rolled them an elegant joint, fitted with its own cardboard filter—the only way in which he'd ever been good with his hands. At seventeen he was a shy virgin. Getting her high seemed the only way he could possibly impress her, his one chance to tell her something she didn't already know.

Some nights they took the hearse to the Star-Light Drive-In. Around them, in parents' automobiles, young couples kissed and groped. Darren and Gia did not touch. They laughed at the third-run horror films, they drank and smoked. She had a boyfriend, a few years older—the lead singer for The Vipers, a local heavy metal act. Darren remembered him clearly from the high school corridor, the cocky swagger, the bleach-blond mullet straight out of a music video. The Vipers were on the road that summer, playing bar gigs on the Jersey Shore. One day after work, Darren and Gia rolled up to her parents' house to find a VW bus parked at the curb. The boyfriend was waiting on the porch, his hair recognizable at fifty paces. Gia bolted from the car, squealing with delight. Darren waited in the driveway with the engine idling, feeling slightly sick, as the two nearly swallowed each other.

The memory returns to him now. "How do you know that guy? Brando." Even saying the name annoys him. "Is that really his name?"

"His last name is Brandon. He works on one of the drill crews. They're in here all the time."

"And he's from—Texas?"

"He was stationed at Fort Hood." Worship in her voice, a kind of dumb reverence, Gia having a patriotic moment, apparently.

Probably there have been others, Gia saluting the flag while lying on her back. "Any more questions, Devlin?"

"Nah, that's all I got. Actually, I have to run." It is literally true: he feels a sudden, powerful urge to flee.

She looks genuinely disappointed. "Promise I'll see you again. I'm here every night, practically." She lowers her voice and leans close to his ear. "Come back, okay?"

Leaving, he feels the whole crowd watching him, whether or not it's true: twenty pairs of jealous male eyes boring into his back. Everybody wants her, still and always. For him this has always been her appeal.

Outside dusk is falling. One by one the streetlights come on, lit like birthday candles.

He still has no house key.

Parked on the street is Gia's battered hatchback—same sheepskin seat covers, same pine tree–shaped air freshener dangling above the dash. In the rear compartment, a set of jumper cables lies on the floor.

DICK DEVLIN TURNS SEVENTY-SIX THAT SUNDAY. To celebrate, Rich hosts a birthday barbecue on his deck. In prior years the birthday barbecue was a raucous affair, burgers and beer drinking and illegal fireworks, a mob of kids playing baseball in the yard. Now—his mother dead, his sisters and cousins moved out of state—the Devlins fit easily at a single table, a depressing thought.

He is scraping the grill with a wire brush when his cell phone rings.

"Tell Shelby to count on one extra," says his father. "Your brother's home."

The revelation stops him cold. "You're joking." There is more, much more he could say, but the words don't come.

"It's been a long time, Richard. He's overdue for a visit."

"Fine," says Rich. "What the hell does he eat?"

"He brought some of those tofu hot dogs. They're not bad, actually."

"You're joking," Rich says again.

The doorbell rings precisely at noon, Dick and, lurking behind him like a sulky teenager, Darren with his package of tofu hot dogs. He looks okay, a little skinny: concave chest, his pale arms slender as a girl's. For this summer barbecue he wears black jeans and a black T-shirt.

"Welcome," Rich says in his best host's voice.

Darren gives him a limp handshake.

"Darren!" Shelby cries, hugging him.

"Let me get you a beer," Rich says.

Darren passes a hand over his shiny head—smooth as an egg, small and perfectly formed. The head makes him seem an alien creature, an ambassador from some future time when men will no longer need hair—a ghostly scientist or philosopher, delicate and curiously evolved. "Do you have seltzer?"

"We have Sprite."

"Sprite is fine."

They stand around awkwardly while Shelby fusses with the food. Potato salad, baked beans, a pineapple upside-down cake made from his mother's recipe that somehow doesn't taste quite the same.

Darren accepts a can of pop and looks around, blinking. "Wow, I had no idea. I thought you were living in the farmhouse."

"We were. The place was falling down."

"You couldn't renovate?"

"We looked into it." It's more explanation than he owes Darren. "In the end it was cheaper to start from scratch."

Shelby interrupts. "We didn't *exactly* start from scratch. It's a modular home. It comes in two parts, and they just bolt it together. You've seen them on the highway. You know, OVERSIZE LOAD."

Rich thinks, Please shut up.

"Oh. Right," Darren says.

But Shelby, having warmed up, will not stop talking. "We tried living in the farmhouse. *I* tried. But I have terrible allergies."

"Oh. Okay." Darren nods vigorously.

Shelby seems to take this as encouragement. She rattles off a list that's longer each time Rich hears it: dust mites, tree nuts, three kinds of pollen, cat dander, shellfish. "And maybe wheat gluten. Though technically that's an intolerance, not an allergy. With the farmhouse, the main issue was mold."

Rich excuses himself and goes out to the deck to fire up the grill. The morning sun has faded, the wind shifted. In the air is a smell of rain.

Through the open window he hears voices, Shelby's mostly. He closes his eyes and makes the words recede. It's a trick he learned in the navy, a way of shutting out language—a particular switch in his brain that, when activated, makes all words sound like Persian or Arabic or whatever they spoke over there. For his dad to know about Shelby's neuroses is embarrassing enough. Dick, to his credit, has never said a critical word about her, though he must wonder what sort of whackjob his son married. Rich has begun to wonder the same thing. He believed, once, that love would cure her: marriage, children, a normal life. Instead her weird hang-ups have multiplied. To have Darren know this is intolerable.

A door opens behind him, the family traipsing out to the deck. Rich watches their faces as they look out over the yard.

"What the hell is that?" says Dick.

Tact is not a Devlin trait.

"An access road," Rich says.

"You should see what's over the hill," says Shelby, who has not, herself, seen it. *I can't bear to look,* she told Rich, and as far as he knows, she still hasn't. Home all day with the kids, she's never once climbed the hill to see what's happening in her own back yard.

"Come on," says Dick, charging down the stairs. "Let's have a look."

They cross the yard together, Dick, Rich, and Braden leading the way, followed by Darren, Shelby, and Olivia. They climb the rise and look down. Five acres of pasture have been razed and flattened, spread with gravel and marked off with chain-link fence. A dozen vehicles are parked there, at random angles: two trailers, an earth mover, a dumper, pickup trucks.

"Jesus Christ," says Darren.

"It's something," says Dick, with characteristic understatement. "Too bad about the trees."

The scale of the operation is shocking, but not surprising. Rich knew what he was in for, having seen what was done at Wally Fetterson's down the road. The real surprise is the feebleness of his own memory. He can scarcely picture the farm the way it was. The row of hybrid poplars Pap had planted as a windbreak; the mature plums and cherries that even last summer had born fruit. The rolling pasture was as familiar as his own body. As a boy he zoomed across it on the back of Pap's snowmobile, anticipating each rise and furrow. Spray of fresh powder, cold stardust burning his cheeks.

"Gia said you signed a lease," says Darren. "But I had no idea."

"Gia has a big mouth." *And she'll put it anywhere,* Rich does not add.

"When do they start drilling?"

"Who knows? They don't tell us anything. I'm starved," Rich says abruptly. "Let's go eat some burgers." He turns back toward the house, knowing the others will follow. A moment later, they do.

On the deck they gather around the table. Rich takes the platter Shelby hands him and lays out hamburgers and buns and the tofu hot dogs, which stick like wet pink styrofoam to the hot grill.

A faint rumble in the distance. "Is that thunder?" says Darren.

"Oh no!" says Shelby. "What a disaster."

"It'll blow over," Rich says.

He loads the burgers onto paper plates and hands them to Olivia, who enjoys setting the table. She watches Darren in mute fascination. She is shy around strangers, and Darren, her only uncle, falls definitively into that category.

"How many of these, um, items can I serve you?" Rich asks him.

"One is fine."

"I cooked two."

"Two, then."

"Can I have one?" says Braden.

Rich laughs. "Trust me, buddy. You're not going to like it."

A tofu hot dog rolls through the slats in the grill.

"Soldier down," says Rich. "I lost one of your dogs, man."

"That's all right. I never eat more than one."

Rich eyes Darren's shoulders, the knobs of bone poking through his T-shirt, and thinks, Maybe you should.

"You're not eating anything?" Darren asks Olivia.

"No," she says. "Unfortunately." It's one of the first words she ever learned, after *Mommy* and *Daddy* and *cookie*. It had seemed comical then, all those syllables from the mouth of a two-year-old.

"She isn't feeling well," says Shelby.

"Can I go watch TV?" Olivia says.

Darren seems tense, fidgety. His tofu hot dog eaten, he reaches for his cigarettes.

"You're *smoking*?" says Shelby.

"A loyal R.J. Reynolds customer since 1998."

"But it's so bad for you!"

There is a long, painful silence in which nobody points out— because how could you?—Darren's lifelong indifference to such matters. That tobacco is, or has been, the least of his sins.

He returns the pack to his pocket. "That's okay, I can wait."

"Thank you." Shelby flashes him a look of such warm gratitude that Rich nearly drops his spatula. Why is it so easy for other people to get on her good side?

"Your brother's got some vacation time coming," says Dick.

"Eight weeks," Darren says.

"Eight *weeks*?" Two months of vacation is, to Rich, unfathomable. For ten years he's sucked up all the overtime he can get.

"You should take a trip," says Shelby. "A cruise or something." In her eyes, a Caribbean cruise is the height of luxury. She's been bugging Rich about it for years.

Darren reaches again for his cigarettes, then remembers himself. "Maybe. I haven't taken a day off in four years. So, you know, I could use a break."

Rich thinks, A break from what? You barely work in the first place. From his sister Kate—the only Devlin who talks to Darren with any frequency—he has a vague idea of what goes on at a rehab clinic: the hand-holding, the sob stories, the handing out of methadone.

By the time the burgers are eaten, the sky has clouded over. Rich gathers up empty beer cans, paper plates smeared with mustard and ketchup. Inside, Olivia lies on the living room couch staring listlessly at cartoons. He gives her hair a playful swipe.

"What's the matter, kitten? You barely touched your burger."

"I don't feel good," Olivia says.

In the kitchen Shelby is scooping Jell-O into a bowl. "For Olivia," she says.

"She didn't finish her dinner, she gets dessert?" Rich is interrupted by a terrific thrumming from outside. "What the hell is that?"

He hurries out to the deck. An immense truck, larger than any he's ever seen, is climbing the access road, or trying to. The thing moves at the speed of a cruise ship, enveloped in a cloud of diesel fumes.

"What the hell is that?" his father barks.

"The drill rig," Rich shouts. "A piece of it, anyway."

Darren covers his ears. "On a Sunday afternoon?"

In stunned silence they watch the hulking machine inch up the ridge. That it moves at all is a straight-up miracle. It's as though an aircraft carrier has run aground in Rich's back yard.

"It's so *loud*," Darren shouts. "Maybe we should go inside."

"You go ahead," says Rich. "I'll talk to them."

He jogs down the stairs and follows the access road up to the ridge, breathing diesel fumes, easily passing the mighty engine. "Hey!" he shouts, waving his arms.

The driver seems not to hear him, which is no wonder. He can't even hear himself.

From the top of the ridge he spots another vehicle parked at the edge of the gravel lot, a white Dodge Ram pickup with a sign—STREAM SOLUTIONS—on its driver-side door. A guy wearing ear protectors leans against its hood, watching the slow progress of the rig. Rich recognizes him immediately, the sawed-off muscleman he sees, far too often, at the Commercial. A name, *Herc*, is written in cursive over his heart.

"What the hell is going on?" Rich shouts.

Herc removes his headphones.

Rich repeats, "What the hell is going on?"

"Just what it looks like. We're moving in the rig."

"On Sunday? I'm having a barbecue with my family." The engine noise makes Rich's whole body vibrate. They're standing two feet apart, and yet he has to shout to be heard. "You guys were here all day yesterday. You can't give us a break today?"

"That wadn't us. That was the construction crew." Herc moves to replace his headset. "Don't worry, we'll stay out of your way."

"You're joking, right?"

Herc shrugs. "Sorry, man. I can't help you."

"It can't wait until tomorrow?"

"The schedule says we drill you this week. Devlin H1. You're Mr. Devlin?"

Rich nods.

"Mr. Devlin, I'm sorry for the inconvenience. But the show must go on."

OUTSIDE, A CRACK OF THUNDER. Rain hits hard and sudden, a sound like gunfire. Periodic gusts rattle the windowpanes. A horizontal rain batters the aluminum door.

The brothers are standing in the garage so that Darren can smoke. Outside, the engine noise continues. Darren is grateful for the noise, which at least fills the conversational void. He's been hoping all day to get Rich alone—why exactly, he can't now remember. To explain himself? To be forgiven or, at least, to acknowledge his unforgivability? To apologize for his entire life?

They have squared off in opposite corners of the garage, crowded with Rich's possessions, some of which Darren can identify: a lawn tractor, a snowblower, and what might possibly be a table saw. Items Rich must consider ordinary, the kinds of things men own.

Darren tries to make conversation. "It's weird to see the farm again. Not what I expected. I thought you'd have cows and stuff." Wasn't that the whole point, the actual reason Rich had bought him out? Instead his brother lives in a tract house the size of a trailer, and Pap's sixty acres sit unused.

"Soon," Rich says tersely. "Once the gas money starts coming in."

"Right." Darren butts one cigarette and lights another. "Explain it to me again, because I'm missing something. Your kids are going to play next to a gas well. You're fine with this."

"Do you always smoke this much?"

Outside, a crack of thunder.

"Also: since when do you worry about my kids, or anybody's kids? You *are* kids." Rich jams his hands into his pockets, his balled fists the size of grapefruits. "Jesus Christ, they aren't orchids. When I was a kid—"

"Yeah, I know. You played in the strippins." It's a word Darren hasn't thought of in years. In the sixties and seventies, Saxon County was a hotbed of strip mining. Rich Devlin and his friends ran wild in the ruined landscape, riding bikes and motorcycles through gaping man-made canyons, treacherous slopes of loose black dirt. By the time Darren came along, the land had been clumsily backfilled, covered over with grass; but the old strippins was still talked about, tales that took on mythic dimensions. It is the essence of a Bakerton childhood: the foregone conclusion that every worthwhile thing has already happened. The town is all aftermath.

"That place, man. I used to come home black with coal dirt." Rich runs a hand through his hair, still conspicuously thick and wavy. "Mom wouldn't let me in the house. I had to clean up in the basement," he adds, as if Darren might have forgotten this detail. As if it hadn't filled his young self with envy: of the four Devlin kids, only Rich had access to the dank basement shower their father used when he came home from the mines.

The hair, honestly, is a little galling. His brother is over forty. Shouldn't he at least have some gray?

"And that's a good thing," says Darren. "That's a thing that should be replicated."

"Can't be replicated. There will never be anything like it. That's not the point."

"Which is."

"Which is: it didn't kill us. Kids aren't that fragile. What are you going to do, lock them in the house?"

It might or might not have been an oblique dig at Darren's childhood. Which, in point of fact, took place entirely in front of the television.

"Shelby thinks they're made of glass. I refuse to be that kind of parent."

"Yeah, about that." Darren drops his butt into an empty Sprite can. "What's the matter with Olivia?"

"Stomach, supposedly. Tomorrow, who knows?" Rich crushes a

beer can and pops open a fresh one. "It's always something. I think she's just imitating her mother, you want to know the truth. My wife is a fucking hypochondriac."

Wait, *what*? Rich Devlin admitting some sort of vulnerability, some aspect of his life not perfectly under control?

Darren lights another cigarette. His brother's marriage to Shelby has always confounded him. In school she'd been two years behind Darren, quiet, mousy, conspicuously Christian. In a normal-size high school, he'd never have noticed her at all. When his mother told him, a few years later, that Rich was engaged to Shelby Vance, he wondered if she'd made a mistake.

"It's my own goddamn fault for indulging her. Tearing down the farmhouse, for Christ's sake. What a mistake." A muscle pulses in Rich's jaw. "Pollution gives her migraines. Food additives. Power lines, you name it. She needs her own fucking planet. Mold, can you believe it?"

"Actually, it's a pretty common allergy."

Rich gives him a warning look.

"So—a brand-new house. No mold. Yeah, I get it." Darren hesitates. "This is kind of an obvious question, but: she can't live with mold, but she doesn't mind a gas well in her back yard?"

Rich says, "Here we go."

"All I'm saying is, you don't know what all they're pumping into the ground. I've done research." Restless in his father's house, Darren had spent Saturday afternoon on a computer at the Bakerton Public Library. "That is some seriously toxic shit."

"Toxic," Rich repeats.

The word hangs in the air, rich with subtext: *This from a guy who mainlined toxins. Who spent years injecting himself with heroin, or some random substance sold as heroin on the streets of Baltimore.*

Darren drags deeply on his cigarette. "There are like two hundred different chemicals in fracking fluid."

"Two hundred exactly."

"Okay, I made up the number. The actual number now escapes me."

Rich guffaws. "Don't talk to me about chemicals. It's a meaningless term. Everything is made of chemicals. If you eat an apple. If it's on the periodic table, it's a chemical."

"Oxygen, for example."

"Oxygen is a chemical."

Darren marvels at his certainty. It is conversational skill he himself will never master, the tone that invites no argument.

"Look, nothing's perfect. The point is, it's an opportunity. I'm not sitting around waiting for the mines to come back. Unlike some people."

"Seriously?" says Darren. "That's the dream?"

"They were good jobs," says Rich.

"Define *good*."

A long tense silence that seems made up of shorter sub-silences. Darren gropes for a new subject. He wishes he followed a sport. *How about those Pirates/Steelers/whatever the hockey team is called?* To fill the pauses, as men did.

Rain beats at the roof.

"How's work?" Darren asks.

"We're twenty percent over capacity—meth busts, mainly. Dregs of humanity. So I guess you could say business is booming."

Dregs of humanity. He'd use the same words, undoubtedly, to describe Darren's clients at Wellways. That Darren had actually *become*, for a time, the dregs of humanity is a fact neither mentions.

"So there's a lot of meth around here?"

"In *Bakerton*? No way, man. These guys are all from Philly or Pittsburgh."

"They get any kind of treatment in there?"

"There are meetings."

"No individual counseling? Cognitive/behavioral—"

"There are meetings."

Another clap of thunder.

"So you've got some vacation," Rich says. "You can stay and help Dad. I could use a break."

"Yeah, about that." Darren gropes for a way to explain it. To anyone else it would be obvious why he shouldn't work in a bar. "I'm an addict, Rich."

"Again?"

Rich looks genuinely alarmed, and Darren feels for a hideous moment the weight of his brother's concern. A pale shadow, probably, of the worry he's caused over the years, and yet it's enough to paralyze him with guilt.

"Not that," he says hurriedly. "I'm doing okay with that. It's just—I'll always be an addict, you know? It's a lifelong illness."

"So I hear. But you were never much of a drinker."

"That's true." A fact recently proven: he sat in the Commercial for more than an hour watching Gia Bernardi, and hadn't taken a drink.

"So what's the problem?"

Darren considers. Tending bar, while not ideal, doesn't seem particularly dangerous to his sobriety. Certainly it's safer than two idle months in Baltimore, where the precise high he still craves is a phone call away.

Also: Gia Bernardi.

"Sure," he says finally. "I could stay for a little while. You know, for Dad."

Rich smiles so broadly it's a little embarrassing. He claps a heavy hand on Darren's shoulder. "All right, man. That's great."

A click behind them, the side door opening. Shelby's head appears in the doorway. "Ugh," she says, waving away the cigarette smoke. "Darren, what am I going to do with you?"

"I am a lost soul."

"Come have some cake. Regular or decaf?"

"Regular."

The door clicks shut. Not a word for her husband, Darren notes; not even a smile. Rich stares at the floor.

"Did it just get cold in here?"

Rich shrugs. "She's on your side, buddy. Royally pissed at me about this gas thing. She was all for it—the money, anyway—until she got a look at that drill rig parked at Wally Fetterson's. I guess she thought they were just going to conjure it out of the ground."

"Too bad they can't," says Darren.

"Yeah, too bad. But the reality is, it's got to come from somewhere. Fuck it," Rich says, reaching for Darren's cigarettes.

"Oh ho."

"Shut up. The point is, what's the alternative? Send more kids to the Gulf, like I got sent? Or we could build more nuclear." He pronounces it *nucular*. "Though—let me guess—you don't like that either." He inhales deeply, then coughs. "Jesus Christ, menthols?"

"Nuclear is problematic," Darren admits, pronouncing it correctly. "But what about renewables? Wind, solar, hydroelectric?"

"How'd I know you were going to say that?" Rich exhales a long stream of smoke. "Yes, fine, renewables. Let's build a few windmills and sit around in the dark."

Truck noise, traffic, road construction, contamination . . .

HAVE WE HAD ENOUGH YET?
HAVE WE MADE A HUGE MISTAKE?

* If you signed a **gas lease** (or if you're thinking about it)
* If you're **worried** about your water
* If you're **sick and tired** of living in a gas patch

. . . YOU ARE NOT ALONE!

Join your friends and neighbors for an evening of
brainstorming and problem solving
with special guest, Dr. Lorne Trexler of Keystone
Waterways Coalition.
The future of our community is in our hands.

6.

The visitors' line is shortest on Mondays. Like every Monday, Rena dresses carefully: no jewelry, no hair clips, a cotton jog bra (underwires trip the metal detector) beneath her scrubs. Instead of a purse she carries a Ziploc bag with cash for the vending machine, coins and singles only, to buy Calvin potato chips and Snickers bars, the junky snacks she rationed when he was a child. Now, because there's nothing else she can give him, she treats him to this terrible food.

Calvin needs a haircut. Unshaven, he looks tired and dissipated. His chin bristles with a two-day beard.

The visit passes slowly. They all do. Rena asks what he is reading. They discuss the upcoming presidential election, and watch the TV bolted to the ceiling—tuned, always, to a court show, in which an irascible lady judge scolds plaintiffs from the bench.

The people are REAL! The cases are REAL! The rulings are FINAL!

Who chooses the program? The guards, probably. If Rena were in prison, it's the last thing she'd want to watch.

"I have my meeting tomorrow night," she tells Calvin. "About the gas drilling. I'm a little nervous." She'd been hesitant to call Professor Trexler, worried he wouldn't remember meeting her at Ronny's store. (He did.) Nervous that nobody would come to the meeting, or that everyone would, a roomful of strangers who knew too much about her, the defining reality of small-town life.

I've never done anything like this, she told him, as though it weren't obvious.

Don't worry. I have.

They spoke by phone nearly every day, Professor Trexler talking her through each step of the process: reserving the room, printing the posters, alerting the local newspaper. *It's a lot of work,* Rena marveled to Ronny Zimmerman. Having failed for years to engage her in his various causes—the antiwar protests, the hemp rallies—he seemed stunned by her sudden conversion. Still he took full credit for it, as though he'd baptized her himself.

Mack was, if anything, even more astonished. *You want to do what?* Night after night she'd listened, more or less patiently, when Rena came home from the hospital ranting like a lunatic. Steph Mulraney's sudden, violent illness; her eventual miscarriage. The bewilderment of her doctors; their frantic attempts—ultimately fruitless—to determine exactly what she'd been exposed to. Rena herself had spent hours on the phone with slippery PR flacks: at Stream Solutions, the drilling company; then at Dark Elephant, which owned it; then at Darco, which owned *it.* Eventually she'd reached an assistant to the scientific director at Bentonics Chemical, the manufacturer of Flow-Z.

Who told her, essentially, to go to hell.

Rena explains this to Calvin at some length, grateful to have something to talk about. She can tell by his face that he couldn't care less. "Wish me luck," she finishes, lamely.

"Good luck," he says, staring at the TV screen. "How's Mack?"

"Don't start."

Minutes tick away. The plaintiff is suing his estranged wife for four hundred dollars, the price of a tattoo she charged to his credit card. The visits pass slowly because Calvin refuses to discuss anything that matters. Still, Rena tries.

"Have you thought about November?" He'll need a job, a place to live. Staying at the farm is no longer an option, after last time:

twelve hundred dollars missing from the safe; the unexplained dis-
appearance of one of Mack's guns.

He tips his head forward and looks up at her with fierce eyebrows. He's done this all his life, since earliest childhood. Mack and
Rena have a name for it: *Calvin's stinkeye.*

"November," he repeats.

He'd been a late talker. His first-grade teacher noticed that he
rarely spoke in complete sentences. *I can,* he told Rena. *I just don't
want to.* The stinkeye spoke for him. There was never any doubt
when he was displeased.

"I think he'll be reelected," says Calvin.

"That's not what I mean."

"He'll need to make some cabinet appointments."

"I'm talking about your future," Rena says.

There is a knock at the door, the guard returned to fetch her son.
Shamefully, she is relieved.

Calvin gets to his feet. "Attorney general would be my first
choice, but I doubt they'll ask me. I'd settle for secretary of state."

Rena says, "See you next week."

"HE ASKED ABOUT YOU. He always does."

Mack and Rena are lying in bed: Rena knitting, Mack half
watching a fishing show on the Field and Stream channel.

Mack does not respond. She is drifting in and out of sleep. It
annoys her to do two things at once.

"Hello?" says Rena. "Anybody in there?"

Mack takes her hand under the covers. "Yep, I'm right here.
How's he doing?" she asks dutifully, as she does every Monday. To
her relief, Rena has stopped asking her to tag along. Mack's interactions with Calvin go badly. The problem, according to Rena, is
Mack's stubbornness.

"He's about the same. I tried to get him to talk about November,
but no luck. He needs to make a plan."

He can't come here. You know that. Mack doesn't need to say it. They've been through it all before. If Calvin were an addict she might have some sympathy. But he is just a businessman.

Mack's stubbornness isn't the problem. The problem is that Calvin takes after his father. Mack believes in breeding the way she believes in weather, in Rena's goodness. She believes in these things because she sees them every day. A good milker will give birth to good milkers. A bull that's ornery or skittish will pass those traits along.

Freddy Weems was an ornery bull.

Freddy Weems was a piece of shit.

Mack doesn't have moods, interior weather that shifts suddenly, dramatically, for invisible reasons. If she's sad or mad or frustrated, it's in response to external conditions: a sick animal, a leaking roof, a glitch in the milking line. Otherwise she is always the same.

External conditions, such as threats, intimidation, obscene phone calls. Such as late-night visits with no warning, Mack and Rena startled awake by an angry drunk pounding at the door.

Such as withholding child support.

Shooting into their pasture.

Pounding at their door shouting filth no child should hear.

Such as following Rena home from work.

Setting the toolshed on fire.

The suspicious death of Mack's dog.

For several years—for all of Calvin's childhood—Mack kept a .44 pistol in the bedside table, unless Freddy was in jail. Rena, who hated guns, understood that this was necessary. Men like Freddy Weems were what guns were for.

State prison in Ohio and West Virginia—for killing a woman while driving drunk, for stealing a motorcycle, for armed robbery.

Mack kept a pistol in the bedside table, until Freddy was killed by a cop in Morgantown.

Calvin was fourteen then, old enough to be told how his father had died. How exactly they phrased it, Mack can't recall. What she remembers is the boy's reaction. He turned to Rena and glowered, looking up through his eyebrows: Calvin's stinkeye. *I guess you're happy now.*

If anyone else spoke to Rena this way, Mack would clean his clock.

At seventeen Calvin committed his first felony. That summer Mack discovered, in a far corner of her back forty, three dozen healthy marijuana plants hidden behind a copse of trees. Three or four felonies ago.

She can't clean his clock because he is Rena's son.

We could've gone to prison, she told Rena. *We could've lost the farm.*

But we didn't, Rena said.

She has never apologized for Calvin, who'd produced and distributed drugs at Friend-Lea Acres, land farmed by Mackeys for six generations.

His first felony. At least, the first one they knew about.

Marijuana growing on Pop's farm, a thought that fills Mack with shame.

FOR THE FIRST TIME in whothefuckknows how long, Darren has a key to the house.

His dad gave it to him with little ceremony, as though it were simply a question of his own convenience: *I can't be here all the time to let you in.* Sparing them both—Darren saw this, and was grateful— the agony of a conversation they should have had years ago but whose relevance died with his mother. A conversation whose time was past.

What Dick didn't say (though Darren heard it anyway): *You belong here. I trust you. You are still my son.*

Now he sleeps in his childhood bed, smokes cigarettes on the back porch, showers in the familiar bathroom—avocado-colored

porcelain, unchanged since 1972. The house is in every way the
same, and yet, without his mother, feels foreign and cold. Darren
blames, in part, the absence of food smells. The kitchen goes completely unused. Dick eats meals at the Commercial, buys his morning coffee at Sheetz. In the freezer he stores batteries, fishing lures,
ice packs for his knee. It's not so different from the way Darren lives
in Baltimore, his trash full of take-out containers and Starbucks
cups. In this way only, he is exactly like his dad.

His dad moves around the house like a shadow, a precursor to
the ghost he will, in a few years, become. Dick's younger self—
gruff and irascible, barking orders—seems to have disappeared
entirely, leaving in its place this limping old man, frightened of
the future. To Darren he is barely recognizable, the son having
missed some vital transition, the tempering years in between. That
he likes the ghost better seems somehow shameful—as though
he'd wished this fate on his father, the creeping frailness, the years
ticking away.

The sad truth is that he loves his father mainly in Dick's absence.
Their interactions are polite, a little uncomfortable. Only later, alone
in the house, is Darren overcome by emotion, the artifacts of Dick's
old age—the reading glasses left on the kitchen counter, the plastic denture case on the bathroom sink—filling him with a terrible
tenderness.

Surprisingly, it's the Commercial that feels like home to him.
For years, in Group, he's listened to alcoholics pine for their favorite taverns. More than one has dissolved in tears. Now, at last, he
understands it. At a bar addiction is normalized, made to seem a
regular part of living: the warm light and familiar faces, friendship
or the illusion of it. Addicts are lonely creatures. His own addiction
had been a furtive thing, deeply solitary—swooning behind closed
doors, secret shame, private bliss. The isolation amplified his illness. Copping heroin on the streets of Baltimore, he was regularly

scared shitless; but later, in the luxurious solitude of a heroin dream, he could imagine himself a kind of desperado, a romantic outlaw. There was no one to contradict this version of events. High, Darren was whoever he wanted to be.

The illusions without which addiction would be impossible. The stories we tell ourselves.

Night after night, he and Gia close the bar together. He enjoys the sameness of these nights, the pleasant regularity of the petty chores, Gia racing circles around him emptying the ice traps, returning mugs and glasses to their shelves, swabbing counters and floors.

Jesus, what's the rush? he'll sometimes tease her. *Everybody's gone. I'm* not going to tip you.

I want to get the hell out of here, she'll say, giving him a shove. *Anyways, what do you care? Less work for you.*

Anyways. Everyone in Bakerton says it, but to Darren the word is pure Gia. He will feel, for a moment, filled up with her.

Serving drinks at the Commercial, he is conscious of enabling. When business is slow he watches the customers—men mostly, some raucously convivial, others staring dumbly at the TV screen. Undoubtedly some are addicts. And yet—compared with shooting heroin—drinking seems increasingly benign to him. He knows on some level that this is distorted thinking, his inner addict talking. That he's been in Bakerton far too long.

Each morning, after Dick has left for the Commercial, Darren hikes across town to the Bakerton Public Library and plugs in his laptop. At home, in Baltimore, it is never unplugged. Nor does it ever sit in his lap. It rests, *en permanence,* on a flimsy IKEA desk, the Berg or Borg or some such, its portability wasted. He has never joined the coffee-drinking masses at his neighborhood Starbucks, who assemble daily in order to ignore each other completely— humans of every age and description deafened by headphones, staring dumbly at their glowing screens. Each morning Darren studies them as he waits in line for his double espresso. Then he orders his coffee, sweetens generously, and leaves.

The truth is that he doesn't like to move his laptop. In his barren apartment it hums continuously. Evenings, weekends, he spends most hours in front of it. Ambidextrous, he mouses with his left hand and eats dinner with his right.

At his father's house, this isn't possible. There is no wireless signal, no wireless anything. Darren was unprepared for how profoundly this would affect him. With no access to the Internet he feels invisible, intangible, as though he has ceased to exist.

That morning, as usual, the library is empty. Like most buildings in town, it used to be something else. A restaurant, in this case: Keener's Diner, a teenage hangout where his mother had once worked as a waitress. Putting herself through college, young Sally Becker had one day served lunch to a sailor named Dick Devlin, home on break or vacation or whatever the navy calls it when they let you leave.

Darren remembers the story with a pang. His mother was prone to reminiscing in a way Dick isn't. If not for Sally, he'd know nothing at all about his parents.

He boots up his laptop and waits, studying the announcements on the bulletin board, which change with surprising frequency. Used snowblowers for sale, used building materials, used truck parts. All of Bakerton, it seems, is selling itself off for scrap.

Today a new flyer catches his eye.

Truck noise, traffic, road construction, contamination . . .

HAVE WE HAD ENOUGH YET?
HAVE WE MADE A HUGE MISTAKE?

"Darren Devlin?"

He turns.

"I thought that was you. The hair threw me a little."

"Mr. Radulski." Darren passes a hand over his head. "Wow, it's great to see you." He actually means it. Mr. Radulski had been his high school biology teacher. More than a teacher: he was the father teenage Darren would have chosen, if he'd had a choice.

"It's been a long time, kid. What are you up to these days? Last I heard you were at Johns Hopkins."

"Good memory." Darren grins, remembering that Mr. Radulski had written him a letter of recommendation. When Hopkins said yes, Mrs. Radulski had made a celebratory dinner, a cake with Darren's name on it. It seems so long ago.

"How could I forget? In all those years I had exactly one kid get into Johns Hopkins. Penn State, sure. Pitt if they're lucky. But you blew the curve."

Darren stands there, grinning like an idiot, dreading the next question.

"So what are you doing now? I remember you talking about going to medical school, way back when."

It's worse than Darren imagined: the kindness and goodwill, the palpable admiration and pride. "Well, I took kind of a U-turn."

"Nothing wrong with that. There's more money in research, I'd say. Drug development. Though what do I know?" he says humbly, waiting to be edified.

Darren swallows. "Actually, I switched majors. My degree"—he doesn't say *from community college*—"is in sociology."

Mr. Radulski's smile flickers. He has the sort of face that hides nothing. It's a terrible thing to watch, the disappointment and disbelief.

"I'm an addictions counselor."

In his eyes, a flash of comprehension. Then embarrassment, pity, concern. "Well, now. That must be interesting work."

"It is," says Darren, desperately cheerful. "I mean, it's not science, but I find it interesting. And—" He stops, unsure how to finish this thought. "You know, it's a job."

"Sure," Mr. Radulski says heartily. "There's more to life than work, God knows. How are things otherwise? Married? Kids?"

"Still single."

An awkward silence.

"Well, there's time for all that. Plenty of time." Mr. Radulski glances deliberately at his watch. "Darren, I should get going. Big day today. My daughter is getting married. You remember Leah."

He does. Leah had been a grade behind him, a plain, whole-some, congenitally happy girl determined, for unfathomable reasons, to make him her boyfriend. Though he found her boringly well adjusted, Darren had encouraged her, because Leah was his entry into the Radulski family. He'd spent countless evenings at their house, watching movies, lingering at the dinner table. Then he gave Leah a chaste kiss good night and went home to get high, alone in his room.

"Oh, wow." It should have occurred to him to ask about Leah. "That's—amazing." He grasps, too late, the tactlessness of this remark. "I mean, that's great news."

Mr. Radulski claps Darren's shoulder. "We're happy for them. He's a nice guy. A schoolteacher, like her dad."

"Wow," Darren says again. "Please give her my best."

"SMELL THIS." Shelby stands at the sink, washing the breakfast dishes. "It smells funny."

Rich finishes the last bite of scrambled egg and takes his plate to the sink. He's still in uniform—awake since yesterday, an overnight double. An insistent rain ticks at the kitchen windows. It's the kind of gray morning he hopes for after a night shift, ideal for sleep.

"Funny," he repeats. "Funny how?"

"Like chemicals. How should I know, Rich? It just smells—not clean."

Outside the noise kicks up, a rhythmic clanging. Rich leans over the sink, runs the water and sniffs. "I don't smell anything."

"You never smell anything."

It's true, of course: she's always complaining about odors imperceptible to him. He is married to a bloodhound.

"It's from the drilling. It has to be. Our water was fine before." She turns on the water and inhales deeply. "You need to talk to those guys."

"And say what? My wife smells something funny?"

Naturally—inevitably—he is thinking of the farmhouse. *It smells moldy,* Shelby complained and complained, until he finally gave in. Now he's raising his kids in a prefab tinderbox, one step above a trailer. For ten years he's been led around by Shelby's nose.

"The water is fine," he says.

"You're just being stubborn." Shelby rinses his plate and places it in the dishwasher. "Don't forget, you're picking up Braden tonight. His practice is over at seven-thirty."

"Tonight?" Rich feels for the scrap of paper in his pocket. *Honiger 8 yrs old 40K.* "I was going to meet that guy out in Somerset. Have a look at his Honiger. I guess I could take the kids along."

Shelby does not approve. "That's a long ride for Olivia."

"Oh. Right." His daughter is prone, famously, to carsickness. His truck still smells faintly of grape candy, from the time she vomited copiously on the floor, seat, and passenger door. "Can't you take them with you? Olivia, anyway."

"To my counseling appointment?" Shelby gives her signature twisted grimace. It calls to mind an old, unfunny comedian whose name Rich can't remember. An ugly little man with a bowl haircut, a frequent guest on the TV game shows of his childhood—*Match Game, The Hollywood Squares.*

"Forget it," he says. "I can go to Somerset tomorrow."

The comedian had seemed, always, a little drunk, if not mildly retarded. What the hell was his name? Rich's sister would know. Shelby, of course, is too young to remember, something he hadn't considered when he married a girl twelve years younger.

"Buddy Hackett," he says aloud.

"What are you talking about?"

"Never mind." Buddy Hackett isn't important; Buddy Hackett doesn't matter at all. And yet, in some way Rich can't make sense of, he feels suddenly lonely. It's as though his childhood never happened, because Shelby wasn't there to witness it.

"Pastor Jess says I need to make time for myself."

Rich keeps his mouth shut, having learned that Pastor Jess is a subject best avoided. She has suggested, according to Shelby, that Rich come along for a joint session, an ordeal he has so far escaped. The whole idea of counseling unnerves him. What exactly Shelby talks about for a solid hour each week, what secrets of their marriage she has confided to the preacher, he truly doesn't want to know. And yet he can't object, because the counseling is free and because Shelby has the kids all day, every day. He can't, without seeming like an asshole, complain about babysitting one night a week.

Again the grimace: his wife is Buddy Hackett in a blond wig.

"Are you even listening?" Shelby says.

"All right, fine. I'll pick up Braden." He rises. "I need some sleep."

"Try the earplugs."

"I don't need any goddamned earplugs."

The master bedroom is shaded at all hours, north-facing. Rich chose it with night shifts in mind. He didn't count on having a gas rig two hundred yards away, lit day and night with klieg lights. Even with the curtains drawn the room is shockingly bright.

He closes his eyes and thinks deliberately of nothing.

Outside, a terrific thrumming kicks up.

He has always been a gifted sleeper, a talent that came in handy in the navy: the ability to sleep anytime, anywhere, the sailor's greatest survival skill. But civilian life has softened him. He squeezes his eyes shut and commands himself: *Sleep, goddamnit. Sleep.*

The outside noise intensifies, a mechanized roar like a tropical storm.

He puts in the earplugs. It feels as though he's cramming chewing gum into his ears. Shelby wears them every night, to put up with his snoring. How does she fucking stand it?

He takes the plugs out of his ears.

Pissed, he wanders the house for half an hour, looking for a place to sleep. The kids' rooms have the same problem: the engine noise, the blinding light. Finally he collapses, exhausted, on Pap's old couch, which Shelby had banished to the basement because of dust mites. He sleeps for maybe ten minutes. Then the clanging starts again.

Defeated, he goes out to the deck. The rain has stopped. That the noise isn't any louder outside is a sad testament to the flimsiness of the house.

He looks out over his back yard, what's left of it. With the forest gone, the property looks smaller than sixty acres, stripped and shrunken like a dog in the bath. Behind the house, the crew left a single patch of grass, twenty foot square. Beyond lies a vast expanse of bare earth, dry and cocoa-colored, enclosed with chain-link fence. A bleak view, but not half as bad as what lies over the hill.

The clanging slows and deepens.

Over the hill, mercifully out of view, sit the containment pond and concrete drill pad—surrounded, depending on the day, by a dozen or more trucks. Always there are two construction trailers, one or two tankers.

Now the noise intensifies. Beneath the high-pitched whine is a deeper grinding, some unlubricated-sounding mechanical gyration.

A ray of sunlight cuts through the clouds. The new access road bisects the field like a surgical scar.

AT MIDDAY THE COMMERCIAL is halfway bustling. In the dining room every table is occupied, gas people finishing their lunches. The bar side is empty except for a few locals. Rich's neighbor Wally Fetterson watches NASCAR highlights on TV. Nick Blick and Booby

Marstellar chalk their pool cues like gentlemen of leisure, two middle-aged Duanes with nothing better to do.

"Devlin," Booby calls. "How you been, man?"

"I'm good, Boob." Rich takes a seat next to Wally and watches Darren pull an Iron City. It startles him, still, to see his brother behind the bar.

Darren gives him a wave. "What are you doing here? Shouldn't you be home sleeping?"

"Don't get me started. Where's Dad?"

"Funeral home," says Darren. "Some veteran thing."

Something in the way he says it, a kind of dismissiveness, makes Rich want to pop him one. Not that he's any kind of flag waver. His Gulf War service was so brief, so unexceptional, that he routinely skips the annual Memorial Day parade, feeling like an impostor next to the kids back from Afghanistan and Iraq. After 2003, the ceremony at the War Memorial became a special kind of humiliation, standing at attention as veterans took turns at the podium: Second World War, Korea, Vietnam. In the past, Rich himself had gone to the podium to read a single sentence—*The Persian Gulf War had no local casualties.* A victory lap, the bragging of a generation: on their watch, American warfare had been perfected, the air offense so precisely targeted, so diabolically efficient, that no blood had been spilled. Now Rich's war—officially renamed the First Gulf War—is all but forgotten. Meeting young vets, guys just back from deployment, he feels a strange mix of emotions: relief that he got out when he did; regret, for the same reason. More than anything else, a lingering and powerful shame.

There is a crack of pool balls, Nick's trademark fast break. Booby lets out a holler. Darren's eyes stray to the back of the room. "Jesus, guys, take it easy. Who are those yahoos?"

"Oh, that's just Nick and Booby. You remember them." Then again, maybe Darren doesn't. A toddler the summer of Three

Duanes, he may have no recollection of Rich's brief infatuation with the guitar. As often happens around his brother, Rich feels his age.

Behind him, Gia Bernardi races out of the kitchen with a platter, generating an actual breeze. She's always racing around the bar, as though waitressing were an athletic event. She sets a hamburger in front of Wally Fetterson, her skirt riding up the back of her thighs.

"That looks good," says Wally, who isn't looking at the hamburger.

"Behave yourself." Gia turns her back to Wally and gives Darren a shove, like a bratty kid sister. "*Village of the Damned.* That was the title."

"Holy shit, you're right. I owe you a sixer." Darren grins like an idiot. Gia gives him another shove, her hand lingering on his chest.

It's been a long time, years, since Rich saw his brother smile. He ought to be happy for Darren, and yet their laughter grates on him. Just fuck her and get it over with, he thinks. Everyone else has.

He nods toward Wally Fetterson. "How you been, man?"

"Can't complain." Wally tears into his sandwich. The Fettersons are among the town's new millionaires, or so everyone believes. After his well came in, Wally took an early retirement from the post office. Now he tools around town in a brand-new Humvee. He and Lois are known for extravagant summer barbecues—last year, a pig roast—around their new in-ground swimming pool.

Another hoot from the back of the room. Nick and Booby circle the pool table—joined, to Rich's surprise, by the ugly punk he's seen here before: Gia's friend from the parking lot, the skinhead with all the tattoos.

"I hear they're drilling you, finally. Lois saw Shelby at church." Wally drinks deeply. "How you holding up with the noise?"

"It's pretty loud," Rich says.

"Trust me, you'll forget all about it when those checks start coming in." Wally cups a hand to his ear and pantomimes. "Noise?

What noise?" He's gained weight, his face round as a Frisbee, his nose and cheeks rosy. One P.M., and he's a drunken Santa Claus.

"I was out Number Twelve Road the other day," he tells Rich. "On the ATV. There's orange flags all over Swedetown. I guess Randy Thibodeaux is next."

"*Thibodeaux?*"

"I hear he got a thousand an acre."

They eye each other in silent calculation. Neither will ask the question neither wants to answer. *How much did you get?* The truth is unspeakable: an inbred hillbilly like Randy Thibodeaux held out for a thousand dollars an acre. Rich Devlin had settled for twenty-five.

"We need to have you over for a barbecue," Wally says through a mouthful of hamburger. "The kids can swim in the pool."

"Sure. That sounds great." Rich lowers his voice. "You haven't had any problems with your water, have you?"

Wally stiffens. "There's nothing wrong with it. Hell, we swim in it all the time."

"Not now," Rich says. "I'm sure it's fine now. But how about back when they drilled you? Shelby thinks ours has a weird smell."

"I wouldn't worry too much," says Wally, licking ketchup off his fingers. "I was a kid when your pap dug that well. Prolly time for a new one."

"Maybe so," Rich says.

Down the bar, Gia reaches into Darren's shirt pocket and takes out a pack of cigarettes. She leans close and whispers in his ear, something that makes him laugh, then heads out the back door. A moment later the skinhead goes out the front. Darren seems not to notice. He is bent over the register, still wearing a moronic grin.

Rich gets to his feet. "I've got to get going. I'm babysitting tonight." He nods toward the door. "Darren, man. You know that guy?"

Darren looks up. "What guy?"

"Gia's boyfriend."

"They're just friends," Darren says.

Rich thinks of the night he surprised them in the parking lot, Gia popping out from beneath the guy's dashboard, squinting in the headlights. He's replayed the memory so often it's a little thread-bare.

"Just friends. Says who?"

"Says Gia."

Rich eyes him with pity. His little brother is no match for the Gia Bernardis of the world. In her practiced hands he is helpless as a child.

Darren leans in confidentially. "So what's this about your water? Sorry. I couldn't help overhearing." The raised eyebrow, the smug half-smile. Again Rich wants to pop him one.

"My water is fine," he says.

"That's good. Though I should probably tell you, there have been documented cases of contamination . . ."

Rich stares at a point across the room as, in Persian or Arabic, his brother talks and talks. A moment later Gia returns through the front door. The skinhead, a few paces behind her, heads directly for the john.

"There are people out west who can set their tap water on fire," says Darren. "I'm dead serious."

Gia slips behind the bar, tugging at her skirt.

Be careful, man, Rich would say to anyone but Darren. But his brother, as always, has all the answers. He deserves whatever he gets.

7.

They meet in the basement of the Bakerton Public Library. The small room is crowded, loud with chatter. Neighbors call greetings to one another. They eat Rena's oatmeal cookies and drink coffee from styrofoam cups.

You could come with me, she'd told Mack, knowing it would never happen; knowing better than anyone Mack's horror of attracting attention, her outsize fear of crowds. Fifty years old, and self-conscious as a teenager. In any social situation, Mack froze like a deer.

At five after seven Rena takes the podium. Lorne Trexler stands slightly behind her, waiting to be introduced. On tiptoe, she speaks into the microphone. "Thanks for coming, everyone." Her knees are actually shaking.

"Speak up, honey," someone yells.

Rena checks the microphone and sees that it isn't turned on. She turns it on.

"That's better. Now can everyone hear me?" There is a chorus of no's from the back of the room. She leans closer to the microphone, which makes a humming noise. "The purpose of this meeting is to talk about our experiences with gas drilling, positive and negative."

From the back of the room, a hoot.

"Okay, not so much positive. If they were positive, you probably wouldn't be here." She is making a mess of this; she is.

Lorne Trexler reaches around her to adjust the microphone. "Relax," he whispers. "They're just your neighbors."

It's exactly the right thing to say. Rena picks out a janitor from the hospital, her second-grade teacher, Peachy Rouse from down the hill.

"Anyways, you didn't come to hear me," she says, more calmly. "Dr. Trexler is a geologist with a special interest in the Marcellus Shale. He is co-chairman of the Geology Department at Stirling College and a founding member of the Keystone Waterways Coalition. He's here to talk to us about what they're doing to our land, and what we can do about it."

She takes a seat in the first row as Trexler adjusts the microphone. A lock of hair falls over his brow.

Lorne Trexler is obsessed—this is clear from the start—with water. "Fracking isn't good for our land. It isn't good—you already know this—for our quality of life. But what it does to our water is truly criminal. So let's start there."

Pennsylvania, he explains, has water everywhere, eighty thousand miles of streams and rivers. "We have so much water that we take it for granted. Out west—they've fracked the hell out of Colorado and Wyoming—folks pay attention to water, because they have to. You mess with their water, and people get mad." He is an effortless talker, relaxed and charming. He talks the way sprinters run and dancers dance, an elite athlete. He talks as though he was born to talk.

At the back of the room, the door swings open. "Come on in," he calls. "We're just getting started."

Heads turn as the latecomer, Shelby Devlin, creeps in on tiptoe, blushing violently. *Sorry,* she mouths. She is dressed for business: high heels, a skirt and jacket. The rest of the crowd wears gender-neutral shorts and T-shirts, blue jeans, flannel shirts.

"Welcome. We're glad to see you. Somebody find her a seat."

Arvis Kipler slips out the back door and returns with a folding chair.

Unfazed by the interruption, Trexler explains the process of hydraulic fracturing, a million gallons of water pumped into the ground at unimaginably high pressure—"enough to peel the paint off a car"—to break up the underground rock.

"Also—and this is important—fracking fluid isn't just water. It's mixed with sand and whatever chemical cocktail they think is going to work. Which chemicals exactly, we have no idea, because the gas companies won't tell us. Rena, is there something you want to say about that?"

It is, of course, the entire reason she organized the meeting. She gets to her feet, her stomach churning.

"We had a situation recently, in the Emergency Room at Miners'. Some fluid was spilled at a drill site, and a worker came into the ER covered head to toe in the stuff. He's fine, thank goodness, but the nurse who treated him ended up in Intensive Care." The grim details of the story—Steph Mulraney's spiking fever, her sudden contractions—she doesn't go into. She doesn't need to. All of Bakerton already knows. "We tried to find out what exactly she was exposed to, but the companies wouldn't tell us anything. They acted like it was none of our business."

She takes her seat.

"The industry claims these are trade secrets, like the recipe for Coca-Cola," Trexler continues. "They say it will destroy their competitive advantage, if they tell us what kind of poison they're pumping into our land. Of course, if you're a first responder, you're expected to treat their injured workers, no questions asked, anytime there's an accident. Which—trust me—happens *all the time.*"

He talks about the problem of flowback, the uncountable gallons of wastewater hauled—in immense tanker trucks marked PRODUCED WATER—to ordinary sewage treatment plants. "Sewage treatment plants use disinfectants to kill bacteria. The disinfectants react with bromides in the frackwater and give you brominated trihalomethanes, which are known carcinogens. You know what that means, right? They cause cancer. And they're in your rivers and streams."

There is a murmur at the back of the room.

"You think I'm kidding? A few years ago there was a big discharge into the Monongahela. That's where half of Pittsburgh gets its drinking water."

"That's *legal*?" says Rena—forgetting, for the moment, that an audience is present. It's as if Lorne Trexler is speaking to her alone.

And, for a moment, he does: "Rena, I'm glad you asked. In 2005, Congress approved something called the Halliburton Loophole. Anybody recognize that name? Halliburton?" He smiles grimly.

"Anyway. The bill exempts fracking fluid from the Clean Water Act. This is the shell game they're playing. You've seen those billboards, right? *Clean Energy for America's Future*? The industry wants you to believe that natural gas is better for the environment than coal or oil. And it is, on paper. But when you factor in all the emissions from thousands of truck trips, the methane that's vented or lost from gas lines—"

He goes on this way for nearly an hour. At first Rena takes diligent notes: names of congressmen, senators, pieces of legislation. After a while she simply watches Lorne Trexler, his floppy hair and lively dark eyes, his wrists turning in the cuffs of his denim shirt. She has never heard a man talk so much. Terseness, in Bakerton, is a masculine virtue. The local men—farmers, ex-miners—seem congenitally silent, and Mack is no different. Rena has taken to playing the radio at suppertime—*Open Mike*, the local call-in show—just to hear another voice.

In this way and others, Mack is entirely too much like a man.

"Questions?" says Trexler. Immediately a dozen hands shoot into the air. "One at a time. Everyone will get a chance to speak."

The complaints are many and elaborate, though most are not actually environmental. Crowding is discussed, lines at the gas pumps, the shortage of downtown parking spaces. The massive tanker that ran out of gas on Drake Highway, tying up traffic for hours. The smaller truck, hauling produced water, that ran over the Marstellars' dog.

A man gets to his feet—Davis Eickmeier, who runs Dickey's Dairy. "What I want to know is, what are them explosions I'm hearing? Out Deer Run somewheres. Scaring the hell out of my cows."

The same had happened at Friend-Lea Acres. For a full week the milking schedule was disrupted. Mack came back from the barn swearing like a soldier.

"That's seismic testing. They bore holes in the ground and blast them with dynamite to figure out where the deposits are." Trexler points to another raised hand, and Rena remembers that he is a teacher.

"My back yard looks like the Grand Canyon," says Arvis Kipler. "They must of carted away a couple tons of dirt. I was down Johnstown visiting my daughter. I come back and half the yard is gone."

"Nice, right?" Trexler nods energetically. "And it's all perfectly legal. If you signed a lease and didn't read the fine print, the company might have the right to build roads and pipelines on your property, or take water from your pond or inject wastewater into your well. They don't even have to tell you they're doing it. And, of course, they won't be paying you anything extra." He points to someone at the back of the room.

Shelby Devlin gets to her feet. "I have a question." A quaver in her voice; she seems ready to cry or faint.

"Speak up," a man yells from across the room.

"Sorry. I'm a little nervous." She takes a deep breath. "What you said about the water. Ever since they drilled us, ours has a funny smell. My husband says it's nothing, but I'm worried about my little girl."

"What's the matter with her?" Trexler says.

"Her stomach, mostly. I thought it was food allergies, but her doctor says no." Shelby rattles off a list of symptoms, relaxing visibly, relieved to be on familiar ground. "I've tried everything. Ask Rena. The doctors and nurses are sick of seeing us."

Chicken Little, Rena thinks. *The sky is falling.* Steph had laughed about it on her last day in the ER.

"Stomach issues aren't typical. But let me do some research." Trexler scribbles on a notepad. "What about breathing problems? That's usually what we see in cases of methane contamination."

"She has asthma," Shelby says.

Trexler's face lights. "There's a known connection between asthma and methane migration." His enthusiasm is unsettling. Rena thinks of Steph, still out on sick leave, the lost baby girl she'd already named.

"I knew it!" Shelby says.

"This is potentially helpful. Risks to human health. The DEP pays attention to that kind of thing." More scribbling. "Come talk to me after the meeting. We have a lot of work to do."

After three full hours the meeting adjourns. Rena and Trexler perch on the table at the front of the room, watching the crowd file out.

"I'm sorry to keep you so late," say Rena. "I wasn't expecting so many questions. The whole laundry list of complaints. The Marstellars' dog."

"Jesus, the dog! It's like a country-western song gone bad."

"It's my fault. Those stupid flyers! I was asking for it."

"Don't be sorry. People need to hear each other's experiences. It's the first step in organizing any kind of collective action. People need to understand that they're not alone." He gives her shoulder a squeeze. "You did a great thing tonight."

Is he flirting with her? She has no recollection of how men flirt.

"I wish I could clone you. I'd send a Rena Koval to every gas patch town in Pennsylvania."

Of course he's flirting with her. Rena feels a slight buzzing in her ears. She can still feel his hand on her shoulder. It's disappointing when Shelby Devlin approaches, and also a relief.

"Here's the lady of the hour. Have a seat," says Trexler, pulling up a chair. "Thanks for speaking up."

"I wasn't going to, but Rena's my neighbor." Shelby is flushed, her eyes very bright. "She already knows Olivia, so, you know, that made it easier."

"How is she feeling?" says Rena. "Is the Reglan helping?"

"Hard to say." Shelby leans forward in her chair. "Every once in a while she has a good day, but then something makes her sick. I can't figure it out."

"We need to get your water tested." Trexler takes, from his back pocket, a worn business card. "These guys are trustworthy. They're based in Pittsburgh, but they might be willing to come out here. If not, let me know and we'll figure out Plan B." He scrawls a number on the back of the card. "That's my cell. Any problems, give me a call."

"Can't I just call Rena?"

"Sure, if that's easier." Trexler barely pauses for a breath. "In the meantime, we need to get Olivia in front of a doctor." He writes another number on the card. "This is my friend Ravi Ghosh at Pitt. Environmental medicine is his specialty. Tell him I sent you."

"*Pittsburgh?*" Shelby looks horrified. "How am I going to get her to *Pittsburgh?*"

"It's not Afghanistan."

"I can drive you," Rena says.

"You'd do that?" Shelby's fervor is nearly comical, her outsize gratitude, as though Rena has offered an organ for transplant.

"Sure," Rena says.

Shelby gets to her feet. "Okay, then. I need to get going. Rich is babysitting. He's probably wondering what happened to me."

RENA AND TREXLER SIT IN A CORNER BOOTH at the Pick and Shovel, the dining room closed now, the lights dim. On the table between them is what's left of their dinner—a single slice of pizza, a half-empty pitcher of beer. Hank Williams on the jukebox: *Why don't you mind your own business.* Hank the gaunt cowboy who was never young and never got old, who died drunk at twenty-nine but hasn't stopped singing, preserved like a scarab in his premature middle age.

"This place is great." Trexler eyes the junk hanging on the wall—miners' helmets and headlamps from different eras, tin lunch buckets, actual pickaxes and shovels.

"It's been here forever. My whole life, anyway. I guess you don't get this kind of thing in the city."

"Stirling is a pretty small town."

"I thought you lived in Pittsburgh."

"Not officially. But when I'm not teaching, I get the hell out of Stirling. This summer I'm basically living out of my car." His knee bounces under the table. He's the sort of person who can't sit still. "I go where I'm needed. All over the state, communities are organizing. What you did tonight, that kind of grassroots effort, is going to turn the tide. Shelby Devlin is a godsend. The DEP doesn't care about our rivers, but even those idiots can't ignore a sick kid."

Are there other men who talk this much?

"I was surprised to see her," says Rena. "Her husband was one of the neighbors bugging us to sign a lease. Are you going to eat that?" She takes the last slice of pizza. "We were the last holdouts on the Dutch Road. We pissed off a lot of people. And it was all for nothing, because they're drilling anyway. We're surrounded. It's happening so fast."

Why don't you mind your own business.

"That's no accident," says Trexler. "That's exactly what the industry wants. The faster they drill, the less oversight they have to contend with. The DEP is pathetically understaffed, and the people they have aren't very good. The gas companies can afford to hire the best and brightest. Some of my most talented students have gone over to the dark side. There was one girl in particular—" His voice trails off. For the first time, he seems at a loss for words.

"What happened to her?" Rena says.

"Last I heard she was a consultant. They're all consultants. The dirty truth is, there would be no fracking if scientists didn't cooperate. They need geologists to tell them where to drill." He pushes away his plate. "Enough about that. I'm starting to depress myself. Tell me about your farm. You grew up there?"

"Mack did. It's been in their family for six generations. I'd hate to be the ones to drop the ball."

"Mack is your husband?"

She hesitates only a second. "Yes."

The lie she can never take back. And yet it seems, in that moment, that *husband* is as good a word as any. The English language has no actual word for what Mack is to her.

"That's too bad." Trexler gives her his slow smile. "Sorry. Did I say that out loud?"

How everything can change in an instant.

He reaches across the table, briefly touches her hand. "I'm making you uncomfortable."

"No. Well, a little, but that's okay."

She is sorry when he takes his hand away.

It's been a long time, years, since she felt drawn to a man, which makes things simpler. By the time they're Rena's age, Bakerton men are physically unappealing; and motherhood has made it difficult—impossible, really—to be attracted to a boy. But Lorne Trexler is her own age, older maybe, and still handsome. He moves like a young man—lean, impatient, with conspicuous grace.

"Sorry. I'm acting like a teenager. You were saying." Again the slow smile. "Something about a farm?"

Once, years ago, Ronny Zimmerman had asked her: *Have you always been gay?* It was at the time—and would be now—an unanswerable question. The truth is both simpler and stranger: she has never been attracted to another woman. Never been attracted to a woman at all, unless you count Mack, and Rena doesn't. Mack is a man to her, and a man to herself.

When Calvin was small she tried to explain it: *Sometimes you just meet a person.* She has only one way of loving. Before Mack, she'd loved men—had loved Freddy Weems—in exactly the same way.

"Yeah, the farm. It's kind of a high-wire act," she says, recovering herself. "We've had a few close calls. There was one bad year, back in the nineties. Calf scours. Not while we're eating," she says, seeing his frown. "Going organic saved us. Though I don't see how we can keep it up, if our cows are grazing in a gas patch."

"I won't let that happen."

There is a silence.

"Organic or not, it's a hard life, and we're not getting any younger." Rena chews thoughtfully. The cold pizza is a little greasy, the cheese gone waxy. "I mean, what happens when there are no more Mackeys? We're the end of the line."

Trexler grins. "That seems like poor planning on your part. I thought all you farmers had a dozen kids."

"I have a son," Rena says, "from a prior relationship. But Calvin isn't cut out for farming." The words come haltingly. She's out of the habit of talking about him. She and Mack avoid the subject, which is fraught with unspeakable truths.

That Mack will never forgive him.

That Rena will never stop.

"Is he in school?" Trexler asks.

"He dropped out." *Of high school,* she does not add. Her face is hot with shame.

"Well, not everybody has to go to college."

"I didn't," she admits, "and I've always regretted it. Nursing school isn't the same."

She is talking too much.

"Calvin was a bright kid. He loved to read and draw. I wanted him to go." Having said his name, she can't seem to stop saying it. It's as though she's conducting a séance, conjuring forth an earlier Calvin, the small boy who needed her, the brooding teenager full of potential. Calling him back from the beyond.

"He didn't want to?"

"No. And maybe he was right. Even with an education, there's nothing around here for young people to do. No, thank you." A hand over her glass to keep him from refilling it. "When I was a kid it was different. My dad worked at Baker Twelve—a huge mine, eight hundred jobs, all union. Now there's only strip mining. Part-time, no benefits. And you have maybe five guys on a crew."

Because he asks, she talks about Calvin's father. "I met him at the Firemen's Festival. That's a big deal around here. I was sixteen. He was twenty-three, and he had ID. I needed someone to buy me a beer."

Trexler grins. "That's when the magic happened."

"He was a volunteer fireman. He had a car and a mustache."

"Marriages have been founded on less. Not good marriages. What kind of car?"

"Even back then I couldn't have told you. It was the fact that he had one. The adultness."

"Plus the mustache," says Trexler.

"See, you do understand."

She could talk to him all night.

"And then what? He courted you. Took you dancing."

"He took me to watch him shoot bottles at the dump."

"To impress you," says Trexler.

"He was a pretty good shot."

The pleasures of confession, a memory from childhood: the all-knowing priest behind the curtain, absolving her of all she is and all she's done. Face-to-face with a near stranger, Rena tells a story she hasn't told in years. Halfway through her senior year in high school, she outgrew her school uniform and found an old one in her sister's closet, her sister who wore a size ten.

"I knew a girl who'd done it, but she was bigger to begin with. I couldn't really hide it. I don't think I fooled anyone." She changes her mind and refills her glass. "I wore a maternity dress to graduation. I sat in the audience with my mother, because they wouldn't let me graduate. They wouldn't even read my name. I got my diploma in the mail."

Trexler's jaw drops open in cartoon amazement. "They wouldn't *let* you? I'm pretty sure that's illegal."

"For a public school, maybe. This was Our Mother of Sorrows."

"It was called that."

"For good reason. The sorriest part was making me sit through the ceremony. I was required to go. A parent today wouldn't tolerate that," she points out. "A parent today would raise holy hell."

"Yours didn't?"

"Are you kidding? My mother felt sorry for me, but basically she agreed with them. Because, you know, I'd brought it on myself."

"So you went to graduation undercover," says Trexler. "In plain clothes, as they used to say. Do cops still wear plain clothes?"

"Because how would it look, six pregnant girls waddling across the stage, getting their diplomas from Our Mother of Sorrows?"

"*Six?*"

"In a class of two hundred. Which, as a percentage, averages out to not good. Actually, there should have been eight. The other two dropped out before graduation."

"This was what year?"

"Seventy-five."

"So you had options."

It's true, of course: she could have borrowed the money from someone, begged a ride to Altoona to catch the bus to Pittsburgh. She hadn't even considered it. To her young self, abortion had been unthinkable in the most literal way. Her mind couldn't hold such a thought.

"Did I? It didn't seem that way."

Her mother would never have forgiven her, her mother who wore, on the collar of her winter coat, an embroidered rose the size of a quarter. The roses were sold in the church vestibule, a fund-raiser for the Legion of Mary. Each January they hired a bus to Washington to join in the March for Life.

"What about the fireman?" says Trexler. "The fireman is strangely absent from this story."

"We were supposed to get married. It didn't work out."

(The time he locked her in the apartment until her face healed.)

"But he was happy about the baby?"

"Sure. He liked to brag how I got pregnant the first time we did it. It wasn't true, but it was a good story."

It's still a good story. The story is in the editing, in what you don't say: that Rena's pregnant body made Freddy inexplicably angry. That he made her do things she no longer wanted to do, and perhaps never had. He liked to screw in public places—in the woods, behind the ball field. He liked it precisely because Rena hated it. Her misery excited him—her mortification and discomfort, her terror of being caught.

He made her talk to him. *Say it. Say, I am a filthy little whore.*

Rena said, *I am a filthy little whore.*

Saying the words was like giving him permission: she was already so dirty she couldn't be made dirtier, so whatever he did to her was her own fault. Of course, she has never told anyone this.

In her second trimester he broke her nose.

"Anyways, it turned out all right," she adds—as she is supposed to, as she must, and in a way it's true. She loves Calvin more than her own life. Her decision was not unselfish; she had chosen the lesser anguish. Understanding, even then, that regret was inevitable; that either way, a life would be lost.

There's more, much more, she could say. How Freddy, dead twenty-three years, still appears in her dreams; how Mack seemed, for a minute, the answer to a riddle: Rena needed protection. Any man strong enough to protect her was not to be trusted. Mack, Rena, and Freddy. It's startling, now, to think how young they all were.

Behind her the barman begins stacking chairs on tables.

"I think he's trying to tell us something," Trexler says.

The parking lot is empty except for her truck and his Prius. A sultry summer night, redolent of cut grass, humid from the afternoon's rain. He walks her to her car, his hand at her back. She is aware of his parameters, the dimensions of his body. He is shorter than Mack, his shoulders narrower. Rena's eyes are level with his chin.

"Thanks for coming all the way out here," she says, to fill the silence. "I don't know how to thank you."

Trexler stares over her shoulder. "My God, will you look at that?"

"They're lightning bugs." It's not the sort of thing she expects a grown man to notice. Long ago, when Calvin was small, he'd amused himself for hours trying to catch them in jelly jars.

"I know what they are. I've just never seen quite so many. You could light a small city. Listen," he says. "Is that water?"

"Carbon Creek runs out this way."

How it happens isn't entirely clear, but a moment later they are crossing the parking lot, walking hand in hand into the woods.

The ground is a little muddy. Rena steps carefully, worried about her shoes. A breeze kicks up, rattling the wet leaves. A shower of cold raindrops shocks her arms and neck.

Trexler charges across a rusted footbridge, nearly hidden among the trees. Twenty feet down, at the foot of a steep embankment, Carbon Creek roars like a rushing river, echoing through the concrete pipe that carries it beneath the road.

They stand in the middle of the bridge. Night sounds: frogs, crickets, a lone car rolling down Number Six Road. The forest is alive with random pinpricks of light.

"Astounding," says Trexler. "But I guess you see this all the time."

A mosquito whines near her ear.

"Yes and no," she says, slapping it away. "You kind of stop looking." She drives down Number Six Road every day, and never once has she noticed this footbridge. It's the fundamental problem of a life lived in one place: sooner or later, everything becomes invisible.

The sky flickers with electrical misfires.

he criminal, the terrorist, the predator, gravitates naturally to the dark.

Eighty yards north of the Amway store, just behind the tree line, Chief Carnicella crouches low. Over his camo pants and jacket, he wears a Defender IV Tyvek security vest and a Gen II Night Vision Monocular, helmet-mounted. His patrol rifle lies at his side.

The ability to see in the dark delivers a superhuman-like feeling of invincibility.

The Amway parking lot is dimly lit, a single bulb trained in exactly the wrong direction, illuminating a giant Dumpster near the back door. Twenty yards away, two fertilizer tanks hold enough anhydrous ammonia to make a mountain of methamphetamine, enough to get all of Bakerton high and keep it that way for a month.

The tanks sit in darkness, unlabeled; but the meth heads aren't fooled. Last week he found the smaller tank fitted with a black hose and tape. Someone, between the hours of 6:00 P.M. and midnight, had siphoned off five gallons. If he'd arrived just a few hours earlier, an arrest might have been made.

The meth heads are smarter than he once gave them credit for. The chief's approach, at first, was sloppy: he kept watch from the comfort of his vehicle. Now he parks unobtrusively a quarter mile down the road. He is careful to vary the time and day; his current domestic situation affords him ultimate flexibility. If he were still married, overnight stakeouts would be impossible. Terri had never taken his career seriously.

The Defender vest is a little tight.

The stakeouts haven't, so far, yielded any actual arrests. Still, it's a better use of his time than staring at the TV in his empty trailer. This was his thinking when he canceled the satellite dish. Without the dish he gets two and a half channels, so TV no longer tempts him. After supper he plays the radio and pedals his old Exercycle and studies catalogs.

Technology that used to be available only to the military is now within the grasp of law enforcement, or any non-felonious U.S. citizen!

The money he saved on the dish went toward a Gen II NVD—a clear improvement over his old gear, a clunky Starlight Scope, Vietnam era, that Cob Krug had sold him for cheap. He paid for the Gen II himself, two grand out of his own pocket. The town has no budget for NVDs, no budget for anything. The budget barely covers the chief's paltry salary and the part-time secretary he shares with the Sewer Authority.

In bigger towns there is money for enforcement. In Allegheny County two deputies caught a thief a quarter mile from a feed store, with a scuba tank full of anhydrous. The arrest made the local news, the deputies—kids really, half the chief's age—interviewed by a sexy blond reporter. Watching, the chief was filled with longing, frustration, anger, and resolve.

The meth heads—the chief knows this—are better equipped than he is. In addition to the scuba tank, the Allegheny deputies confiscated a police scanner from the vehicle. Their perps wore camo and NVDs—not a crappy Gen II like the chief's, but the NightSniper 900 thermal sight.

Thermal technology is the wave of the future! End your dependence on available light.

The NightSniper detects body heat—any living thing, a person or animal, will show up as a ghostly silhouette, glowing white. With the

NightSniper you can see in absolute darkness. You can see through rain, snow, fog, and smoke. Its color display shows differences in temperature, useful for distinguishing a concealed weapon. The 900— top of the NightSniper line—can even detect residual heat: the tracks left when a gun dealer in the basement of a Best Western walks across a carpet, or a strung-out meth head sprints across a cornfield with a three-gallon jug in his hand.

You are the Predator! Project your will to the 1,000-yard range.

Last spring, at a gun show in Pittsburgh, he had held one in his hands. The dealer led him into a darkened room in the hotel basement, which had been set aside for showing NVDs. With the NightSniper, in pitch darkness, a subject's facial features can be distinguished at a hundred yards. Small differences in body heat are apparent. If the subject is sweating or feverish or stoked on methamphetamine, the NightSniper will know.

A weapon-mounted NightSniper runs fifteen thousand dollars, half the chief's annual pay.

He settles in for the night. The rain stopped hours ago, but the ground is still damp. Even with the army blanket spread out beneath him, his ass feels clammy, his legs numb with cold.

During a stakeout the mind wanders.

The chief imagines himself in another time, another country— smoking Vietcong in the jungle of the Mekong Delta, as his older brother had done.

He imagines himself in the old life, with all its comforts: the split-level residence bought and paid for, the two-car garage, the water bed Terri hated but, when she kicked him out, refused to surrender. A few days later he drove past the residence. Thursday morning, trash day. His deflated water bed sat at the curb.

No question, it was a low point: the chief kicked out of his residence, sitting on the divorce papers but not signing, Terri nagging him via text message and e-mail, his wife having embraced the twenty-first century, a brave new era for nagging. Their entire married life she'd issued a steady stream of instructions, what to eat and wear and how to spend his free time, the never-ending series of projects around the residence. It was a reality of his life, a fact like weather—until, abruptly, the nagging stopped. The silence was disorienting, like driving over a hill and losing your radio station completely. An annoying station, talk radio, with a host who bugged the shit out of you; but at least it kept your mind occupied. Cursing the voice on the radio, you stopped noticing the endless miles of highway, the soul-crushing void.

He still has trouble deciding what to eat and wear.

He should have taken the water bed.

Now, by every measure, things are looking up. A year ago, every dime he earned went straight to Penn State so that his son could flunk out of mechanical engineering, then business administration, then the university as a whole. Now, the flunking completed, Jason assembles hoagies at a Subway sandwich shop—a job which, if not lucrative, is at least free.

So the chief has a little more pocket money. He has his stakeouts. He has twice fucked the part-time secretary he shares with the Sewer Authority.

She is a likable woman, kindhearted. *What happened?* she once asked him. *With you and Terri. After twenty-some years, what could go wrong?*

She got tired of being married, is what happened, the chief said.

What also happened: so slowly he didn't notice, Terri lost a hundred pounds. Over the years she'd tried many diets, none of which lasted. But this time she followed exercise videos in the basement. She portioned out her cereal with a measuring cup. She went—and possibly still goes—to weekly meetings of overweight women, where she stood on a scale and was scolded if she'd gained and applauded if she'd lost.

An even hundred. The chief doesn't mention this to the part-time secretary, who is moderately overweight. Not as big as Terri at her largest, but quite a bit bigger than Terri is now.

The truth is that her weight never bothered him. After a while he simply hadn't seen it, the way he'd stopped hearing her nag. What mattered was she was there when he got home at night.

He closes his eyes for just a moment, or so it seems. When he wakes he is disoriented, hugging the army blanket around him, so cold he is perspiring. The Defender vest is cutting off his airflow. An eerie sound in the distance, the fluty note of an owl. Glancing at his watch, he is shocked to see that two hours have passed.

With a feeling of foreboding he approaches the tank. Fresh tracks in the mud, the grass trampled. He stops short.

The tank has been mended with black electrical tape.

8.

Pastor Jess is wearing perfume. Shelby smells it the instant she walks in the door. The synthetic floweriness makes her eyes itch, but she keeps quiet. Though she would like to, she can't exactly scold the pastor for what she wears in her own house.

"Excuse the mess," says the pastor. "I wasn't expecting you until seven."

In fact the house isn't messy. Except for two empty wineglasses on the coffee table, Shelby sees nothing out of place.

"Oh, I'm early! Sorry," says Shelby, though she isn't. She came early on purpose, hoping for an extra fifteen minutes. Always the hour passes far too quickly, and this week has been particularly eventful. She fears running out of time.

They go downstairs to the church office. Shelby sits in her usual chair. The pastor's cell phone—she notices this immediately—lies on the table between them.

"I want to apologize for last week," says Pastor Jess. "I hate to cancel at the last minute, but something suddenly came up."

"What?" says Shelby.

"I'm sorry?"

"What came up?"

Pastor Jess seems flustered. "I had a—prior commitment. It completely slipped my mind."

Shelby, whose appointment is at the same time every week,

doesn't see how that's possible. "It's all right," she says graciously, though it isn't. "Anyways, you won't believe what happened. First, I went to the meeting. I almost chickened out at the last minute, but I went."

"Meeting," Pastor Jess repeats.

Is it possible that she doesn't remember?

"At the library. You know, about the gas drilling. I told them everything. The noise, and the water. Rich doesn't believe me, but it has a terrible smell."

It isn't so easy to describe a smell. Shelby knows this from experience. Still, she tries.

"And they believed me! They think for sure our water is contaminated."

"For sure? Don't you have to, I don't know, have it tested?"

"I was getting to that part." It's disconcerting to be rushed. For the first time in years—since Braden's surgery—something momentous is happening to her. Shelby wants to savor the story, its twists and turns and surprising developments. Is that too much to ask?

"Dr. Trexler—he's the scientist—told me to call this lab in Pittsburgh. Which I did. But *they* said they couldn't drive all the way out here, so I called another lab, and—"

Again the pastor interrupts. "What does Rich have to say about that?"

Shelby isn't thrilled with this question.

"I haven't told him yet. I'm waiting until the results come back. Then he'll *have* to believe me."

"Are you sure that's a good idea?" Pastor Jess leans forward in her chair. "Shelby, I'm happy to keep meeting with you, but I do think it would be more helpful if we got Rich involved."

Which would be a reasonable suggestion, if Shelby were married to someone else.

"If child care is an issue, maybe someone could stay with them for a couple hours."

"A babysitter?" Shelby feels her face heat. It's exactly what Rich is always saying: *They don't need you with them every minute of the day.* Every month or two, he bugs her about getting a job, not understanding that she already has one. That looking after a sick child is the hardest job on earth.

"A friend or relative," says the pastor, as though it were just that easy. "Your mother lives in town, doesn't she? Can't she look after Braden and Olivia for an hour or two?"

Shelby gropes for an answer. Her mother is a subject she avoids at all costs. Also: she is fairly certain that Roxanne stole twenty dollars from her purse.

"She's pretty busy. Anyways, I'd be nervous leaving Olivia with anybody."

"How is she feeling? Is the medication helping?"

"A little, I guess. But it doesn't solve the underlying problem. Remember how I thought it was food allergies? Dairy and corn? Now I know: she's sick from drinking our water! At the meeting—"

The pastor's cell phone buzzes, scuttling across the table like a bug.

"I'm so sorry," she says, coloring. "Let me turn this thing off." She reaches for the phone and turns off the ringer, though not without sneaking a peek at the screen. "So—the water. You're sure that's it? What does your doctor say?"

"Well, that's just it. Olivia needs to see a specialist. There's a doctor in Pittsburgh who knows all about this kind of thing, but I couldn't get an appointment until August twenty-eighth. I was thinking you could come with us. For moral support."

"To Pittsburgh?" The pastor looks surprised. "Well, sure. You know, schedule permitting."

"August twenty-eighth," Shelby repeats. If she were Pastor Jess, she would write down the date. "How come you never had kids?"

Pastor Jess looks startled by the question.

"We planned to, eventually. Somehow it was never the right time. There was so much else to do."

"Like what?"

It occurs to Shelby—not for the first time—that Pastor Jess is selfish.

"Building the congregation, mainly. By the time we got around to trying, Wes wasn't feeling well. A few months later he was diagnosed."

Trying, Shelby thinks. Her face is very hot.

"I didn't mean to upset you," says the pastor. "I know you and Wes were close."

Shelby looks around the room, which had once been his sickroom. After his death Pastor Jess had redecorated, removing every trace.

Shelby says, "Pastor Wes would have made a great father."

There is a silence.

"You too," she adds quickly. "A great mother."

"Thank you." Pastor Jess smiles briefly. "But that's enough about me. This is your time, Shelby."

Yes, Shelby thinks. It is.

JESS WATCHES THE MINIVAN DRIVE AWAY. In its back window is a diamond-shaped plastic sign: BABY ON BOARD. A relic of Olivia's infancy—barely legible, now, the letters faded by the sun.

"Wes, what am I going to do with her?"

Their marriage is a conversation that hasn't ended, just grown one-sided. Jess talks to Wes the way other people talk to God, her own version of prayer.

In the kitchen she pours a glass of wine, exhausted by the work of listening. In two years of counseling, the content of Shelby's monologues has varied little: her fears and neuroses and frustrations, her abiding and insistent needs. Shelby needs a friend, a mother, a babysitter for her children and possibly for herself. A divorce lawyer might come in handy, and a psychiatrist wouldn't hurt. Despite her best efforts, Jess is none of these things.

"What exactly does she want from me? What am I not doing?"

Wes, if he were here, would know the answers to these questions. Shelby had been a project of his, a stray to be rescued: Youth Group, an after-school job in the church office. In summer there was Vacation Bible School, Shelby's camp fees paid from the pastor's own pocket.

She has a mother, Jess reminded him.

I've met the mother. Trust me, said Wes. *We're all she's got.*

She did trust him. If he'd been a different kind of man, she might have questioned his intentions, his active interest in a lost girl who loved him blindly. But he was Wesley, unimpeachable. The purity of his motives was beyond all doubt.

He had never lost patience. This earned him Shelby's lifelong gratitude, a fervent loyalty that is nearly religious. Shelby the faithful disciple, keeper of his memory. Once a month she places flowers on his grave and makes a point of telling Jess, which should not be annoying.

A project left unfinished, like so many others. Her husband's unfinished life.

Shelby never misses a counseling session, even when she has nothing to report. At such times, like a TV host in a slow news cycle, she fills out the hour with a human interest story—a stranger's tragedy, the more grotesque the better. The pregnant Florida woman in a coma, the Siamese twins joined at the heart. Shelby maintains a lively interest in the agony of strangers, their wrenching moral dilemmas. (If the twins are separated, one will die instantly. If not, both have a fifty-fifty chance of survival. *Pastor Jess, what would you do?*)

Possibly she's imagining it, the implied criticism: that she isn't the pastor Wes was, that she was never the wife he deserved. Shelby studies her knowingly, as though she's guessed a secret: that Wes and Jess had argued about her; that their marriage wasn't perfect. That Jess—married too young to a boy who loved her too much— had sometimes wished for a different kind of love.

The intimacy of young marriage. Their first apartment was two cramped rooms above a picture-framing shop: ugly wallpaper, a loud refrigerator, clanging radiators that were always cold. The poor divinity student and his wife washed their clothes in the bathtub because the Laundromat cost a dollar. They showered together because they could. They ate meals side by side, from the same plate. She will never be that close to anybody again.

If the twins are separated, which one gets the heart?

Wesley had been the center of his mother's life, and from Jess, expected nothing less. Their marriage was exclusive in all ways. An hour on the phone with her sister was an hour stolen from him. He was, clearly, an only child.

They were exactly the same size—a tallish woman, a smallish man—and wore jeans and sweaters interchangeably. For most of their courtship, both were virgins. They waited two full years, as long as human beings could possibly wait. Later, because their Christian college demanded it, they kept up the charade of separate apartments but spent every night in Jess's twin bed, curled around each other like puppies. They fell in love in childhood, and in some way had remained children. In the shower they sang together. He had a beautiful voice.

An only child. Jess has known others, of course—only children of unexceptional temperament. But onliness, for Wes, was determinative. He was the onliest of children, the onliest child she had ever known.

A couple could sleep in a twin bed as long as neither moved.

At a certain point you had to move.

At a certain point you wanted your own plate.

Jess feels at times that Shelby is baiting her, daring her to lose patience, as if that would prove something.

She takes the cell phone from her pocket and listens to the message. *I'm finishing up some paperwork. I'll be there at nine.* Herc's voice is low and rumbling, an ordinary man's voice. He is nothing at all like her husband. For Jess, this is part of his appeal.

For her birthday he'd bought her lingerie, something Wes would have been embarrassed to do.

"I'M NOT ALLOWED," OLIVIA SAYS.

Rich pauses in midscoop. He stopped at the Food Giant for a quart of chocolate chip, the kids' favorite. A *Batman* movie is in the DVD player. He employs this strategy every Thursday night while Shelby is at counseling: the same movie week after week, the same ice cream. He is grateful for his children's dependable enthusiasm, their appetite for sameness, their immunity to boredom.

"I got sick last time," Olivia says.

"That was just a stomach bug. You're allowed. I say so." Rich fills her bowl. "Just don't tell Mom."

It is nearly dark, Braden and Olivia installed in front of the TV with bowls of ice cream, when he hears a crunch of gravel. He glances out the kitchen window. A truck idles in the driveway—a beat-up Ford 150, the same model he drives.

He steps out onto the deck and comes around to the front. At the wheel is his neighbor Rena Koval.

"Hey, Rich, how's it going?" she calls out the window, as though they're old friends. Neighbors for nine years, they have never, in his memory, actually spoken. They have a waving relationship. The one time he visited Friend-Lea Acres, with Carl Neugebauer, she was nowhere in sight.

She cuts the engine and steps out of the truck—a tiny thing, maybe five feet tall. He never realized she was so little. Does she sit on a phone book to see over the hood?

"Rena. What can I do for you?"

"Is Shelby around?" She is a pretty woman, curly haired, in faded jeans and shit-kicker boots. Older than Rich, probably, though she looks younger—the freckles maybe, or just the weird youthfulness of the very small.

He knows her from somewhere.

"Nah, she had an appointment." He can't bring himself, somehow, to say the word *counseling*.

"Oh, okay. I was wondering if she had any luck with the lab. The first one she tried—"

"The what?"

"The lab that does the water testing. She didn't tell you." It isn't a question. It must be clear from his face that he has no clue what she's talking about. "At the meeting she was saying how—"

"What meeting? When?"

An awkward silence.

"We had a community meeting Tuesday night at the library," says Rena. "About the drilling. She didn't tell you?"

"Oh, that," Rich says, coloring. Shelby had told him she was going to Bible study.

Through the flimsy walls he hears the *Batman* soundtrack, gratingly familiar. He hates the music and yet finds himself humming it at odd moments. The *Batman* soundtrack will haunt his dreams.

"Anyways," says Rena, "she was talking about your water, and—"

"What about my water?" He is aware of the edge in his voice.

"She said there was an odor. A chemical smell. Arvis Kipler has the same problem. I've done some research, and—"

"My water is fine," he says through his teeth. "Shelby's just being neurotic. I wouldn't pay any attention."

Another silence.

Rena asks, "How is Olivia feeling?"

The *Batman* soundtrack rises in pitch.

"She's fine."

Another silence.

"She had a stomach bug a while ago, but it was nothing. You know kids." Finally the realization dawns. "Wait, you think my *water* is making Olivia sick?"

He listens in disbelief as Rena explains, finally, the reason she's standing in his driveway.

"Let me get this straight," he says, with deliberate calm. "You're trying to shut down the drilling." He can actually feel his blood pressure rising. It is in every way like listening to his brother: the sanctimonious tone, the clear assumption that other people don't understand what's good for them and must, like children, be protected from what they want.

"Rena, are you out of your mind? This town is dying. It's the first glimmer of hope we've had in thirty years."

"And drilling is going to save us? It's killing my business."

"I don't hear anybody else complaining."

"Nobody else is doing organic. *You* try and sell organic milk when your cows are grazing in a gas patch. Pretty soon we won't be able to give it away."

The *Batman* soundtrack builds to a sweeping crescendo, Hollywood's version of waterboarding.

"I don't know anything about that," he admits. "But nobody's making you do it, right? Organic." The word sounds awkward coming out of his mouth. "That's your own choice."

From the back yard comes a grinding noise. Rena covers her ears. "Good Lord. They never stop, do they?"

The grinding gives way to a mechanical shriek.

"Look, Rena, I get it." He has to shout to be heard. "You think I like listening to that? I haven't had a decent night's sleep in weeks. So if people want to get together and bitch about it, knock yourselves out. Just leave my kid out of it. There's nothing wrong with my water. And Olivia is fine."

The shrieking vibrates his hands and feet.

"Listen, I know there's problems. I look out my kitchen window and I think, what the hell are they doing to my land?" He has never admitted this to anyone. "But I'm trying to be patient. A lot of good could come out of this. Look around, Rena. Half this town is out of work."

"Name me *one local person* who's gotten a job on a drill rig. All those guys come up here from Texas or wherever."

(The drunken yahoos at the Commercial, the parking lot full of out-of-state plates.)

"Well, maybe so," he admits. "But what about all these trucks on the road? *Somebody's* driving them. If I needed a job, I'd get myself a commercial license. Some people in this town are just fucking lazy," he adds, thinking of the Nick Blicks, the Booby Marstellars. "If they're out of work, maybe it's their own goddamn fault."

Abruptly the noise stops. The silence is somehow shocking. They stare at each other, blinking.

As he watches her drive away, Rich remembers the strippins.

The old strippins, not yet backfilled. Beyond the sooty moonscape lay woods and lake and rusted track, an old rail bridge where teenagers congregated. They left behind a trail of graffiti and used rubbers, beer cans and cigarette butts.

He remembers a summer evening just before twilight, jumping bikes with Booby Marstellar on the ramps they'd made, stolen planks and cinder blocks lugged from a building site. Rich ducked into the woods to take a leak and saw movement on the rail bridge, a flash of white. He was nine years old and didn't, at first, understand what he was seeing. A shirtless man crouched on his knees, bareassed, pants around his ankles. Pinned beneath him was a half-clad girl. He held her by the throat.

That winter, hunting with his pap, Rich had bagged his first doe. This girl was as still as the deer in his crosshairs. Her bare feet were dirty. Her arms and legs were white. When she saw him her head jerked sideways, and he understood that she was telling him to run and he ran.

The girl held by her throat. To this day he isn't sure what he witnessed: horny teenagers going at it, or a sexual assault in progress? He remembers thinking, She could get away if she wanted to.

(her feet dirty, as though she'd already tried)

He didn't tell Booby what he'd seen. He didn't tell anyone. The boys rode home grimy and sunburned on the cinder path along the railroad tracks—two little shits on bicycles, a long time ago.

IT'S NEARLY DARK when Shelby gets home. The house, predictably, is a shambles: a greasy fry pan left for her to wash, bowls and spoons piled in the sink. Honestly, how is it possible? Two hours ago she left the place in perfect order. Now there is clutter everywhere, piles of junk mail, toys and small shoes littering the floor. To Shelby, who spends much of her day returning items to their proper places—dolls to the toy chest, scissors to the kitchen drawer—the level of chaos is unfathomable. She thinks of Pastor Jess's tidy house, the two empty wineglasses on the coffee table. What passes for messy when you don't have kids.

In the living room Braden and Olivia lie on the floor in front of the TV.

"You shouldn't watch in the dark," she says, flicking on a lamp. "It's bad for your eyes. Where's Daddy?"

"Basement," Braden says.

She finds Rich sprawled on the old couch, staring at his laptop.

"Where were you?" he says.

"Where am I every Thursday night?"

"That's a great question, Shelby. I *think* you're at counseling. Then again, I thought you were at Bible study on Tuesday." Finally he looks up from his screen. "Your pal Rena Koval came by to see you. She wanted to know how you made out with the lab."

Shelby feels suddenly faint.

"I was going to tell you about it. I knew you'd be mad." How much had Rena told him? She sits on the dusty couch, clutching her stomach. "I don't feel well."

"Goddamn right I'm mad. Now the whole town thinks there's something wrong with our water."

"There *is* something wrong with our water."

"You," he says very slowly, "have completely lost your mind."

"Oh, really?" she says. "They didn't think so. They said it happens all the time."

"Who said?"

"Dr. Trexler, at the meeting. He's a scientist. There's people out west who can light their tap water on fire. Did you know that?"

"If one more person tells me that, I'm going to put my fist through a wall."

"It's a true fact." The couch is making her eyes itch.

"And what's this about having the water tested?"

Rena had told him everything.

"They came this morning," Shelby says with a pounding heart. "From Pittsburgh. We should have the results in a few weeks."

"Exactly how much is this going to cost me?"

Shelby hesitates. In all the excitement, she had forgotten to ask the most basic question. "I'm not sure. They're going to send a bill in the mail."

"Jesus Christ."

She has never seen Rich's face this color. He looks like he's about to have a heart attack. "Calm down," she says. "You're scaring me."

"I will not calm down. You're making a fool of yourself. Of us both. What did you tell them about Olivia?"

"The same thing I've been telling you. The same thing I've been telling *everybody*." Shelby is near tears. "Rich, she *isn't getting better*. Something is seriously wrong."

"Not according to Dr. Stusick."

"Dr. Stusick doesn't know anything. She needs a *specialist*."

Nothing to lose, now; she might as well tell him everything. "There's a doctor in Pittsburgh. Environmental medicine. I made an appointment."

"Let me guess. Something else I'm supposed to pay for?"

"Oh no," she says quickly. "They take Blue Cross." This is an outright lie. In truth Shelby has no idea whether insurance will pay for the visit. Another question she forgot to ask.

CLOSING TIME AT THE COMMERCIAL. Gia wipes down the counters while Darren swabs the floors. In the back room he fills a bucket with hot water and Pine Sol. Above the sink his brother has posted a list of instructions—terse commands, no articles, all caps. AT CLOSING: 1. SWEEP KITCHEN. 2. MOP FLOOR. 3. EMPTY DISHWASHER. 4. TAKE OUT TRASH. It's more or less the way Rich speaks in life.

He takes the bucket out front. "MOP FLOOR," he tells Gia.

"WIPE COUNTER," she answers. "Your brother is an asshole."

Out of embarrassment or solidarity, some weird filial allegiance left over from childhood, Darren keeps quiet. What is there to say? That Rich is perfectly reasonable, as long as you do exactly as he wants?

Gia swipes briskly at the bar. "Why do you think Shelby goes to counseling? I'll tell you why. Her husband is an asshole."

"Wait, what? There are therapists in Bakerton?"

"At her church. I don't know if it's doing any good, but at least she gets a break from the kids. It's the only time she ever leaves the house."

"I was over there on Dad's birthday," he says, enjoying the gossip. "Definitely some marital tension in the air. Shelby's a little—intense."

"Shelby's a little nuts." Gia finishes wiping and gives the rag a rinse. "I think she might be anorexic, or that other one. The puking one."

"Bulimic?"

"The girl eats like a lumberjack. She never gains an ounce."

"You're one to talk. You used to have a little more meat on you," he says, pinching her arm. Her tanned skin is surprisingly warm, as if saturated with sun.

"Baby fat. Don't remind me."

"Seriously, Shelby's bulimic? Why would you think that?"

"Next time you're over there, look in the medicine chest."

"Look for what?" he asks, but Gia has already disappeared into the kitchen.

When she returns they empty the ice traps into the sink. "Remember Mr. Radulski?" says Darren. "I saw him the other day, at the library."

"That dickwad?"

"He was a nice guy."

Gia snorts. "To the smart kids, maybe."

"You're smart," says Darren.

"You know what I mean."

Darren runs the hot water. There is a satisfying crackle of ice melting. "It was pretty awkward. I never know what to tell people."

"About what?"

"My wasted potential. My utter betrayal of anyone who had hopes for me. We didn't talk very long," he says quickly, realizing he's said too much. "He had better things to do. His daughter was getting married."

"Leah? Wasn't she your girlfriend?"

"Er, no. I wouldn't say that. We were friends."

"You're a terrible liar."

"She liked me," he admits. "I wasn't really into it."

Gia howls. "You did her!"

"Nah," says Darren, his face heating. Recently he'd found, in his dad's basement, his own high school yearbook, its inside cover inscribed in the exuberant rounded cursive—*Friends forever! Dar-*

ren, U R the coolest. Have fun in college!—of girls who didn't want to sleep with him. For reasons he still can't fathom, Leah had been the exception. At high school graduation they were both still virgins—despite a close call in the Radulski basement, an awkward clinch interrupted by Leah's little brother.

Gia, of course, hadn't signed his yearbook. He hadn't had the nerve to ask.

"I was kind of a jerk," he admits. "Leah was super nice. My mom loved her." His mother had never liked Gia, though she'd been careful not to say so. When Gia rolled up to the house in Rocco's cast-off hearse, the open windows pouring heavy metal and cigarette smoke, Sally offered only the mildest sort of criticism. *She seems like a wild girl.* She seemed to understand that Gia could break Darren's heart, or maybe already had.

"Do you think my dad's okay?" he asks. "He seems lonely." It isn't precisely true. Dick doesn't seem any way in particular, unless Darren supplies the subtext. What he really means: *We are equally lonely.* Age is the only difference. Darren's youth allows for certain illusions, the implicit hope that life could change.

"Ah, Dick's all right," says Gia. "Now that he's got you to kick around."

"I guess." It's a disconcerting thought, that his father's well-being depends in any way on his own presence. "But, you know, I can't stay forever."

"Why not?"

He starts to say that it's an unnatural arrangement, a person of his age living—even temporarily—with an elderly parent. He stops himself, remembering that to Gia it's perfectly normal. Except for her brief teenage marriage to Steve Yurkovich— *the worst five minutes of my life*—she has lived, happily it seems, with her widowed father. Rocco Bernardi is older than Dick, his health questionable. How much care he requires, Darren isn't sure.

"You've never thought about moving out?" he asks as they empty the dishwasher.

"And pay a grand a month for some shithole?"

"In Bakerton?" The number seems impossible. He pays only a little more in Baltimore.

"Rents are out of control. Those gas guys have money." Gia polishes the Iron City tap, which is already gleaming. "Remember my old place? That dump above the hair salon?"

"The stove didn't work." It's his sole memory of Gia's marriage: getting high in her kitchen, lighting joints off the stove's only working burner while Steve, a long-distance trucker, was on the road.

Gia squeals. "God, remember my hair when my hair caught fire?"

It is possibly the most vivid memory of his life: Gia leaning over the gas stove, the sudden flash of light, the strange airy noise like opening a can of tennis balls.

"Sorry, no," he says. "I can't recall."

Gia shrieks with laughter. "I didn't know what the hell happened. I couldn't figure out why you were smacking me in the head with a magazine."

"I had to extinguish you."

Gia laughs soundlessly.

"You had half a can of Aqua Net in your hair. You were like a Molotov cocktail. We could have been killed."

Gia wipes a tear from her eye. She's the only person he knows who actually laughs until she cries. "Jesus, that place. I know for a fact it hasn't been painted since we lived there. Me and Steve paid four hundred. Now it goes for twelve. Crazy, right?"

"Unbelievable." Most nights Gia's tips are double his, for obvious reasons (her lightning quickness, the denim skirt). But even with the generosity of the drilling crews and the occasional twenty-dollar bill from Wally Fetterson, a thousand a month would be beyond her reach.

"Anyways, I like living with Rocco. If my mom were still

around, that would be a different story. But the old fart would be lost without me. You know he still makes me toast and coffee every morning?" Gia hangs up her towel. "Why would I move out when I have everything I need?"

"But doesn't it make things difficult?" It's the question he's been dying to ask. "Dating, and so on."

"*Dating?*" she says, laughing. "And *so on?* Devlin, you are such a girl."

His face feels heated by a blowtorch. Gia gives him a shove. "I'm just messing with you. Guys mostly have their own places. And if not, there are ways."

Tell me about the ways, he might have said, if he were not Darren Devlin, stone-cold sober. If they were people other than Darren and Gia, with everything that implied.

He bags the trash and carries it out to the Dumpster. When he comes back she's standing in the doorway to the stockroom. Behind her is the bulletin board where Dick pins confiscated fake IDs.

"Come here," she says.

As kisses go it's a knockout, thorough and probing. He leans against the doorframe and pulls her in, thinking, *I am kissing Gia Bernardi.* Her body feels somehow familiar—for no other reason, probably, than he's been thinking about it for so long.

I had to, she'll tell him later. *We'd both be eating Jell-O at Saxon Manor if I waited around for you.*

Which, of course, is absolutely true.

According to Dick Devlin, there are two kinds of work: the kind where you shower before and the kind where you shower after. His elder son has always done the second kind—roofing, soldiering, hauling oxygen tanks for Miners' Medical. Now, compared with Deer Run, those seem like clean jobs. More than ever before, Rich looks forward to his afterwork shower, scrubbing away the prison with the hottest water he can stand.

Outside the rig noise stops abruptly, a small miracle. He undresses at full speed and stuffs his uniform into the hamper. With luck he'll be asleep before the racket starts again. Sunday sleep, the best of the week: with Shelby and the kids at church, it's the only time he can be reliably alone in his own goddamn house.

Two kinds of work. When you're as old as his dad, everything you say is familiar. At what age does a person stop having new thoughts? Dick has gone years—decades, possibly—without saying anything he hasn't said a hundred times before.

Rich turns on the taps and right away is struck by the odor. Shelby is right: the water smells like something. Lighter fluid, maybe? At the sink he hadn't noticed. Now, with the spray blasting down on his head and shoulders, it's impossible to ignore.

He takes an abbreviated shower, breathing through his mouth. The drain is a little slow—he's been meaning to snake it—and he stands, watching the tub empty. The water is cloudy. A rainbow film clings to the surface, like a spill of gasoline.

THE RIG IS LIT, around the clock, with klieg lights. From a distance it radiates a sulfurous glow, like a football stadium at night. Several trucks idle loudly. Up close the diesel smell is overpowering. The engine noise makes his whole body vibrate. He sees no sign of human presence. It's as though the giant machines are running themselves.

He stands at the base of the platform, looking up, and finally sees workers. He counts exactly five men—from his vantage point, small as children. Given the scale of the operation, it isn't much of a crew.

"Hey!"

He waves his arms to get their attention, his body vibrating with sound. The noise is epic and surprisingly complex, layered like music: a low grinding he feels in the base of his spine, a shrill whine like the world's largest table saw. There is a metallic tapping, sharp and regular, and behind it all, a titanic whoosh of air.

"Hey!" he calls again, starting up the stairs.

Finally one of the men notices. He descends the staircase, gripping the handrail. It's the same guy as last time, the beefy little bulldog Rich has served at the Commercial.

"You can't come up here," Herc shouts. "It's a hard-hat zone. I'll meet you in the trailer."

In the construction trailer the noise is not quite deafening. The temperature is maybe a hundred degrees. Herc takes styrofoam plugs from his ears. He wears work gloves, a hard hat, grimy coveralls.

"Something's wrong with my water," Rich says. He describes the smell, the cloudiness, the rainbow film. Herc listens without comment. Then, finally, he speaks:

"I can tell you right now, that wadn't us. Your well is what, a hundred feet deep?"

"About that."

"We're nowheres near your well. We're drilling a mile down."

His voice is surprisingly deep for a guy his size. His eyes are level with Rich's collarbone.

"My grandfather dug that well. It's been good for fifty years. Now it just happens to go skunky a week after you start drilling. That's some fucking coincidence."

"I don't know what else to tell you."

"You haven't told me anything so far."

They stand nearly toe to toe, arms crossed.

"What are capturing charges?"

Herc frowns.

"On my statement. You charged me a thousand bucks for capturing charges."

"*I* did?" Herc laughs. "I didn't charge you anything. You'll have to take that up with Dark Elephant."

"I thought you *were* Dark Elephant."

"We're Stream Solutions. We're subcontractors."

Nothing, nothing is simple.

"Whatever," Rich says through his teeth. "I don't care who you are. I'm having my water tested."

"That's your right. I can recommend a company, if you want."

"No thanks. I'll find my own."

Herc goes to a cluttered desk and riffles through a drawer. "When you get your test results, call this guy." He hands Rich a business card: QUENTIN TANNER, DIRECTOR OF COMMUNICATIONS.

"Who the hell is this?"

"He handles environmental concerns. But I'm telling you, you're wasting your time."

LORNE TREXLER CALLS, always, after midnight. It's a little late for Rena, who's been up since dawn. Still, the timing offers certain advantages. By midnight Mack is long asleep, the house quiet, and she can be alone with Lorne's voice. She prepares for these calls as she did, long ago, for chemistry and biology classes. Nearly every day, he sends her links to articles—pending lawsuits, drilling mishaps, legislative efforts in Pennsylvania and elsewhere. She reads carefully, knowing he'll question her later. He assumes, always, that she'll have an opinion, something no one has ever expected her to have.

He is an education.

"What do you think of *Silent Spring*?"

He'd given her the book when he walked her to her car. *Have you read this? Required reading for the environmental activist.*

I haven't read anything, Rena said.

"I haven't started it yet," she admits. "Tomorrow for sure."

She tries to picture where Lorne is calling from, the rented house a few miles from campus. He lives alone, something Rena has never done. Like her brothers and sister and everyone else she knows, she lived with her parents until she got married, or whatever she is, to Mack.

(Mack. Is that your husband?)

"Guess," he says, when she asks what his house looks like.

"Neat. You're very organized. And you have books everywhere. Lots of books."

"Guilty on the books. Otherwise, I gotta tell you, you have no future as a psychic. I'm a fucking slob."

If Rena lived alone she'd stay up late and watch movies all night and eat cold cereal breakfast, lunch, and dinner—something she can never do, because Mack has a gigantic appetite and skipping meals makes her cranky. She never had a mother to cook for her and so attaches undue importance to such things.

Lorne doesn't ask what Rena's house looks like, which is just as well. Tonight she sits in the cluttered parlor, at the scarred rolltop desk where Pete had done the farm's bookkeeping, or pretended to. After his death they found the dusty ledger he'd kept under lock and key. The most recent entry was six years old.

Lorne talks about a public forum in Washington County, a promising e-mail exchange with a state senator, his upcoming meeting at the DEP. He speaks admiringly of the governor of New York, who's placed a temporary moratorium on gas drilling. Rena is only half listening. She looks around the room, trying to see it through his eyes: the faded floral wallpaper, the old-fashioned divan piled with seed catalogs, junk mail, unpaid bills. The few books belong to Mack, well-thumbed paperbacks (*World of the Soil, Alternative Treatments for Ruminant Animals*) grubby with farm dirt.

The many lives she will never get to live.

Watching Lorne drive away from the Pick and Shovel, his red taillights disappearing down Number Six Road, Rena thought, Take me with you.

"I stopped by Shelby's the other night. I wanted to ask her a question, but she wasn't home. Her husband wasn't too happy to see me. He claims there's nothing wrong with their water."

"Denial. That's a pretty typical reaction. And—let me guess. His daughter is in perfect health."

His voice—warm, resonant—fills a space inside her. She doesn't need to touch him or even see him. His voice is enough. Often, in passing, he mentions women by name—students, colleagues, an ex-wife with whom he remains friendly. He has never mentioned a girlfriend. Rena listens for subtext.

"He didn't say *that*, exactly. But here's my question." She hesitates. "I looked up Olivia's medical record. Shelby brought her in to the ER on March first and again on May thirtieth. Same symptoms, nausea and vomiting. But they didn't start drilling at the Devlins' until June."

Unusually, there is a pause. Normally he starts talking the instant she stops, as though he's been waiting his turn.

"Does that bother you?" he asks.

"It doesn't bother *you*?"

"It's not ideal," he admits, "but let's say she did have a preexisting condition. It doesn't mean the water *isn't* contaminated. Ravi will know better than I do, but isn't it logical that a kid with a lousy immune system is going to be more affected by bad water than a healthy adult would be? Pregnant women, the elderly, people who are already ill—they're always the canaries in the coal mine."

Rena, a healthy adult, thinks again of that day in the ER. If she'd been exposed to Flow-Z, she might have felt sick for a day. Instead she'd let a pregnant woman treat the patient. For the canary, the consequences had been grave.

"That's true, I guess. She's had four emergency room visits this year, two in the past month."

"So they're getting more frequent."

"Exactly. No admissions, but still. Also, her lab results—" Rena stops short. Patients' medical information is supposed to be confidential. "Let's just say the numbers are all over the place. I can't make any sense of it. I'm trying to get a copy of her record so we can take it to Dr. Ghosh."

"About that," says Lorne. "It looks like you and Shelby will have to go without me."

"Why?" She is embarrassed by the plaintive note in her voice.

"The Coalition is taking a busload of people up to Lincoln County, and I have to be there. The county commissioners are about to vote on a drilling ban—which, if it passes, would cover all the unincorporated land in the county."

"Great," says Rena, because a response seems necessary. "That's great news."

"Potentially. They're holding a public forum before the vote, and our people will be out in force. I wish you could come, but it's more important to get Olivia in front of Ravi ASAP."

The intensity of her disappointment is mortifying. She is fifty-four years old.

"You and Shelby will manage fine without me. And in the meantime, I have a proposition for you."

Immediately she feels lifted, her mood reorganizing itself.

"There's a thing in New York next month. Upstate, on the SUNY campus. We're rallying in support of the moratorium."

She speaks without thinking: "Who's we?" He could have another Rena, many Renas, in New York State, a whole platoon of sad farm wives waiting for his call.

"A coalition of local groups, plus as many students as we can wrangle the first week of the semester." He pauses. "It might be interesting for you to see how it works. We could drive up there together. What do you say?"

MACK HAS BEEN SLEEPING POORLY. She lies awake, listening to the clock. Somewhere a phone is ringing, which is not unusual. Lately Rena's cell phone rings more or less constantly: at mealtimes, at night when she's paying bills or staring at the computer and Mack is supposed to be sleeping.

Rena has a restless nature. Every so often, she'll get an idea in her head—nursing school, organic farming. She and Mack could raise goats or llamas, breed sheepdogs, study cheese making; the County Extension offers classes online. They could make their own yogurt, bottle and sell it. All they need is a website and something called a Twitter.

Sure, baby, says Mack. *Sounds good to me.*

The ringing stops. Mack gets out of bed and stands at the top of the stairs, listening.

There is a very long pause. For a moment she thinks they've hung up. Then she hears Rena's laugh, like some exotic birdcall.

Mack puts on her old flannel bathrobe and pads downstairs. Rena is in the parlor, which doubles as Friend-Lea's business office. Her cell phone lies on the desk beside her. She sits at the computer, reading glasses sliding down her nose.

"You're awake?" Rena looks astonished to see her. Mack, historically, is a heroic sleeper. They have never found an alarm clock that can rouse her. No matter how loud or shrill, the ringing simply becomes part of her dream. Each morning the alarm wakes Rena, who then shoves Mack out of bed.

"I heard the phone."

"That was Dr. Trexler," says Rena—unnecessarily, because it's always Dr. Trexler, often around midnight. He is nocturnal, the way Rena used to be and would still be, if Mack hadn't talked her into farm life. She was the sort of person who might have gone any-where, been anything—unlike Mack, who was born to be a farmer. There was nothing else she wanted to be.

"We need to get the Devlins' water tested. The trick is finding a company that will come all the way from Pittsburgh. The labs around here don't have the right equipment, or something."

"So why is he calling you?" Is it her imagination, or is Rena blushing?

Rena's eyes dart toward the computer screen.

It isn't her imagination.

"He says Shelby trusts me. Which is true, I guess. The drilling was her husband's idea. I don't think she had any say in the matter."

Mack knows the feeling. It's her own fault, of course: back when the neighbors were signing gas leases, she'd happily left the decision to Rena. *Sure, baby. Sounds good to me.* It wasn't until Carl Neugebauer came calling that Mack began to wonder: What would Pop do?

"Come to bed," she says.

"Soon. I need to send one more e-mail." Rena's eyes dart back toward the screen.

Restless.

Upstairs, the sheets are still warm. Mack settles into her spot with a series of deliberate adjustments, like a dog bedding down.

What would Pop do?

She recalls a story he used to tell, the one time in his life he had a little extra money. During the war, long before his daughter was born, young Pete Mackey had dug the coal out of his back forty and sold it on the QT. Men came after dark and hauled it away by the truckload, town people who'd used up their ration stamps and run short on house coal. It was a lucrative side business for a farmer—a *country bank*, Pop called it. All the neighbors knew what he was up to. Those who could, did the same.

Mack sees, now, that Carl Neugebauer was right: Pop would have signed a gas lease. He was the sort of person who did what he had to do.

She flops onto her stomach and places the pillow over her head.

Her sleeplessness is a recent development. For most of her life she has drifted off effortlessly, her limbs heavy with the good tiredness of a full day of farm chores. Her insomnia started a week ago, the night of Rena's meeting. After Rena left for the library, Mack fell asleep in front of the TV. At 11:00 P.M. she startled awake. The house was dark and silent. Rena had not come home.

Mack was surprised but not worried, until she saw the Friend-Lea delivery van still parked in the driveway. Rena had taken the pickup—prone, lately, to overheating. When Rena didn't answer her phone, Mack pulled on boots and set out driving. She flicked on her high beams and drove slowly, keeping an eye out for the truck. She drove the entire length of Number Six Road, past the library—closed now, its windows dark—and all the way into town, where she made a U-turn in the empty street.

No Rena.

Had she'd taken the shortcut home? Number Six Road crossed under Drake Highway and had, until recently, been the fastest route from town to farm. Now, with new detours every week, the shortcut was no longer quite so short.

Mack took it anyway. The road ran alongside Carbon Creek for several miles, then crossed over. At the crossing sat the Pick and

Shovel, a dark little roadhouse where she and Pop had sometimes drunk a beer, on a Sunday afternoon when the Steelers were playing. The Pick and Shovel was winding down for the night. A handful of cars were left in the parking lot.

Including Rena's truck.

Was she dreaming? Mack waited for the distant alarm clock, Rena shooing her out of bed.

She pulled over to the side of the road. From the shoulder she had a clear view of both the parking lot and the bar's front entrance. She cut the engine and waited—for what, she wasn't sure. One by one, cars and pickup trucks clattered out of the parking lot, until only three were left. One was an old Corvette, famous around town, the prized possession of a local mechanic. Parked on either side of it were Rena's pickup and a red Toyota Prius.

Wide awake, her mind blank, Mack waited and waited, until finally the door opened. She saw them in silhouette, a middle-aged couple crossing the parking lot. The man—not tall, notably skinny—walked close behind Rena, steering her by the elbow, in the way men were allowed to do.

They looked like a couple because they were a man and a woman.

Mack was not allowed to walk with Rena in this way.

She watched them cross the parking lot and pause next to the truck. Then a remarkable thing happened. The man took Rena's hand and led her into the woods.

Mack gets out of bed. In the bathroom she swallows one of Rena's sleeping pills—prescribed years ago, during Calvin's trial. The first and last time Rena took one, she slept for sixteen hours; but on Mack, who is twice her weight, the pills have little effect. Maybe, after sitting in the medicine chest for four years, the pills have lost their potency, because Mack still has trouble sleeping.

She does, however, have a lot of nutty dreams.

She dreams of swimming with Lindy Najarian, her college roommate, in what might or might not be Garman Lake, Lindy in a normal bathing suit, Mack in her boots and overalls, as though she'd rushed into the water to save a drowning swimmer. They are playing a game where Mack is chasing Lindy. The object of this game—what exactly will happen when Lindy is caught—is thrillingly unclear. Lindy darts through the water, quick as a minnow, and Mack feels her own disadvantage, her heavy boots filling with water. Then Lindy dives beneath the surface. Bubbles surround her: miraculously, she is able to breathe underwater. Mack follows, holding her breath until she can hold it no longer.

She wakes gasping.

The next day, after Rena leaves for the hospital, Mack stations herself in front of the computer, something she rarely does. Rena had left the machine running. Mack reads:

> *Lampyridae* is a family of insects in the order *Coleoptera*. They are winged beetles, commonly called <u>fireflies</u> or lightning bugs for their conspicuous crepuscular use of <u>bioluminescence</u> to attract mates or prey.

Lying awake wondering what Rena was doing at the computer, Mack couldn't have imagined she was reading about fireflies.

She opens a new window and types into the search field: Lindy Najarian. How many can there possibly be?

She'd been the team's star distance runner, Mack's training partner. Mack's roommate, best friend, and drinking buddy, until the Friday they stumbled home, very late, from a bar downtown. Drunk, Mack reached for Lindy in the way she'd always wanted to, and Lindy pulled away and called her terrible things that weren't all true but mostly were. The next night, a Saturday, Mack came home to find their bedroom door locked and bolted. Laughter behind it, murmuring voices. When she knocked, no one opened the door.

The boy wasn't important. She knew it even at the time, through her dumb hurt and mortification and rage. Lindy had chosen him almost randomly. She was simply making a point.

In B Quad lounge Mack waited. When the boy stumbled out of the room at 5:00 A.M., she followed him across the quad and up the hill.

He would have been fine if he hadn't taken the shortcut.

Shadowing him up the hill, Mack thought of hunting with her dad, the silent dawn forest, the damp mudsmell, the night sky gradually bluing. Her mind was curiously empty. Her pop's favorite hunting dog was a bluetick coonhound named King. What was King thinking on those cold mornings as he nosed through the underbrush? Nothing. He was simply doing what he did.

The shortcut snaked around the library, unlit, the path worn by a thousand pairs of sneakers.

Unlit.

The boy was down in an instant, stunned and silent. A second later Mack was on him, his long narrow body pinioned between her thighs. Like Lindy he was a distance runner, greyhound-thin, aerodynamic. No match for a shot-putter who threw fifty-six feet.

For the rest of her life the sound would haunt her, the peculiar cracking. Making popcorn or chopping firewood, she'd recall the sensation: the smooth motion of her champion shoulder, the boy's ribs snapping like twigs.

In the shadows behind the library he looked slender as a girl.

Dawn was breaking as she returned to B Quad. Lindy had already left for the gym. Her bed had been stripped, the sheets stuffed into the hamper so Mack could see the naked mattress, a spiteful reminder of what had transpired the night before. Mack filled her gym bag with a few clothes and trudged across campus, stopping briefly at the athletic building to leave a note under Coach's door. Her last night in State College, she slept in the Greyhound station, waiting for the only bus to Bakerton. The next morning she bought a copy of the local paper and saw a small item at the bottom of page 2. A Penn State student had been attacked behind the library by an unidentified assailant.

An unidentified assailant.

In his place she'd have lied about it, too. Mack, too, would have found it humiliating to have her clock cleaned by a girl.

Her search for Lindy yields a single result, a blog called Marathon Moms. Lindy Najarian-Holtzmann is something called a contributing editor.

We are a community of moms committed to active parenting, sunscreen, good nutrition and achieving our personal best.

Mack scrolls through the site. One user, WatertownMom, posts almost daily: family photos, times and distances, inspirational mottoes accompanied by sunsets. Clicking through these posts, Mack finds at last, a photo of WatertownMom in a singlet and running shorts. Blond now, her face leathery, she is still tiny. Still unmistakably Lindy. Her body hasn't changed in thirty years.

In the search field Mack types **Lorne Trexler**.

Immediately, the search returns hundreds of results. Mack is stunned. A search for anyone she knows—herself, Rena, anybody in Bakerton—would come up empty, or nearly so. She understands, then, that Lorne Trexler is in a different category of person, a man of consequence in the world.

She clicks on the first link, the home page of the Stirling College Geology Department. *Dr. Trexler's teaching and research interests include aquatic ecology, watershed assessment and management, operational models for grassroots community organizing, resource management, and public policy.*

Mack studies the photo on the screen. He's older than she expected, shaggy-haired, gaunt in the face. Is this what Rena finds attractive, this aging hippie? A skinny little guy, badly in need of a haircut? It seems improbable. But Mack is no judge of male horse-flesh.

The second search result links to *Time* magazine.

A CONFLICT OF INTEREST?

To the Editor:

"The Big Frack" raises compelling questions about the proper relationship of the Academy to industry. Dr. Amy Rubin, the geologist quoted in the piece, is in fact a paid consultant to Darco Energy, a gas and oil conglomerate that has—coincidentally?—endowed a new geology facility at the SUNY campus where Dr. Rubin was recently granted tenure. Such fiduciary relationships have calamitous effects on the integrity of scientific inquiry. Dr. Rubin's corporate underwriters have a direct financial stake in the outcome of her research. When a scientist accepts money from industry, it's reasonable to ask what industry expects in return.

Lorne Trexler, Chair

Department of Geology

Stirling College, Stirling, PA

Links and more links. The home page of the Keystone Waterways Coalition. Lorne Trexler at community meetings, antifracking rallies, a fund-raiser for something called the Planet Fund. Lorne Trexler in a jacket and tie, testifying before the Pennsylvania State House.

A man of consequence in the world.

THE BOY
IN THE BUBBLE

1988

The bus rolls eastward on the highway, long and white, the words *STIRLING COLLEGE* emblazoned in green on both sides. Lorne Trexler stands in the aisle, talking and gesticulating, in violation of posted safety rules. Early spring by the calendar, though winter hangs on in the patchy snow with its gritty inclusions, the salt scrim dusting the pavement, the tin bucket sky.

These weekly lab trips are the cornerstone of Earth Science. ATTENDANCE MANDATORY, NO EXCUSES is printed in boldface on the syllabus. Still, his students try. Family emergencies, mononucleosis, dead grandmother, the usual euphemisms for *hangover* and *laziness* and *still drunk from the night before.* Classic excuses, time tested. In their feints and dodges—in all things—they are traditionalists.

Stirling is a safety school, a respectable fallback for the duller offspring of wealthy parents—children of privilege, raised on television.

Their excuses are hallowed, archetypal, handed down through the semesters like the myths of a primitive tribe.

Trexler makes his way down the aisle to see who's awake. Honestly, it's hard to tell. The students are barely sentient, flipping through magazines or nodding to whatever commercial tripe is streaming through their headphones.

The lab trips are tied, thematically, to the earth science syllabus—sites chosen for reasons never precisely articulated, though the students sense, vaguely, that Trexler is making a point. On lab trips he climbs hills and shimmies up ladders and, once, scaled a security fence at a co-generation plant. Amy Rubin's camera caught him in midstride, one worn boot wedged into the chain-link, the sternly worded sign—TRESPASSERS WILL BE PROSECUTED—half obscured by his denim thigh. When she gave him a copy, he taped it to his office door, a fact noticed and commented upon.

Not magazines, Trexler notes. Several of the students—more than a handful—are reading catalogs.

Amy Rubin and her friends have commandeered the back of the bus. Caroline Minturn is a willowy blonde from Greenwich, Connecticut, the outlier. Suki Lee and Amy are small brunettes.

"Look who's coming this way," says Suki. Earth science had been her idea, a lazy way around the science requirement. To Amy, the daughter of a theoretical physicist, it was a radical notion. *That counts as science?*

They watch Professor Trexler make his way down the center aisle, loose and nimble, grasping each seat with a rhythmic motion, hand over hand. Aside from his long hair, it is his most notable quality: his obvious pleasure in the movement of his body, his kinetic and masculine grace.

They are best friends—three versions of the same girl, in the eyes of Stirling College: a pretty girl too busy for study, a party girl much in demand. Because it's a Friday, they wear blue jerseys printed with Greek letters. To the casual observer their differences are not apparent: Suki's years at American schools in Paris and Tokyo, the lonely daughter of diplomats; Amy the late-life child of scholarly parents, dour Russian émigrés mistrustful of pleasure. Suki and Amy, roommates, have concealed these histories even from each other. It took a third party to cement their friendship, a third girl to envy and adore. Caroline is normality perfected, her sunny childhood a thing to be coveted, the summer camps and licentious boarding schools, the horses and tennis and recreational drugs. Amy and Suki copy her style and manners, borrow liberally from her vast collection of sweaters. Caroline is the antidote to their own dubious pasts, their weird foreign families, their hidden, shameful strangeness.

"I'll bet you anything he sits next to Amy," Caroline says.

Trexler despairs of these students, he weeps for them—at once spoiled and neglected, raised on TV so bad he can't believe it exists, even worse than the dreck he watched as a child: the broad comedies and sentimental morality plays; the old cowboys, heroes of genocide, trapped in the terrible immortality of eternal syndication in spectral monochrome. Today's television is at once emptier and more malignant. There are many shows—an entire genre of TV drama—concerned mainly with real estate. The characters, ruthless tycoons and their conniving offspring, are incidental. The true protagonists are the vast and ostentatious houses of the rich, a crass American fantasy of elegance.

All of America is watching, even the young.

At their age, Lorne Trexler did not watch television. He was on fire then, a crusader against injustice—a long-haired jagoff farting opinion and argument, in the eyes of his father. His mother was more oblique, wondering aloud why Lorne sided, always, with the downtrodden, the dusky-skinned reliefers who lived off the system. In their convictions his parents never wavered: stalwart, incurious, impervious to doubt.

His parents, if they were still alive, might enjoy *Lifestyles of the Rich and Famous,* a show that people actually watch.

At the back of the bus the girls giggle and whisper.

"Is this where the cool kids sit?" Trexler nudges Amy's foot with his. "What news from Greece?"

Amy flushes. He never misses an opportunity to rib her about Theta: the hokey rituals, the lame community service projects in which she has failed, so far, to participate. *I don't do any of that,* she says, knowing it's a weak defense. That she's never mentored a low-income child or tutored illiterate adults, that her "service" has been limited to a single afternoon picking up litter along the highway, makes herself and Theta seem even more pathetic.

"What are you reading?" he asks, just to bust her chops. He sees something in this girl, a quickness, a flicker of deeper intelligence she seems determined to hide. A mirage, probably. He's been wrong before.

He takes the catalog from her hands. "Explain something to me. Are you actually planning to *buy* these"—he squints at the page— "extraordinarily tight hundred-dollar blue jeans with the corporate logo on the right butt cheek?"

"No," she says. "I mean, probably not."

"So this is just your reading material. This is *entertainment*." He explains with weary patience the slim but vital difference between a catalog and a magazine, which at least hides the ads between celebrity interviews and gossip columns. A catalog makes no secret of its purpose. The difference (he thinks but doesn't say) between a stripper and a whore.

"Slide over, Rubin. There's something I want you to see."

He sits beside her, adopting her own crouched posture, his body blocking her off from her friends, and points to the four towers in the distance, bell-shaped and glowing white. "There it is. Scene of the crime. It was supposed to be a miracle. Power too cheap to meter."

He doesn't wear a wedding ring.

"That's it?" she says. "It's still running?"

"Amazingly, yes. Half of it, anyway. That's Unit One in the foreground. Unit Two is where it happened."

"Can we go see it?"

His jaw drops open. "You're kidding, right? Seventy-five kids in their prime reproductive years? You'll take your fucked-up sperm and eggs back to campus and screw like bunnies. You'll pass along mutations science has never seen."

Amy slides lower in the seat.

"Did I embarrass you? Sorry," he says, briefly touching her leg.

He doesn't wear a wedding ring but is known to be married. Once Amy saw him walking in town with his wife. Mrs. Trexler was tall and skeletally thin, with a long equine face. She wore her hair in the unfortunate Dorothy Hamill cut, popular ten years ago.

"So it's still—contaminated? Even ten years later?"

"*Rubin.*" He sounds truly angry. "The half-life of plutonium two-three-nine is *twenty-four thousand years.*"

Shame floods her, the visceral memory of past disgraces. In junior high she herself had attempted the Dorothy Hamill cut, a style ill-suited to curly-headed Jewish children. Her face fills with blood. "Sorry. I'm a moron."

"You're not," he says, more gently. "So don't act like one. The point is, ten years—nine, actually—is nothing. In geologic terms, it happened a minute ago."

"But don't they have to clean it up?"

"Can't be done. Not really. Though they're putting on a good show. Guys in hazmat suits making six bucks an hour. Nonunion, of course." Organized labor is one of his favorite topics: the air traffic controllers, President Reagan's shameless union-busting. "Those poor bastards have no idea what they're handling."

"That's legal?" Amy is sometimes skeptical of his pronouncements, but ill-equipped to argue. Always he seems in possession of inside information, a complex understanding of the world she will never have.

"Oh, sure. Some lawyer hands the guy a list of radioactive compounds he's never heard of, and he signs a piece of paper that indemnifies the company against any wrongdoing. Ten years from now, when he's got leukemia or thyroid cancer, a secretary pulls that waiver out of a file cabinet. Presto. No lawsuit."

"I was a kid when it happened," says Amy. "I remember my parents talking about it. I didn't understand anything."

"Nobody did. Half the core melted, and there wasn't even an

evacuation. People down the street were out mowing their lawns. Finally the governor told them to close their windows. Like that was going to make a difference." Trexler shifts in his seat. "It was my last semester at Rutgers. My buddy had a van, so a bunch of us drove up to demonstrate."

Amy listens, enraptured. She has never been to a protest of any kind, a notion she associates with hippie times. In that moment she feels keenly her own misfortune, the injustice of having been born so late, when all the world's problems are already solved.

"It was pandemonium. Protestors from all over, kids mostly. The locals hated us. You believe that? There was a hydrogen bubble in the reactor that could have exploded. These people are living next door to a potential nuclear meltdown, and they're pissed at *us* for disrupting their lives." He shakes his head, still incredulous. "Fucking sheep. We stayed a couple days, then drove into the city for the benefit concert. Ended up panhandling in Times Square, begging for gas money back to school. Worth it, though, to see Carly Simon. Ever heard of her, Rubin?"

Amy rolls her eyes. "Please. I know who Carly Simon is." It is nearly true. She knows there was a Carly and a Carole, a Joni and a Janis. In her mind they are all the same woman, earnest, woolly-haired.

"Good times, Rubin. You'd have loved it. All evidence to the contrary, I think you have a hippie soul." He gets to his feet.

"Wait. I need you to sign something." Amy fumbles in her backpack and hands him the triplicate form—INTENT TO PURSUE MAJOR COURSE OF STUDY. Her heart races pleasantly.

"Seriously, Rubin? Geology?"

From across the aisle comes a squelched giggle, Caroline or Suki.

"What was your old major?"

"Undeclared," Amy says.

"You know what this means, right? You're mine now." He signs with a flourish. "See you at field camp."

IT WAS THE SUMMER OF ASTONISHMENTS, plural and various—the end of one thing (the classroom with its endless note-taking, its accumulation of unconnected facts) and the beginning of multiple others. A summer of extraordinary events, rare conspiracies of altitude and weather; of totemic apparitions beginning with the land itself, the West in all its sprawling actuality, its arid strangeness: the undulating anticline, the reddish moonscapes spiked with sage. For Amy Rubin—apartment raised, congenitally asthmatic—it was like tumbling through a portal. She was reduced, daily, to a state of dumb marvel, as though she'd spotted a dodo back from extinction, a creature modern humans weren't meant to see.

They came from the cities and comfortable suburbs, Rochester and Philadelphia and Montclair, New Jersey; Long Island and Westchester and Dutchess County, New York. At the baggage claim in Denver they eyed one another warily, four girls and twenty-six boys in laundered blue jeans and fresh T-shirts. (They wouldn't be this clean again in weeks.) There were a few loud reunions, kids from the sponsoring institution, a large SUNY campus. The rest, like Amy, came from liberal arts colleges with tiny departments and no field programs of their own.

She stood a little distance from the conveyor belt, her duffel bags piled at her feet. The group did not interest her, the gum-chewing undergraduates in college sweatshirts. They were not the reason she'd come.

"Amy, right?" said Dave or Mike or some other male syllable, a guy she recalled vaguely from a mineralogy class at Stirling. His face she barely remembered, but his body was familiar—well formed in the way of short men, long waisted, square in the shoulders. She had always recognized men by their outlines.

"I thought that was you. I didn't know you were a geo major." He studied her like some rare specimen. Tim was his name, the male syllable.

"Amy Rubin!"

She turned to see Lorne Trexler coming toward her—unshaven, radiantly sunburned. Under the airport lights his face was the color of canned ham. His eyes looked pale as litchi nuts, luminous—the enraptured gaze of a pilgrim back from the hajj.

It's you, she was about to say when he spoke.

"Don't tell me that's all yours." He pointed to her luggage—contemptuously, as though she'd messed on the floor. "We said two small packs. That's three, and they're huge."

"But one is a tent," she protested, feigning innocence. In truth she had overpacked knowingly, willfully disregarding the rules.

"A tent counts as one bag. We explained this. The other one is for your clothes."

"For five *weeks*? That's impossible." Impossible, too, to explain the battles she'd already won, the hundred small victories that allowed her to leave the apartment with *only* three monstrously large duffel bags. Her mother hovering as she packed, sneaking in contraband when Amy's back was turned: extra socks and underwear, eardrops and eyedrops, a small pharmacopoeia of ointments and pills.

You get seasick, she protested when Amy handed back the Dramamine.

I'm going to the desert, Amy said.

"Rubin, what am I going to do with you?"

"One extra bag makes that much difference?" The force of his exasperation dismayed her. It seemed beneath them to haggle over luggage.

"Do I really have to explain this? If everyone brought three, we'd have to hire an extra van." He squeezed the bridge of his nose; she was giving him a headache. "Sorry, Charlie. You're going to have to leave some things behind. We keep a storage locker at the airport."

Amy stared at him uncomprehendingly.

"Sort through them, if you need to. Pack and repack. Just be quick about it."

"Here?" Amy eyed the grimy floor. A wad of blue chewing gum stuck to the tile like a plasticated snail. "It's disgusting."

"Honey, it's the cleanest surface you'll see in weeks."

He stood watching as Amy knelt and emptied a duffel onto the floor: folded shorts and T-shirts, a box of Tampax, her shampoo, moisturizer, and hairspray.

"Good Lord, is that a hair dryer?"

Her face filled with blood.

An hour later they were driving west into blinding sunlight, a slow caravan. Each van carried ten students; a fourth was packed with their rucksacks. The final truck, the chuck wagon, was driven by the cook herself. Amy stared out the window, memorizing road signs: WILKERSON PASS 9,502 FEET. She hoarded this information like words of a new language. There was an interest in the altitude of things.

TRUCKERS: DON'T BE FOOLED! 4 MI OF STEEP DESCENT AND SHARP CURVES AHEAD.

TRUCKERS: YOU'RE NOT DOWN YET! 1 MI OF STEEP DESCENT AND SHARP CURVES TO GO.

They drove and drove. The road dipped and fell. "Holler if you need a pit stop," said Trexler, "but only if you need it. We want to make camp before dark."

The blinding sun was nearly overhead. "It's, like, one in the afternoon," said Amy.

"Correct," Trexler said.

LOST BRAKES? DO NOT EXIT. STAY ON HIGHWAY.

Dipping and falling, dipping and falling. Amy thought, regretfully, of the Dramamine. By the time they climbed out of the van and lined up outside a gas station restroom, she'd lost all interest in Lorne Trexler. She longed for a dim apartment, muted street noise, her own familiar bed.

They made camp east of Durango, near the Ute reservation. Shouldering their packs, they climbed a steep ridge. Trexler came up behind her. "You okay, Rubin? You look a little green."

"I have a headache." It seemed an absurd way to describe the pulsating pain lodged beneath her eyeballs, her skull encircled by a tourniquet.

He handed her a plastic water bottle. "Keep drinking. You're coming from sea level, remember. Altitude sickness is no joke."

She took the bottle and drained it in one go.

"Wow, nice technique. You must be formidable at those sorority chug-offs."

She flinched.

"Sorry. I'm an asshole. You really do look a little green. Here." He touched his thumb to her forehead and, to her astonishment, rubbed in a circular motion between her eyebrows. You couldn't call it sexy or romantic or even affectionate, and yet the touch nearly undid her.

She closed her eyes.

Later she would forget the beginning; the beginning wouldn't matter. She'd remember, instead, the Wingate Formation mesas, the anticline eroded in the middle. The abandoned gold mines— the Mayflower, the Old Hundred—with their ghostly names. Mapping horst and graben near Split Mountain—a hammer in her pack, a hand lens, a Brunton compass, everything she could possibly need.

The rainstorm in the Salt Lake Valley.

The Ute woman in Moab who lent her a pair of scissors.

The Green River, breathtakingly cold, where she jumped in shirtless. As though she'd seen a rare creature back from extinction, or become one herself.

The roadside motel where she studied her body in the shower: her blistered feet on fire, her arms burned brown by the sun. Filthy water circling the drain, the color of weak tea. She unwrapped a motel soap and washed until it disappeared.

The Laundromat run by a Ute woman, who sat clipping items from a newspaper. Amy chose the heavy-duty cycle and ran her jeans through twice.

The steakhouse on the highway, which catered to large groups. Vans and tour buses idled in the lot. She pulled up a chair and ate as though she were starving, Rocky Mountain oysters with Tabasco chasers, and Lorne Trexler touched what was left of her hair.

In Moab she stopped wishing, stopped waiting. She cut off her hair and ate ravenously. She might have done it weeks before if only she'd known.

The beginning didn't matter. The ending she'd remember forever, the roadside motel in Moab. As she might have done at any point, she simply knocked at his door.

1992

The Penn State campus has mushroomed, doubled or tripled in size. "We could ask for directions," Rena says as Mack drives, embarrassingly, in circles.

"It's been a long time. Nothing looks the same."

"That's okay. He's getting the lay of the land. Right, sweetie?"

In the backseat Calvin mumbles, "Whatever, Mom." The smart-aleck tone, the roll of the eyes: Mack, as a kid, had been smacked for less. She studies him in the rearview mirror. *Don't push your luck,* she tells him silently. *I'm watching you.*

They find the admissions building and park in a visitor space, ten minutes late for the campus tour. Another family is already waiting, a cute redhead and her well-dressed parents. Their tour guide is a chubby talkative girl dressed head to toe in Penn State–licensed apparel: hat, scarf, jacket, sweatpants. Even her tiny gold earrings are lion-shaped. She glances uncertainly from Mack to Rena. "Mrs. Weems?"

"Well, no. But close enough," says Rena. "I'm Calvin's mom."

They set out across a parking lot, the tour guide up front, followed by the redhead and the two mothers. Calvin and the father linger several paces behind. Mack walks alone, halfway between the men and the women, where she can hear both conversations at once without having to talk to anybody.

Rena is studying a campus map. Her eyes are bright, her color high. "Sweetie, that's the art building," she calls over her shoulder. "Calvin is considering an art major. He's very talented."

"Jesus Christ, Mom," Calvin mutters under his breath.

The kid is begging to have his clock cleaned.

"Awesome! Is this your first visit to Happy Valley?" the tour guide asks no one in particular.

"First time for me," says Rena. "Mack went to school here."

Did she? All the new buildings confuse her, the anonymous boxes of glass and brick. Every single one looks vaguely familiar, even those still under construction. Her memory, clearly, is not to be trusted.

"Oh, no kidding," says the tour guide. "What class?"

"I didn't graduate," says Mack, her breath steaming in the cold.

Behind her, the redhead's father is talking to Calvin. "Farma's been good to me. Vacation place in Hilton Head. We put three kids through school, all thanks to Farma."

Mack wonders: Who the hell is Farma?

They cross a grassy quadrangle, snow-flecked. Mack feels, finally, a gut punch of recognition: they are kitty-corner from B Quad. "That was my dorm," she tells Rena, pointing. "Over there, behind the gym."

"The new gym is on the other side of campus," says the tour guide. "Your partner means the old gym." *Partner.* She pronounces the word with a big smile, proud of her open-mindedness.

Mack blushes scarlet. When she and Rena refer to each other this way, they're talking about farm business. When other people use the word—Rena's sister in Akron, who blames Calvin's attitude on their *lifestyle*—it never means anything good.

They climb the hill to the library. "How's it going back there?" Rena calls over her shoulder. "It must be weird for you. Lots of memories."

"Yeah," says Mack, thinking, I beat the tar out of a guy behind that building. She has never told Rena this, Rena who despises violence. Who covers her eyes during action movies when an actor pretends to be shot.

The redhead explains that Penn State is her safety school.

"Right now Presslo is our bread and butter," her father tells Calvin. "For hypertension. A year from now it's going to be Lumox. You heard it here first."

"That's very interesting," Calvin says. For a moment Mack sees him through a stranger's eyes: a bright, articulate teenager, confident and self-assured, willing to make conversation with adults. It's a version of Calvin she never gets to see.

They round the bend to the cafeteria. One winter morning after breakfast, Lindy had slipped there on a patch of ice, twisting her ankle. As a joke Mack carried her home to B Quad. Lindy clung to her shoulders like a well-designed backpack, filled with soft things.

Calvin is willing to make conversation with adults, as long as they aren't Mack and Rena.

"Pharmaceutical sales is an interest of mine," he says, just loud enough for Mack to hear.

She could've knocked him sideways. It's hard to remember what he used to be: her hunting buddy, her fishing buddy. A long, long time ago.

"I wish my son could meet you," says the father. "He graduated last spring and still no job. I could get him in at Centex, but he's set on sports management. He's twenty-three. Believe it or not, Joe Montana hasn't called."

Calvin laughs politely.

At age fourteen he turned on her. Would it have been better if she were a man? Rena thinks it would've been worse. She blames the hormone storm of puberty, but the truth is darker and more complicated. The hunting and fishing ended when Calvin's father died. In some way that made no sense, he seemed to blame Mack for Freddy's death. *I didn't kill him*, Mack wanted to say.

Though of course she would've, given the chance.

Pharmaceutical sales. Mack would never have known if she hadn't run into her neighbor at the barbershop. Hank Becker was an old friend of her pop's. *Susan, I could swear I seen a fox in your back forty. Maybe go have a look. You don't want it getting in your coop.*

Mack took a look.

She made short work of Calvin's plants, swinging a sickle like a sturdy Cossack. The clippings looked like perfectly good forage, but was it safe for a cow to eat marijuana? Mack took no chances. She gathered the plants into trash bags and drove them to the dump.

On her way home, she stopped by the Beckers'. Hank was sitting on the front porch. *I saw that fox. I took care of it,* she called from the truck. *Thanks for letting me know.*

She didn't tell Calvin what she'd done. She let him figure it out on his own. He took a walk after supper and returned looking stricken. *You cut down my fucking plants.*

Mack said nothing. Just this once, she let the expletive slide.

You owe me for lost revenue, he said. *Six thousand dollars.*

Are you kidding? You're lucky I don't call the cops.

You wouldn't do that, said Calvin, but Mack could see in his eyes that he wasn't sure. *Are you going to tell Mom?*

That depends on you.

She believed, at first, that she was managing the situation. The threat would be enough to make him straighten up. He'd be grateful for his second chance and eventually, inevitably, they'd be buddies again. Later she saw how easily he'd played her, having sensed her weakness: her pathetic hope that he'd love her again, a secret Mack had kept even from herself. *You'll never tell Mom,* he said when some weeks had passed. *She'd never forgive you for lying to her.*

The tour ended, they head back in the direction of the Admissions Office. The pharmaceutical salesman falls into step beside Rena. "That's some kid you've got."

Rena looks ready to kiss him. "I'm very proud of him. Whoa!"

The salesman reaches out a hand to steady her, just in time, as she slides on a patch of ice. Rena seems not to notice his hand lingering at her back.

He was flirting with you, Mack will tell her later. She's seen it before, Rena's effect on men: the bearded young veterinary assistant, the horny fertilizer salesmen who stop by unannounced and dawdle on their porch for half the morning. Even Pop had come alive when Rena fussed over him. *She's a nice girl, Susan. She'll keep you company when I'm gone.* He was frail by the time Rena moved in, hadn't climbed the stairs in a year and maybe never knew that they were sharing a bedroom. Though even if he'd known, he'd have thought nothing of it. They were both girls.

It's nearly dusk as they turn onto the highway, the early dark of deep November. Rena turns in her seat. "Well, what did you think?"

In the backseat Calvin shrugs. "It doesn't matter. I'm not going."

Rena looks stunned.

"Even if I wanted to—which I don't—I can't apply this year. I didn't take the SAT."

"What do you mean, didn't take it?" says Rena. "For God's sake, why not?"

There is a silence.

"Well, it's only November," says Rena. "The application isn't due until January. You have plenty of time."

"Actually, I don't." Calvin smiles unpleasantly. "They only give the test on certain days. The next date isn't until spring."

Rena turns to Mack. "Is that true?" As though Mack's semester and a half of college have made her some kind of expert.

"I think so." Mack avoids Rena's eyes. Her disappointment is too painful to watch.

Mack studies Calvin in the rearview mirror, understanding that her mission has changed. For years she protected Rena from Freddy Weems. Her job, now, is to protect Rena from Freddy's son.

Pennsylvania History

Second Period

Oct. 1, 1995

"William A. Smith: Unsung Hero of the Pennsylvania
Oil Rush"

By Shelby Elizabeth Vance

When the world's first oil well was drilled, right
here in western Pennsylvania, Colonel Edwin Drake
was given all the credit. As a result, people think
that Colonel Drake (who was not actually a Colonel)
rolled up his sleeves and drilled the well all by
himself. Nothing could be further from the truth. In
fact, the driller of this historic well was a man by
the name of William A. Smith, known as "Uncle Billy."
(He was not actually any kin to Colonel Drake.)

"Uncle Billy" was trained as a blacksmith and
saltwater driller. His specialty was "fishing," that
is, recovering tools that were lost or broken inside
a salt well. When Colonel Drake came to Pennsylvania in 1859, he heard of "Uncle Billy's" reputation
and hired him (for $2.50 a day!) to come and drill
his well.

Progress was slow because of conditions around Oil
Creek. The groundwater was close to the surface. The
soil was a mixture of clay, sand, and gravel almost
forty feet thick. When "Uncle Billy" tried the tradi-

tional methods of drilling, the well would fill with water and it's walls would collapse. The story goes that Colonel Drake came up with the idea to drill inside an iron pipe pounded into the ground. This kept water from coming in and kept the well from collapsing. This "drive pipe" as it is now known was a unique invention that had never been used before.

In later years "Uncle Billy" claimed the drive pipe was his invention, but history, once again, gives the credit to Colonel Drake. Who really came up with this idea remains a mystery. The world will never know.

Colonel Drake may have a major highway named after him, but "Uncle Billy" is, in my opinion, the real hero of the Pennsylvania Oil Rush. He was married a total of three times and had nine children (one of whom died while he was working for Colonel Drake, another aspect of his life that is little known). In spite of his personal tragedy, "Uncle Billy" continued to drill wells in the oil region until 1870, when he retired to a farm in Butler County. He never earned any large sum of money from his work (or his farm for that matter), and lived on charity until his death.

The surviving children were named James, William, Samuel, Margaret, Ellen, Adeline, General Grant, and General Washington. ("Uncle Billy" did not actually serve in the Civil War, but was a lifelong patriot.)

It is not an exaggeration to say that the drilling of the first oil well transformed life in America. Though it is best known as a source of heat and light, petroleum also plays an important role in creating medicines that lessen suffering and make life more pleasant today. In addition, it is used in the making of plastic. If you look around a typical American home, you will see an amazing variety of products made of this material. It is literally impossible to imagine modern life without plastic.

In conclusion, it is important to remember the legacy of "Uncle Billy" as one of the "mysteries of history." Life is not always fair. When he died in 1890, "Uncle Billy" had the personal satisfaction of knowing he had drilled the world's first oil well, but also the heartbreak of seeing another man take all the credit.

2004

The days begin at seven. Beds are made, showers taken, breakfasts eaten. It is, arguably, the most useful part of the program, the dumb animal normality of living in daytime, sleeping at night. For years Darren has kept junkie's hours, nodding off at 9:00 A.M., at midday, at dusk.

After breakfast, meds are given. Men file in and out of the nurse's office, where the magic Jell-O shooters are dispensed. In light of his last, spectacular failure, Darren is not invited to the party. He is given a multivitamin and a cup of herbal tea that smells like socks.

He takes a small, sad pride in his bed making.

The tea is made from milk thistle, an ambitious herb that is going to detoxify his liver, or at least try.

Fortified with sock tea, he attends his morning group, which is called Steps. This is to distinguish it from the afternoon group, which is called Group.

At Steps, twenty guys work the program. They admit they are powerless over drugs, that their lives have become unmanageable, that a Power greater than themselves can restore them to sanity. They turn their lives over to the care of said.

You might find this hard to do, if you've ever considered yourself powerful. If you're Darren Devlin—as, regrettably, he is—this is not a problem. The first three steps are easy enough.

Step Four is the searching and fearless moral inventory, which is where the trouble begins.

This time around, Darren has a head start. His last time in rehab—two shortlong years ago—he made it all the way to Step Eight: *We made a list of all persons we had harmed, and became willing to make amends to them all.*

Willingness was not the problem. He was willing enough. The problem was the list itself, which included every person he had interacted with since the age of fourteen. The list contained multitudes. The day after he completed his searching and fearless moral inventory, he walked out the front door, caught the 12 bus at the bottom of the hill, rode sixteen blocks, and wandered the neighborhood until he ran into Nelson.

Faced with such a list, an unending litany of shames and failures, anyone—anyone—would want to get high.

Nelson was his best friend, an old junkie. How old exactly, and whether Nelson was his first or last name, Darren never knew. With a few notable interruptions—hospitals, prison—Nelson had been fixing since the seventies, the golden age of Baltimore heroin. When the supply dried up in the eighties, he'd actually gone to live in Afghanistan, where his colossal habit could be maintained for pocket change. Before the terrorists and American soldiers had ruined everything, Kabul had been the junkie's Mecca, his Medina, his Lourdes. Someday, when the bullets stopped flying, Nelson and Darren would travel there together.

Afghanistan was Darren's exit strategy, his plan for the future. High, he'd been impressed by his own foresight.

There was power in having a plan.

THE NAMES ON HIS EARLIER LIST carry forward like a bad debt.

His senior year in high school, the Bakerton Rotary Club had awarded Darren a small grant, called the Hope Scholarship. Placed in the context of a massive tuition bill from Johns Hopkins, it was more than nothing, but only a little more.

The Rotarians were big on ceremony. They presented the award at a special banquet. Darren was called to the stage and handed a giant replica of his thousand-dollar check, printed on poster board.

The Hope Scholarship existed because of his father. Years earlier, when Darren was still in junior high, Dick Devlin had sold his fellow Rotarians on the idea of funding a scholarship in the sciences. *I was thinking ahead,* he admitted to Darren later. *I thought it might come in handy for you someday.*

For years Dick had been laying groundwork, so that Darren could receive the Hope Scholarship. It is—well, sobering—to think.

Arnold Wu had been his first lab partner in Organic Chemistry—a shy, serious kid from Southern California who shattered all Darren's assumptions about that place. Their first experiment involved recrystallization. They'd written the report together, an all-nighter fueled by Red Bull and two Adderalls Darren had bought from a guy in his dorm.

The second week's experiment involved melting points. Darren had been late for class, but Arnold had started without him. He'd given Darren his notes to copy, the calculations written in mechanical pencil, in Arnold's careful hand.

The third week's experiment, Darren can't remember. Whether he'd gone to class high, or had gone only in his imagination, was impossible to say.

O-Chem was a weed-out class. By second semester the class had shrunk by a third. Thanks entirely to Arnold Wu, Darren was not weeded out. His second lab partner in Organic Chemistry was Holly Gillman and this was much, much worse, because Holly Gillman had loved him.

She was not a pretty girl, for what that mattered. As Leah Radulski had in high school, Holly chose him for her own inscrutable reasons.

At the end of freshman year he was invited back to the Rotarians' banquet, to give a speech on his experience at Hopkins. Darren promised to attend. He'd had every intention of going. He had even borrowed Holly's car.

His academic adviser, at that time, was a woman named Greta Schenkel. That summer she paid him—generously—to house-sit and watch her cat while she visited her parents in Stuttgart. For an entire month he enjoyed the professor's stereo and projection TV, usually with total strangers—people who'd given or sold him dope, or promised to.

One night he returned to Greta Schenkel's and found a smashed window. He never got around to reporting the robbery. That night— that entire summer—he was in no shape to deal with cops. He called Nelson instead.

When he crashed Holly's car he had called her in a panic. There were no witnesses to the accident. He convinced her to tell the police that she, not Darren, had been driving.

He slept with her because it made her easier to deal with.

He still owes Holly Gillman several thousand dollars. More, possibly. He has no idea—he's never asked—what she pays for car insurance.

He is not entirely sure when the cat ran away.

The stories are numberless.

THE SCHEDULE SETS ASIDE two hours for phone calls. From eleven to noon is Phone Out. From five to six P.M. is Phone In.

Twice a day Darren stations himself at an actual pay phone, the kind that used to exist in the world and now is found only in rehab, where cell phones—with their treasure troves of stored numbers, the suppliers on speed dial—are not allowed.

He starts small. All things considered, he doesn't feel too bad about Arnold Wu, who'd requested, and was assigned, another lab partner. Arnold, at least, had the stones to save himself.

Now a post-doc at MIT, he doesn't at first, and possibly not even later, remember who Darren is.

"Oh, *Darren*," he says finally, in a parody of remembering. "How are you, man?"

As though the words *I'm in heroin rehab* don't answer that question.

"No sweat," he says, when Darren explains his reason for calling. "Actually—this is kind of funny—my lab partner after you? You remember Wendy?"

Darren thinks, Did Wendy sell smack? No? Sorry, don't remember.

"We're married now. With a baby on the way. So I guess I should be thanking you."

You're welcome, Darren thinks as he hangs up. I'm so glad my addiction has worked out for you.

Greta Schenkel no longer teaches at Johns Hopkins. Possibly she went back to Germany, says the indifferent graduate student who answers the phone.

Gia Bernardi's cell phone number is stored in his own cell phone, which had been confiscated at Intake. From some remote part of his brain undestroyed by opiates, he conjures forth her parents' phone number, where he'd phoned her every day for an entire summer, a lifetime ago.

Rocco is winded, a little wheezy. He sounds very old. "Hang on," he rasps. "I'll get her."

"Hello?" says Gia. "Hello?"

Darren remembers clearly the first time they got high. Without him she would never have picked up a joint. Of this he is utterly sure.

He hangs up the phone.

The first time he calls Holly Gillman, she hangs up on him. The second time she weeps. The third time she hangs up again. None of this is the actual problem.

The problem is that he can't call his mom.

THE NEXT DAY he tries again. This time, Gia herself answers. His contrition seems to amuse her.

"Sorry for what? We had a fucking blast that summer. Anyways," says Gia.

And just like that, she changes the subject. About Darren's Eighth Step—his moral imperative to make amends, his paralyzing guilt and shame—she has nothing to say.

"You doing good?" she asks. "What do you do for fun in there?"

"Fun is discouraged."

"I was really sorry to hear about your mom."

The words cause him physical pain.

"It was a beautiful service. Stoner's did a great job. Even Rocco said so, and he's critical."

The pain lodged in his throat like something that could choke him.

"She looked good. She was pretty banged up, you know, but they covered everything."

Darren swallows very deliberately, searching and fearless.

"They tried so hard to find you. Your dad even called *me*. He thought I'd know how to reach you. I tried your cell, but it wouldn't let me leave a message. The mailbox was full."

Darren had been, at the time, unfindable. This was no accident. This was completely by design.

They tried for days to find him. He learned, some months later, that his brother Rich had come to Baltimore to track him down. He was seen lurking around the old apartment in Charles Village, a big blond guy who looked like a cop. Darren was by then locked out of his apartment. He heard the rumor third-hand from Gary Beasom, who lived in the building and sold substandard weed, cheap quarter-ounce bags of seeds and stems. *They're watching you, man*, said Gary, a conclusion Darren recognized as pot smoker's paranoia but did not dispute. It was in some way flattering, that he was important enough to be watched by cops. It never occurred to him that his brother would come looking for him, or why.

That spring, like every spring, Sally's daffodils would bloom before the snow melted.

The family postponed her funeral as long as possible. Finally, the day before Christmas, they put his mother in the ground.

2005

Because somebody really should, Wesley ponders the question of water.

Two million gallons spilled during the accident; untold gallons contaminated during the cleanup. (The radioactive crust packed into underwater canisters. The water sprayed by wheeled robots at the basement walls.)

Untold because no one is asking. Fucking journalists! Wesley is outraged by their slapdash methods. They never ask the questions he wants them to.

The basement of the reactor building was too hot for humans. Cesium-137, a by-product of atom splitting, had soaked into the floor and walls. In spraying them, an untold volume of water was contaminated. Which, of course, had to be disposed of somewhere.

"Fuck," Wesley says.

It's his new favorite word, deployed when anything aggrieves him: shoddy reporting, night sweats, or, today, the childproof cap on his Lumox, which is nearly impossible to open even with two adult hands. At least twice a week the cap defeats him completely. He pries it off with psychotic force, sending a shower of (blue, 10 milligram) capsules flying. Jessie refilled his Lumox just yesterday. This morning ninety capsules—a full month's supply—landed on the bathroom floor.

"Fuck," Wesley said.

The mess was, in that moment, too much to face. He closed the bathroom door and returned to his desk. The half-life of Cesium-137 is thirty-three years. He has, somewhere, a monograph on its other properties, though he can't remember where it is. In the spare bedroom are four full-size filing cabinets, each half-filled. On the floor, the desk, the nightstand, the bed, a dozen piles of documents are waiting to be filed. There are newspaper items and engineers' reports. There are memos on the letterhead of the Nuclear Regulatory Commission—made public under the Freedom of Information Act, acquired over several trips to the Pennsylvania State Archives in Harrisburg. There are full issues of his favorite periodicals, *Radiation Oncology* and the *Journal of Environmental Medicine:* double-blind, placebo-controlled studies of treatments that don't work, and longitudinal population studies that prove this is so. Jessie has offered to help organize his papers, but Wesley has, so far, resisted. Once something is filed, it is lost to him forever. He has a problem letting go.

He returns to the bathroom to gather up his Lumox, handling the capsules gingerly. After insurance, he pays a dollar a pill. At his new daily dosage of 30 milligrams, he can't afford to toss them in the trash. He can't afford to consider what sorts of microbes are living on his bathroom floor.

The containment building flooded with reactor water—two, maybe three million gallons, highly radioactive. Where the fuck did it all go?

He began cursing one morning as they drove away from the hospital, a morning of bad news. Jessie was at the wheel—even before his illness, a near constant in their marriage. She had always been the better driver.

"Fuck," Wesley said.

Reflexively she hit the brake. "What did you say?"

"Fuck," he repeated wonderingly. "You know, I don't believe I've ever said that out loud."

This occurred seven weeks ago. He was—still is—thirty-three years old.

He marvels, now, at his old prudery, his lifelong rejection of strong language. Why had he denied himself the pleasure? His parents had believed in godly speech. His father, especially, tolerated no lapses. It was his main grievance against television, which he judged full of profanity, portentously changing the channel when an actor said *hell* or *damn*.

Thirty-three was Jesus's age at Crucifixion. The half-life of Cesium-137 is thirty-three years. The most ordinary sort of coincidence, and yet from long habit Wesley probes it for significance, some deeper meaning hidden in the number. He recognizes the ridiculousness of the impulse. Years of Bible study have turned his brain to mush.

The containment building contained a container, which contained other containers.

He curses behind closed doors only, out of respect for his congregation. He does it badly, with no ear for the nuances. *What the shit?* he once fumed, when a minivan cut them off in the hospital parking lot. Jessie had laughed herself purple. He had married a laughing woman, the best decision of his life.

Supplying meaning where none exists is a rare cognitive skill, useless except in certain professions—fortune-telling, advertising. For the biblical scholar it is a necessary aptitude—the only one, possibly. Nothing can be allowed to mean only what it means. Numbers, especially, are fraught with subtext. (Seven: completion, perfection. Forty: the time needed for God to act.) The ultimate test of this ability being, of course, the book of Revelation—a bedtime story for the fanciful, the desperate, the paranoid, the mad.

He returns his Lumox to its amber plastic bottle—WESLEY PEACOCK LUMOX 10 MG TAKE 3X DAY WITH FOOD—and places it on the shelf. When did it become *his* Lumox? It is terrible to contemplate, this intimacy with the drug, an arranged marriage brokered by Big

Pharma. Courtship happens in thirty-second increments, between segments of the evening news, a grim variation on speed dating: the ailing elder introduced, night after night, to a series of drugs, any one of which might become *his*. A true match depends on a constellation of factors: symptoms, side effects. Like all romances, it comes down to chemisty. *Talk to your doctor,* the avuncular voice-over advises.

The evening news is lousy with these commercials, in which lively active seniors enjoy their grandkids without worrying about acid reflux or hip fractures, atrial fibrillation or sudden stroke.

Wesley will never have grandkids.

The ugly truth is that he resents them, these spry happy oldsters with their pharmaceutically generated erections. Their dogged pursuit of health seems the worst kind of greediness.

"Seventy or eighty years: that isn't enough for you?" he asks the handsome old gent pushing his granddaughter in a swing.

"Die already," he tells the screen.

With the clinic staff he is surly, unpleasant. After twenty-six irradiations to the head and neck, he is questioned about side effects. "How does your skin feel?" he was asked this morning, by a pretty young nurse who looked nearly old enough to drive.

"It feels burnt."

"Like a sunburn," she said, making a note in his chart.

It will be the defining memory of his time in treatment, this unending talk of sunburns, which began at the initial consult. By week three, the radiation oncologist explained, most patients noticed a slight flushing of the treated area. *Like a sunburn,* he added with a wave of the hand. At the time it seemed a reasonable comparison, if unhelpful. Wesley had rarely spent more than ten consecutive minutes in the sun.

This morning, finally, he had enough. "You people need to stop saying that."

The child nurse looked up from his chart.

"I understand it's a useful shorthand. You all say it, and I'm sure you believe it." Wesley's heart worked loudly; his face felt hot. Like a sunburn, he thought.

"Maybe nobody's ever told you, or maybe you don't care, but in case you're interested, it feels nothing like a sunburn." And there is no Santa Claus, and no comfort and no justice. All that you cling to is false.

The child nurse looked at him as though he'd lost his mind.

At week three the skin begins to redden.

At week four the skin begins to weep.

His cancer, caused by radiation, is being treated with radiation. The irony does not escape him. The irony is nearly too much to bear.

He has learned that the dying are not saintly, a shattering discovery. In his years of ministry, he regularly visited hospitals to comfort the sick. Now the memory shames him, the scripture verses he regurgitated, the hollow platitudes spoken in the smugness of health. He believed, then, what all healthy people believe: that the dying are critically, profoundly different from themselves.

Now that it has left him definitively, he understands the true nature of faith.

The day of his first treatment, an intake nurse had asked his religious preference. He explained that, to his great surprise, he rarely thought of the afterlife. Now that it was just around the corner, eternity held no fascination at all. It was the present that called to him, the physical world that had never interested him until he was about to leave it.

He explained that faith is the child of fear, a primal terror shared by all animals, the dread of our own negation. Desperate to believe himself eternal, man will embrace the wildest fiction: the ultimate redemption, the final justice, the godman who walked the earth. Faith, in the end, is human stubbornness on a heroic scale—the passionate denial, the absolute and abiding refusal to die.

"Religious preference?" she repeated.

"None," Wesley said.

NUMBERS, ESPECIALLY, are fraught with subtext.

Twenty-six years ago, at the time of the disaster at Three Mile Island, the boy Wesley Peacock was seven years old.

The mean latency of radiosensitive solid tumors is twenty to thirty years.

Even Jessie doesn't understand the impulse, his need to know what killed him. Note the past tense: in every way that matters, Wesley is already dead. And yet, thanks to technology, he is a corpse in possession of abundant information. Each day he adds to his store.

He nearly says it aloud one night at dinner. *I died in the Golden Age of terminal illness.* Jessie's face stops him, because he loves her terribly. Because, even enraged, he is not cruel.

In the spring of 1979, President Carter appointed the Kemeney Commission to study the accident. Politically, the timing was delicate. With the election looming, panelists were chosen carefully. The main criterion for selection was a lack of conviction about anything. Carter lost the election anyway.

Four days after the accident, he toured the site in yellow booties, to keep from contaminating his shoes.

In 1979 the Pennsylvania Department of Health set up the Three Mile Island Population Registry, a list of people who lived, at the time of the disaster, within five miles of the plant. The list is compared each year against the state's record of death certificates. Of the 32,135 names in the Population Registry, three are Wesley, Eugene, and Bernadette Peacock. Wesley Peacock is dying. Eugene and Bernadette are already dead. Both names have been ticked off the Registry, the cause of each death duly noted: Cardiac Arrest and Undetermined. Their deaths were not attributable to Three Mile Island.

Radiation at levels above 5 millirem will cause fogging of high-speed photographic film.

Wesley's father suffered a heart attack a week after his retirement. The timing is not unusual, in men especially. Death comes when a man loses his higher purpose—in the case of Gene Peacock, the selling of animal feed.

The Registry makes no distinction between Gene's death and that of his wife, who on March 28, 1979, was pregnant and didn't know it; who wouldn't live long enough to develop leukemia or breast cancer and so, according to the Registry, was no more a casualty than Gene. At the time of her miscarriage, Bernadette failed to see a doctor, and so the Population Registry doesn't account for the unhatched Peacock, the baby desperately wanted and grievously lost.

Undetermined is, possibly, a misnomer. Wesley strongly suspects—he will never know for certain—that his mother was determined to die.

That summer, engineers from Eastman Kodak went door-to-door in the neighborhood, collecting undeveloped film. Bernadette, who didn't own a camera anyway, heard the doorbell but was too tired to move. She had finally seen a doctor, who prescribed Valium to help her relax.

Carter lost the election because of the hostages.

None of the film showed unusual fogging.

She took a fistful of Valium and drifted off to sleep.

Years later, after Chernobyl exploded, a team of Russian scientists appeared in Pennsylvania to ask questions. They made phone calls and knocked on doors. The Russians took blood samples from twenty-nine people and performed cytogenetical analysis. Their findings are not known.

(Fucking journalists: why those twenty-nine people? What were the principles of selection? What dark, inscrutable Soviet knowledge drove such choices? Dead Wesley wants to know.)

In Pennsylvania, four dead Peacocks.

The spring after Chernobyl the starlings never came.

Like all legit catastrophes, Three Mile Island has been explained by academics. The Theory of Normal Accidents: an unanticipated interaction of multiple failures in a complex system. The disaster was unexpected, incomprehensible, uncontrollable, and unavoidable, according to people who know.

Hundreds of photocopied pages, studies of studies. The studies look at rates of various cancers, of stillbirth and miscarriage, and arrive at the same conclusion: there was no significant increase in cancers, stillbirth, or miscarriage. (All calculations assume minimal exposure to radiation, a condition imposed by the courts.)

Wesley replaces the childproof cap and gets to his feet and feels, too late, a precious blue gel cap crushed beneath the heel of his slipper. Four months from now, his name will be crossed off the Registry. His anaplastic thyroid cancer, diagnosed seven weeks ago, will not be attributed to the accident at Three Mile Island.

If minimal exposure is assumed, a statistically significant correlation is impossible. Which raises the question—

(*You're making yourself crazy,* Jessie tells him periodically.)

Which raises the question—

(*Please stop,* says Jessie.)

Which raises the question: If the study design makes it impossible to disprove the null hypothesis, why do the study at all?

(His wife is grateful to go to work each morning.)

Why do the study at all?

To Dead Wesley the answer is obvious. Do the study to have done the study. To have pages of data suitable for photocopying, for filing away in a drawer.

NUMBERS, ESPECIALLY, are fraught with subtext.

The ten-year survival rate of papillary thyroid cancer is 93%.

The ten-year survival rate of follicular thyroid cancer is 85%.

The ten-year survival rate of medullary thyroid cancer is 75%.

The ten-year survival rate of anaplastic thyroid cancer is (no data).

None of the film showed unusual fogging. And yet, in Harrisburg, the infant death rate tripled. Hundreds of people reported skin sores and lesions, a metallic taste in the mouth.

SLEEP ELUDES HIM. He can't do enough to make himself tired. Late at night, after Jessie is in bed, he creeps downstairs to watch TV. Of the 146 channels, one is as good as another. Sitcoms and infomercials, the Home Shopping Network. He simply wants to hear a human voice.

One night, flipping through the channels, he finds a movie already in progress—one made for TV, in the seventies probably. He can tell this at a glance, without knowing how he knows. The lighting, maybe—like pale, watery sunshine—or the fuzzy resolution of the videotaped image. Was this the way all television used to look? Wesley remembers, vaguely, that fine-tuning had been required. If the actors looked a little green, you fiddled with the TINT knob. If the picture jumped, you adjusted HORIZONTAL HOLD.

This movie he recognizes immediately. *The Boy in the Plastic Bubble* conjures, in an instant, the whole of his childhood. For that reason and others, it is nearly too painful to watch.

The film is far, far stupider than he could have imagined, dreadful by every measure: the cheesy sets and insipid music, the acting embarrassingly sincere. Its premise—the child born without an immune system, confined to a sterile wing of his parents' suburban ranch house—now seems ludicrous, though as a kid he'd accepted it without question. Had been, in fact, haunted by it: for months or maybe years afterward, the characters had appeared in his dreams.

What did this say about the boy Wesley Peacock?

Watching, he is haunted all over again, not by the idiotic film but by his young self: an indoorsy boy prone to childhood ailments, afraid of the larger world and, especially, of other kids. A boy who craved the sober company of adults, his mother specifically. Bernadette had been his best friend and nursemaid, her attention to his colds and earaches well worth the discomfort of a runny nose. Sickness had seemed to him, then, the height of luxury—the cherry-flavored cough syrup, the lozenges. His mother bringing his meals on a tray.

More than anything he'd wanted to be an invalid, to be cosseted and cared for, a horrible realization. To Dead Wesley the irony is nearly intolerable. It is, truly, too sharp to bear.

He forces himself to keep watching. The problem with the acting, he sees now, is the players' great conviction. They seem not to understand that the story is preposterous. Instead of making their performances better, this only makes them seem pathetic, gullible actors fooled by some fast-talking director into embarrassing themselves.

You know, the Bubble Boy tells his doctor, *I'm not so unhappy in here as all of you think.*

He recalls, now, that *The Boy in the Plastic Bubble* was also a love story. The teenage Bubble Boy spends most of his time staring through binoculars at the girl next door, until finally—improbably—she invites him to a beach party. The scene is exactly as Wesley remembers it, and no wonder—as a kid, in the age before VCRs, he replayed it in his memory a thousand times: the Bubble Boy wheeled to the beach on a gurney in an airtight glass case; the girl in her bikini riding up on horseback. As a boy he'd found the image electric. It was, in fact, the first erotic fantasy in which he had cast himself: the girl riding toward him, breasts bouncing. Himself safe in his glass box like a giant corsage.

Weird. Beyond weird.

Weirder still is that even now, the scene stirs him. Not the teenage actress, whom he barely recognizes. In his fantasy he'd recast her as Jessie, his own girl next door. The only girl he would ever love.

The beach scene, it turns out, is the highlight of the film. Dead Wesley watches, slightly bored, as the Bubble Boy attends high school, first on closed-circuit television and later in person, wearing a polyester space suit with a battery on his back. The scene is excruciating to watch, the one moment where the film bears any resemblance to actual life. Against his will he remembers the trauma of finding himself, for the first time, in a public school classroom, surrounded by kids his own age—boys and girls in the throes of puberty, buzzing with some strange energy he didn't understand.

He turns off the TV.

He has no desire to relive the film's maudlin final scene, the boy stepping out of his bubble to ride off on horseback with the girl (and, presumably, fuck her before she goes off to college, an implication Wesley was too innocent to grasp at the time). As a kid he'd hated the ending, which struck him as a betrayal, an affront to bubble-dwellers everywhere. To Dead Wesley it is a different kind of outrage.

He turns the TV back on.

The truth is that anger is invigorating. In his final months it is the only emotion that makes him feel alive. The laughable climactic scene—the boy's blithe departure from his bubble—was clearly written by an obnoxiously young and healthy person. Who else could take survival so lightly? Who else could imagine throwing away—for love or sex or freedom; for any reason whatsoever—his precious only life?

EACH DAY AT NOON, he puts a bathrobe over his pajamas and listens for a car in the driveway, Shelby Vance coming to give him his lunch. Shelby Devlin, now, though Wesley has trouble thinking of her as a married woman, a wife and mother. As an adult of any kind. *She seems a little simple,* Jessie has said more than once, but that isn't it, exactly. Shelby is as unguarded as a child. You never know what's going to come out of her mouth.

"How are you feeling?" she asks when he opens the door. It has replaced *hello* as their standard greeting.

"Fine. A little sunburned." He is surprised to see her without Olivia, whom she normally hauls along in a bassinet, awkwardly, like a pail of wash water. At first Wesley found the baby's presence irritating. He was—still is—unnerved by infants, their incessant demands. And yet today he is disappointed not to see her. When they run out of words, he and Shelby watch Olivia like television. Without her, there will be even less to talk about.

"It's Rich's day off," says Shelby. "I asked him to babysit."

Is it possible to babysit one's own children? Wesley doesn't ask. He has met Shelby's husband only once, and finds them an unlikely couple. Rich Devlin is Wesley's age but seems older, a gruff man who, oddly, reminds him of his own father. Shelby, as far as he can tell, has changed little since age fourteen.

"How hungry are you? I can make two sandwiches."

"One is plenty," says Wesley, who hasn't been hungry in months.

He watches her move around the kitchen, locating bread, butter, canned soup. She knows the kitchen as well as Jessie does.

"He can handle them one at a time, just not together. So this is kind of an experiment." Shelby places his cheese sandwich in the pan. "Of course, in a couple weeks it won't matter. Braden is starting preschool."

"That will be nice for you," says Wesley.

"Oh, no," she says gravely. "I'd keep him home with me forever if I could."

"Be careful what you wish for. I was homeschooled. I'm pretty sure I drove my mother nuts."

Shelby looks astonished. "You can do that?"

"Sure. A lot of people do." He is regularly amazed by what she doesn't know. "For religious reasons, mainly. They don't necessarily agree with what's taught in the public schools."

"Is that why your parents did it?"

"I guess so." Oddly, he has never wondered. The flip side of Shelby Devlin: the question that startles. "It was probably my dad's idea. He had opinions."

"Did you like it?"

He is reminded, again, of the idiotic movie, the Bubble Boy in his ludicrous space suit, tormented by his classmates. Mood swings are a common side effect of Lumox. Absurdly, he is near tears.

"Loved it. Though in retrospect I'm not sure it was good for me. You look nice," he says to change the subject. Instead of her usual jeans and sweatshirt, Shelby wears a skirt and blouse, her waist cinched by a wide belt of red leather. The belt strikes him as part of a costume, the crime-fighting gear of a cartoon superhero.

"It feels good to dress up once in a while. I never get a chance anymore."

"Me neither," Wesley says, but Shelby doesn't even smile. She has no sense of humor, not even a bad one, a quality he finds slightly exotic.

She places his grilled cheese on a plate, the plate on a tray. She pours him a glass of milk and a glass of water, and sets out his Lumox. Her skirt is very short. On another woman it might be sexy. Shelby seems, simply, to have outgrown her clothes.

Shelby plus anyone makes an unlikely couple.

She returns the milk and butter to the fridge. "It's good to see you up and around. Do you want some company while you eat? I have a whole hour. If I'm gone longer than that, Rich panics. He's afraid he'll have to change a diaper."

"Don't worry about me," says Wesley. "Tell Rich I said hello."

He walks her to the door. Her legs are long and skinny; is that a good thing? He has never understood the fascination with women's legs.

"Thank you for coming," he tells her. "It helped."

She takes a small step toward him. "Are you sure you don't need me to stay?"

Dead Wesley studies her, puzzled. It is an indicator of his dead-ness that he does not, at first, understand her meaning.

She takes another step.

I have lost my mind, he thinks as he lets Shelby kiss him. The realization is less troubling than it should be. He has already lost everything else.

They kiss with abandon, an expression that once baffled him and now makes perfect sense. He abandons hope, honor, the illu-sion of consequence. The doomed boy steps out of his bubble, into the very short future.

They kiss with abandon, as the living do.

He leads her downstairs into the basement office. The futon is piled with documents he will never file. With abandon he knocks them to the floor.

He kisses her with what's left of him. Her skin feels powerfully alive, shockingly warm beneath her blouse.

Their undressing is dyssynchronous. Wesley wears pajamas, easy on, easy off, like a giant baby who requires frequent changes. Shelby's outfit is a gauntlet of complicated fasteners: the Wonder Woman belt with its multiple buckles, the bra and garter stockings. All this takes time.

"What's the matter?" says Shelby.

"Nothing. I'm sorry," he says. "It's not your fault."

She flushes nearly purple. "Did I do something wrong?"

"I'm taking a lot of medication," he mumbles. "Nothing really works anymore."

"That's okay. I should get going anyway." Quickly, furtively, she reassembles her elaborate armor. He has never seen anyone dress so fast.

Dead Wesley walks her to the door. When he finishes dying, 122 days from now, the time he failed to make love to Shelby Devlin will be the only secret he ever kept from Jessie.

The dying are not saintly.

In a kind of trance he watches her drive away, Shelby who'd been willing—eager—to lie down with a dead man. Understanding, at last, how truly exotic she is.

An unanticipated interaction of multiple failures in a complex system. Was there ever a better description of human life?

Based on the assumption of minimal exposure, no ill effects were observed.

THE
COLLECTIVE NEED
AUGUST 2012

9

Do you have a persistent, nagging problem? Do you have too many to count?

All over the Commonwealth, the deleterious effects of gas drilling are coming to light.

Does your tap water have a foul odor? Is it cloudy or greasy-looking? How is your health?

If you and your family are caught in a fracking nightmare, you have valuable legal rights.

Dizziness, nausea, diarrhea. Skin irritations are common. Do you have unexplained boils or rashes? Insomnia or excessive sleepiness? Do you find it difficult to breathe?

For more than forty years, Attorney Paul Zacharias has stood up for the little guy. We strive to maximize your financial recovery.

Headaches, memory loss. Cognitive symptoms are not uncommon. Are you easily confused?

Among gas patch workers, injuries are rampant: falls, explosions, toxic spills, automotive accidents. Attorney Paul Zacharias has fought and won generous settlements in the areas of Personal Injury, Wrongful Death, and Product Liability (due to defective machinery/equipment).

What is the general state of your livestock? Have you noticed birth defects or decreased fertility?

Attorney Paul Zacharias has been awarded a "Pre-eminent 5

out of 5 rating" representing "the highest level of professional excellence." Call today to arrange a free and confidential assessment of your claim. Can't come to us? No problem! Let us come to your home, hospital, or union hall.

Attorney Paul Zacharias is your ally. Together we can hold the frackers responsible. We call it Frackountability™.

Are you confused yet?

Each revelation is to be acknowledged with applause.

A BELL RINGS: ten-minute movement. A ding is escorted to the Ding Wing. Correctional Officer Devlin—now back on day shift— makes his rounds.

Visiting hours begin at 2:00 P.M., though for most inmates— resented by wives, abandoned by lovers, scorned by children—this is largely theoretical. *The world goes on without you,* Hops explained to him once. *You been gone so long they forgot you was ever there.*

In Devlin's block only two inmates have visitors. He stops first at Wanda's cell.

"Officer Devlin! What a pleasure. I was expecting Officer Mulraney."

"He's out sick," Devlin says.

Wanda is looking rough. Literally, in fact. Devlin notices it mainly on second shift: by midafternoon her chin is shadowed with beard. It is said that Mulraney has stopped slipping her birth control pills. Possibly he has other things on his mind: his wife still on disability, plagued by mysterious symptoms the doctors can't make sense of. Losing the baby, it is generally agreed, was a blessing. In her current state she couldn't take care of another one.

Of course, no one has ever said this to Steph.

He unlocks Wanda's cell. She has a new hairdo, a ponytail high on her head like the leafy crown of a pineapple.

"Officer Devlin. You're looking expecially handsome this morning." She lowers her voice theatrically. "I hope Mrs. Devlin appreciates you."

"I hope so, too." It's as close as he will allow himself to banter.

He leads her down the corridor to the visitors' room, where the sister—a pretty, round-faced teenager Wanda calls Ray Ray—is already waiting. She is a shorter, plumper version of Wanda: same high cheekbones, same wide painted mouth. A girl who once had a brother and now has a sister; who makes the long bus trip from Philadelphia (five hours, two transfers) to smuggle in nail polish.

In the world—and especially in prison—love is weird-looking.

"Girl," says Ray Ray. "What you did to your hair?"

Devlin leaves them, the door clanging shut behind him. He returns to the block and finds Weems lying on his bunk, reading a magazine.

A tip is a gang is a ganga is a clica. A waterhead is an outcast, a guy without homies. A guy who can't or won't tip up.

"Weems. You have a visitor."

He unlocks the cell and they walk silently down the corridor. Weems is small and slight, a head shorter than Devlin and fifty pounds lighter. Not the sort of guy who fares well in prison, a fact he should have considered before doing dirt that would get him locked up. Devlin came to a similar conclusion some years ago, when his brother was on drugs. Locked in with animals like Offill and Cholley, Darren would have been an easy target, a handful of chum tossed to the sharks.

A hog is an angry hoodlum who won't back down, always looking for a fight.

If I were Weems, Devlin thinks, I would definitely tip up.

"All right, then. Have a good visit." He unlocks the door and sees, through the Plexiglas, his neighbor Rena Koval, dressed in hospital scrubs.

"Hi, Mom," Weems says.

HIS SHIFT ENDED, Devlin changes out of his uniform—he has taken to showering at the prison—and gets into his truck.

He knows nothing, nothing at all, about his neighbors.

Years ago, the world was different. Pap had been friendly with Pete Mackey, Mack's father. Each winter, at slaughtering time, the Beckers and the Mackeys had gone in together on a beef cow. It was more meat than either family could eat on its own.

Had Pap known Pete's daughter was a lesbian? Is *lesbian* even the right word?

It's hard to think of Mack as female. Last summer, when Rich was building the deck, he twice saw her at the lumberyard, a big snuff-chewing woman in overalls. She acknowledged him with a curt nod, as a man would do.

Years ago, neighbors were neighborly. Rich believes this firmly, though the exact source of his belief is not clear. People pitched in at barn raisings, shared equipment, looked after each other's kids and animals. (Also, they ate a lot of meat.) Pulling into Walmart, he wonders how often Rena visits her son. It's possible she's at Deer Run every week, and Rich, who for years worked mostly night shifts, simply failed to notice.

He can't, without a deliberate and tactical leap of imagination, think of Mack as female.

He ignores the old coot greeting visitors at the door.

At the back of the store Rich loads his shopping cart. The water comes in five-gallon plastic tanks. He pays for his water and wheels it out to his truck, wishing he had a bed liner. Each tank should last two days, by his calculation. And yet—somehow—he was here just yesterday. It's his third Walmart trip this week.

Rena Koval doesn't look like a lesbian. And anyway, you don't expect a lesbian to have a son.

It occurs to him that Walmart is part of the problem. His grandmother bought shoes at Meyer's, furniture at Friedman's, fabric at the five-and-dime. Pap was a regular customer at the hardware store in town. As a boy Rich had sometimes gone along with him. Pap, a sociable guy, always ran into someone he knew. All those stores are gone now.

Rich is not, himself, a sociable guy.

At Walmart you never run into anyone you know.

He pulls out of the parking lot. His brother has some vague moral objection to Walmart. The actual reason is mysterious, constantly changing: child labor maybe, or sweatshops in China. Like all Darren's convictions, this one falls apart under pressure. It gives like rotted wood.

The water is for drinking and cooking only. And yet the plastic bottles empty at a sickening rate. Rich had to buy an entire extra trash can, for the express purpose of transporting them to the dump.

It's just like Darren to worry about poor people in China while giving no thought to poor people in America, who need Walmart because they can't afford to shop anywhere else—a losers' club Rich feels, eternally, on the brink of joining, if he hasn't already. Financial ruin is the bogeyman of his adulthood, the subject of every nightmare. His wife has never understood this, Shelby who spends his money as though she earned it herself. Once, in the heat of an argument, she called him a cheapskate. She'll never know—he's never told her—how deeply this wounded him, an insult he can't forget.

He pulls onto the highway. The day is unseasonably cool, more like September than August—the afternoon summer-warm, a tinge of mourning in the air. The sky vibrant blue like the day the planes went down.

As everyone does, he remembers the day vividly. He was driving, then, for Miners' Medical, heard the news on the radio as he was making his rounds. He and Shelby—his girlfriend then—sat shoulder to shoulder in front of the TV, staring at the same grisly footage over and over. The catastrophe seemed far away until one of the planes crashed in Shanksville. Watching, Rich thought of calling his brother, but at the time it was impossible. Darren had been drifting away from the family for years. Even in a crisis, he could not be reached.

A massive tanker truck squeals past in the left lane. It is clearly labeled—RESIDUAL WASTE—as though someone is proud of its contents.

The day the planes went down. In some way Rich would have been embarrassed to explain, September 11 changed his life. In October he made an offer on Pap's farm. On the front porch of the farmhouse he proposed to Shelby, ready for his future to begin. They married quickly, which raised suspicions, but Shelby wasn't pregnant. Rich was the one rushing them to the altar. He was—still is—decisive by nature. He knew what he wanted, and saw no point in waiting around.

He couldn't have imagined all the ways she would change, the danger of marrying someone so young. A year later, when she was pregnant with Braden, Rich held her hand during the sonogram, staring at the screen: the unformed mass that would become his son, a swirl of paisley that would, in a few months, resolve into a human shape.

He had married an unformed mass, a swirl of paisley. There was no telling what a nineteen-year-old girl might become.

His mother had tried to warn him—*she's a little young, isn't she?*—but Rich wouldn't listen. His previous attempt at marriage, to a girl his own age, had ended badly. A girl he barely knew and never should have married, a girl who couldn't be trusted. They met in a bar a mile from base and married four months later, a soldier's mistake: you wanted someone on the other end, waiting for your return.

He proposed to Shelby on the front porch of the farmhouse. Three years later, at her insistence, the farmhouse was razed.

Rich pulls into the driveway. In the mailbox he finds bills, a
vitamin catalog, and an official-looking envelope: *Pennsylvania
Department of Environmental Protection.*

> *Re: Act 223 Section 208 Determination*
>
> *Carbon Township, Saxon County*
>
> *Dear Richard Devlin:*
>
> *The Department has investigated the possible degradation
> of your water supply, located on Number Nine Road in
> Carbon Township. Our analysis indicates the presence of
> natural gas in your water supply. Our findings are enclosed
> here for your records.*
>
> *Methane is the predominant component of natural
> gas. Drinking water standard limitations have not been
> established for methane gas. In general, methane levels in
> water wells are under 5 mg/L. The level of concern begins
> above 28 mg/L methane, called the saturation level, at
> which, under normal atmospheric pressure, the water cannot
> hold additional methane. At these levels, gas may escape
> the water and concentrate in the air space of your home or
> building. There is a physical danger of fire or explosion due to
> the migration of natural gas into water wells or through soils
> into dwellings where it could be ignited by sources present in
> most homes/buildings.*
>
> *Please be aware that methane levels can fluctuate. Even
> with a relatively low level of methane, you should be vigilant
> of changes in your water that could indicate an increased
> concentration of methane.*
>
> *All water wells should be equipped with a working vent.
> This will help alleviate the possibility of concentrating these
> gases in areas where ignition would pose a threat of life or
> property. Please note that it is not possible to completely*

eliminate the hazards posed by natural gas in the water
supply, simply by venting the well.
    The presence of dissolved methane in your water supply
appears to be related to background conditions. At this time,
our investigation does not indicate that gas well drilling has
affected your water supply. The cause of the gas migration
is currently unknown and remains under investigation by
DEP.

A lab report is attached. Rich's eyes slide over the columns of figures, values for methane, ethane, SMCLs. He has no idea what he's looking at. For just a moment he thinks of his brother, who before flunking out or withdrawing or simply wandering away from Johns Hopkins had earned half a degree in chemistry. I could call him, Rich thinks, knowing he never will.

He reads the letter again, then shoves it into his pocket. Inside he finds Shelby standing at the sink. He wouldn't have believed it unless he'd caught her in the act. "What the hell are you doing?"

She turns to him red-faced. "Washing dishes."

"In *bottled water*? Are you fucking kidding me?" He feels, for a moment, flooded with emotion. Anything seems possible. He could knock Shelby sideways, or have a heart attack, or simply weep.

"Drinking and cooking only," he says through his teeth. "We agreed."

"*You* agreed," Shelby says.

This, he reflects, is how it happens. Deer Run is full of guys who've been slapped with domestics, men who—drunk or drugged or, like Rich, stone-cold sober—simply snapped.

"Jesus Christ, Shelby. I can't be running to Walmart every fucking day."

"You're the one who canceled Poland Spring."

Which was true enough: their first (and last) monthly bill had given him chest pains.

"Do you know what that was costing us?"

A different kind of wife would feel a responsibility to help. A different kind of wife would get off her ass and get a job, something Shelby will never do.

"Well, what am I supposed to do? I can't do the laundry without getting a headache."

"You use it for *laundry?*"

"Just the kids' clothes," says Shelby.

For weeks, now, he's made phone calls. There is no one left to call.

Pastor Jess's car is in the driveway, as always; and yet the house looks deserted, the windows dark. Shelby rings the doorbell and waits. Later she won't recall making a decision. She will remember only that the doorknob turned easily in her hand.

"Hello?" she calls.

The house is quiet inside, but the stillness seems phony—as though party guests are hiding in the closets, ready to jump out and yell *surprise.*

"Hello?"

She climbs the little staircase to the living room and promptly sneezes. She understands, then, that the place is empty. She can tell from the sound of her sneeze, shockingly loud in the silent house.

Shelby has never been alone in this house, and yet the feeling is familiar, from dreams. In the dreams she is herself, but younger—a girl, always. She lives here with a mother who is definitely not Roxanne and a father who is and isn't Pastor Wes.

She does not, in general, like the smell of other people's houses.

In her dreams Crystal is always alive.

The living room is sun filled and homey, plants hanging at the windows, colorful pillows strewn across the couch. The plants look green and healthy, and yet there is a gravity to the empty room, as though something terrible has happened here. On the coffee table is an empty mug, a string hanging over the rim. Somewhere a clock is ticking. Shelby thinks of the Israelites fleeing the Angel of Death, skipping town right in the middle of supper, and sneezes again.

Compared with her own house, the living room seems complicated, layered with artifacts. She studies the framed photographs on the wall. Pastor Wes and Pastor Jess on a roller coaster. On horseback. In college sweatshirts. In wedding clothes. Pastor Wes looks out from each photo in mute comprehension, as though he sees Shelby moving through his former house and is glad she's come.

She moves aside the pillows and stretches out on the sofa.

If she lived in this house, she would instantly become a different type of person, an effect she has experienced before. In the farmhouse she felt paralyzed by other people's tastes and opinions, the sturdy ghosts who'd picked the curtains and laid the carpet and hung the clock on the wall. In the farmhouse any sort of change was inconceivable. She'd been unable even to move a chair.

Three sneezes in a row: a wish, a kiss, a disappointment. She blames it on the books piled everywhere. Even if you dusted every week, books were impossible to keep clean.

A brand-new house had seemed, at first, a rare opportunity. For months, a year, she studied furniture catalogs, the Home Shopping Network, trying to think a home into being. The task was more difficult than she'd imagined. The new house was like a blank sheet of paper, waiting for her to write on it. In the end she had nothing to say.

She wanders through the dining room, the kitchen. The bathroom smells of shampoo, a recent shower. A book, *A Prairie Home Companion,* sits on the back of the toilet. Shelby opens the medicine chest and studies the bottles on the shelves, Midol and contact lens cleaner and Clairol Natural Effects, which according to its label covers gray instantly.

She is more than surprised, she feels somehow deceived, that Pastor Jess dyes her hair.

A wish, a kiss, a disappointment. They said it as children, she and Crystal, when either of them sneezed. What exactly did it mean?

When Crystal was sick, and again in the weeks before Braden's surgery, the entire congregation had prayed for Shelby. Each Sunday morning she felt lifted up in their arms, a kind of sacred crowd-surfing. At the social hour she no longer stood alone, awkward and tongue-tied. Women approached her and asked solicitous questions. She was kissed and hugged, praised and blessed.

A wish, a kiss, a disappointment.

She peeks into the bedroom. The bed is unmade. More books are piled on the nightstand. Bits of discarded clothing—a sock, pink underpants—dot the floor like bird droppings.

At Crystal's funeral the praising and blessing reached a glorious crescendo. It was in many ways the best day of Shelby's life. Not because she wished her sister dead. (She didn't.) Because it was finally her turn.

She has never told anyone this.

In the kitchen she studies the contents of the refrigerator, bottles of skim milk, diet cola, salad dressing, and wine. She stands there a long time with the door open, something she is always scolding Braden for doing.

If she lived in this house, she would become the type of person who read books while sitting on the toilet.

In the distance a car door slams.

Shelby is startled but not afraid. Voices outside, chatting, laughter. She takes a seat at the dining room table just as the front door opens, and thinks, *surprise*.

Pastor Jess looks shocked to see her, her hand actually fluttering to her heart. "Shelby! Goodness, you scared me. What are you doing here?" She wears sunglasses and a flowered sundress, her arms bare. Behind her is a short man Shelby doesn't know.

Shelby waits.

Finally the realization dawns. "Did we have an appointment? Oh, no! Shelby, I'm so sorry. It completely slipped my mind."

Still Shelby waits.

"It's my fault," says the man, his hand at the pastor's back. "I'm the one that stole her away."

Shelby thinks, *Who are you?*

"This is my friend Marshall," says Pastor Jess, as though she hears the question. "This is Shelby Devlin, from the church."

"Devlin," the man says. "You live out Number Nine Road? That's my crew that's drilling your well."

That contaminated your water, Shelby thinks. That poisoned your daughter. Pastor Jess is consorting with the enemy, the worst kind of treason.

Another silence.

Marshall looks adoringly at Pastor Jess—who is, frankly, not even all that pretty. He gives her shoulder a squeeze. "I should go. I have an early morning tomorrow."

No one has ever looked at Shelby that way.

"No, wait." Pastor Jess lays a hand on his arm. "Shelby, let's reschedule for another night—tomorrow, maybe?"

The request is stunning. Shelby has explained a dozen times that Thursday is Rich's day off, the only day she can possibly come. Now, with Rich on day shift, she could theoretically come tomorrow, but she isn't about to make it easier for Pastor Jess. It's the principle of the thing.

"I can't," she says firmly.

"Oh. Okay." Pastor Jess glances at her watch. "It's getting late. Let's just plan on next Thursday. I won't forget, I promise." She offers a conciliatory smile. Shelby would like to slap her.

"Okay," Shelby says.

Again Pastor Jess touches Marshall's arm. (So much touching!) "You wait here. I'll walk Shelby to her car."

Shelby follows the pastor down the stairs and out the front door, ignoring Marshall completely. In addition to being short, he has a small stain, ketchup maybe, on the front of his shirt. His very ordinariness offends her.

Envy and jealousy are not the same thing.

Pastor Jess closes the door behind them. "Shelby, I have to say, I wasn't expecting to find you sitting at my kitchen table."

Envy is coveting what a person has. Jealousy is wanting to be chosen over someone else.

"The door was unlocked," says Shelby. "I was worried."

"Why?" Pastor Jess looks confused, as though she truly doesn't remember (maybe she doesn't) that it was Shelby who found Pastor Wes, alone in the house, on the day he died; Shelby who called 911 and rode with him in the ambulance, holding his hand. How could you forget a thing like that?

Shelby stares at her mutely. There is so much she wants to say. She thinks of Marshall waiting inside for Pastor Jess. She is envious of them both, jealous of them both.

She wonders if he knows the pastor dyes her hair.

"I'm sorry about tonight. I truly am. We can talk about it next week," says Pastor Jess. "I'll see you in church on Sunday, Shelby. Drive safely."

Shelby gets into the minivan and closes the door.

10.

ack is leaning over the kitchen sink, her sleeves rolled to the elbows, her forearms pink from scrubbing. She looks startled when Rena comes downstairs in her uniform.

"It's Friday," says Mack.

"That's the rumor."

"You never work Friday."

"It's just until Steph comes back. I couldn't say no, considering I'm off all next week."

"You are?" Mack looks genuinely surprised, as though this is new information. As though Rena's work schedule isn't hanging in plain sight, stuck to the refrigerator with an udder-shaped magnet.

"I said I'd drive Shelby and Olivia to Pittsburgh. And"—casually, as though it's just occurred to her—"there's that rally in New York."

"With Dr. Trexler?"

"Yes," Rena says.

There is a silence.

"He wants me to learn about the process. To see how it works." She isn't asking permission, exactly. She is simply explaining herself.

"Why?"

There's more, much more, Mack could say. In her eyes Dr. Trexler is no better than a politician, a TV preacher, the Jehovah's Witnesses who periodically come calling.

"Your meeting at the library, that's different," she says slowly.

"We live here. Our farm is here. But if people in New York want to lease their mineral rights, what does that have to do with Dr. Trexler? He doesn't even live there." For Mack it is quite a speech.

Rena thinks, He lives in the *world*. He cares about the *world*.

Mack thinks, Don't leave me.

"Is his wife going with you?"

Rena feels a sudden dread, as though she's been caught in some misdeed. Naturally she said that Lorne was married. It's the sort of white lie she tells reflexively, to manage Mack's anxieties. At one time these deceptions seemed harmless. Now she isn't so sure. When Calvin was small, he won a carnival goldfish in a tiny bowl. When they replaced the bowl with a larger one, the fish grew to fill it. Mack's jealousy has grown to the size of a sturgeon, because Rena has made room for it.

Rena says, "I'm not sure."

Her instinct, always, is to avoid strife. Conflict paralyzes her, the barest whiff of anger or discord. She will lie outrageously, if necessary, to make other people comfortable. It's a quality she deplores in herself, an impulse Mack would never understand—Mack who was born brave, a hero in her heart.

"We haven't worked out the details yet."

Mack eyes her with suspicion, or maybe Rena is imagining it. Being questioned alarms her: sick in her stomach, her ears pounding. Panic chokes her like a hand around her throat. Mack has no idea, of course. How could she? There's so much Rena has never told her.

(I am a filthy little whore.)

Mack looks around for a towel and, finding none, dries her hands on her dirty overalls. "But you already told him you're going." It isn't a question.

"Yes," Rena says.

SHE IS LATE FOR HER SHIFT, something that never used to happen. Time has become slippery. Distracted by daydreams, she loses minutes or hours. She moves through the day in a fog, a delicious slow heaviness she remembers from long ago, a time in her life that now seems imaginary: the wild improbability of Mack in her bed, Mack who was a girl and a boy at the same time, every lover she could possibly want.

Young Rena had been electrified by her own audacity. Making love to Mack was the bravest thing she'd ever done—the only one, really. At the time it seemed a revolutionary act. Only later did she understand that Mack was not so different from the gruff coal miners she'd known all her life, stubborn silent men their wives complained about or made excuses for but basically accepted, because that was how men *were*. Men were nothing like the heroes in romance novels, the grubby paperbacks her mother bought by the dozen at rummage sales and read compulsively—with the covers torn off, as though anybody was fooled.

(Her mother, who considered Freddy Weems quite a catch. Who seemed not to notice that Rena had grown clumsy—falling down stairs, walking into doors.)

Teenage Rena read the same books, not understanding, yet, that the Lances and Brads were female creations. They bore no resemblance to actual men—who were, more or less, like Mack.

She had never met, or even imagined, a man like Lorne.

She parks in the staff lot and waves to Jo, the charge nurse, who sits on the steps near the loading dock, smoking a cigarette and reading a newspaper.

"You made the *Herald*," Jo calls.

Rena approaches, shading her eyes. She has never spent any time on the steps, which the nurses call *the smoking lounge*. Ten feet away, a delivery truck idles loudly; a cafeteria worker tosses trash into a giant Dumpster. An air duct blows a hot breeze, kitchen noise, a smell of dishwashing. It's hard to imagine a more unpleasant place to sit.

Jo reads: "'Rena Koval, a local dairy farmer and a nurse at Miners' Hospital, called the meeting to order.'"

The Dumpster lid closes with a metallic thud.

"Look, I know you don't agree with what we're doing," says Rena, "but we're meeting again next month. Maybe you should come check it out before you make up your mind."

"Why?" Jo looks mystified. "What's that going to do for me? I don't have a gas lease."

"You're part of this community. The entire community is affected." It's what Lorne is always saying, though the words sound less convincing coming out of her own mouth.

"Anyways," she says lamely, "you're welcome to come."

She circles around to the front entrance and crosses the lobby to Medical A, where a nurse named Agnes Lubicki mans the desk. She is older than Rena, a plain, sturdy woman with a heavy brow and no time for chitchat. Rena has never met a less charming person, or a more capable nurse.

A call light rings.

"Uh-oh. It's Chicken Little," Agnes says with a rare smile.

Even Agnes is in on the joke.

"Wait, *what*? Shelby Devlin is here?"

"The daughter was admitted last night. Chicken Little brought her in to the ER. Dr. Stusick discharged her this morning. I don't know why they're still here."

Rena hurries down the corridor toward the children's end. She finds Olivia sitting up in bed, wearing a pink quilted bed jacket over a frilly nightgown. Her hair, still damp, shows comb marks. Shelby sits beside the bed, reading *Prevention* magazine.

"Rena! I thought you worked in the Emergency Room."

"I work everywhere. Shelby, what happened?" Rena takes Olivia's chart from the foot of the bed. "How are you feeling, sweetie? Don't you look pretty."

"I ate all my breakfast," Olivia says.

"Good girl. I hear you're going home today."

"No, we're not," says Shelby, a weird tremor in her voice. "We're going to stay here until somebody helps us."

Rena replaces the chart. "I'm going to step out in the hallway and talk to your mom for a minute. She'll be right back."

Shelby follows her out of the room. "Dr. Stusick came to see her early this morning. *Very* early. I wasn't here yet. I think he's avoiding me."

"I'm sure that's not true," says Rena, who is not at all sure.

"But I didn't even get a chance to *talk* to him! How can he send her home if we still don't know what's wrong?"

"Look, I understand your frustration. But she's holding down her breakfast. We can't keep her here if her symptoms have resolved."

"But I told Dr. Stusick about the water. I *told* him! I made a copy of the test results and everything. Methane migration. It says so in black and white. He still didn't believe me."

"He said that?"

"Not in so many words, but I could tell. Maybe we could talk to him together. He'll listen to you."

"He usually comes by in the afternoon." Rena glances at the clock. "Technically Olivia has already been discharged, but if you can sit tight a while longer, I'm sure he'd be happy to talk to you. He's a good doctor, Shelby. I trust his judgment."

"Well, *I* don't." Shelby's face is very red. "What does he know? He's never spent more than two minutes with Olivia. I'm her mother. I can tell she isn't all right."

BACK AT THE NURSES' STATION, Agnes is eating a salad. Jo flips through a supermarket tabloid, stopping to study a photo spread: *STARS WITHOUT MAKEUP.*

"Can I help you?" Rena asks the old man approaching the desk.

"I'm looking for a patient," he says, and gives a name. "I understand he was brought in a few days ago."

"He's on Medical B. This is Medical A." The hospital is all on one floor, its five wings—the ER, the ICU, Surgical, and two Medical—connected by a central hub. "I can take you there."

She leads the man down the corridor. "You look familiar. Have we met before?"

"It's possible. I'm up here all the time." He hands her a business card from a silver case. PAUL ZACHARIAS, ATTORNEY-AT-LAW. "You must see quite a few worker accidents in the Emergency Room. Falls, that kind of thing." He takes more cards from the case. "The next time it happens, maybe you could pass these along."

"We're not allowed to do that," Rena says.

At the dinner break she takes her cell phone out to the lobby. She listens to a message from Mack, about a livestock sale in Somerset County. Then she calls Lorne Trexler. The call goes straight to voice mail. *Hey, it's Lorne. You know what to do.* Despite having heard this greeting more times than she can count, she thrills at the sound of his voice.

"I'm at the hospital," she tells his voice mail. "Olivia was admitted last night. She seems fine now, but I'll know more after I talk to the doctor. Call me tonight?"

Tonight. With Mack at the livestock sale, they can spend the entire evening on the phone, something Rena wouldn't normally do. Normally she'd make room for Mack's jealousy.

Back on Medical A, she finds Shelby Devlin lurking near the nurses' station.

"Rena! I've been looking everywhere for you. Dr. Stusick still hasn't come, and I have to go pick up my son."

"Easy," says Rena. "Take a deep breath. I have your cell phone number. I'll call you the minute he comes."

"I already told her that," says Jo. "But she insisted on talking to you."

Shelby grasps Rena's arm. "My pastor is coming to see Olivia.

She'll be here any minute. Can you tell her to wait for me? Please just tell her I'll be *right back*."

"Good Lord," says Agnes, watching her go. "Someone give her a Valium."

"She's a little high-strung." Rena recalls, vividly, the time two-year-old Calvin caught bronchitis, his spiking fever, her own panic. There's no misery in the world like having a sick kid—an anguish Jo and Agnes, both childless, simply don't understand.

"That old guy in the suit," says Jo. "He's been here before."

"You didn't recognize him? From TV?" says Rena. "You know: *For forty years I've stood up for the little guy.* That billboard on Drake Highway."

"Great. Lawyers." Jo looks truly angry. "Are you happy now?"

"That's not the point. The point is, *someone* needs to—" She feels a hand on her shoulder.

"Rena," says Dr. Stusick. "Can I borrow you for a minute?"

He leads her into an exam room, closing the door behind them.

"You just missed Shelby Devlin," she tells him. "She's very anxious to speak with you."

"What else is new? She calls my office every day with some new theory or other. Now it's the drinking water." He pauses significantly. "Of course, you know this already."

Instantly Rena's face goes hot.

"I understand you told her the water was making Olivia sick."

"I didn't say *that*, exactly." Rena's scalp is sweating, her chest, her lower back. "But, well, they *are* living on top of a gas well. Have you driven out Number Nine lately? You can see it from the road. It's maybe two hundred feet from the house."

Dr. Stusick doesn't respond.

"Their water has been tested by two different labs. Did Shelby tell you that? They both found high concentrations of methane."

Still no response.

"I know she's a little—emotional," says Rena. "But the Devlins aren't the only ones having problems. Her neighbor down the hill had his well tested, and it's the same story. Methane migration. Two weeks after they started drilling, both of those wells went bad."

She notices, then, the tiny red marks on her left arm. Faint scratches, crescent shaped, left by Shelby's fingernails.

"Look, I don't know anything about gas drilling," says Dr. Stusick. "I have no opinion one way or the other. But when it comes to effects on human health, there isn't a lot of data."

"Okay, but *something* is making her sick. Isn't it at least *possible* the water has something to do with it?"

"Anything's possible, but there's nothing in the literature. If there's any connection between methane in the water supply and acute pediatric gastritis, nobody has written a paper on it."

Rena, who has done the same literature search, knows that this is true.

"Rena, you're a fine nurse. What you do on your own time is your business. But when it starts to affect patient care, we have a problem." He glances at his watch. "I should go. I have rounds to finish. But I want you to be careful with Mrs. Devlin. She isn't a rational woman."

THE DRILLERS ROLL DOWN the Dutch Road in the company truck, Herc at the wheel, Mickey Phipps riding shotgun. The afternoon sun is high overhead, the one advantage of starting work at dawn: at quitting time there's plenty of daylight left. Rolling landscape, green hills in the distance. Mickey is on his cell phone, talking to his daughter. Herc whistles under his breath.

"You're in a good mood," Mickey says when he hangs up.

"I guess I am," Herc says.

They are turning the corner onto Number Nine Road when Herc spots the green minivan idling in the Devlins' driveway. He slows as the wife steps out, followed by a blond-haired boy in a baseball uniform. Herc recognizes her immediately, the strange silent girl they'd found sitting at Jess's kitchen table, awaiting her return like a faithful dog.

I've been counseling her for two years, Jess told him later. *I don't think it's helping.*

I met the husband when we were out there drilling. I see why she needs counseling, Herc said.

He feels, suddenly, that he knows too much about this town. The interconnectedness of everyone and everything is making him claustrophobic. He is not cut out for small-town living.

"Cute kid," says Mickey. "Your Levi's age, maybe. He still playing ball?"

Mickey's always trying to get him talking about the boys, as if Herc might need a reminder (maybe he does) of his fatherly responsibilities.

"Not this summer," Herc says, hiding his irritation. "Maybe next year." Levi is ten and, for reasons Colleen doesn't understand, losing interest in baseball. To Herc it couldn't be clearer: the kid is small for his age and not happy about it, a feeling he recalls exquisitely. His shortness is yet another paternal failing, a curse he's passed on to his son.

Right on cue, Mickey says, "I bet he misses you."

He could've said a lot worse; Herc knows this. Still, the self-righteousness is grating, Mickey the model husband and father.

"I guess they're still having water troubles. The Devlins," Herc says, to change the subject.

"Not our problem."

"I know it," Herc says, but does he? He's drilled hundreds of wells—thousands, maybe. Can he recall any one of them distinctly? His memory is like an old videotape, warped from constant reuse. He tries, again, to remember: was there anything even the slightest bit unusual about Devlin H1?

"Could be the conductor casing. I've seen it happen. Not often, but I've seen it."

"That's the cement crew," says Mickey. "That ain't even us. Don't go borrowing trouble."

Herc remembers, then: his regular cement crew had been tied up with Neugebauer. He'd had to call in a different crew, one he'd never used before. He hadn't watched the actual cementing.

"I'm the rig manager," he tells Mickey. "I'm going to feel responsible, even if it isn't my fault."

Of course, if he *had* watched the actual cementing, he'd have seen nothing. The hole was a mile deep. The crew pumped cement between the casing and the hole wall. When it squirted up the sides, the job was pronounced finished. What actually happened down-hole was anybody's guess.

"We could've run an intermediate casing."

Mickey says, "Not our call." As, of course, it isn't. It's a lesson Herc has learned time and again, that ten different operators will drill the same well ten different ways. Bern Little, Dark Elephant's company man, chose a cheaper and faster solution, a liner string held in place with hangers. The rig manager had no say in the matter. Why should he, when Dark Elephant was footing the bill?

They ride awhile in silence. When Herc's cell phone rings, he knows without even looking that it's Jess calling.

"You need to get that?" says Mickey.

"Nah, that's all right." With Legrand or Jorge he wouldn't hesitate, but Mickey's basic decency unsettles him. Only around Mickey does he feel shame.

"Are you sure? It could be an emergency."

"I'm off the clock," Herc says—realizing, too late, that Mickey isn't talking about the rig. Again he feels the weight of Mickey's righteousness. A responsible husband and father always picks up the phone.

Against his better judgment, he does.

"Hercules?" says Jess.

Even with Mickey in earshot, her voice thrills him, warm and resonant and somehow intimate, as though she's confiding a deep secret.

"Speaking." He tries to keep his voice neutral.

"Change of plans here. I've had a long day and I don't feel like cooking. Meet me at the Pick and Shovel?"

"Now?" He glances at Mickey. "I thought you had to stop by the hospital."

"The what? You're breaking up."

"The hospital," Herc repeats.

"Ack, you're right! It completely slipped my mind."

"Did you say 'ack'? I don't believe I've ever heard a person say that."

"I'll go tomorrow, I promise. Pick and Shovel in half an hour?"

"With bells on." He hangs up and stows the phone in his pocket. Mickey, who is Christian, stares deliberately at the road. Disapproval rises off him like fumes.

"That was a friend," says Herc.

"None of my business," Mickey says.

The night is very dark, foggy, the moon hidden. Two vehicles zip along a country road, crashing through puddles. The air is alive with fireflies. The first car, a red Toyota Prius, whips smoothly around the sharp corners. The second driver, unfamiliar with the road, lags a few car lengths behind.

Three or four car lengths. To Mack it seems a discreet distance, but what does she know? She's never followed anyone before—not in a car, anyway. Stealth doesn't come naturally to her.

But Lorne Trexler, luckily, is distracted. He drives with one hand, the other holding a cell phone to his ear. A more observant driver would have noticed the headlights in his rearview mirror, the same white pickup truck following him across campus, through quaint downtown Stirling and into the countryside beyond. Now the road—Walnut Creek Bottom, according to a sign a mile back—is nearly deserted. In the last ten minutes they have passed only one car.

Trexler hits the gas and guns it up a steep hill. Mack does the same, impressed, in spite of herself, by the Prius's acceleration. For a little car—a hybrid, yet—it has a lot of kick.

She is prejudiced against small cars the way she is prejudiced against small dogs—unapologetically, with deep conviction.

Is it possible he hasn't noticed the pickup truck following him? Mack has memorized his license plate. His face is lit by the bluish glow of his cell phone.

The prime function of bioluminescence is in sexual selection.

Forty miles per hour, fifty, sixty. The road is slick from the afternoon's rain. The Prius turns a sharp curve, too fast for conditions. Mack feels this in her body, a creeping sense of danger, as though a line has been crossed.

This is what she's thinking when the deer darts into the road.

THE DAY BEGAN WITH A LIE, and would end with one.

That morning, after Rena left for work, Mack again visited the Stirling College website. Quickly, before she could lose her nerve, she called the phone number on the department home page.

Geology, said a very young female voice.

Mack cleared her throat. *Um, is Dr. Trexler in?*

He usually stops by his office in the evening. Are you a student?

A former student, said Mack, the story she had rehearsed. *I'm passing through town today. I wanted to stop by and say hi.*

Next she left a message on Rena's cell phone. *I forgot to tell you. I might not be here when you get home. There's a sale in Somerset.* This was true, as far as it went. At the John Deere she'd seen a notice on a bulletin board: DAIRY CATTLE OF ALL AGES, MILKERS AND BREEDING STOCK.

Mack didn't actually *say* she was going to the auction. Technically, it wasn't a lie.

The drive to Stirling took longer than expected. The tiny campus, once she found it, looked nothing like Penn State and very much like a college in the movies: old buildings of matching gray limestone, some covered in ivy, arranged around grassy lawns. An ancient-looking limestone wall marked the perimeter. Even the trees were old. Mack located Winger Hall and parked in a space marked FACULTY. She killed the engine and settled in, aware of how wrong she must look in her battered farm truck, its rear end caked with mud and decorated with bumper stickers common in Bakerton but probably not on a college campus. NRA NOW. COOL COUNTRY FROGGY 101. SUPPORT OUR TROOPS.

She just wanted to see him.

She wasn't in the habit of lying. Telling the truth was hard enough. Rena often joked that Mack's natural state was silence, a Mackey family trait. Like her pop, her grandpop, she was unskilled at idle chitchat, talking for talking's sake.

She fumbled in the glove box for her snuff, keeping her eyes on the door.

If she were a different person, she might simply have asked: *Are you in love with Dr. Trexler?* But if she asked the question, Rena would answer it. And maybe Mack doesn't really want to know.

She recognized the car immediately, the red Prius she'd seen at the Pick and Shovel. Trexler parked in the next row over and hurried into Winger Hall. He was carrying a backpack and talking on a cell phone.

Mack waited. The time passed slowly. She wished she had brought a snack. Hungry, queasy from too much snuff, she watched the door.

NOW THE DEER DARTS INTO THE ROADWAY. The Prius slows, brakes screeching, then swerves violently in the exact wrong direction.

"Idiot!" Mack shouts, smacking the steering wheel. Whom she means—herself or Trexler—is not clear.

The Prius misses the first deer but hits the second. Mack knows—doesn't everybody?—that deer rarely travel alone.

The second deer hits the passenger side, the front quarter panel, with a sickening thud. Brakes screeching, the Prius spins out, nosing into the guardrail. Finally it rolls to a stop, its back end blocking the road.

Mack pulls over to the shoulder and gets out of the truck. "Are you all right?" she calls.

The Prius's hood has popped open. Its headlights are still on, its engine steaming in the damp. Lorne Trexler is still behind the wheel, pinned by the airbag.

"Fucking deer!" he shouts, as though the deer were at fault. The airbag fills his car like a giant bubble of chewing gum. "Can you call 911?"

As though the deer had behaved irresponsibly.

"I don't have a phone," Mack says.

"Mine is in here somewhere. On the floor, I think. Can you find it?"

At that moment a telephone rings.

"That's my friend calling back," says Trexler. "We were on the phone when it happened. She must have been scared to death."

Again the phone rings.

Mack kneels beside the car and feels around on the floor, around and between Trexler's feet. The strangeness of the situation is overpowering.

Again the phone rings.

Finally she finds it, still warm, and hands it over. He waves it away, covering his face with his hand. "Tell her I'm fine. Tell her to call 911."

"Hello?" Mack says into the phone. For a second she holds her breath, but the voice on the other end is not Rena's. "Lorne's had an accident. He's okay, but the car's in bad shape. Can you call 911?"

"Walnut Creek Bottom!" Trexler shouts. "Right past the reservoir."

"Did you hear that?" Mack says.

After she hangs up, Trexler eyes her strangely. "How did you know my name?"

"That's what she called you," Mack lies.

Finally Trexler wriggles out from beneath the airbag. He's lucky to be small and skinny. A man Mack's size would be trapped inside.

He scrambles to his feet. The top of his head is level with Mack's earlobe. "Jesus. This thing is totaled."

"Doesn't look good." Mack rolls up her sleeves. "Come on. Let's move it."

Trexler looks dumbfounded.

"It's a blind curve," she explains, as though talking to a child. "You don't want to cause another accident."

The Prius is astonishingly lightweight. Piece of junk, Mack thinks, putting her back into it. Together they push the car onto the narrow shoulder. Trexler isn't much help. He's a little guy, skinny and narrow-shouldered. Mack thinks, I could take him.

(As if that would solve the problem. As if being clocked by a total stranger, *an unidentified assailant,* would somehow keep him away from Rena.)

"That's better," she says. "It's still in the road, but you should be able to swerve around it." To herself she adds, *if you're not driving like a jackass.*

They stand a moment looking at each other. The next thing can now happen.

IT'S NEARLY MIDNIGHT when Mack turns down the dirt lane to the farm. The fog has lifted. In the half-moon light the barn is clearly legible: CHEW MAIL POUCH TOBACCO TREAT YOURSELF TO THE BEST. In Depression times, a traveling painter from Ohio had turned it into a billboard. In return her grandpop got a free paint job and a few dollars a year.

Except for a light in the bedroom, the house is dark. In the kitchen she takes off her boots, looks in the refrigerator, chugs a glass of water. She climbs the stairs in stocking feet. Rena is in bed, asleep but still wearing her glasses. A paperback book—*Silent Spring*—lies open on her chest.

She wakes with a start. "Where have you been? I was worried. You forgot your phone."

"Sorry," says Mack, who always forgets her phone. "There was an accident."

"Are you okay?"

"I hit a deer. The truck's okay—not a scratch—but it shook me up a little."

"Sweetheart." Rena slides over and Mack, fully dressed, climbs in beside her. This is all she wants, all she can imagine wanting. She recalls how, standing face-to-face with Lorne Trexler, she heard an odd rustling somewhere behind her. She stepped over the guardrail and knelt in the underbrush.

"It was still alive," she tells Rena. "A yearling." A young male bleeding at the head, stubby antlers coming in, one back leg kicking. A fluttering heartbeat visible in the white fur of its chest.

Where are you going? Trexler said as Mack jogged toward her truck.

I can't just leave it like that.

She came back with her Remington and placed the shot carefully, square in the middle of the animal's chest.

The report rang through the forest. A moment later Mack heard a siren in the distance. *There's your ambulance,* she told Trexler.

She got into her truck and drove away. When she looked back, he was talking on his cell phone.

THE STAR-LIGHT DRIVE-IN is unchanged since 1999. When Gia pulls up to the ticket booth, Darren reaches for his wallet, but the kid in the booth—a mute longhair in a Metallica T-shirt—waves them inside. Darren wonders: Does Metallica still exist? Gia would know, but he doesn't ask her. He understands that he's fallen through a black hole, a portal to his lost youth. Asking the question would somehow break the spell.

Just as they used to, they take Gia's car. When Darren suggested taking his smart car, she laughed so hard she cried.

The crowd is small for a Saturday night. The midnight movie has already started, the second of a double feature. It is, altogether, a familiar feeling, with one critical difference: Gia's hand on Darren's, her lips nuzzling warmly at his ear.

The movie is an old one, from an endless series of bloody stories about a plastic troll doll possessed by demons. Darren recognizes the doll but can't name the sequel.

Gia is aghast. "You don't remember *Bride of Chucky*?"

He can taste her perfume. "Should I?"

"We saw it! The summer we were working at the Manor."

"We did?" It was entirely possible. They'd seen any number of horror films that summer, drunk on beer or wine coolers and pleasantly stoned.

"Yep. You and me, cowboy. I can't believe you don't remember."

"I can't believe you do."

She reaches into her purse, takes out rolling papers and a Ziploc bag.

"Gia, come on. You know I don't do that anymore."

She gives him a sly smile. "Yeah, I know, and good for you. Seriously. I'm proud of you. But it's been ten years, for Christ's sake! You don't get any time off for good behavior?"

"Eight," says Darren. "It's been eight."

"Eight years, you can't loosen up a little? You know, for a special occasion."

The air hums between them, the long-awaited occasion, the fragile moment. He has wanted her for as long as he can remember.

"Not coke or heroin or anything. Just a joint here and there.

Something not so bad." Gia gives him a small smile. "Don't listen to me. I'm an idiot."

"You're not an idiot. Never say that." Darren hesitates. "Actually, you're not far off. There is one treatment philosophy— it's called 'harm reduction'—that recognizes a hierarchy of addictiveness."

"I said *that*?"

"The idea is that if you're addicted to hard drugs—heroin, for example—having an occasional drink or a joint or whatever can function as a release valve, and actually help you stay clean. It's controversial," he adds, which is putting it mildly. If anyone at work heard him talking, he'd be quickly out of a job. Harm reduction, at Wellways, is treated as the worst kind of heresy. And yet the Wellways model recognizes a place for methadone and buprenorphine. No one seems to find this hypocritical.

"Whatever," says Gia. "I don't care if you smoke or not. I just thought it would be fun."

He watches as she sprinkles a little weed into the paper. Her technique is still clumsy. Just as she used to, she leaves a gap in the center of the joint. The thing isn't going to burn properly. It's a waste of what smells, anyway, like perfectly good weed.

"Give me that," Darren says.

He rolls quickly, remembering how he'd always taken the first hit. *Taking a commission,* he'd called it.

The first hit does nothing for him, nothing at all. Ditto for the second. The third reminds him of the first time he ever smoked, a complete misfire, three nervous fourteen-year-olds drinking beer at the Huffs and pretending to be stoned, on bad homegrown weed bought from Calvin Weems.

"Nothing," he says, exhaling.

Gia laughs soundlessly.

"That's funny? Why is that funny?"

"Just: you're a born-again virgin." Gia inhales deeply. "Girls know this. After eight years it grows back. Medical fact."

This is much, much funnier than it should be, which should have been his first clue. He takes another hit and feels his senses dilate and is filled with gratitude.

They stare enraptured at the screen.

Ooh, Chucky, the blond actress croons, stroking his plastic cheek. Which should not, under any circumstances, be sexy.

Darren is grateful to be alive and stoned and kissing Gia Bernardi.

He is grateful to be spared the awkwardness, the punishing self-consciousness, of sober sex. For their first time, anyway. For just this once.

Gia nuzzles at his ear. "Back in a minute," she whispers. "I have to piss like a racehorse."

In a kind of daze Darren watches her go. He hadn't even considered bringing a condom. It would have seemed wildly optimistic.

Somewhere inside the car, Gia's cell phone rings. He tries to ignore the cloying electronic ringtone, the opening bar of a song he doesn't recognize.

The phone rings and rings.

The ringing is coming from inside the glove box. Darren sticks his head out the window, but sees no sign of Gia. Who is calling her at midnight?

(His brother's raised eyebrows when she ducked outside with Brando: *Just friends? Says who?*)

Gia's phone, briefly quiet, rings again.

Against his better judgment, Darren reaches into the glove box. He can't help himself. He simply has to know.

The phone's display shows a number with an unfamiliar area code, 210.

He returns the phone to the glove box, which is full of female junk: hand lotion, a hair clip, a tampon. Sunglasses, a CD case, Gia's lighter and cigarettes. And, at the bottom of the pile, a blackened glass pipe, long as his hand and bulbous at one end—obscenely, scrotally bulbous.

Oh, Gia.

Gia lightning quick, skinnier than she used to be, tearing around the Commercial as if her hair, once again, is on fire.

What else had he failed to notice?

Somehow it hadn't occurred to him to ask: *Why were you looking in Shelby's medicine chest?* It's classic addict behavior, a truth Darren knows intimately. This is exactly why it hadn't seemed strange to him. He is still—and forever will be—that kind of person.

The mysterious Brando, who at least once during her shift stopped by the Commercial, though never for very long.

He is still holding the pipe when the car door swings open. Gia's face freezes. "What are you doing in my glove box?"

There is a terrible silence.

"What?" says Gia. "It's not like I do it all the time."

Darren waits.

"It's a party drug, you know? Not, like, a daily thing. I quit for two months once. I can quit whenever I want."

"You know everybody says that."

(*It isn't heroin,* says another, treacherous part of his brain.)

Gia leans in close to him. "Well, I'm not everybody. I know you're an expert and all, but have you even tried it?"

They stare at each other a long moment. He is aware of his heart working.

"No," Darren says.

FROM HIS CHILDHOOD BED Darren watches the sun rise, *The Big Book of Alcoholics Anonymous* open on his chest. After some hours there is a knock at the door, brisk, official-sounding. "Darren, buddy, are you awake?"

"Yeah, Dad. I'm up." In fact he's been awake for thirty-four hours. He's never been so awake in his entire life. He pulls on jeans and a sweatshirt and, because he can't immediately come up with an excuse not to, opens the door.

His dad—shaved, showered—eyes him uncertainly. "I thought you were going to help Bud open. Are you all right, buddy? You look a little—" He hesitates. The words for how Darren looks (*punked, tweaking, shitslammed*) are not in Dick's vocabulary.

"I was sick in the night. Some kind of stomach bug." It isn't true but will serve as a useful cover, an explanation for whatever noises Dick might have heard.

(Creeping up the stairs with Gia behind him. *Take off your shoes,* Darren whispered, and she did.)

Is he imagining it, or does Dick look skeptical?

"All right, then. Get some extra shut-eye. You can go in later, if you feel better. If not, your brother can cover. Gia's off today."

Darren's stomach lurches at the sound of her name. He hugs the sweatshirt around him, shivering, and closes the door.

The night at the drive-in comes back to him in a wave. He barely remembers making love to Gia the first time. Thirteen years of longing and he barely remembers it, the furtive coupling in the passenger seat.

At such times he is supposed to call his sponsor. He didn't call his sponsor. His sponsor has left the program.

They didn't make love, they fucked. Then they smoked more meth.

He pages through his *Big Book.*

In our daily lives, we are subject to emotional and spiritual lapses, causing us to become defenseless against the physical relapse of drug use.

The second time they fucked in his childhood bed, where he'd once slept in footie pajamas.

Dick takes out his hearing aid at night, a mercy. Possibly he heard nothing.

Darren's sponsor is no longer in the program, being dead.

By the time Gia got dressed the sky had lightened. Four A.M., an hour Darren hadn't seen in years.

It's important to remember that the desire to use will pass. We never have to use again, no matter how we feel. All feelings will eventually pass.

His sponsor's name was David Grady. Like soldiers, they called each other by last names. Devlin and Grady. Darren had enjoyed that, the manly camaraderie he'd never before felt. If only he could talk to Grady at this moment. *I fucked up. I relapsed on meth.*

He knows exactly what Grady would advise.

I can't just leave, Darren would tell him. *Who else is going to help her? I'm a fucking drug counselor.*

You're a fucking addict, Grady would say.

Downstairs, Dick is puttering around in the kitchen. Darren hears water running, a scrape of cutlery. His dad will be gone all day, at the V.A. hospital in Latrobe, where his buddy Chuckles is having something—a knee? a hip?—replaced.

When Grady relapsed, he relapsed on heroin.

The long drive to Baltimore, his silent apartment. In a few hours Darren will be sitting in a meeting. He will admit to God, to himself, and to other human beings the exact nature of his wrongs. He will do this in some unfamiliar church basement out in the county, among suburban strangers. At any meeting in the city of Baltimore was someone he'd counseled, copped from, or used with. In this one way Baltimore is, like Bakerton, a very small town.

The subterfuge troubles him. The subterfuge is a little squeaky.

As we grow, we learn to overcome the tendency to run and hide from ourselves and our feelings. When we feel trapped or pressured, it takes great spiritual and emotional strength to be honest.

The subterfuge is unavoidable. If anybody at Wellways caught wind of his relapse, he'd be quickly out of a job. He allows himself to imagine it, month upon month of empty days. It is not an exaggeration, it is entirely accurate to say that the free time might kill him. His fear of free time was the entire reason he'd come back to Bakerton in the first place.

Where he relapsed on meth.

He steps into the shower, his heart still racing. Is he having a heart attack? How much meth did they smoke, exactly? Five hits, ten, fifteen? Is five hits a lot of meth?

The feeling is not pleasant.

The feeling is vaguely familiar, a distant cousin of the jangly desperation he remembers from snorting coke, a drug he tried—long ago, with considerable tenacity—to like.

It isn't Bakerton's fault. In *life* addiction is normalized: the chocoholics, the shopaholics. He had simply picked the wrong substance. He wishes he were hooked on phonics. That he had chosen shopahol.

In the kitchen he forces himself to eat a piece of toast. He doesn't want a piece of toast, which is not heroin. Meth, like toast, bears little resemblance to heroin. So why does it make him crave heroin?

Because everything makes him crave heroin.

Because he is a fucking addict.

He loads up the car and sets out driving. He is maybe a quarter mile from his brother's house when he hears a faint clanging in the distance.

The clanging grows louder.

By the time he pulls into Rich's driveway the noise is breathtaking, a shrill duet of machinery, *Concerto for Jackhammer and Dentist's Drill*. To a person in his fragile state it is nearly sickening. He cuts the motor and steps out of the car. A moment later his brother's front door opens. Rich stands on the doorstep, shading his eyes, and yells something unintelligible.

"WHAT?" Darren shouts.

Rich comes toward him—dressed, unusually, in pressed trousers, a button-down shirt, and tie. "Darren, man. That's some vehicle you've got there."

"It's a good car."

"For an elf." Rich peers inside. Darren's duffel bag is on the passenger seat, *The Big Book* lying atop it. "Going somewhere?"

The racket makes Darren's teeth hurt. "Can we go inside for a minute? I can't hear myself think."

They go in through the front door. Even indoors, the noise vibrates his spine.

"Ignore the mess." Rich kicks aside a child-size sneaker. "Shelby took the kids to church."

"You're not going?"

"You're joking, right?" He loosens the tie around his neck. "This isn't for church. This is something else. There's coffee left."

There may be some substance on earth Darren needs less than he needs caffeine. He can't, at the moment, imagine what that might be.

"None for me. Just a glass of water, maybe?"

"How about a Sprite?"

"Sprite is fine." Darren passes a hand over his head. "I can only stay a minute. I need to get on the road. I'm going home."

Rich looks baffled. "You *are* home."

"No. *You're* home." His brother the good son, the husband and father. I'm not you, Darren thinks. I will never be you.

"I need to get back to Baltimore," he says. "To go back to work."

"Don't you have another month of vacation?"

"Two weeks. But that's not the point. There are other considerations." Outside, the clanging reaches a crescendo. "I was supposed to work at the Commerical tonight. Maybe you could cover?"

Rich sighs. "Yeah, sure. Fine. It's not like I have anything else to do."

"I'm sorry," Darren says.

"What's the rush? You got a girlfriend down there?"

He ignores the question. "I've been here six weeks. That should count for something."

The roar outside sharpens to a shriek.

"It does. It's been great for Dad. For me, too." Rich frowns. "I don't get it. You looked like you were having fun. You and Gia."

Gia.

"When's the last time you shaved?" says Rich. "You look like a bum."

Darren thinks, I'm high on meth. A shave won't help.

"Thursday? I don't remember. Look, I can't just *stay* here. It wouldn't be good for anyone." Does his brother even see him? It's a truth every addict knows, one Darren briefly forgot: *No one is paying attention.* In the interests of science, try it at home. Spend a solid week stoned, dopedumb, strung out on crack. Barring some out-size catastrophe, some grievous loss of life or limb, your nearest and dearest will not notice.

His brother looks startled by the edge in his voice, which is natural enough. Darren is a shrugger, not a shouter.

"I'm sorry I missed Shelby and the kids. Can you tell them good-bye for me?"

The brothers stand.

"I'm sorry for everything," Darren says.

All feelings will eventually pass.

He takes a circuitous route to the highway, bypassing town entirely, wondering what Gia is doing at this moment. Even through sunglasses the glare is blinding. He drives in a lazy circle, the mean-dering country roads where his father taught him to drive.

This place, this place.

He accelerates around a curve and there it is, the old strippins—high and sloped, machine-graded to an angle not found in nature. The land looks sicker in the harsh light, backfilled acres that were supposed to recover. They haven't recovered. What's left is a treeless expanse, empty as a Russian steppe, the dry summer grass lit blond in the morning sun. The grass looks plausibly healthy, but what lies beneath is altered forever. It will never be the way it was.

RICH WATCHES HIS BROTHER drive away, the ridiculous toy car disappearing down Number Nine Road, which leads to Drake Highway. Which leads to the turnpike, the interstate, the Baltimore Beltway, Darren's unknown life.

Caught off guard, he hadn't said what he wanted to say. *Please don't go.* As often happens when it comes to his brother, he wishes for a do-over.

He heads back into the kitchen and empties Darren's pop into the sink. Outside, the noise kicks up again. It's no wonder he fails to hear the car in the driveway, no wonder he's startled when the doorbell rings.

His do-over.

This time he'll say what he really means. *Darren, man. I'm glad you came back. It's good to have you around.* But when he opens the door, the guy on his doorstep is not his brother.

"Mr. Devlin?" The man is older than he looks on television— liver-spotted hands, eyes deeply circled. He hands Rich a business card. "I'm quite early. My previous appointment canceled. I hope that's not a problem."

"Nah, it's fine." Rich studies the card. Paul Zacharias looks old enough to be his grandfather. He feels like an asshole, now, for asking an old man to drive all the way from Pittsburgh. "Sorry to make you come all this way."

"Not at all. It isn't far."

Rich thinks, It isn't? "I'm not much of a city driver," he admits. He's been to Pittsburgh maybe five times in his life.

At the kitchen table he hands over a sheaf of papers: his contract with Dark Elephant, the two lab reports, the letter from the DEP. "Like I said on the phone, it's been tested twice. Both times it came back skunky."

Zacharias takes half-glasses from his pocket and flips quickly through the contract. Rich has never seen anyone read so fast. Despite his stoop, his drooping eyelids, there is something youthful in his quickness. His darting eyes seem expressly built for scanning contracts, like some advanced machine.

"You're married?" he asks, glancing at the signature page. "Will your wife be joining us?"

"She's not home. I can fill her in later." Rich hesitates. "She's pretty upset about everything. She thinks it's all my fault."

"She was opposed to signing the lease?"

"Hell, no. She was all for it. We both were. I've been trying to get the farm up and running. The extra money came in useful." There is more, much more he wants to say: about his grandfather, his brother, what this land has cost each of them, the great price paid all around. It takes some effort to stick to the facts.

"Shelby was the one who first noticed the water. I didn't believe her at first. Then I had it tested. It's all right there in the report."

Zacharias flips through the pages. "Who else has seen this?"

"This guy. Quentin Tanner." Rich takes the business card from his pocket. "One of the guys on the rig gave me that number. They asked me to fax a copy of the report. Which I did." He pauses for a breath. "Right away this Tanner guy tells me they want to do their own testing."

"That's standard."

"I was a little worried, but the numbers came back basically the same, so I figure I'm home free. Pretty cut-and-dried, if you ask me: they contaminated my well, and they need to make it right."

"Let me guess. They're saying the water was dirty to begin with."

"How did you know?"

Zacharias shrugs. "It's a negotiation. Dark Elephant has been down this road many times. Their opening offer is always the same: exactly nothing. That's why I tell landowners to have their water tested *before* they sign a lease. Then, if something goes wrong, you have some baseline numbers to point to."

How did I not think of that? Rich understands, too late, the depth of his own disadvantage. Two years ago he'd barely glanced at the contract, which—he sees now—might as well have been written in a foreign language. In the end he simply scanned for numbers. It had never occurred to him to hire a lawyer.

"Nobody told me that."

"Of course not. It's in their interest to keep the landowner in the dark." Zacharias scribbles something on a yellow pad. "The truth is, these well contaminations aren't as rare as the industry would have us believe. A well bore is lined with cement casing. If something goes wrong in the cementing phase, gas can migrate into the groundwater. Darco will contest that point. The industry has taken the absurd position that there have been no documented cases of gas migration. But it simply isn't true."

Rich recalls, again, the morning he found Bobby Frame sitting at his table, in the same chair where the old man sits now. Bobby Frame had played him. He'd give anything to get his hands on Bobby Frame right now.

"The thing is, I don't see how they *could* fix it. Even if they wanted to. I already had a guy out here to drill me a new well. He went down five hundred feet. Still dirty. My wife won't even wash clothes in it." Rich hesitates. "There's one other thing. I wasn't going to mention it, but my daughter—she's seven—has a lot of stomach problems. She spent the other night in the hospital. My wife thinks it has something to do with the water."

Zacharias makes a note on his pad.

"She made an appointment with some doctor in Pittsburgh, a specialist. Environmental medicine? I think that's what she called it."

"It must be Ravi Ghosh. He's the best in the field." He makes another note on his pad. "You're still using the water?"

"For some things. Laundry, showers. For drinking and cooking we get bottled water from Walmart. It's costing me a fortune."

"Save your receipts. At minimum, Darco should reimburse you. No guarantee, but we can try."

"That's good, I guess. But it doesn't solve my problem." Rich gropes for the right words. "This was my grandfather's land. I'm not farming it right now, but I plan to. That's why I bought it in the first place. That was the whole point of signing a gas lease." He's never actually said it aloud before. Now that he's said it, the words won't stop coming. He talks about Pap's old tractor, which he's finally got running; the farmer in Somerset County with his eight-year-old Honiger. He babbles like a teenage girl.

"With those royalty checks I can just about afford to quit my job. Buy some animals. But how do I raise them without a supply of clean water?"

"You can't," Zacharias says.

The truth sits between them like a turd on a plate.

"So this land is basically no good to me."

"Not at the moment, no."

"Fuck it. I'll sell it, then." Does he mean it? In fact, selling never occurred to him until he heard the words come out of his own mouth.

"It's not that simple. To sell, you need a clear title. And once you've signed away your mineral rights, the gas company can file a lien against your property. What we've seen in Washington County—I don't want to scare you, Mr. Devlin, but we've seen it—is that the lien is typically grossly inflated. Often it's greater than the market value of the property. In which case—" He pauses significantly.

"What?"

"You wouldn't be able to use the land as collateral—for example, to get a home equity loan. And you certainly couldn't sell it."

"How is that possible? It's *my land*."

363

"Yes and no." Zacharias riffles through the sheaf of paper. "Your lease is with Darco?"

"Dark Elephant."

"Same difference. I should tell you that the news on this particular company isn't good. They finance their drilling operation by borrowing billions of dollars, so they're carrying an enormous debt load."

Nothing, nothing is simple.

"What does that have to do with me?"

"When did they start clearing your land? A couple months ago? You wouldn't know it, but you've had several different subcontractors working on your property. Logging crews, road crews. If I were a betting man, I'd wager that those workers haven't been paid yet. Dark Elephant has a reputation in the industry for paying their contractors late, or not at all."

"You're saying they're deadbeats?"

"Essentially. Of course, if I'm a contractor, I don't care who's at fault, as long as I get my money. If Dark Elephant won't pay up, I can file a mechanics' lien against your property."

"That's legal?"

"Absolutely."

The truth dawns slowly. "So I can't farm it, and I can't sell it." Blood in his mouth: he has bitten the inside of his cheek.

"Not at the moment, no."

The lawyer keeps talking, but Rich isn't listening. He doesn't want a lawyer. He doesn't want to go to court. He wants his old farm back.

All he wants is to make it stop.

11.

Gia sits at the kitchen table, watching Shelby fill the coffeemaker. "Bottled water?"

"For now. You know, until we drill a new well." Shelby sits, still in her bathrobe. It looks, to Gia, like a sleeping bag with sleeves. "Rich finally believes me. I've been telling him all summer the water was bad, but he's so stubborn."

Their friendship is a curious thing, surprising to them both. Gia doesn't make friends with women. Shelby doesn't make friends with anyone.

The house is quiet around them—no cartoon music, no Braden noises. "Where are the little monsters?"

"First day of school. Doughnut?" Shelby says, to change the subject. To forget the cold and terrible dread of standing at the foot of the driveway, watching the yellow bus take her children away. When she came back inside, the emptiness of the house was nearly sickening. She was grateful when Gia called.

"Did I tell you Olivia was in the hospital?" Shelby picks out a jelly doughnut and lays it on a plate. "They kept her overnight and everything. But they still can't tell me what's wrong."

The friendship is a relic of their days at Saxon Manor—Shelby working for Larry Stransky in Medical Records, Gia managing the laundry room. For two years they shared a lunch table, weekly Happy Hour at the Pick and Shovel, a place Shelby would never have ventured alone. That she met Rich Devlin at the Pick and Shovel, and thus owes her whole life to Gia, is a truth she avoids thinking about.

"I'm taking her to Pittsburgh, to see a specialist. My neighbor is going to drive us. Olivia isn't happy about missing school already, but she knows it's important."

Predictably, Gia isn't interested—waiting, as usual, for a chance to talk about herself. Her busy social life is like a trashy TV series Shelby devours in secret, one Braden and Olivia wouldn't be allowed to watch.

But Gia seems, this morning, to have nothing to tell. In the bright light she looks as though she slept in her makeup, her eyes ringed with smudged black liner. In high school she'd been a kind of celebrity, the queen bee of Bakerton High. Now she looks older than she ought to. This morning, Gia is showing her age.

"Is Darren sick?" she asks. "He didn't come to work yesterday."

"He didn't tell you? He went back to Baltimore." Shelby hugs her bathrobe around her. "He stopped by the house, but I was at church. I didn't get to say good-bye."

Gia looks stunned.

"That's crazy. When is he coming back?"

"He isn't. He didn't tell you?"

Gia is suddenly, inexplicably busy, sorting through her pocket-book. "I guess he used up all his vacation." She knows it isn't true. He had two more weeks.

"That's too bad," says Shelby, chewing at a cuticle. "Rich thought for sure he was going to move back here. You know, to help Dick. I told him it would never happen."

"Why not?"

"Can you imagine Darren living in Bakerton?"

Gia doesn't answer. She can easily imagine Darren living in Bakerton. Also: he had two more weeks.

"I'm glad you're here. I need a second opinion." Shelby springs out of her chair and takes a shopping bag from the broom closet. "My secret hiding place. I don't think Rich has opened this closet even once." From the bag she takes a child-size plaid jumper and a purple sweater dress. "For Olivia's appointment. Which do you like better?"

"The purple. Definitely."

Shelby holds the dresses at arm's length. "So cute! I was going to return one, but maybe I'll keep them both. Poor Olivia never gets any new clothes. Rich says she hasn't outgrown her old ones. Which is true, I guess. But it doesn't seem fair."

She returns the dresses to the bag and stashes it in the closet. Gia drinks her coffee in silence. Their friendship is made possible by the fact that neither envies the other in the slightest, while believing the other envies her. Gia's life, to Shelby, seems lonely and desperate: the long series of throwaway boyfriends, the sad job as a barmaid. To Shelby it's a familiar story, with a grim ending.

Gia thinks Shelby married an asshole.

"How's the counseling going?" she asks.

"I quit."

"Why? I thought it was helping." Gia imagines, idly, what it must be like to live with Rich Devlin. Does he leave Shelby lists of instructions? EMPTY DISHWASHER. TAKE OUT TRASH.

"It was. Pastor Jess—oh, it's a long story." Shelby selects a second doughnut. The complexity of the situation overwhelms her. She hungers to tell someone—not Gia, but *someone*—about the pastor's stunning duplicity, her fall from grace. Her own outrage and disappointment, her sense of betrayal: normally she would hoard these feelings, save them up to share at her next counseling session. Because Pastor Jess, in the end, is the only person she wants to tell.

"Rich said he'd go with me. He promised! But now he's being a butt. And Pastor Jess is wrapped up in her own life. She didn't even visit Olivia in the hospital. The *hospital*," she repeats for emphasis. "Anyways, if Rich won't go with me, there's really no point. And

if he *did* go with me—which he would never—who would watch
the kids?"

"I'll come hang out with them. I love those little monsters."

Shelby would never in a million years leave her kids with Gia.

"You know all those gas guys, right?" she says, changing the
subject. "From the Commercial. Have you ever met one named
Marshall?"

"Nope," Gia says.

"Are you sure? He was one of the guys who drilled our property.
A short guy, but kind of muscular. *Very* muscular. Like a weight-
lifter."

"Oh, you mean Herc." Gia laughs. "Sure, I know that whole
crew, Herc and Vince and Brando. Herc and me, we're like this."
She crosses her fingers.

Shelby finds the gesture confusing. "You've dated him?"

"Nah, I'm done with old guys." Gia remembers, too late, that
Shelby's husband falls into that category. "Anyways, Herc's married.
With kids! I draw the line at kids."

At this Shelby makes a remarkable face. Gia has never seen anything like it, a *grand mal* seizure of horror and disbelief. *"No!* Are
you sure?"

"Positive. His wife's name is Colleen. I helped him pick out
earrings for her birthday." Gia leans in, smelling gossip. "Why? You
like him?"

"Are you crazy?" Shelby wonders for a moment what world Gia
lives in. "I have a husband, remember?"

"Oh. Right," Gia says.

THE SUNY CAMPUS IS ALIVE AGAIN, roused from its summer coma.
A week ago the only sounds were lawn mowers. Now the backpacks
have returned. Lost freshmen, rowdy sophomores, cool juniors,
jaded seniors. American youth with its palpable hungers, its summer suntans, new haircuts, resolutions, anxieties, plans.

In the quad they note signs of foreign activity, above and beyond the new-semester bustle: a stage set up at one end, flanked by loud-speakers; tour buses parked along the winding campus road. Men and women in legible T-shirts, of parental age and older, set up tables on the lawn: the Empire State Sustainability Coalition, the Green Future Society, Antifrack Nation New York.

The old in their relaxed-fit blue jeans, potbellied and pear-shaped, earnest, thick-bodied, gray. Lorne Trexler moves through this crowd like an impresario. These are his people. Everybody knows Lorne. He is accompanied, today, by a woman no one recog-nizes, which is not unusual. The activist community is fluid, perme-able. It runs on coalitions and alliances, unions of all kinds. Today, for example, Keystone Waterways is partnering with Frackless Future—an offshoot of Fracklash!, which coorganized the event.

His hand at the woman's back, Lorne points out the key play-ers. Watershed Watch, the Greater Catskill Food Co-op, the Zero-Impact Collective, the Hudson Valley Livestock Network. Joined today, in a show of solidarity, by sundry others, seen wherever crowds are gathered—the antivaccinators, the hemp activists, the Falun Gongsters. These are the movement's peculiar relations, its distant cousins. Their connections to gas drilling are strategic, or metaphysical, or perhaps totally imaginary. Gluten-Free Living, the drumming circle from Philmont. The La Leche League, Fur No More, TransAction, the Jews for Jesus.

The connections are not easily explained.

Lorne squeezes Rena's shoulder. "Well? What do you think?"

She thinks the day is passing far too quickly. It seems only min-utes ago that she met him in the Days Inn parking lot. The meeting had the feeling of an assignation: the neutral location, separate from either of their lives; the roadside motel in her peripheral vision, with its concrete promise of sin. It was hard to look at him. His face didn't quite match her memory, the recollection she'd fingered and worried all these weeks like a string of rosary beads.

When she arrived he was waiting in a nondescript Ford Taurus. *The Prius is in the shop. I hit a deer.*

They're bad this year. Mack hit one, too.

The intimacy of riding in a car together, the enforced closeness. She could smell the cinnamon gum he chewed, the fabric-softener freshness of his shirt, as they crossed a border to a place she didn't live.

"I love it," she says.

"I knew you would." Lorne waves to someone across the quad. "I wanted you to see what can happen when we speak truth to power. Trust me, this would never happen in Pennsylvania."

"Why not?"

He shrugs, as though the question is unanswerable, or simply of no interest. "You tell me. Personally, it makes me crazy. The fatalism. The lack of, I don't know"—he gropes for the word—"*outrage.* It's like they *expect* to have their land and water polluted." He seems to have forgotten that Rena is part of this *they.* "Like they're just waiting to be screwed."

They make their way through the crowd. The drumming circle stakes out a territory near the food trucks. A bearded man hands Rena a pamphlet. **ARE YOU WAITING FOR THE MESSIAH?**

On the makeshift stage a man approaches the podium, a movie actor in a plaid shirt.

A burst of applause, cheers and whistles, a rattling of home-made placards.

NOT ONE WELL

STOP FRACKING NOW

GOV. CUOMO: HOLD THE LINE!

The actor is young and scruffily handsome. He might play Lorne Trexler in the movie version of his life. He holds up a jar of what looks like greasy dishwater and says, "This is why I'm here."

A woman in a knitted beanie hands Rena a pamphlet. *Immunization and the Autism Spectrum: What Big Pharma Doesn't Want You to Know.*

"We are in a spiritual war." The actor is not generally famous. He is indie-famous, which is better. "I got this out of a family's well that was poisoned by frack drilling that's within two hundred yards of their home."

Signs in all colors, on plastic sheeting, on poster board, on butcher paper.

MOTHERFRACKERS, GO HOME!

I SPEAK FOR THE TREES!

"Who in New York would take a sip of that?" the actor demands. "Who in New York wants to wake up in the morning and bathe in *this*? I mean, if there aren't any problems with frack drilling, how come there's so many problems with frack drilling?"

DON'T FRACK WITH OUR FUTURE

HOME IS NOT AN INDUSTRIAL ZONE

"We're in a battle, and a battle has refugees. Today we're joining with refugees from Pennsylvania, which, let's face it, is ground zero for hydro-fracking. I don't care how prodrilling you are, you still want your water and your air clean."

Lorne grasps Rena's shoulder and points to a sign in the distance: PENNA. WAS THE EXPERIMENT. THE PATIENT DIED.

"I'm here today for my kids and your kids and the kids in New York City. Don't get me wrong. I want the farmers to survive. I think it's a shame they can't make a damn fine wage in this community."

Rena appreciates the sentiment, though she has never heard of this actor. An Asian girl with a crew cut hands her a pamphlet. **WHAT IT MEANS TO BE TRANSGENDER.**

"New York isn't ready for this. *Pennsylvania* wasn't ready for this. *Every single community* where they've done the drilling is seeing water contamination. In *every single community* they're poisoning the rivers, the lakes, the air."

The crowd goes wild.

"Is that true?" Rena asks, but Lorne doesn't hear her. Her question is lost in the noise.

"For every person here, there's a thousand more who feel the way we do. Do you think we *like* schlepping all the way up here?" The actor pauses, as though he expects an answer. "I'm not getting paid to do this. My land isn't leased. So why am I sticking my nose in?"

Rena blinks. It was Mack's point exactly, the same question she'd asked about Lorne.

The actor spreads his hands. "I have no angle here. I'm here because I care."

To Rena it is a moment of pure marvel. How the very same question can have two conflicting answers, both incontrovertibly true.

The actor is winding up for his big finale, a hearty call-and-response. "Now we're going to take the energy—"

The crowd repeats: *We're going to take the energy*

"That we've created here today—"

That we've created here today

"We're going to carry it to Albany—"

We're going to carry it to Albany

"We're going to carry it to Cuomo—"

We're going to carry it to Cuomo

"We're going to carry it to President Obama—"

We're going to carry it to President Obama

"And tell him enough is enough!"

And tell him enough is enough!

The actor bounds from the stage to shouts and whistles, a controlled roar of applause. Music pours from the loudspeakers, the loping rhythm and bright upbeats of what might as well be the only reggae song ever recorded. *Get up, stand up. Stand up for your rights.*

"Now what?" Rena shouts over the noise. "It's over?" Across the quad, two Jews for Jesus are folding up their table. The drumming circle piles into a Dodge Caravan.

"Looks that way," Lorne says.

"Maybe we should get on the road," she says, not because she wants to. Because Mack, because her whole life, is waiting.

"Not yet," he says. "There's someone I need to see."

THE EARTH SCIENCES BUILDING is tall and sky lit, filled with sunlight. Lorne Trexler crosses the hallway to study the directory, an alphabetical listing affixed to the wall. *Dr. Amy Rubin, Associate Professor of Geology.*

At that moment, across the lobby, doors open. Amy Rubin steps out of the elevator, rubbing at her blouse with a napkin. She looks stunned to see him, stupefied: the mute peasant girl in a Balkan village who sees the face of the Virgin floating in a cloud bank, or burnt into a slice of toast.

"Unbelievable. It's like you sensed I was in the building. Some unseen force pulled you into the elevator and delivered you to me like a pizza." Lorne treats her to the slow smile she once loved and later hated. "Hi, Rubin."

"What are you doing here?" It takes her a moment to collect herself. Because this doesn't happen every day, your past coming to find you. The fuse that started everything, the blast that birthed the world.

He's aged, no question. His hair, still long, is more gray than black. The lines around his eyes are new, the deep grooves from nose to mouth. And yet Lorne will never be old to her. She sees him as he once was, an involuntary parallax. It's all that's left of her adolescent infatuation, this glitch in her vision, a reflexive generosity he doesn't deserve.

"Oh, right," she says. "The protest."

"You saw it?"

"For a second." She is miserably aware of the coffee stain spread across her sternum, the reading glasses hanging from a chain around her neck.

"Pretty good turnout, for the first day of classes. We had at least a thousand people."

"You organized it?"

"That would be overstating. I gave some advice here and there." Lorne tips back his head and stares up at the vaulted ceiling. He whistles low like a rube in the city, a broad pantomime of looking. "Some digs you've got here, Rubin. You must have generous benefactors."

"So you've said."

A silence.

"I saw your letter to the editor," she says, because why pretend? "How did you phrase it? *Calamitous effects on the integrity of scientific inquiry?*"

"A direct quote. I'm flattered."

"Dr. Rubin's corporate underwriters have a direct financial stake in the outcome of her research."

"Tell me I'm wrong. Bearing in mind that we're standing in the Oliphant Earth Sciences Center. I drove up here today with a dairy farmer from Saxon County. She's waiting for me in the student union. You ought to come and meet her. Her cows are grazing downhill from a well contaminated by Dark Elephant. Small world, no?" He studies her. "You look good, Rubin. Corporate skullduggery suits you."

The comment is pure Lorne: first the caress, then the wallop. Somehow, Amy forgot this.

"You know nothing about my life."

"I beg to differ. That first paper on the Marcellus was quality work. Don't look so surprised. I've been following your career— lately, with a kind of morbid fascination." He takes a step toward her. "I can accept that you're a lost cause, but what is this saying to the next generation? I met some of your students today. Despite your uninspiring example, they still believe they can make a difference."

Amy thinks, Get a haircut.

"Oh, *that's* what you're doing! Shaping the next generation. Like you did with me."

"I seem to recall you had a hand in that."

It's true, of course. She knocked at his door.

"I was nineteen."

"People go to war at nineteen, make babies at nineteen. It's fashionable, now, to treat them like helpless children, but that's ahistorical. I looked for you at the rally," he says. "I figured you'd at least come check it out. Weren't you even curious?"

"Please. I've seen demonstrations before. Last fall we had a couple hundred Occupiers sleeping in cardboard boxes. Apparently it's what democracy looks like."

"What's happened to you? They say the eyes are the first thing to go"—he glances meaningfully at the reading glasses—"but I say it's curiosity. People hit middle age and they stop questioning. That's aging. That's the beginning of the end."

"*Questioning*? Give me a break. You figured out the world in 1979, at a Grateful Dead show probably, and haven't questioned anything since. Well, demonstrate all you want, if it makes you feel righteous. But trust me, that's the only benefit."

"*Rubin*. Read the papers, will you? There is concerted, organized opposition in this state, and it's been remarkably effective. New York has a moratorium on drilling, the last time I checked."

"And Pennsylvania?"

In the tall vaulted foyer of the Oliphant Earth Sciences Center, a satisfying silence.

"Pennsylvania is a conundrum," he admits. "Pennsylvania makes no fucking sense."

"Well, let me enlighten you." Amy's heart races pleasantly; there is pleasure in this. Oftener than she'd ever admit, she has practiced this speech in her head. "You're so busy being right that you refuse to acknowledge a basic fact. Which is: *People want this*."

"People are idiots," he snaps.

Aha! she thinks. Lorne Trexler the famous populist, champion of the working classes until they dare to disagree with him.

"That's a heartwarming sentiment. But before you dismiss the entire population of Pennsylvania, at least consider the possibility that they know something you don't."

"Which you're going to explain to me," says Lorne.

"Good God, somebody should." Her voice echoes in the cavernous space. "Has it occurred to you that virtually every dollar that's ever come into Pennsylvania is an energy dollar?"

"You're exaggerating."

"Yes, but not much. Even Beth Steel would never have set up shop there, if it weren't for the coal."

"Beth Steel? *That's* your argument? Jesus, look how well that turned out."

"But it *did*! It did until it didn't. Nothing lasts forever." Not youth or love or wonder, not anything.

Once, long ago, she knocked at his door.

"Look, it's got to come from somewhere," she says wearily. "You taught me that. So what's the alternative? Keep on burning coal?"

"That's a spurious argument and you know it. Drilling the Marcellus is costing billions. If we invested *half* that much in renewables, we'd have a permanent solution to this mess instead of swapping one fossil fuel addiction for another. Gas is no more sustainable than coal or oil. At best, we're postponing the inevitable."

"*Life* is postponing the inevitable."

They stare at each other across a wide chasm, a frozen lake of incalculable depth, the scene of a mortal accident: the drowning of Amy Rubin, her youthful idealism, the way she once loved him. Her young self is possibly still down there, trapped beneath the ice.

"Lorne, this is bigger than all of us. You can't stop it. Nobody can, when there's this much money involved."

"My God, you're cynical."

"I'd like to know what world you live in, if you're not."

A silence.

"It's not a perfect technology," she admits. "I know that. Everyone knows that."

"Not everyone. Every day I meet people who sign leases and have no idea what they're in for. That's what we're fighting against. We won't change everybody's mind, but we can make sure they know the facts. That's my mission." Again the slow smile. "What's your mission, Rubin? And don't give me that I'm-a-scientist crap. I didn't just roll off the turnip cart."

"I don't have a mission."

And there it lies, the fundamental difference between them. The way other people believe in Allah or Jesus, Lorne Trexler believes in his own power, his ability to affect outcomes. Amy has a sudden vision of him twenty years older, a hippie in his dotage, still fighting battles long ago lost, or long ago won.

The outcomes have already been decided.

The collision of large forces, or their collusion. The machine that can't be stopped.

The point of dynamism moves inexorably. Only its wake is discernible, the atmospheric waves and eddies. Kip Oliphant is living, now, in the divorce apartment, the furnished penthouse suite of Gulf Vista. Ten years ago it was the best address in Houston—thirty glittering stories of mirrored office tower, built in the boom years when the sky rained money. Now Gulf Vista stands nearly empty, a bleak lesson in the laws of the universe, the unseen, inexorable workings of the game.

Seasons of fortune and decay.

In the divorce apartment—the apartment associated with this particular divorce—he begins each day precisely as he did when married, with the 24 Hour News Network.

His hunger for news is reflexive, insistent. It rouses him like a morning erection. He reads the paper while listening to the TV, a habit his last wife found confounding: *All that bad news first thing in the morning! It's so depressing.* In eleven years of marriage, Gretchen had failed to grasp a basic reality: sleep, to Kip, was unwelcome. After five hours he woke in a blind panic, as though he'd dozed off behind the wheel. An infusion of news was then necessary, an immediate debriefing on all he'd missed during his regrettable nightly lapse.

"America's middle class has endured its worst decade in modern history, according to the Pew Research Center." The morning anchor, Meredith Culver, wears a tailored jacket with a camisole underneath, as though she's come straight from her boudoir. Her mouth is her most notable feature—blossom-shaped, plump as fruit.

He ignores the cell phone ringing in his pocket.

A weather forecast crawls across the bottom of the screen: sunny in Kansas City, tornado warnings in Omaha.

Kip attacks his *Chronicle*, rearranging the sections in order of interest: Business, National, everything else. He has a habit of marrying the wrong kind of woman. Next time he'll choose one interested in the world, a Meredith Culver type. He puts down his paper and studies the face on the screen—the dewy skin, the tumescent mouth. The camisole is silky and wine colored, the same shade as her lips. She is a product of the 24 Hour News Network, native to the studio, conceived and raised there. Kip imagines her a precocious child, an awkward teenager, coming of age against the vibrant blue background, clear and luminous as a desert sky at dawn.

Seattle is reporting rain.

The crawl at the bottom of the screen turns from blue to red. His tech stocks are up, his Intel and Apple. He watches the crawl, waiting for the number.

That mouth could sell lip gloss or toothpaste.

His cell phone rings and rings.

Finally the number comes crawling. Dark Elephant is trading at twenty-two dollars a share.

"Son of a bitch," Kip says aloud.

From the high windows of the divorce apartment, he watches calamity rain down.

SEASONS OF FORTUNE AND DECAY. The weather changes with little warning. Kip has learned to look for signs, like an Old Testament seer dreaming of wheat.

The current season began two months ago, disgustingly. A backed-up toilet was the harbinger of his doom.

More than he misses his ex-wife, Kip misses his ex-bathroom, the granite-and-marble temple designed to his exact specifications: halogen lighting, heated floors and towel racks; a glass-enclosed spa with six showerheads aimed strategically (a vision he described to the architect by telephone, while driving through an automated car wash). Opposite the spa sat the bathroom's showpiece, a limited-edition angular toilet, the signature design of an Italian sculptor with a three-year waiting list—Enrico Scarpacci, toiletmaker to the stars. Kip's Scarpacci has been featured in swank design magazines: *Houston Living, Urban Homestead.* Visitors to the house regularly asked to see it. Like a marble saint of the High Renaissance, the Scarpacci sat majestically in a recessed apse, beneath a custom-built arch that mirrored the tank's contours.

Two months ago, on a Tuesday morning, Kip had flushed thoughtlessly. Looking back, he is touched by his own innocence. He flushed in pure naïve faith, never imagining the ruinous chain of events he was about to unleash.

Beginning, horribly, with the befouling of his personal sanctuary. *Plumber!* he shouted to no one in particular. *Somebody call a plumber!*

Already running late, he closed the door on the mess and ducked into his wife's bathroom, where every surface was littered with female clutter, as though a high-end hair salon had been devastated by an earthquake.

Spitting out his toothpaste, he noticed, at the edge of the sink, a plastic compact of birth control pills.

He found Gretchen in the sunroom running on the StairMaster. He'd bought her a half-dozen new cardio machines over the years, but she always went back to the StairMaster, which delivered a more unpleasant and thus more effective workout.

"What are these?" he demanded.

His wife was flushed with guilt or, perhaps, simple exertion. The machine was at its highest setting. "My pills. What were you doing in my bathroom?"

"Never mind that. Why did I get a vasectomy, if you're taking pills?" He was so angry he could barely speak. The procedure had nearly killed him, his balls swollen grapefruit-size by a freak infection. Ten years later, the misery and indignity were still fresh.

"I was nursing Allie then. I couldn't take them."

"Why do you need them?"

She explained that the pills improved her complexion. Also, they made her boobs bigger.

"Your boobs are fake," Kip said.

Which, honestly, was a matter of record: Kip had paid for the surgery himself. None of it made sense until, a few days later, he viewed the footage, shot from a hidden camera. Years ago, when Allie was small, the sunroom had been her playroom. The security system was installed at Gretchen's insistence, so she could keep an eye on the revolving cast of nannies who came and went. The system was fully automated. They had simply never bothered to turn it off.

The footage was a little grainy. Kip didn't, at first, recognize Gretchen's trainer. He barely recognized Gretchen herself, naked except for socks and sneakers, awkwardly straddling a weight-training bench.

Now, in the divorce apartment, his cell phone rings and rings. Kip glances at the display: his broker, Taffy Campbell. It's only 7:00 A.M. in New York, which implies some urgency.

He hits the Ignore button.

In the current cycle, it's wise to stop and think before picking up the phone.

"SUING ME," HE REPEATS DUMBLY. "What do you mean, suing me?"

He is sitting in the downtown offices of Mahenny, Garner and Bunch. His attorney—known to the wide world as Piggy—hands over a sheaf of paper.

"Not you. Dark Elephant."

"I *am* Dark Elephant."

"Not legally, you're not, praise the Lord. Or praise me, if you are so inclined."

Kip scans the paper. The print swims before his eyes. "What am I looking at, Pig?"

"In a nutshell? This group of shareholders is claiming that you—that Dark Elephant—overstated the value of some acreage in Arkansas."

Kip stares in disbelief. "I made these people a fortune."

"They don't see it that way. They see you playing fast and loose with their money, is what they see."

"MY MONEY TOO!" he shouts. "I never asked anybody to take a risk I wouldn't take myself."

"Don't get excited."

"What's this going to cost me?"

Piggy reaches into the desk for his tin of lemon drops, a nervous habit. "Nothing, I hope. In your current situation you can't afford it. How's the divorce going?"

"Better than the last one." Last time Piggy had recommended a lady lawyer: *You'll do better with female counsel.* By the time it was all over, Kip had lost a Mercedes, a Land Rover, and one of his houses. With male counsel, would the judge have taken his teeth?

"I hate to kick a man when he's down, but there's more bad news. Water problems up in Pennsylvania. Also, a group of shareholders is claiming you've been using the company jets improperly."

"Horseshit," Kip says.

"That's your official position? Because I'm here to tell you, it may be untenable. They have proof."

"Of what?"

"In an unfortunate confluence of events, there is a separate complaint."

Kip sinks low in his chair. "Just give it to me, Pig. Don't make me guess."

"The incident in question happened on a flight to Bermuda. The plaintiff is Megan Somebody. Ring any bells?"

"Bermuda?" Then, suddenly, Kip remembers: last spring Gretchen had thrown a bridal shower there for one of her friends.

"That one's a personal injury suit. Facial disfiguration."

"What?"

"According to the complaint, this lady was having an injection in her face aboard a Dark Elephant company jet. I guess they hit some turbulence. You're a codefendant, along with something called Serenity Day Spa."

"Fine. Let her sue." Lawsuits do not rattle him. He's been sued for breach of contract, for nonpayment. He's been sued by six separate municipalities in the state of Texas, and for divorce by four separate wives.

"I'm not so worried about that one. That one we can probably settle for cheap. But the shareholders—" Piggy hesitates. "It's worse than you think, Whip. They've named you in the suit. They're going after your personal assets."

Kip is dumbfounded, stung by the ingratitude. Men who'd made their fortunes off his nerve and hard work, his unerring instinct, his willingness to imperil himself. For two years, nearly three, they had bathed in money.

"You'll need counsel," Piggy says. "Technically I represent Dark Elephant. I can't represent you personally. Jill could do it."

Another lady lawyer.

"No, thank you," Kip says.

"Also, you're carrying a lot of debt."

"Me-me? Or Dark Elephant-me?"

"Both," Piggy says. "I warned you about this. All those new wells are costing you a fortune. You-you."

"I know it." The Columbus Clause had been Kip's own invention, a provision unheard of in the industry. Piggy had groused about it, but in the end wrote the language into Kip's contract, a clause that let him buy a two percent share in every Dark Elephant well. The terms are simple, elegant. Two percent of the operating costs come out of his own pocket. In return, he gets two percent of revenue when the well comes in. His instinct and ingenuity, his unflinching nerve, have made fortunes for other people. It seems only fair that he keep a little for himself.

"You need cash, amigo. No two ways about it."

Rigs to maintain, supplies to buy, crews to pay. Two percent of expenses doesn't sound like much, until you drill five or ten thousand wells.

Kip says, "Let me make some calls."

AT WORK HE STEPS LIGHTLY. His stepfather's office, on the eighth floor, is serviced by a high-speed elevator. Kip takes the stairs. It seems prudent, even with Dar out on sick leave, to avoid the executive washroom, the company cafeteria, anyplace his stepfather is likely to go.

"You're out of breath." Kip's secretary eyes him up and down. "Dar is looking for you."

In his pocket the cell phone vibrates.

"I know it," Kip calls over his shoulder. "Tell him I'll catch him later."

He turns the corner to his office and sees, too late, Dar sitting behind his desk.

"Catch me now."

Kip manages a weak smile. "Hey, stranger. What are you doing here?"

"Aging."

"Sorry. I was just over to Piggy's. You're looking good."

Dar looks like hell. Last week he keeled over on the golf course, surprising no one. The actual surprise came later—his death implausibly postponed by an emergency angioplasty, unsettling all who knew him, Kip's mother especially.

"Don't give me that." Dar clutches his side. A girdle of bandage is visible between his shirt buttons. The paramedic who administered CPR broke two of his ribs. "We need to pull the plug on Pennsylvania. For now, anyway. The bubble has burst."

"You can't be serious."

"You see me laughing? It's been a long time coming, buddy. I've given you plenty of rope."

"You're talking about a third of our business. You can't kill it just like that."

"Watch me." Dar eyes him levelly. His left one looks milky, the beginnings of a cataract. "I would've done it a week ago, but I been otherwise occupied."

"You got a good scare." Kip lowers his voice, a trick that sometimes works with horses. "I understand that. Don't let it make you lose your nerve."

"Nerve's got nothing to do with it. These Marcellus wells are putting me in the poorhouse. I blame myself. I never should have let you run off half-cocked." Again Dar clutches his side. "Time to circle the wagons, buddy. Get back to our core business."

Kip says, "Oil's in the toilet."

"It'll come back. Always does."

"Gas will come back, too. I made you a lot of money, Dar."

"Cost me plenty, too."

Kip thinks, *You are not my father.*

HE IS DRIVING AWAY from the office when the phone rings.

"Here's the situation." Taffy Campbell speaks at the speed of a cattle auctioneer. "You are fatally undercapitalized. With Dark Elephant trading at twenty-two, your shares don't have enough value to back a loan of this magnitude."

"Give me a week," says Kip. "One godblessed week. I guarantee that number is going up."

"There are no more weeks. I need cash now, or I'm going to have to sell your stock. We're out of options."

Kip swerves into the passing lane.

"We talked about this," says Taffy. "I warned you this could happen."

"Fine," he snaps. "What can you do for me?"

There is a silence.

"I can't help you, Whip."

"What do you mean, can't? I thought you were the law in those parts."

"Only in Personal Wealth Group," says Taffy. "This came from upstairs."

THE POINT OF DYNAMISM is a construct, useful only when it is useful.

Fatally undercapitalized.

Facial disfiguration.

The packet of birth control pills at the edge of the sink.

Multiple points of dynamism, darting randomly, fleet as june bugs, their demented trajectories known only to the Creator himself.

Driving, Kip has a realization that nearly makes his brain burst.

The point of dynamism is me.

When Rena pulls up to the house, they're waiting on the porch: Olivia in a plaid jumper, Shelby in a severe navy blue suit like an old-school airline stewardess. Shelby buckles Olivia into the van's backseat, then climbs in beside Rena. There is a chill in the air, a rumor of fall.

"I thought your pastor was coming."

"She couldn't make it. It's a long story. Oh, can you stop right here? I need to mail this." Shelby takes an envelope from her purse.

"What about Rich? We have plenty of room."

Shelby lowers the window and leans out to open the mailbox. "He's not a very good passenger. Anyways, he's on day shift. Oh, wait! I forgot the flag."

She steps out of the van and hurries back to the mailbox, raising the red flag.

"Where's Dr. Trexler?" she asks when she returns.

"He couldn't make it. Something came up."

"People are always saying that." Shelby reaches over the seat and hands Olivia her cell phone. "You look tired."

"I'm fine." Objectively, it's true. There's nothing wrong with Rena beyond a kind of psychic hangover from her day with Lorne—a creeping soreness, vaguely muscular, as though she threw out her back while shoveling snow.

The long and complicated day, in all its electrifying strangeness. After the rally he'd left her sitting in the student union for nearly an hour. *I have to see a colleague in the Geology Department. I won't be long.*

In the student union Rena waited and waited, wishing she'd brought *Silent Spring.* In her bag she found a pamphlet folded in thirds. She'd had a vague idea of saving it for Mack.

Gender identity is a person's internal sense of being

- **a woman,**
- **a man, or**
- **a person outside the gender binary.**

Not all gender-nonconforming people identify as transgender, nor are all transgender people gender-nonconforming.

Rena thought: Sometimes you just meet a person.

She threw the pamphlet in the trash.

Lorne's moodiness on the drive home, the unexpected silence that was somehow nothing like Mack's. How was it possible, that two people could say nothing in entirely different ways? Mack's silence was negative space, an absence of anything. Lorne's was rich and complicated, fraught with unknowable meanings, a pot simmering on the stove.

By the time they crossed over the border—PENNSYLVANIA WELCOMES YOU—she understood the depth of her foolishness. She had misread the situation completely. Lorne cared nothing for her.

As they turned into the Days Inn parking lot, he seemed to remember she was there.

I wish I could go with you tomorrow, he said. *To see Ravi. I'll be thinking of you. Call me, okay?*

He leaned over and kissed her cheek.

Now, in the backseat, Olivia plays a game on her mother's phone. She stares at the tiny screen, rapturously absorbed. Shelby is chatty, animated, full of questions: Did Rena grow up on the farm?

Did she have brothers and sisters? Had she always wanted to be a nurse? Does she belong to a church?

No, yes, yes, no. Rena answers the questions at length, with copious details. Why not? She has nothing else to do but drive.

Were Mack and Rena best friends since childhood? What was Mack's real name, actually, and why did she go by Mack?

Rena answers: No. Susan. Nobody remembers why.

Shelby asks, "Have you ever been married?"

There is a simple answer to the question, and a complicated one. Rena opts for simplicity. "No," she says.

"Has Mack?"

Rena studies her, fascinated. Honestly, how is it possible? What goes on in Shelby's brain is a flat-out mystery. At times it's like talking to a precocious child. At other times, a slow-witted adult.

"No," she says.

Shelby nods sagely. "I used to be afraid of that. Being—an old maid, or whatever. No offense. But now I think it wouldn't be so bad. Marriage isn't all it's cracked up to be." She stares out the window. "I think Dr. Trexler likes you."

Rena says, "I like him, too."

IN THE WAITING ROOM Rena flips through a magazine, trying to picture where Lorne is at this moment. She thinks, I am lovelorn. An old-fashioned word she hasn't heard in years.

She leaves a message on his cell phone: "Shelby and Olivia are in with Dr. Ghosh. They've been in there awhile." For half an hour she's kept her eyes on the door next to the reception desk. Somewhere behind it, Shelby and Olivia are sitting in an exam room.

At that moment the door opens. Shelby, red-faced, leads Olivia by the hand. Behind them, a nurse signals to Rena.

"Call me later, okay?" she tells the voice mail. "I have to go." She hangs up and gets to her feet. "Shelby, what happened? Are you all right?"

Shelby shakes her head mutely, her eyes welling.

The nurse asks, "Are you Rena Koval? Dr. Ghosh would like to see you."

"Sit tight, Shelby. I'll be right back."

The nurse leads her down a long corridor to an exam room. Dr. Ghosh—a tiny wizened man, hairless, ageless—offers his hand. "Lorne has told me a lot about you. Please have a seat. Have you spoken with Mrs. Devlin?"

"Not yet. She seemed upset, though. What happened?"

Ghosh closes the door. "I examined Olivia and looked at her labs, and I'm afraid I can't help her."

"You mean it's not the water?"

"No."

"But you've seen the lab reports, right? Two different labs said there was methane migration."

"I have no doubt the well is contaminated. But as I told Mrs. Devlin, it's extremely unlikely that has anything to do with Olivia's GI symptoms."

"I was afraid of that," says Rena. "Poor Shelby!"

"Is she always so volatile?"

"No. Well, sort of." How to explain Shelby Devlin? "It's just that she was hoping for answers. She was convinced—we all were—that the water was the problem. Lorne, especially. He was absolutely sure."

"Lorne is an activist, not a doctor."

"That's true. But, you know, *something* is making her sick. And I'm worried about Shelby. This is taking a toll on her."

The doctor seems to hesitate. "How well do you know Mrs. Devlin?"

"Not very. Why?"

"Something else occurred to me. It's only a theory. Less than a theory; let's call it a possibility. I have absolutely no proof."

IT'S NEARLY DUSK when Rena drives into Bakerton. She drops Shelby and Olivia at their house and immediately dials Lorne's number.

"Hey, it's Rena. Can you please pick up?"

She remembers, then, that he can't hear her: she's talking to a cell phone, not an answering machine. Does anybody have an answering machine anymore?

She deletes the message and tries again.

"So, hi there, it's Rena calling. I know you're busy, but this is *important*." She is surprised by the tremor in her voice. "I talked to Dr. Ghosh and—"

Words fail her.

"Can you please call me, please?"

UNSPEAKABLE.

In Melbourne, Australia, a toddler was brought to the Emergency Room with projectile vomiting, fever, diarrhea. He weighed no more than a year-old infant. He was diagnosed with failure to thrive.

The term "factitious" describes symptoms that are artificially produced rather than the result of a natural process. GI symptoms can be produced with emetics, laxatives, and many common substances.

The Australian boy was put on an elimination diet. For six weeks he ate only boiled chicken.

The deliberate production or feigning of symptoms in another person who is under the individual's care.

The Australian boy was fitted with an NG tube.

The mean number of symptoms per victim is 3.25.

By the time of his death, at age four, the Australian boy had been seen by a pediatrician nearly three hundred times. His autopsy showed profound deterioration of the heart muscle.

"Come to bed," says Mack. "You've been on that thing for three hours."

"In a minute," Rena says.

The mother in North Carolina caught on videotape, injecting salt water into her son's IV.

The British mother who contaminated her baby's urine sample with drops of her own blood.

The daily disasters of the ER, the heart attacks and car accidents, seem benign in comparison. Nursing in the Information Age: a catalog of horrors at your fingertips.

THAT NIGHT LORNE DOESN'T CALL. Again and again Rena tries his cell phone.

Hey, it's Lorne. You know what to do.

He's wrong, of course. She has no idea what to do.

THE NEXT DAY SHE ARRIVES EARLY for her shift and corners Dr. Stusick in the hallway. "I need to talk to you about Olivia Devlin."

"I only have a minute."

Rena thinks, What else is new?

She leads him into an exam room and closes the door. Sometimes there's no way to say a thing, except to say it.

"You think she's poisoning her own child?" Dr. Stusick stares at her as though Rena—not Shelby—were the monster. As though she's grown claws and scales.

"It's not just me. I took them to Pittsburgh yesterday, so Olivia could see Dr. Ghosh." Rena's heart beats loudly. "I didn't believe him at first. Then I thought about the last time Olivia was admitted. Shelby didn't want her to be discharged. She was really upset about it. I left them alone for maybe ten minutes. As soon as Shelby left, Olivia was vomiting again." She pauses for a breath. "She could have given her something."

Dr. Stusick frowns. "Even if she were capable of it—and I'm not prepared to believe she is—I don't see how it's possible. With all the labs we've done, something would have come back hinky."

"Not necessarily. Not if she used an emetic. Ipecac, maybe?"

Dr. Stusick blinks, a look she's seen before: the mute amazement of a doctor confronted with evidence that nurses actually think.

"There was a case in Australia," she says. "I did some research."

He seems to consider this. "Ipecac is undetectable, as far as I know. So even if it *were* true—"

"We couldn't prove it. Dr. Ghosh said the same thing."

There is a silence.

"I've read about these cases," says Dr. Stusick. "From what I understand, parents do it to get attention from medical staff. And Mrs. Devlin has never seemed terribly interested in what I have to say."

"I had the same thought," says Rena. "But, you know, what if we're not the ones she cares about?"

Somewhere a clock is ticking.

"This guy in Pittsburgh," says Dr. Stusick. "Ghosh. Did he confront her?"

"No. He just wasn't sure. Neither am I," she adds quickly. "But if I suspect a child is being hurt, I'm legally obligated to report it." *So are you,* she thinks but does not say.

She doesn't have to; Dr. Stusick grasps the subtext. "Let's be clear, Rena: these are *your* suspicions, not mine. If you want to report it to ChildLine, I'm not stopping you. This is your call."

There is a knock at the door.

"Two seconds, Agnes! I'll be right there." Dr. Stusick eyes her intently. "Reasonable cause, Rena. That's the standard. Do you have reasonable cause to believe Mrs. Devlin is harming her child?"

(Dr. Ghosh: *It's only a theory. Less than a theory; let's call it a possibility. I have absolutely no proof.*)

"No," she admits. "Well, maybe. I honestly don't know."

"That doesn't inspire confidence." He goes to the sink and turns on the water. "These are very serious allegations. Have you thought about what happens if you're wrong?"

In the past twenty-four hours she has thought of little else.

He literally washes his hands.

RENA IS DRIVING BACK to the farm when, at last, her cell phone rings.

She signals and pulls off the highway. Hand over one ear, she lets Lorne complain about the dullards in his Intro course, his ongoing feud with the registrar's office, the gas-guzzling rental car, his wounded Prius still in the shop. She lets him talk, knowing that once she says it, there will be no unsaying it. That nothing, ever, will be the way it was.

"Listen," he says finally. "I want to apologize for the other night. I had a lot on my mind."

It takes her a moment to remember what he's talking about. The long, awkward drive back from New York seems very long ago.

"Remember that girl I told you about? The consultant? Well, I saw her. I gotta say, it messed with my head. I don't know if I told you, but we were lovers. A long, long time ago."

"You didn't mention that." Only yesterday she would have been sick with jealousy. Now his words wash over her like water. None of it matters anymore.

"Lorne, we have a problem. It's Shelby."

He listens without comment as she explains about the boy in Australia, the mother in North Carolina. "There's a name for it. Munchausen syndrome by proxy. You can Google it."

Finally he speaks: "Are you sure?"

"Well, *no*. That's my whole point. Ipecac, if that's what she's using, is untraceable. It has kind of a weird smell, like grape candy, but I've never smelled that on Olivia."

"So we can't prove it."

"No," Rena says.

He exhales audibly. "All right, then. It's still *possible* the water is to blame. For our purposes, that possibility is enough."

"I don't understand." Heat washes over her, a hot flash to end all hot flashes. She rolls down the window. The stagnant air smells of catalytic converter, the truck's imminent demise.

"Look, I'm no doctor," he says. "And I'm sorry, my dear, but neither are you. We deal in perceptions. Our role is to raise questions, Cassandra sounding the alarm. That's all we *can* do. And if we do it right—loudly, with great conviction—it just might be enough."

The heat makes thinking impossible. Rena turns the key in the ignition, fiddles desperately with the vents. The broken air conditioner bathes her in lukewarm air.

"I'm a mandated reporter." She hears the quaver in her voice. "If I suspect a child is being harmed, I have to call Child Protective Services. That's the law."

"Of course. But it's a judgment call, right? There's a gray area. If there weren't, Ravi would have reported it himself."

"But we can't keep *encouraging* her! Don't you see that? If she really is making Olivia sick, all this attention is exactly what she's after."

"*If,*" says Lorne. "*If.*"

A horrible silence in which Rena understands: *He doesn't care.*

"Look, you said yourself that we can't prove it," he says calmly. "And if we can't prove it, neither can they."

"*They?*"

"Darco. The DEP. The huge fucking propaganda machine that's telling the world fracking is safe. Trust me, Rena. You have no idea what we're up against."

The nights are getting cooler. The chief shivers in his summer-weight camos. In another month he'll switch to heavier gear, long underwear. In two months he'll wonder if there's any goddamn point.

During a stakeout, the mind wanders. Three weeks ago, on a Sunday evening, the chief noticed a strange vehicle, a late-model Ford Explorer, parked outside his ex-wife's residence.

The next day, while the part-time secretary was on her lunch break, he attempted to run the plate, an operation that would have taken two minutes if the chief knew anything about computers. He was still at it when she returned. "What are you doing at my desk?" she asked.

"Running a plate."

She sat beside him. "It's pretty easy, really." And within thirty seconds the chief was copying down a name and a Texas address.

"Who's Bernard Little?" she asked.

"I'm not at liberty to say."

For the next three days he surveilled, driving past at all hours. The Explorer never moved, as though it had grown roots in the driveway. The windows of the residence were always dark. On Day Four he tried using his key, and found that Terri had changed the locks.

Finally he stopped by Subway on his lunch break. "How's your mom these days? More cheese," he told Jason through the sneeze guard.

"Pretty good, I guess." His son, wearing plastic gloves, added an extra slice of mozzarella to the chief's usual, a twelve-inch Meatball. "She's in Hawaii."

It was not the answer the chief was expecting. He and Terri had always been homebodies.

"All by herself?"

"Nah. Bernie took her. Her boyfriend."

Through skillful questioning the chief learned the following facts: Bernie Little lived at the Days Inn and managed a drill rig. Terri had met him at Weight Watchers. For her birthday he'd bought them his-and-her motorcycles.

The interrogation was cut short by the lunch rush. "I have to go, Dad," said Jason, who didn't charge him for the extra cheese.

He'd never imagined that men went to Weight Watchers.

Changing the locks was Terri's right, of course. Probably she'd done it months ago. The chief had been happier when he didn't know.

Is it his imagination, or does he hear a noise? The chief holds his breath. There is a rustle of leaves, the dry grass crunching. A flash of white catches his eye.

He powers on his NVD. The image is murky, but the movement is unmistakable. Two white males in dark clothing sprint across his field of vision. The tall skinny one carries a propane tank, the size used for a barbecue grill. The other, shorter and heavier, holds a length of hose.

For a moment the chief is paralyzed. Buzzing in his ears, his arms and legs humming. Then professionalism and training take over. He gets to his feet.

"Hold it right there." His weapon hand is a little shaky, his NVD askew.

The meth head reaches into his pocket.

The chief will reflect later that thermal imaging would have come in handy at this point. As he has long suspected, his Gen II isn't up to snuff. Also, he needs a sturdier helmet mount to hold the fucking thing in place.

He won't remember raising the Remington to his shoulder, only the exhilarating kickback. And, a moment later, the single ragged syllable he shouted at the meth heads.

RUN.

AFTERLIFE

A soundstage at the 24 Hour News Network. At the anchor desk sits MEREDITH CULVER, blonde. She wears a suit jacket over a camisole, showing notable décolletage. Beside her is TY SLATER, a suntanned man with white teeth.

MEREDITH: Today, in our Energy Spotlight series, we'll take the temperature of the natural gas industry, where unexpected volatility has left investors in a panic. To make sense of what's happening on Wall Street, here's our in-house energy industry expert, Ty Slater.

TY: Thanks, Meredith. Boys and girls, energy is and forever will be a numbers game. Right now the numbers don't work. They don't even *almost* work. The past few years we've seen a massive rush to drill, and now we're *drowning* in natural gas. The market is so glutted they're practically giving the stuff away. Trouble is, drilling for gas in these particular formations is hella expensive. With gas at a buck ninety, they can't cover their operating costs.

MEREDITH: Let's talk about what happened last week, what I'd call the dark elephant in the room.

Ty offers a shit-eating grin.

MEREDITH: After the very public firing of founder and CEO Kip Oliphant, the company had this to say. (*Reading*) "The board of directors would like to thank Kip for his many years of visionary leadership. We wish him well in all his future endeavors." That's from Dark Elephant's communications director, Quentin Tanner. Ty, what aren't they telling us?

TY (*glancing at his watch*): How much time do we have?

Meredith *titters* appreciatively.

TY: Well, for starters, Oliphant is being investigated by the SEC, for running a private hedge fund out of the Dark Elephant headquarters. Which—*wait for it!*—trades gas and oil futures. Conflict of interest, anyone? Not to mention the fact that his own shareholders are suing him—

MEREDITH (*gleeful*): —for misusing the company jet!

TY: Look, Kip the Whip has been pulling these stunts for years. When gas was at four fifty, nobody cared what he did with the jet. But DE is undercapitalized and overextended. The Whip is on the hook for personal loans to the tune of a billion dollars. Let's review: last year he took home twenty million dollars in salary, stock, and bonuses. So why does he need to borrow a billion dollars? Does he have a secret drug habit?

MEREDITH: Ty, you're terrible! Our lawyers are going to have a field day with this.

TY: My point is, Kip Oliphant *is* an addict. He's addicted to drilling. His contract made him part owner of every well the company drilled, as long as he covered his share of the drilling cost. He's drilled so many wells in the last couple years that he's hemorrhaging money.

MEREDITH: So he took out a *loan*?

TY: And put up his DE stock—thirty million shares!—as collateral. Trouble is, with the company's share price in the toilet, they're no longer worth enough to back a billion dollars in debt. He had to come up with hard cash, fast, so he sold some stock.

MEREDITH: A *lot* of stock.

TY: Yeah, baby! Ninety percent of his interest in the company! By the end, those shares were selling for ten bucks apiece. If you're a shareholder—and Meredith, I seriously hope you are not— your DE stock lost twenty percent of its value in a single week. Naturally you want the guy bounced. (Another *shit-eating grin*.) Personally, I hate to see him go. Everybody in Houston has an Oliphant story.

MEREDITH: Okay, I'll bite. What's yours?

TY: Remember when they built the new corporate campus? The Whip wanted skylights in the company cafeteria. He left the architect a voice mail, and then billed his own company for design services.

From Meredith, peals of *laughter*.

MEREDITH: So what's going to happen to Kip Oliphant?

TY: Stay tuned, kids. I wouldn't count him out yet.

Winter comes early to Saxon County. At Friend-Lea Acres, cows are switched to stored feed.

Mack renews her hunting license in time for rabbit season. It arrives in the mail with a leaflet from the State Game Commission, a list of helpful tips:

```
*   Do not hunt around or from atop natural gas
    production equipment. This includes storage tanks.

*   Random shooting near drilling sites, compressor
    stations, and pipelines is dangerous and unlawful.

*   Identify your target and what is beyond it.
    Industry personnel may be wearing fluorescent
    orange, or may not.
```

Trick-or-treating takes place in a full-on blizzard. The witches and goblins wear scarves and mittens. Braden Devlin, grumbling, shares his candy with his sister, who spent the evening watching TV in her princess costume. They sort the candy into two piles. Their mother checks labels for rogue ingredients: wheat, dairy, peanuts, corn.

By the time the candy is divided, the snow is a foot deep. The calendar calls this mid-autumn, but on whose authority? Where, exactly, does winter begin on December 21?

In whiteout conditions, amid horizontal snowfall, the drill rigs roll out of town.

Rena doesn't understand, at first, what's happening. Nobody does. One by one the drill sites go silent. Roads under construction are left unfinished. DETOUR signs disappear. At Sheetz, shorter lines at the gas pumps; on Baker Street, a sudden abundance of parking spaces. She includes these observations in a long, complicated e-mail to Lorne Trexler. It takes her three days to write.

When he doesn't respond, she leaves a message on his voice mail. *Either I'm going crazy, or they're done with us.*

Late that night, her cell phone rings, Lorne sounding jubilant. *Congratulations, my dear. We won.*

He talks about the workings of democracy, the role of an informed citizenry, the awesome power of collective action. He talks and talks.

They do not discuss Shelby Devlin.

We won, he says, but did they? The citizens' group had met twice and built a website. Their e-mail campaign—targeting state legislators, the governor, the state DEP, and the Environmental Protection Agency—had scarcely begun. Now, suddenly, the fight is over. Dark Elephant has left town and nobody, not even Lorne Trexler, knows why.

Instead drilling ends the way everything ends, inscrutably. As when the mines closed; as when Beth Steel pulled out of Johnstown and Rena's brother lost, in rapid succession, his job, his house, his wife and kids. Nobody ever tells you why.

AT THE CAMP ON COLONEL DRAKE HIGHWAY, roughnecks are packing their bags.

"This is booshit, man," says Jorge, who is twenty-four and caffeinated and owes child support.

Brando, who always has money, grunts in agreement or dissent.

The layoffs, as always, come out of nowhere. For the middle-aged and elderly, the shock lasts one minute exactly. Roughnecking has forever been a cyclical business: drilling, not drilling. In a week they'll be watching college football and collecting unemployment. They will eat and drink immoderately, like athletes breaking training. They will go joyfully to seed.

In the parking lot Jorge and Brando shake hands good-bye, a series of complicated grips. Jorge gets into Mickey Phipps's truck, tossing his duffel into the bed. Mickey hunches over the wheel, looking rough. His top lip is swollen, his right eye bruised.

"Thanks for the lift, man. Jesus, what happened to your face?"

Mickey, who is Christian, can't help flinching. He sees no reason to take the Name in vain. "Nothing. It's a long story."

They ride awhile in silence.

"How long you going to hang out here?" Jorge asks. "If you don't mind my asking."

Mickey does mind. It's none of Jorge's goshdarn business.

"It's a complicated situation," Mickey says.

At the camp on Drake Highway, when the last key has been surrendered, Brenda Hoff closes the front office. Denny Tilsit locks the door and activates the alarm. In light snowfall they say their good-byes. Brenda's new job, running the deli counter at the Food Giant, starts tomorrow.

"Don't get too comfortable," Denny tells her. "My guess is, this place will open up again before too long. I'll tell them to give you a call."

He gets into his camper van, packed with everything he owns. He'll spend the next two days driving to North Dakota. There's a new Logistix camp in the Bakken shale.

THE FLIGHT TO HOUSTON IS CROWDED. Herc stares out the window during takeoff, Pittsburgh getting smaller and smaller, the snaking rivers, the small square houses like rows of tiny teeth.

I'll be home in time for dinner, he told Colleen.

I'll believe it when I see it, she said.

The flight takes three hours exactly. By the second hour he's already tanked. He lines up the miniature bottles on his tray table and rings the flight attendant for one more. His hand is a little sore, the knuckles bruised where they made contact with Mickey's jaw.

For nearly a week Jess had dodged his phone calls. Finally, in desperation, he parked outside her church on Sunday morning and waited for her to appear.

They sat in his truck a long time, watching the snow fall.

Who told you?

The letter came, unsigned, to the Living Waters P.O. Box, an address anybody might have seen printed on the church newsletter. Each Sunday Jess leaves a hundred copies on a table near the front door.

He thought immediately of Mickey Phipps. Though the whole Bravo crew knew Herc was married, only Mickey was likely to care.

My buddy wrote that letter. Must have. The one I first came to your church with. He's the Moral Majority type.

Were you ever going to tell me?

He sat staring at his hands, his silence answering her question.

So I guess your buddy did me a favor. I guess I should thank him.

The words hit him like a slap.

Do you feel like thanking him?

Not yet, she said.

His flight lands ten minutes early. At George Bush International the airport bars are busy, travelers crowded in to watch Texas Tech beat Oklahoma State. Herc bolts a shot of bourbon, then makes his way to baggage claim. Colleen is there waiting, in high heels and a tiny denim skirt. When he kisses her cheek, she smells the liquor on him. "I see you did a little early celebrating."

Marriage in middle age, the sequel. Herc imagines the Hollywood subtitle: *Back in the Shit House.*

He follows her to the parking garage, still warm and loose from the drink.

"I guess I better drive," she says.

"Whatever you want." He'd surrendered his company truck in Pennsylvania. Judging from the little pile of potpourri she keeps in the ashtray, his Bronco now belongs to Colleen.

She gets behind the wheel, the skirt riding halfway up her thighs. "Can you believe Mickey and Didi? I'm still in shock."

"What are you talking about?"

Colleen looks surprised. "They're splitting up. I figured you already knew."

Herc stares at her, dumbfounded. Mickey Phipps, getting divorced? Mickey who'd spent untold thousands of dollars flying back and forth from Houston. Mickey who wouldn't look at another woman if she burst into flames.

(The satisfying collision of fist and jaw. Mickey dazed and blinking, like he didn't know whether to shit or go blind.)

Colleen says, "I heard Didi met someone."

It's a gift certain women have, that magical power to sober up a drunk man. After five minutes with his wife, Herc's bourbon flush has left him completely. It's as if the tiny bottles contained nothing but water.

He understands that this is the moment to tell her everything. *There was a lady in Pennsylvania. I fell in love with her.* Recent events have taught him the power of truth-telling, and its limits. If he doesn't tell her now, he never will.

He turns on the radio and scans the dial for the game.

AT HALFTIME TEXAS TECH is leading by a healthy margin. They're so far ahead that there can be no catching them. Reassured, Kip turns his back to the TV.

"I need some land," he tells the kid beside him. "I hear you're the man to help me."

They meet, at Kip's suggestion, in a location both public and private, an empty hotel bar near the airport. This is a strategic choice. His new office—the worldwide headquarters of Whiplash Energy—lacks certain amenities. A receptionist, for example. He's trying to keep overhead to a minimum. His main expense, at the moment, is Amy Rubin. Her monthly retainer is an investment in the future. Only a fool cuts corners on the science, a lesson he learned long ago.

Kip says, "We're on the verge of a new inflection point."

Bobby Frame drinks soda water and eyes him levelly, unimpressed. Kip wonders what he has heard.

Kip explains that from a land perspective, the Marcellus is over. Any land worth having is already under contract. Let the others fight over the crumbs. Whiplash is looking forward, not back. The Utica Shale is theirs for the taking, the point of dynamism moving westward.

The Next Big Play.

"I want you to run my land program," he finishes grandly.

"You're offering me a job?" Frame looks skeptical—as though he's got something better to do; as though Dark Elephant hasn't already sent him packing, along with the rest of its land team. It's a basic truth Dar never understood: the energy business is really the land business. Land is the only commodity of lasting value, the one true wealth.

"I know what you're thinking," says Kip. "Gas is in the toilet. Well I, for one, hope it stays there." This isn't true, not remotely. But it makes Frame sit up straight.

"As long as gas stays at a buck ninety, no one else is buying leases. We'll be the only game in town. Any questions?"

"Just one. Can you afford to pay me?"

Kip does not fluster. "I've got a half billion in financing." It's only a slight exaggeration: he has promises. "You'd be my first hire. Right now I got nobody else to pay. I hope you're ready to travel."

Promises from Taffy Campbell, from Personal Wealth Group. From Amy Rubin, who knows where the gold is.

Bobby Frame says, "I keep a toothbrush in my truck."

THANKSGIVING MORNING AT WELLWAYS. Group, predictably, runs long: Bodily Debacles, holiday edition.

Darren settles in with a cup of coffee. Everybody's got a Thanksgiving story: the family fisticuffs; the poorly timed opiate nod, face-first into the cranberry sauce. So begins the season of anguish, the High Holy Days of addiction. In the coming weeks, Group sharing will take on an escalating urgency, the pulsing shame of remembered humiliations: boozy high jinks at the office party, the inebriated pratfall on the church stairs. Christmas comes loaded with childhood memories, tender and monstrous. There is forced communion with disapproving relatives (the heartbroken parents, the smug siblings, the fucking in-laws). All leading, inexorably, to New Year's Eve—for the recovering addict, the most dangerous night of the year.

Darren's cell phone vibrates in his pocket. Gia, he thinks, without knowing how he knows.

He thinks of her at odd moments: yesterday, absurdly, when a hearse passed him in the street. Driving to work, he's stopped listening to the radio. Nearly any song released in a certain era is attached to some memory of her.

She won't leave a message. She never leaves a message.

The session ended, his clients linger, reluctant to leave the safety of the room.

In the hallway he bumps into Patricia. She looks surprised to see him. "Darren, sweetie, you better get on the road. Seventy is already backed up. I saw it on Traffic Cam."

"I'm not going anywhere." Like every year, he will eat Thanksgiving dinner at Wellways. The cook makes him his own tofu turkey, a solid mass the size and shape of a man's shoe.

Patricia frowns. "Oh, funny. I don't know why I thought you were going to Pennsylvania."

Thanksgiving in Bakerton: his father's silent house, his mother's empty chair. Even without Gia Bernardi, it's much, much more than he can handle sober.

"Maybe next year," he says.

LONG AGO, WHEN JESS PEACOCK WAS A PASTOR'S WIFE, every holiday was a performance. Each year after his service, she and Wes had hosted a Thanksgiving dinner in the church basement. Some years half the congregation attended: families, elderly widows, lost souls like Shelby Devlin who fit into no category Jess could identify. Sitting shoulder to shoulder with her healthy husband, toasting with glasses of grape juice, Jess lamented the overcooked turkey, the lumpy mashed potatoes. Only later did she understand that those were the best Thanksgivings of her life.

This year she canceled her Thanksgiving service. If anybody minded, she hasn't heard about it. She isn't feeling particularly thankful.

She wishes, now, that she had kept the letter. That she hadn't, in a fit of blind rage, burned it in the sink.

```
Dear Pastor,
I am writing in the spirit of Christian
friendship. There is a person in your life who
isn't what he appears to be.
```

Jess refills her wineglass and glances at the clock. In her current state, driving to the Devlins' is a bad idea. Had she really intended to go in the first place? The Devlins will have a houseful of people. Maybe her absence won't be noticed. Still, she really ought to call.

```
This man has a wife and children in Texas.
```

Calling the Devlins is only going to get more difficult. A second bottle is chilling in the refrigerator. She hadn't expected to need it.

```
I understand that you are lonely. Widowhood at
a young age is a heavy cross to bear.
```

She needs it.

```
But that is no excuse to steal the poor man's
ewe lamb.
```

Would a man who worked on a drill rig write such a thing? Would *anybody*? And yet, somebody had.

Herc was nothing at all like Wes. Even before his illness, her husband had been a slender man. In his arms she had wished herself smaller. With Herc she felt delicate, exquisite, herself perfected. His strength delighted her. He lifted and turned her effortlessly, all sweetness and grace.

She is always canceling on Shelby. What on earth can she say this time? *I can't make it after all. I'm feeling under the weather.* The *th* sound is problematic. Would Shelby notice if she slurred her words?

She never intended to go in the first place.

The birthday lingerie she'd worn only once.

She takes the second bottle from the refrigerator. She doesn't need the letter. She remembers every word.

It was the last line that enraged her. The last line made her strike the match.

```
Your husband, if he were alive, would tell you
the exactsame thing.
```

How is such a thing possible? The question does not plague him. It's the main advantage of being dead, the only one, really. The dead are—at the very least, at the very last—unplagued.

He watches Jessie pour a glass of wine. She's drinking too much.

In the months after his mother died, the boy Wesley Peacock had a powerful sense of being watched. In the classroom, the dreaded school bus, he felt Bernadette's presence. The feeling faded over time, though it did not disappear entirely. Even as a grown man, on rare occasions—his wedding day, for example—he sensed her gaze. Early in his marriage, he worried that she could see him making love to his wife. Jessie had laughed at him, but he knows, now, that he was correct.

On a bright day when he was very small, his mother took him walking in the snow.

He doesn't completely understand the interface. The Bubble Boy is confined to his house, as he once wished to be. He can see Jessie and anyone else who enters—see them, as you might naturally suspect, from above.

Watching her make love to another man was not painful, though he's still able to feel pain. It's one of the surprises of the afterlife, one of many. The afterlife, frankly, is not as advertised. Wesley hasn't met God or anyone resembling Him. Though he would dearly love to, he hasn't seen his mother or father or any other of the dead.

Only once, since dying, has he felt pain: the night Jessie discussed him across the dinner table. *By the end he had file cabinets full of papers. Medical studies and so on. But nobody believed him.*

Did you? the man asked.

I believe he believed it, Jessie said.

She had never believed him. And yet even in death Wesley is convinced. Even in death he knows he was right.

Through all his research, his despairing and febrile months of study, he had never grasped the full mystery. Uranium-235, enriched to 4 percent: he added up the digits and got fourteen, a number that meant nothing. His mind was by then a blunt instrument. He blamed hermeneutics, homeschooling, the dulling effect of Lumox, the hot grief of leaving her.

The reaction itself was impossible to visualize. What did an electron even look like? Wesley's drug-addled brain saw jelly beans, candy hearts, the small sweet treasures that are childhood's currency, its only wealth. Tiny hearts colliding and dividing, orange, yellow, cherry-pink, split down the middle into matching halves, a mad burst of heat and light.

The splitting of the hearts.

Alive, he had no head for abstraction. Now, of course, he has no head at all. Bodiless, headless, heartless. The dead are pure vision. Their only occupation, the only power left them, is to see.

The terrible gift of clear vision. If you'd had it when you were alive, you'd have done everything differently. If you'd had it when you were alive, it would have killed you.

Hearts splitting like cells dividing, the child he and Jessie might have had, if only he'd known. But Wesley was just a boy, would never be anything but a boy. It was unimaginable that he could be anybody's father, and so he hadn't imagined it.

His mother took him walking in the snow.

It's too late, now, for Jessie to have a baby. The years when it might have happened, so few really, she'd wasted loving him. Nursing, burying, and mourning him. Too late, too late.

A hard snow in radiant sunlight. The brightness hurt his eyes. The brightness was strange and misbegotten, a glorious confusion in the heavens.

Now he sees only Jessie, who remembers him.

This is all there is.

THE BUILDING LOOKS INNOCUOUS in the afternoon light. Squat and square, of municipal construction. It could be a warren of government offices, a junior high school. As instructed, Rena drives around to the side entrance and waits.

This morning President Obama granted the traditional Thanksgiving pardon to Cobbler and Gobbler, the official White House turkeys.

She turns off the radio. For four years she has, quite literally, dreamed of this moment. Not every night, but several times a month, her sleeping brain conjures some iteration of what is about to happen. Now, absurdly, she is filled with dread. She wishes Mack were with her, because sometimes you don't want lively conversation. Sometimes—now, for example—Mack's silent, solid presence is exactly what you need.

Lorne Trexler is never silent. *Occupational hazard,* he jokes. According to his ex-wife, he once told Rena, he gave lectures in his sleep.

She doesn't miss him, exactly. She misses the idea of him.

If they'd met when they were younger, in a different time and place. If she had never met Freddy Weems.

Freddy changed her in ways that are not reversible. (*I am a filthy little whore.*) If she'd never met him, there would be no Calvin. She would never have fallen in love with Mack. Instead other things would have happened—what things, Rena will never know. Too much time has passed, too many choices with consequences that led to more consequences that led to more consequences, her path spiraling off in a direction no one could have predicted. Impossible, now, to rewind it; to picture those other lives she might have lived.

Silent Spring sits unread on her bedside table. She understands, now, that Lorne was only trying to fix her, like the home ec teacher who decided, when Mack was in ninth grade, to take her shopping for a bra. *You're already a B cup. Congratulations!* Mack carries the memory like a tingling scar: the hot misery of that shopping trip, the silent mortification. The teacher failing to grasp the most obvious fact, that Susan Mackey had never wanted breasts of any size.

Mack's memories are Rena's memories. They move her as though she lived them herself. It seems to her a working definition of love.

They live on the farm as though it were an island. Rena thinks, often, of Mack's mother—Pete's second wife, twenty years younger, the one frivolous decision he ever made in his life. She ran off with a man her own age, also married, for reasons Rena can easily imagine: the loneliness of farm life, Pete's meager company. At the end of the day, when Mack is tired, Rena sees him in the set of her shoulders, the aging lonely man who loved and was left, silent because he knew no other way to be. In the months after Pete's stroke, it was Rena who fed and dressed and bathed him. He could not thank her. By then his words had dried up, what few there'd been. How long had it been since anybody had touched him?

Sometimes, as she cut his hair or shaved his bristled chin, his eyes would tear.

The grinding effort of farm life, waking at dawn like a monk doing penance. To love Mack is to live this life forever, something Rena has always known. She's put her life into somebody else's farm, decades of labor, every dollar she's ever earned. If she left Mack she'd have nothing, but this isn't the reason she stays.

Last week, driving down the Dutch Road, Rena glimpsed a towheaded child in the Devlins' driveway, bouncing a tennis ball off what looked like a giant plastic cistern. A boy, Olivia's brother probably. A normal, healthy child playing outdoors.

Shelby came to the door in a pink bathrobe.

I was driving by and I thought of Olivia. How is she feeling?

Shelby seemed delighted to see her. *She had a good day yesterday. She's still sleeping, or we could go say hi.*

I'm watching you, Rena wanted to say. I know what you're doing to that child.

(Except that she doesn't, not really. Except that it's still possible she is wrong.)

Now she glances at her watch. The warden's secretary told her to come at four. To save time she came straight from work, still dressed in her new uniform. At Saxon Manor, the entire nursing staff wears the same scrubs, a pale blue smock and pants, printed with tiny butterflies. The pattern seems, to Rena, a little juvenile. As though the clients were born-again children, consigned to a kindergarten for the very old.

Except for the scrubs, the new job suits her: no overnights, no weekends. Her new patients are adults with long lives behind them. Their infirmities are inevitable, wholly expected. She never has to see a sick kid again.

Her coworkers were stunned when she quit: Jo, Agnes, Steph Mulraney (back to work now, temporarily unpregnant), and even Dr. Stusick, who alone knew the reason. By the time Child Protective Services requested copies of Olivia's medical record, Rena Koval was no longer an employee of Miners' Hospital.

In the end she made the call anonymously. It was Mack who helped her decide, Mack who urged her to pick up the phone. A lifetime ago, when Rena was in danger, only Mack had come to her rescue. Now Mack's bravery makes Rena better.

This is the reason she stays.

At that moment the truck pulls in beside her and Mack steps out, still in her orange vest—as though, in thinking of her, Rena has conjured her from the air.

Rena gets out of the van. "You came."

They stand shoulder to shoulder, not speaking, squinting into the sunlight. At last the side door swings open. Calvin is underdressed for the weather, in a cheap windbreaker and khaki pants. He carries a plastic bag.

Just for the holidays, they tell each other. Until he gets on his feet.

SHELBY BRUSHES OLIVIA'S HAIR, counting the strokes.

"Pastor Jess will be here any minute. She'll be glad to see you. She's been worried about you." Her hands are shaking a little— nerves, probably. Except for Sunday services and a brief sighting at the Food Giant, she hasn't seen the pastor in months.

Olivia squirms. "Is Granny Rox coming? I want to show her my shoes."

The child's fondness for her grandmother is, to Shelby, mystifying. Roxanne who forgets birthdays and ignores Christmas, who shows up irregularly, reeking of cigarettes and Jean Naté. *She smells beautiful,* Olivia once said.

"I don't think she can make it, sweetie." Shelby parts Olivia's hair and begins braiding. Inviting Roxanne is never more than a formality. Any minute now the phone will ring, her mother canceling— assuming, of course, that she remembers to call. "She has to take care of Peanut."

Olivia laughs delightedly. It's a reliable source of mirth, for a seven-year-old, that a grown man could have such a name. "Peanut can come, too."

Shelby does not respond to this. She has never actually met Peanut, though she's seen him from a distance—reclined, always, in the passenger seat of his van, which Roxanne leaves idling while she runs into the liquor store. He's not the sort of man you want around children.

She says, "You can show your shoes to Pastor Jess."

There's so much she wants to share with the pastor, months' worth of worry and frustration and, yes, trauma. If ever in her life Shelby needed counseling, it was after the surprise visit from Child Protective Services, the greatest shock of her life. For weeks it seemed that the world was caving in around her: the menacing letters on official stationery, the humiliating questions. Olivia was interviewed twice. What exactly the social worker asked her, Shelby isn't certain; she wasn't allowed in the room. Though Shelby begged her not to, she insisted on interviewing Rich. He's going to leave me, Shelby thought; but incredibly, the opposite happened. For the first and only time in ten years of marriage, her husband came to her defense.

She's an excellent mother. She lives for those kids. What's the matter with you people?

He has a temper, no question. For once his anger was directed at someone else, and it was marvelous to watch.

Shelby's husband believed her—and so, in the end, did everyone else. In October she received a letter in the mail: the accusation against her had been ruled Unfounded. The interfering busybody who reported her (Dr. Stusick? the specialist in Pittsburgh?) was simply wrong.

Unfounded. That was all: no apology, no official acknowledgment of the injustice she'd suffered, the insult and anguish and breathtaking shame. Rich went back to being Rich, bossy and critical. He worked overtime and went hunting on Sundays, determined to pretend that nothing had happened. To him, nothing had.

Then, last week at the Food Giant, Shelby spotted Pastor Jess pushing her cart down the frozen foods aisle. Even at a distance she looked terrible, her eyes deeply circled, her hair graying along the part, and Shelby recalled—vaguely, like some memory of a past life—that Pastor Jess had been wounded, too.

It was hard to keep track of other people's suffering.

The pastor looked surprised to see her. She took Shelby's hand in both her own. *I should have called you weeks ago. Forgive me, Shelby. You deserve better.*

The touch warmed her, but it was the words that mattered. The words pierced her like an injection, a lifesaving antidote. In that instant the pastor's many transgressions, the slights and careless cruelties (the counseling appointments she'd canceled, the hospital visit that never was, the wasted and ultimately disastrous trip to Pittsburgh) simply unhappened. Shelby could actually feel the anger leave her, draining away like blood from a wound.

I had some personal business to deal with, said the pastor. *But life is finally getting back to normal.*

Shelby has a forgiving nature.

That's all right, she said generously. *I understand.*

A Thanksgiving miracle, a blessing she never expected: Pastor Jess has come back to her. In an hour she'll arrive on Shelby's doorstep. They'll hold hands around the table as the pastor says the blessing.

Shelby ties off Olivia's braids with blue ribbon. A mother is judged by her child's appearance. This is a known fact.

BUSINESS IS SLOW AT THE COMMERCIAL. On Thanksgiving there is no lunch crowd to speak of. Rich Devlin wipes idly at the counter. Gia hangs silver tinsel in loops along the bar.

"Jesus, already? You can't wait till after Thanksgiving?"

She frowns, as though he's a minor irritation, a dog barking. "Another day? Seriously, that would make a difference to you?"

He studies her in the mirror above the bar. For a long time, years, she was his own personal definition of sexy. Lately, though, something has shifted. He can't put his finger on why, exactly; but Gia is looking bad.

She asks, "What's Darren doing for Thanksgiving?"

Has she always been this skinny?

"Beats me. I haven't heard from him in months." His brother's life in Baltimore is a mystery. Once, long ago, Rich had gone there looking for him. For two days he walked the streets around Johns Hopkins, showing Darren's picture to strangers. Then, as now, Darren didn't want to be found.

Gia frowns. Her forehead is creased in a way he's never noticed, two diagonal lines like lightning bolts. She's ten years younger than he is; how can she possibly look old to him? Too thin, scrawny around the neck and shoulders. The word, he thinks, is *frail.*

Are you okay? he nearly asks. It's not a question he typically puts to women. He doesn't need to. Shelby keeps him constantly apprised of her own and Olivia's symptoms, the endless series of imaginary ailments. There's never any need to ask.

He glances at the television. The local news is playing: Andy Carnicella in his dress uniform, shaking hands with a man in a suit. A crawl across the bottom of the screen reads *POLICE CHIEF HONORED.*

Gia shrieks with laughter. "Turn it up! I want to hear this."

Rich fumbles under the bar for the remote.

In our local heroes department, Bakerton police chief Andrew Carnicella got a shout-out from the Saxon County commissioners, for saving two lives in the line of duty.

"Oh, for Christ's sake." Rich hits the Mute button.

"No! Give me that." Gia grabs the remote from his hand.

The chief was on an undercover mission at this farm supply store when two men, identified as Nicholas Blick and Robert Marstellar, both of Bakerton, were allegedly seen siphoning off fertilizer from an outdoor tank.

Two mug shots flash across the screen, Rich's old buddies. Transformed, now, into a couple of middle-aged thugs. He thinks, Don't make me see it.

The other two Duanes.

"Can we turn this off, please?"

"Not on your life," Gia says.

The chief is credited with driving both suspects to the Emergency Room at Miners' Hospital, after the fertilizer tank was punctured during a shootout. Anhydrous ammonia is a hazardous substance that can cause serious injury if inhaled. Thanks to Chief Carnicella's quick action, no one was seriously hurt.

"Let me get this straight," says Rich. "The idiot shoots a fertilizer tank, and he's a hero for taking the guys to the hospital?"

Gia's shoulders shake with laughter, her eyes actually tearing. The chief is beaming at the camera. It is, clearly, the proudest moment of his life.

The broadcast cuts to a commercial. *For forty years I've stood up for the little guy.*

Rich studies the man's face. He looks better on television, slightly younger and healthier. The commercial might be ten years old, or twenty. Paul Zacharias has been chasing ambulances for a very long time.

"I need to get going," he tells Gia. "Shelby's cooking Thanksgiving. She has a whole list of chores she wants me to do."

"Tell her to call me, will you? I haven't heard from her in ages."

"She's had a lot on her mind."

At that moment the front door swings open. The tattooed skinhead takes a last drag on his cigarette and drops it to the sidewalk.

"Hey, girl," he calls to Gia. "What up?"

Gia looks suddenly alert. "Jesus, finally. I've been calling you all morning." She steps out from behind the bar.

"Where are you going?" says Rich.

"Back in a minute," Gia says.

A HAZE OVER SWEDETOWN, what looks at first like fog but turns out to be woodsmoke. The Prines or Thibodeaux have built a bonfire. There is a smell of burning leaves.

Driving, Rich thinks again of the two mug shots: Booby dull and bloated, Nick gaunt and vacant-eyed, both obviously (obviously!) high. Nick, especially, looked wasted by meth, starved and not quite sane. And yet the last time Rich saw them, shooting pool at the Commercial, no such thought had crossed his mind.

In his line of work it's a question of survival: *Don't make me see it.* He thinks of the soldiers back from deployment, swapping their best stories around the bar at the Commercial, forgetting the rest with the help of drink. In this one way, the prison is not so different from Afghanistan. If you looked, really looked, at what was going on around you, you wouldn't last a week.

A county sheriff's cruiser whizzes past, blue lights flashing, and rolls down Thibodeaux Lane.

Rich is dumbstruck. Jesus Christ, is it possible? Somebody called the law on Randy for burning leaves on his own property, out in the middle of nowhere? To Rich it's yet another example of government sticking its nose in. More and more, the government seems to be the source of all his problems. First the Department of Environmental Protection failed to protect his environment. Then a couple of county bureaucrats attacked his wife and threatened, for a terrifying moment, to break up his family. When you needed help desperately, government abandoned you. When you didn't, it wouldn't leave you the fuck alone.

His wife isn't perfect: an overprotective mother, a hypochondriac. In practical matters she has no more sense than a child. Her pessimism makes him crazy. She greets each new day by cataloging every catastrophe that could possibly happen, as if naming them will somehow protect her against the worst. But she would never in a million years hurt their kid.

She had a sister who died. Rich learned this only recently, by accident: Gia Bernardi mentioned it once in passing. (*Crystal. She was younger. Leukemia, maybe?*) Until that moment he'd believed Shelby was an only child.

If it's strange that she never told him, it's a type of strangeness Rich understands. There's plenty he's never told her—the humiliating way his first marriage ended, the wife who betrayed him. It's a subject he feels no urge to discuss.

Shelby isn't perfect, but she can be trusted.

He sees her, now, with different eyes. Her fears and failings, her vigilance against disaster, now seem logical. If a child could die, no one was safe.

Shelby isn't perfect, but she is his.

He passes his driveway and turns down the access road. Stripped of its function, it's a runway to nowhere, though it comes in handy as a parking space. Between Shelby's minivan and the water tank, there's no room in the driveway for his truck.

He heads into the house. The tank—his lawyer calls it a *water buffalo*—holds five thousand gallons. A plastic pipe connects it, through a basement window, to the house's plumbing. At the end of the month, a tanker truck will come to refill it. The service costs two thousand dollars a month. For now, anyway, Dark Elephant is footing the bill. The guy on the phone, Quentin somebody, called it *a good neighbor gesture.*

You're not my neighbor, Rich thought.

Infuriatingly, the company has admitted no wrongdoing. The water delivery implies no responsibility for the contamination of his well. Rich signed a paper to this effect, though only after checking with Paul Zacharias.

It doesn't commit you to anything, his lawyer explained. *We can still negotiate for a real settlement. But in the meantime, you'll have water to drink.*

In the kitchen he opens the refrigerator and pours a glass of something. "What is this stuff?" he asks Shelby, who stands at the stove studying a cookbook.

"Peppermint tea."

"Tastes like toothpaste."

She puts down the book. "Your dad will be here any minute. Can you put the leaf in the table?"

"Do we need it?"

Shelby does her Buddy Hackett grimace. "Us plus your dad, that's five already. My mother probably won't show, but you never know. Oh, and I invited Pastor Jess." Defiantly she meets his eyes, daring him to ask the obvious question.

He asks it anyway. "What the hell for?"

"She doesn't have anywhere else to go. And, well, I get the

feeling she's under a lot of stress." She covers a pot with a lid and wipes her hands on her jeans. "Can you give this a stir once in a while?"

"I guess. Remember, Shel, don't say anything about—"

"I know, I know," Shelby says.

Rich heads out to the garage and comes back with the leaf. He isn't ashamed of the lawsuit, exactly; but he feels no urge to broadcast it. He's never considered himself the kind of person who would sue.

Dark Elephant contaminated his water and stole his future. No question, he has been well and truly screwed. Still he can't shake the feeling that he's responsible for his own predicament, that his greed and gullibility made him an easy mark. Nobody forced him to sign away his mineral rights. That was his own cursed decision, motivated by fear of poverty or simple greed. Where one began and the other ended was not clear.

At the time it had seemed a simple choice. There was the Bakerton of his father's day, a thriving boomtown that reeked of its bony piles; or the Bakerton his own generation had inherited and largely fled, a ghost town that was perfectly clean.

Bakerton Coal Lights the World.

He turns the dining room table on its side and slides in the extra leaf, thinking of his father. At Rich's age he'd been lost, jobless, hopeless. Compass north—mine and Mine Workers—was gone forever. Dick's generation had lost its stars. And yet, against tall odds, he'd built something, a business to pass on to his children. This is the official version of events, the Devlin family gospel father and son repeat to each other, forgetting, always, the other character in the story: Rich's uncle Pat, wasted by mesothelioma. The settlement from Erie Door and Window let him buy the Commercial on his deathbed, just in time to leave it to his brother. All their lives, Dick and Pat had been working stiffs—a coal miner, a factory slave. Pat's lawsuit is the sole reason the Devlin family now owns a business. For a long time Rich had resisted drawing certain conclusions, which now seem indisputable.

The only way to get ahead is to be grievously wronged.

He still keeps, in his glove box, a grubby slip of paper: *Honiger 8 yrs old 40K.* Exactly why he keeps it, he isn't sure. He will never be a farmer. When his settlement comes—*if* it comes—he could, in theory, buy another farm. He knows he never will. The point was to work *this* land—Pap's land, bought and paid for with his own hard labor, ten years of overtime at Deer Run. With the pain and suffering—entirely self-inflicted—of his very foolish little brother.

Who'd been the bigger fool, Rich or Darren, was impossible to say.

MORE THAN MOST PLACES, Pennsylvania is what lies beneath.

Accidents of geology, larger than history, older than scripture: continents colliding, seas encroaching and receding, peat bogs incubating their treasures like a vast subterranean kiln. In the time before recorded time, Pennsylvania was booby-trapped. Blame the gods for what lies beneath—the old pagan gods, discredited now, vaguely disreputable, the unwashed old men who struck a backroom deal before Jesus was invented.

What lies beneath.

Rich Devlin recalls, often, a famous TV commercial of his childhood: the Indian chief looking out over a trash-strewn highway, a single tear sliding down his cheek. A public service announcement, designed to make people stop littering; but the ad hadn't turned him into a tree hugger, as it was clearly meant to do. It sparked, instead, his fascination with American Indians—who, he discovered, weren't the villains the old westerns had made them out to be. At nine years old, for the first and last time in his life, he read voraciously: adventure stories, encyclopedias, anything with an Indian in it. Apache, Seneca, Cherokee, Chickasaw. How he loved the sound of those names, the cascading syllables. Reading, he imagined waking up in a teepee or a pueblo to a different life entirely, in which boys weren't forced to take spelling tests or deliver newspapers or learn catechism, the daily gauntlet of responsibility that had already begun for him and wouldn't end until he was too old to hunt or track or fish, too old to do anything but watch TV commercials and fall asleep in his chair.

How the world must have looked then, in Indian times: his own corner of the world before roads and bridges, tipples and steel mills, the sprawling strip mines that blackened the earth like char. As a boy he imagined it, vividly. As a man he learned it didn't matter. If not for the mines he'd be someone else, somewhere else. He'd never know this place existed, and so, for him, it wouldn't. His great-grandfather came here the way everyone did, washed up in Bakerton like so much flotsam: a man who owned a single pair of shoes, a man willing to mine coal.

Long ago, in the navy, Rich Devlin learned his place in the world, his basic and inescapable smallness. Military life taught you this truth. He turned nineteen aboard the SS *Roosevelt*—the Big Stick, they called it, a ship so massive it seemed to be standing still as it carried six thousand men, three times the population of Bakerton, to the Persian Gulf, a distant and desolate place that mattered for one reason only. When he thinks of it now, he imagines the Big Stick gliding across a vast sea of other people's money, a thought that didn't occur to him at the time.

We are all sailors.

ACKNOWLEDGMENTS

Much has been written on the subject of gas drilling. I am indebted to Seamus McGraw's remarkable memoir, *The End of Country;* Gregory Zuckerman's *The Frackers,* and Josh Fox's two-part documentary *Gasland,* which offer three very different—and to my mind, essential—perspectives on the issue.

Heat and Light is a book about the world. Writing it demanded many different kinds of knowledge no novelist actually possesses. I am indebted to those who schooled me.

Pamela Twiss at California University of Pennsylvania and the Northern Appalachia Network shared valuable insights about what gas drilling means for communities. But for our conversation several years ago, and others since, this book would not have been written.

Atul Gawande, Lori Wirth, and Ben Scheindlin answered my incessant medical questions. Kenneth Cain and Mike Konior taught me about crime and punishment. Liz Diehl gave me a crash course in organic dairy farming. Mike Brennan, Mike Jennings, Andy Rodriguez, and Brian Fink shared their experiences of working on a drill rig. Greg McIsaac helped me understand the peculiar geology of western Pennsylvania. Carrie and Michael Kline taught me to listen in a new and powerful way.

My editor at Ecco, the great and good Daniel Halpern, helped me build a better mousetrap. Dan Pope, Sheri Joseph, Dorian Karchmar, and Megan Lynch waded through early drafts and helped me through the weeds.

Rob Arnold believed in the machine.

Julian and Patti Adams gave me Truro in a blizzard, the greatest writing retreat of my life. The Corporation of Yaddo, the MacDowell Colony, the Danish Centre for Writers and Translators, and the Dora Maar Foundation provided optimal writing conditions and stimulating fellowship. It's a miracle I ever left.

Finally, a special thanks to my publishing family at Harper-Collins, especially Michael Morrison and Jonathan Burnham, for their understanding and support. *Heat and Light* owes a particular debt to two books that came before it, *Baker Towers* and *News from Heaven*. Neither would have come into the world without the immeasurable generosity of Claire Wachtel at Harper. My gratitude is unending.